SOMETHING GOOD

A Novel

D0036214

VANESSA MILLER

THOMAS NELSON
Since 1798

Published in Nashville, Tennessee, by Thomas Nelson. Thomas Nelson is a registered trademark of HarperCollins Christian Publishing, Inc.

Thomas Nelson titles may be purchased in bulk for educational, business, fundraising, or sales promotional use. For information, please email SpecialMarkets@ThomasNelson. com.

Scripture quotations are taken from the King James Version. Public domain.

Library of Congress Cataloging-in-Publication Data

Names: Miller, Vanessa, author.
Title: Something good : a novel / Vanessa Miller.
Description: Nashville, Tennessee : Thomas Nelson, [2022] | Summary: "When three women find their lives inextricably linked after one terrible mistake, they must work together to make the most of their futures and the challenges before them"-- Provided by publisher.
Identifiers: LCCN 2021046105 (print) | LCCN 2021046106 (ebook) | ISBN 9780785256724 (trade paper) | ISBN 9780785256731 (ebook) | ISBN 9780785256816 (downloadable audio)
Subjects: BISAC: FICTION / African American & Black / Christian | FICTION / Family Life / Marriage & Divorce | LCGFT: Novels.
Classification: LCC PS3613.I5623 S58 2022 (print) | LCC PS3613.I5623 (ebook) | DDC 813/.6--dc23
LC record available at https://lccn.loc.gov/2021046105
LC ebook record available at https://lccn.loc.gov/2021046106

Printed in the United States of America

22 23 24 25 26 LSC 5 4 3 2 1

To my niece, Diamond Underwood, whom I love dearly

And to all those who thought dreaming was a luxury
you couldn't afford. It's time to dream again . . . believe
God will bring something good into your life.

PROLOGUE

SIX MONTHS AGO

Glancing at the clock on her dashboard, Alexis Marshall bit down on the back of her lower lip. She had exactly twenty minutes to get across town to pick up the twins. Traffic was always terrible on Pineville-Matthews Road. She would be cutting it close. When she was a kid, this road had nothing but trees as far as the eye could see. Now, shopping centers and one eatery after another lined the street, and cars and more cars.

A car cut in front of her. She almost didn't have enough time to put her foot on the brake. Pressing hard on the horn, she yelled, "What are you doing?"

When she stopped at the red light, her phone beeped, indicating she had a text message. It read: Your mother is missing. We can't keep doing this.

"No! No! No! Not again." She slammed her hand against the steering wheel. Her mother was always pulling stuff like this. This was the third in a year. Alexis picked up her phone and called her husband. He wouldn't like it, but he'd have to pick up the kids. She had to go find her mother.

"Hey, hon, can you make it quick? I have a meeting to get to."

Okay, she was going to make it really quick. "I need you to pick up the kids because my mother has left the nursing home and they don't know where she is."

"Again?"

She heard the contempt in his voice, but she didn't have time for it. "I've got to go. Don't forget about the kids." Hanging up, she texted her mother's nurse. On my way.

She put on her left signal, needing to move into the left lane to make a U-turn. A black Audi beeped at her as she merged into the lane. She waved at the driver as she pulled over one more time to get into the turning lane. Traffic was coming and going so fast that she had to wait for the light to turn yellow to make her turn. She made sure that there was a safe gap between the oncoming cars. After checking her blind spot she turned the steering wheel all the way to the left, made the U-turn, and headed back to the nursing home she had left not more than ten minutes ago.

She was speeding, and her heart felt like it was trying to jump out of her chest. She needed to slow it down, but the last time her mother pulled her disappearing act, they didn't find her for twenty-four hours. It wasn't until the hospital called, letting them know she had been admitted, that they found out where she was.

Her cell phone beeped again. Had they found her mother that fast? She picked up the phone, but it slipped out of her hand. Trying to catch the phone before it hit the floor, she bent over to grab it.

Her car swerved.

Oh no! She straightened in her seat, but the steering wheel jerked. She tried to grab hold of it and right the car again, but as she tried to put her foot on the brake, she accidently pressed down hard on the gas. The car jumped the median, and she went spinning and spinning into oncoming traffic.

Her eyes darted back and forth in horror, watching as she spun past the Pineville shopping mall, Red Lobster, and Wells Fargo Bank. Her foot got entangled between the gas and the brake. Her twins flashed before her eyes. She still remembered the day she gave birth to them. They came out all wrinkly and red, but the biggest surprise of

SOMETHING GOOD

all was that she delivered not just a son but a daughter. They were only ten years old now, too young to live without their mother.

The car in front of her tried to swerve. Cars were on every side. There was nothing she could do and no way to clear a path. She screamed.

Bang!

Her head jerked back, and the air bag exploded as she felt the impact of the crash. Eyes fluttering. Head hurting. Then . . . nothing.

CHAPTER 1

These gluten-free, avocado-toast-eating, green-smoothie-drinking, bougie country folk got on Marquita Lewis's last nerve.

"Um, excuse me, but did you just roll your eyes?"

That Britney Spears song, "Oops! . . . I Did It Again," popped into Marquita's head. She wasn't trying to get fired from another job. She just got this waitress gig six weeks ago and had already been late five times. The last thing she needed was some bougie customer complaining about her because of some dumb breakfast order.

And it wasn't really her fault anyway. She didn't roll her eyes to be rude. It was an involuntary condition, brought on whenever she was in the vicinity of stupid. I mean, come on. How you gon' ask for all these extra accommodations, then get mad because it costs more?

"I don't think I rolled my eyes," Marquita said back to the woman. "I'm not sure what you saw, but I'm just trying to get your order right."

The woman's friend lifted a finger to get Marquita's attention. "Oh, and make sure there's no pesticides in my smoothie. I only eat organic greens."

"You did it again! How dare you roll your eyes. Is my order too difficult for you?" Bougie jumped out of her seat, grabbing her purse. "Come on, Lisa. We are not eating here. I have never in my life dealt with such a rude waitress."

"Wait. Sit back down. I'll put your order in. I'll even throw in a gluten-free nut bar. And they are yummy." The last thing Marquita needed was to cause a scene. She had already been put on probation because of her tardiness.

But now, all of a sudden, they didn't care about the gluten-free extras. The woman got up, and the two of them three-inch heeled it out of the restaurant.

Marquita yelled, "It's like that, huh? Y'all probably weren't going to tip anyway. Go on to Burger King and get a sandwich you can afford."

It wasn't until she heard the gasps at the surrounding tables that she thought, *I shouldn't have done that.* Rent was due next week. She was already behind and expecting an eviction notice any day now. She just hoped her manager was outside on another one of his gazillion smoke breaks and didn't see what she'd done.

"Can I speak with you in my office, Marquita?" the manager said as he came up behind her.

Dog and double dog. Her nosy coworkers turned their heads—all up in her business. "Ain't none of y'alls name Marquita, so there's no need to look this way. Mind your business. Take orders."

"Marquita!" the manager snapped. "Now!"

"I'm coming. I'm coming." She sullenly walked behind him, taking note of the shirt sloppily hanging from the back of his pants as he slue-footed his way to the office. Marquita wanted to kick herself. She had just messed things up again for her and her son, Marcus. Since she was fourteen years old, Marquita had been working and taking care of herself. She'd had Marcus two months ago, a week before her nineteenth birthday.

They stepped into her manager's Cracker Jack–box size office. Marquita took some boxes off the chair in front of his desk and then sat down. She'd been through this drill a dozen times since she took on her first job five years ago because her mother was in rehab again, trying to kick a habit she never should've had in the first place. So it became Marquita's responsibility to make sure her younger sister and brother were able to eat.

"I'm letting you go, Marquita."

He said those words with such calm, as if no check for Marquita didn't mean eviction and that she and her son wouldn't be on the street with no place to go.

"You can't. I need this job." She was close to tears as she stood. *Why does this keep happening?*

He shook his head. "We can't afford to lose customers. I've had too many complaints about your behavior, and now you're causing customers to walk out the door. You've got to go."

"Look, I'm sorry about those customers, but they were too bougie for me." She snapped her fingers. "I couldn't help how I responded to them, but I promise I'll do better. Just give me another chance."

"I've given you too many chances. Most of you young girls weren't raised right. I know y'all don't know how to act on a job, so I try to work with y'all." He stood, walked around his desk, and opened the door.

Marquita's neck rolled as her hand went to her hip. "Who don't know how to act? You don't know nothing about how my mama raised me." But her mother, Gloria Lewis, hadn't trained Marquita for much of anything, unless teaching her children how to protest evictions and then how to quickly pick up all their clothes and pack them in their cars once the sheriff showed up to throw them out counted as some type of skill.

The manager backed up a bit and conceded. "I don't know your mother, but I've witnessed how you act at work. It's obvious that you have a lot to learn."

Marquita's eyes brightened with a thought. "What about a warning? You can't just fire me without a warning first, right?" She'd received warnings on all her other jobs before getting booted out the door. It wasn't fair not to get one here as well.

"Girl, bye, what did you think you were getting all those times you showed up late and I told you that couldn't continue?"

"But you never said you were going to fire me. How am I supposed to pay my rent? Me and my son don't have nowhere else to go." She was talking loud and knew that the customers and coworkers heard her begging for her job, but what else could she do? She just had to find a way to keep a job so she could pay her bills.

Why did she have to roll her eyes at those customers? Didn't she know better than that? Or was it like her manager said? She wasn't raised right. If so, how could she possibly know how to act on a job?

"Do I need to call the police and have them cart you off my property?"

She scoffed at that. "It's not *your* property. You up in here collecting a check just like the rest of us."

"Oh, okay, but I'm the only one of us"—his finger wagged from her and then back to him—"who's still collecting a check, because you fired, boo. And I will call the police if you don't take that apron off and get out of here."

The last thing Marquita wanted was for the police to come in here and drag her out like they'd done to her mother on multiple occasions. Marquita still had nightmares about neighbors watching them being thrown out of one place after another. Those were scary times, but things got even scarier when Child Protective Services took them away from their mother when Marquita was eleven. They spent an entire year in foster care, waiting for their mother to get out of yet another rehab and find a place they could move into. When Marquita had her son, she promised him that no one would ever take him away from her.

"No, no. You don't have to call the police." She snatched off the apron. "If you don't want me here, then I don't need to be here. It's not like I can't find another waitress job."

As she walked through the eating area, making her way to the front door, she turned and shouted to the customers, "Don't order the chili. Bugs fall in it all the time, and my wonderful manager feeds it to unsuspecting customers anyway."

4

He ran toward her, trying to chase her out of the restaurant, while simultaneously providing the customers a nervous smile. "We don't have bugs. Don't believe a word she says."

Marquita opened the door and ran out. Her manager was a smoker. No way would he catch her.

"Don't think you're going to get a reference from me. You can forget that!" he yelled as she made her way to her 2003 Chevy Cavalier.

Snapping her fingers and twisting her lip as she got in the car, she forgot about needing a reference. She'd been on this job for less than sixty days. Her last job had been almost ninety days because she'd worked up to two weeks before giving birth to Marcus. She'd experienced back pain on that job and had to take a few days off. She probably couldn't get a reference from them either because she'd showed out when they fired her too.

Sighing deeply, Marquita pulled out of the parking lot and headed to her mother's apartment to pick up her son. He was the bright spot of her day. She hated having to leave him at her mom's place while she worked, but day cares were too expensive. Marquita didn't know how people could afford childcare and be able to eat too. It was all just too much.

When she arrived at her mother's place and saw the eviction notice on the door, she was outdone. Marquita lived on her own, so her mother's constant evictions didn't affect her like they used to. But her brother, Mark, was sixteen and her sister, Kee Kee, was thirteen. Where were they supposed to sleep once Gloria was kicked out of yet another place?

Marquita already didn't like bringing Marcus over here because she never knew what kind of drama might be popping off. She didn't have the money for day care, but if her mother went to another women's shelter, she'd have to find it because she was not letting her son step foot into a place like that.

Rolling her eyes, she snatched the notice off the door and entered the apartment. "Why aren't you in school?" she asked Kee Kee, who was sitting on the sofa, bouncing Marcus on her lap.

"Mama wasn't feeling well so I stayed home to take care of my little man." Kee Kee made cooing sounds. She kissed Marcus's cheeks. "Isn't that right, Moochie?"

Moochie was the nickname Kee Kee had given Marcus. Marquita thought it was cute, but there was nothing cute about her sister skipping school. "You are too smart for this, Kee Kee. Out of the three of us, you have a real chance to get a scholarship, go to college, and get out of here. You are not going to mess that up just because I had a baby."

"I'm just trying to help. I didn't want to leave Moochie with Mama today." Kee Kee nervously cut her eyes toward Gloria's bedroom. Then she plastered that same don't-want-no-trouble smile on her face that appeared whenever Gloria got to acting like she needed Iyanla to fix her life.

Marquita figured that her mother must have gone into a rage, for God knows what, and scared Kee Kee so bad that the girl feared for Moochie. Marquita didn't get why Kee Kee wasn't immune to Gloria's antics by now. The girl was just too soft, too good-hearted to be in this family.

Marquita went into her mother's bedroom. Gloria was lying in bed with a heating pad on her head. The heating pad normally came out after Gloria ranted and raved through the house about some perceived injustice. The whole world always against her.

"What happened now?" Marquita asked.

Gloria lifted the heating pad from her head. "Why are you back so soon? Get fired again?"

Marquita tossed her mom the eviction paper she'd taken off the front door. "Yeah, I got fired and you got evicted again. Let me know when I'm saying something that sounds like a surprise."

"You getting fired sure isn't a surprise. It happens all the time."

Gloria sat up, legs dangling from the side of the bed as she turned off the heating pad.

"And you getting evicted certainly isn't a surprise. It's been happening every five months like clockwork since I was a kid. When will you realize that you have to pay rent if you want to keep a roof over your head?" Marquita had no room to talk, since she was a month behind on her own rent and had just lost her job. But she was new to this. Her mother was true to her eviction game.

"I told that landlord that he had to give me another month to come up with the money. He can't just evict me without getting a court order."

Marquita pointed to the eviction notice. "Isn't that from the court?"

"Don't get my blood boiling again, Marquita. They not just gon' throw me out on the street without a fight." Gloria's hands went to her head.

Marquita didn't want to give her mother another headache, but she wasn't finished. "Don't let Kee Kee miss school to keep Marcus anymore, Mama. It's not fair to her."

"I wasn't feeling well after talking to the landlord. Kee Kee asked to help with Moochie, and she did her school assignments while the Mooch slept."

"Kee Kee is smart, Mama. You can't be acting like a raving lunatic around her. That stuff makes her nervous. That's why she stayed out of school. She was afraid to leave you with Marcus."

Gloria waved that comment off. "She's heard me talk to these slumlords a thousand times. She ain't never missed no school because of it before."

She wasn't trying to disrespect her mother, but Marquita's eyes did that thing they do whenever she heard ignorance.

"Roll your eyes at me again, Marquita Ann Lewis, and I'll knock them in the back of your head."

7

"I'm going home." Marquita walked out of her mother's bedroom, packed up Marcus's diaper bag, and then took her baby out of Kee Kee's arm. "Don't miss school to sit with my kid no more. You are better than that."

Gloria came out of her room. "If you don't like the way we keep Marcus, then why don't you go find his daddy and tell him to watch his own kid. But then again, you won't even tell us who the daddy is."

"I'll watch my baby myself, so Kee Kee can go to school. I can't have her falling behind in school on my conscience."

Marquita put the diaper bag on her shoulder and walked out of the apartment with her baby on her hip. Her mother followed her and started screaming, "Go find that baby's daddy!" for all the neighbors to hear as she made her way down the stairs.

"Go back in the house," Marquita shot back at her.

"Why don't you want Moochie to know who his daddy is? Maybe he can take care of that baby, because you sure can't."

"I take care of Marcus better than you ever took care of us. That's for sure."

"We'll see about that." Gloria went back into her apartment and slammed the door.

Marquita opened the back car door and strapped Marcus into his car seat. She got in the car and sat behind the steering wheel. Taking several deep breaths didn't help her calm down. She screamed. Marcus started crying. Then Marquita hit the steering wheel and screamed again, as if screams could change the world.

The baby cried louder.

"I'm sorry, Moochie. Stop crying." She turned and rubbed his belly to soothe him. "And I'm sorry about your daddy. I'd like to take you to meet him, but I just don't see what good it would do. Anyway, he's got his own problems. Don't see how telling him about you is going to change anything."

CHAPTER 2

Pulling herself out of bed, Trish Robinson stretched to get the kink out of her neck and glanced over at her husband's snoring form. He used to give good massages, good hugs, good everything, but that was before everything went left. Rolling her neck from side to side, she looped her fingers together to give her arms and back a stretch, then took a long, deep, do-I-have-to-start-this-day-already sigh.

"I will sing a fruitful song in a barren land." Every morning since the day her precious son was told he might never walk again, Trish sang those words to encourage herself to keep on fighting, keep getting out of bed every morning so she could see how God would turn her midnight into sweet, sunshiny days.

"Mama!"

"I'm coming, Jon-Jon." They lived in a ranch-style home with nine-foot-high ceilings, so sound traveled. Even though their master bedroom was on the opposite side of the house from Jon-Jon's room, she heard him holler her name.

Jon-Jon rarely hollered for her first thing in the morning, but when he did, Trish knew what that meant. She rushed into the bathroom and grabbed a washcloth, towel, wet wipes, and a Depend for her precious twenty-year-old. Long, deep sigh. "I will sing a fruitful song . . ."

Before stepping out of her bedroom, Trish made sure to plaster that same generic smile on her face that she hoped said to her son, "All is right with the world," even though it wasn't. Picking up her smartphone, she pulled up YouTube and put on some praise music. She danced to "You Deserve My Praise" by Tamela Mann as she entered Jon-Jon's room.

"Hey, handsome." He was a younger version of his father, with skin the color of a russet potato. He and his father both sported goatees, but Jon-Jon hadn't brushed his hair in a month. So, where his dad had a low-cut fade, Jon-Jon had a matted, coming-to-America-straight-out-of-Africa untamed afro sitting on top of his head.

"Turn it off, Mama. I'm not in the mood for that this morning."

"Boy, you better give God some praise." She continued dancing, trying to change his mood. The room smelled foul, like soiled diapers mixed with sweat, but she resisted the urge to cover her nose.

"For what?" Jon-Jon flung the covers off his bed, revealing soiled sheets. "Who in their right mind would praise God for this?"

Trish's heart went out to her son. Her only son. A son she had expected to be in his second year of college and on his way to the NFL the following year. At least that's what the scout had told them.

She had expected to attend her son's wedding and welcome grandchildren into her home one day. But life had dealt them such a low and sneaky blow that it was hard to get back up. Trish refused to give up, refused to stop believing that God could change their circumstances.

Trish placed her phone on the dresser and let the music fill the room as she rolled her son to the left so she could unhook the sheets from his mattress. Then she rolled him to the right and unhooked the other side. "What happened to you isn't fair, son. But you woke up this morning and every morning since that horrible accident. That's something to thank the good Lord for, isn't it?"

"You're changing the boy's diaper, Trish. At least let him be angry at God while you're cleaning his behind." Dwayne wiped the sleep from his eyes as he stood in the doorway.

"Tell her to turn the music off, Dad. I'm not in the mood."

Why couldn't Dwayne have just stayed asleep? Why'd he have to come in here, getting Jon-Jon worked up with all his foolish talk about being mad at God? She waved him into the room. "Come help me lift Jon-Jon's waist so I can pull this Depend off."

"It's a diaper," Dwayne snarled.

That deep baritone voice of Dwayne's used to give her that come hither feeling, with fluttering all up in her stomach. Now she just wanted to stuff a rag in his mouth so he would shut up. "Just help me, or get out of here and leave us alone. I'm not doing this with you this morning, Dwayne."

He came into the room, went straight to the dresser where her phone was, and stopped the music from playing. He then put his shirt over his nose as he lifted Jon-Jon's waist.

Snatching the shirt from his nose, Trish wanted to scream at her husband. How dare he treat his own son this way? She side-eyed him, daring him to put that shirt back over his nose as she cleaned Jon-Jon. She then pulled the new Depend up to cover her son.

Dwayne helped her take the sheets off the bed, holding Jon-Jon to one side and then rolling Jon-Jon to the other side while she moved the sheets.

She took a laundry bag out of Jon-Jon's closet, put the soiled sheets in it, and tried to hand it to Dwayne. "Can you take this to the laundry room?"

"Have you lost your mind?" Turning his nose up, Dwayne scurried out of the room like he smelled smoke and needed to put out the fire. Although he had no problem lifting Jon-Jon out of the bed or helping with his physical therapy, he rarely helped her clean Jon-Jon. He said he didn't have the stomach for it. Trish just wished he wasn't so mean about it.

Turning back to Jon-Jon, she playfully nudged his shoulder. "All better. That wasn't so bad, was it?"

She took the dirty linens to the laundry, then came back to

Jon-Jon's room and vacuumed the floor. She wiped off his table and then held out a hand to Jon-Jon. "Now let me get you out of that bed."

He shook his head. "Not today, Mom. Just leave me alone. I just want to be left alone."

She started to object. The doctor said it wasn't good for Jon-Jon to lie in bed all day. He didn't want his muscles to atrophy. But as he turned his head away from her, she saw the tear roll down his cheek. "I'll fix you some pancakes."

No response.

Trish went to her master bathroom, brushed her teeth, took the headwrap off, and let her hair fall on her honey-toned shoulders. Catching a glimpse of herself in the mirror brought on a sigh. Trish's eyes were so puffy that it looked as if she had gone five rounds with Floyd Mayweather and floated like a feather with every jab and uppercut to her face. Exhaustion hung on her shoulders like an old friend. If Jon-Jon didn't need her, she would climb back in bed and sleep as if sleep was money and she was trying to get paid. But sleep was a luxury she couldn't afford, so she made her way to the kitchen to take care of breakfast.

Pancakes were her son's favorite breakfast, guaranteed to put a smile on his face. When he was younger he'd told her that he didn't want his dad's pancakes because, as he put it, "Nobody fixes pancakes like you, Mama." Ever since then, Trish made sure to sprinkle a little extra cinnamon in the pancake mix.

As the cinnamon mixed into the pancake batter, the color change was just a shade darker than her walls. These days, a lot of interior walls were being painted gray, but Trish liked warmer colors. She had picked a color called golden rod, which was a mix between yellow and brown, for her interior color. Because of the high ceilings and the open floor plan, the color worked and didn't darken the house much at all.

Mixing her batter, she added vanilla extract and melted butter, but the cinnamon she had already added was the key to great pancakes.

That, and the extra butter she slathered on the cakes while they cooked in her special pancake-making skillet, like every good Southern mother worth her cooking apron would.

"Make me a few of them cakes." Dwayne sat down at the kitchen counter.

Lip curled, displaying her disgust, she responded, "I know you didn't just ask me to fix you nothing after the way you treated my son this morning."

"He's my son, too, Trish. And if he would put forth a little effort during physical therapy, he'd be able to get himself out of that bed and into his wheelchair. Then he could get to the bathroom on his own."

"He's trying, Dwayne. You just don't care what any of us are going through." She was married to a man who didn't open his eyes to see anybody's needs but his own. He hadn't always been like this though. Jon-Jon's accident had changed him, turned him into someone she barely recognized.

"I'm hungry, Trish. I don't have time to argue with you this morning."

She turned to give him a preview of the cold shoulder he'd be receiving all day long, but that's when she realized he had his work shirt on. He'd just gotten off work at eleven last night and was now going in for another shift.

He'd been working extra shifts as a forklift driver ever since he found this job about three months ago, after being fired from a job he'd held for fifteen years. The company had a no-tolerance policy when it came to attendance and didn't care if Dwayne was at the hospital as his son fought for his life.

While Dwayne was losing one job and searching for another, Trish had taken family medical leave from her fourth grade teaching position. Dwayne had been fine with that, but when Jon-Jon didn't get better and the pay checks stopped coming after two months, he told her to go back to work. But how could she go back to school and teach other kids when her son couldn't even get out of bed without help? So she handed in her resignation.

Dwayne had been smoking mad when he discovered that she quit her job without discussing it with him. Still, he had asked for extra hours on his job so they could catch up on some bills. So if he wanted to eat, she would feed him. "You want sausage links and eggs too?"

"Naw, pancakes are good enough. I got to get going."

Trish put some butter in the skillet and turned her back to Dwayne as she prayed he wouldn't ask . . . *Don't ask. Don't ask.*

"Heard anything from that blood-sucking attorney?"

She put the mix in the pan and turned up the fire a bit. The sooner she got him on his way, the easier her day would be. "Not since he told us that the court case has been postponed again."

"You still think them people aren't trying to pull a fast one? They won't even give us our day in court. Haven't even given our boy an 'I'm sorry,' or a 'Hey, let me pay those hospital bills.'"

Flipping the pancakes and buttering the smooth side, she turned to him. Jon-Jon's room was just off the kitchen, about fifteen feet from where she stood, so she whispered. "If you would let Jon-Jon accept the money from the insurance settlement, we could get some of these bills paid."

"Jon-Jon's injuries and lifetime loss of income is worth way more than that insurance policy they got."

"Yeah, but at least we'd have something."

"Something that didn't cost them nothing. You think rich people like that lose sleep over their insurance premiums going up? What about what my boy lost? They owe us, and all they've done is try to get out of paying for what they did." He slammed his fist against the counter.

She put his pancakes on a plate, handed it to him, and held out the syrup. "Not saying they don't owe Jon-Jon more, but the bills are piling up. You're working all this overtime, trying to cover hospital bills and household bills, like a hamster on a spinning wheel."

Snatching the syrup from her outstretched hand, he said, "That's why you shouldn't have quit your job. Who does that?"

Hands on hips and neck rolling, she fired back, "A woman whose son has been paralyzed for six months, that's who."

Stabbing his fork into his pancakes, Dwayne swirled them around the plate to soak in the syrup and then stuffed them in his mouth.

She sighed, ready to throw in the towel. "Why can't we stop fighting and being so angry? We can't pay for the next surgery Jon-Jon needs. And if he doesn't get it, he has even less of a chance of walking again. Maybe it's time to just take the money and move on with our lives."

Dwayne's lip drew into a snarl. His eyes held disdain for her words. "Forgiveness runs deep with you, don't it? Too deep."

She wished that was true. Since she was a little girl sitting in the church sanctuary, listening to Pastor Greenwald talk about forgiveness like it was the answer to all the ills of the world, Trish had made up her mind to forgive. But, for the life of her, she couldn't find a way to forgive her husband for becoming as mean and surly as a coiling rattlesnake.

She wanted out of this marriage, but every time she decided enough was enough, she'd hear Pastor Greenwald's message ringing in her head. Why had she attended church that day? Pastor Greenwald's words had sounded so reasonable, so just and full of grace. But that was before her son lost the use of his legs and his football scholarship, before she had to give up hope of all the grandchildren she thought she'd have, and before her husband turned into Hannibal Lecter— without the cannibalism, just all the evil.

Wiping his mouth, Dwayne stood and put his plate in the sink while leering at her. "Now you acting like you don't hear nobody. You good at that silent game until you need my money for these bills. You talk real good then."

Why wouldn't he just divorce her already? This misery that crept up on her every gut-wrenching day was becoming too much to bear. Whenever she thought things might be getting better, she'd go to sleep and wake up to the same misery, like that movie *Groundhog Day.*

Slamming the spatula on the counter, nostrils flaring like a lioness who'd found her prey, she attacked. "I have put up with your mess for months now. You want to be hateful for the rest of your life, fine. But here's what you ain't gon' do . . ." Yeah, she was a teacher by profession and was speaking all types of ebonics, but as she got in Dwayne's face, she didn't care about proper English. "You are not going to pull me into your darkness. I don't want to have this conversation with you ever again. You want to know what the lawyers are doing about Jon-Jon's case, then call them yourself."

Leaning back like he wanted to put space between him and Trish, Dwayne said, "You're the one at home. I'm working extra hours, so I don't have time to make those calls."

"I don't care!" she shouted at him, hands flailing in the air.

"Mom, stop yelling!" Jon-Jon called out from his bedroom.

"Oh, so it's like that now?" Dwayne whispered.

Lowering her tone, while still rolling her neck from side to side, she said, "You better believe it's like that. Either tell Jon-Jon to accept the insurance settlement or deal with the attorneys yourself." She plated Jon-Jon's pancakes as she gave Dwayne an I-wish-you-would-say-something-else-to-me staredown.

"You done changed Trish." He shook his head but didn't say anything else.

Trish picked up the syrup and left her husband in the kitchen to fix his own lunch and go on about his business.

When she and Dwayne first married, Trish thought she'd found her little piece of heaven on earth. He'd been good to her, and she'd loved him for it. When the doctors told her she wouldn't be able to have any more children after Jon-Jon was born, Dwayne didn't trip. They were grateful that they had a son, and they made him their world.

Maybe they were wrong for doing that because their world was now crumbling around them, and neither of them knew what to do about all the broken pieces. The only thing it seemed they knew to do was to keep waking up so Jon-Jon would have somebody to take care of him.

She and Dwayne had once been lovers, friends, and confidantes. They were now only civil with each other in front of Jon-Jon, but this morning they couldn't even manage that. She was sure Jon-Jon felt awful and blamed himself for her and Dwayne's problems. She hated the thought of that more than anything.

She heard Dwayne slam the garage door as he left the house. Trish came back into the kitchen, rested her hands on the counter, and shook her head as her eyes watered. Tears in the rain, too many reasons to name, just pain, pain, pain.

CHAPTER 3

Alexis Marshall could hardly believe that her twins, Ella and Ethan, had just turned eleven. The years were moving way too fast. Before she knew it they would be off to college and treating her like an afterthought.

But today they were only eleven, and she was having the time of her life spoiling them. For their birthday party, she and Michael hired face painters, a juggler, a magician, and a Justin Bieber impersonator. With their forty-five-hundred-square-foot open floor plan, they could have just moved some furniture around and hosted the twenty-three kids in the space between the living room and kitchen.

But Ella and Ethan wanted to show off the new pool their dad had installed in the backyard. The pool was a true work of art, so she could understand why the kids wanted to show it off. There were three components to the pool: a circular hot tub, connected to the oval twenty-eight foot pool, and—the third and most eye-catching of all—the mountainous wall that surrounded it.

Alexis put her long auburn hair in a bun on the top of her head. Then she remembered the terrible sunburn she got on the back of her neck last year in this Carolina heat. Today was the eighth day of June and the sun was beaming, so she went to her bedroom and put on the straw hat Michael purchased for her during one of their travels to the Caribbean.

Looking in the mirror, her green eyes smiled back at her. *This is perfect for keeping the sun off of my neck.* She rushed out of the room and back to the kitchen; she had hungry kids to feed.

Michael had grilled the hot dogs and burgers for the party before retreating into his home office to take care of some important business—on his kids' birthday. You'd think business could wait. She tried not to complain. Michael was a wonderful provider, neither the kids nor she wanted for anything. He was in the middle of a deal to sell the tech business he and his business partner started thirteen years ago, and then life would be even sweeter.

So she cut him some slack as she filled bowls with chips and put the hot dogs and burgers in buns. Then she put the food on a tray and headed outside to feed the hungry munchkins in her backyard.

The Justin Bieber look-a-like was standing by the pool, microphone in hand, singing, "Love Yourself." Some of the kids were singing along. Others were swimming and a few were dancing. She caught the looks on Ethan's and Ella's faces and knew she'd done good. They were smiling. They were happy.

Ethan started climbing the wall to dive into the pool. The first level of the structure was built of beautiful rocks and stones. The second level had a waterfall with several stones sticking out of the rock work. There was no diving board because the protruding stones were used for that. At the top of the structure was a thick stone, wide enough to stand on.

"No diving today, Ethan." Alexis pointed downward and Ethan complied. She didn't want the other kids climbing on that wall and possibly hurting themselves.

That structure was the only thing Alexis didn't like about the design. She often admonished Michael to make sure those stones were wiped clean. With the water falling onto them, she worried that they could become slick and someone might slip and fall, but Michael accused her of worrying too much. So she let it go and just let the kids enjoy themselves.

"Come and get it!" She set the food on the picnic table and then moved out of the way as the kids rushed the table. The plates, cups, and juice had already been laid out, so Alexis stood back and watched them fix their plates and then sit or stand around the pool, eating and chatting amongst themselves.

It was a carefree life—the kind Alexis hadn't known until she met and married Michael. Her American prince stepped into her life and opened her eyes to a world of possibilities. She and her children were blessed, and Alexis didn't take that for granted.

Michael walked up to her and placed a hand on her shoulder. He had grayed prematurely, reminding her of a younger Michael Douglas from the movie *Wall Street*. Her Michael had even said the movie's catch phrase, "Greed is good," when he and his business partner joked about the money flowing into their business.

"You hanging out with us?"

"Not yet." He waved a hand, getting the kids attention. "Okay, kids, the juggler and the magician are here. Have a seat around the pool so we can start the show."

"Yay!" The kids got excited.

Ethan came up to his father. "Dad, you said you were going to race me in the pool, remember?"

Michael grinned and gave him a playful punch. "You don't really want me to embarrass you on your birthday, do you?"

Ethan flexed his eleven-year-old muscles. "I've been practicing. I beat Ella last week, and I'll beat you too."

Turning to Alexis, Michael said, "You hear your son? He actually thinks he can beat me."

She shrugged. "He has been practicing."

"Okay, I'll tell you what, son. You take over for your mom for a few minutes. Make sure everyone sits down and watches the show. Then, after the party I will show you why I was a champion swimmer in college."

Alexis elbowed her husband and gave him the not-again side-eye. "You're not going to watch the magic show?"

"Can't right now. And I need you to come into my office with me."

Alexis extended her arm toward the kids in the yard. "I'm kind of busy hosting a party for our children right now."

"Can't one of the other moms take over for a few minutes?"

Her husband had come out to the pool area wearing black slacks, black leather shoes, and a white shirt with the two top buttons undone. Next to him she looked underdressed in her bright-yellow sundress, straw hat, and flip-flops. "And why are you dressed like this on a Saturday afternoon?"

He looked down at himself. "I took my tie off."

She laughed. "That makes it all right then."

"I need you, Alexis."

When she didn't respond, he pulled her into his arms. She purred and snuggled up to him. Alexis loved being in Michael's arms. She felt safe, secure, and fully satisfied. Being with him felt like home, like she was always meant to be with this man. And that cologne—a mix of mint, lemon, vanilla, and cedarwood—tore down her resolve. "You're not playing fair. You know I can't resist your hugs."

"Then stop resisting. Come with me." He kissed her neck and then became serious. "I wouldn't interrupt the party if it wasn't important."

"I don't like being in your office."

Michael lifted his hands, backing up a bit. "It's okay. You can pick up my stapler or touch anything else you want. I promise."

Michael was so protective over every little thing in his office. Alexis still remembered an incident that occurred about seven years ago when she was searching through his desk for a notepad and pencil so she could help Ethan with a drawing project.

She had come across a wallet-size picture of a beautiful African-American baby. The baby looked like a cherub with a tiny black beauty mark next to her nose. When she asked him about the photo, Michael had become agitated. He'd said the baby belonged to a friend of his. Alexis hadn't questioned his honesty about the picture, she just didn't understand why he was so upset that she had found the photo.

She didn't want to go to his office, but the kids were seated, watching the magician. The show would take at least twenty minutes, and then the juggler would dazzle them with his skills. Two of the moms volunteered to chaperone for a few minutes, so she left the backyard.

Michael's office was toward the back of the house. His window overlooked the backyard, so she followed him to his office and then opened the blinds. "Before I listen to whatever you need from me, you have to make me a promise."

Sitting on the edge of his desk, he said, "You know I never agree to anything without all the details."

Ever the businessman. She admired that about him, but there were times when she needed him to just be Michael—her husband and the kids' dad. "I just want you to promise to be present for the kids' next birthday party. Not just in body but all the way in." She folded her arms across her chest. "I mean it, Michael, if I have to put a lock on your office door, I will. They will be grown and gone before we know it. Don't you want to spend more time with them?"

"Babe, I'm sorry about today. But Peter and I are having issues with the sale of the company, and you know that we'll be set for life if this deal goes through."

Alexis nodded. Michael and Peter had been college roommates who created apps that helped users add funny videos and emojis to their texts. Users flocked to the app and now a major player in the business wanted to buy the company. If Michael needed her help, then she was here for him. "What can I do?"

"I just got off the phone with Peter, and he's nervous about our upcoming court case. He thinks if those people go shooting their mouths off about you getting into an accident while texting and driving, that our deal might go up in smoke."

Alexis' heart rate sped up as her mind's eye flashed back to that terrible accident. She rubbed the left side of her chest as she exhaled. "I feel so bad for that young man, Michael. I'm usually a good driver. I should have never reached for my phone like that."

"Don't beat yourself up, babe. Accidents happen. But that kid's father won't go away. He wants his day in court, and we just can't allow that."

"But I thought you said our insurance was more than enough to cover the accident? You told me that you would take good care of that young man." Alexis bit her lip so hard she touched it to make sure she didn't draw blood.

"The insurance money is enough, but the boy you hit was in college on a football scholarship, and those people think his earning potential is higher than the insurance policy. Basically, they know we have money and are trying to cash in."

Those people . . . She didn't like the way Michael said that. "The father's name is Dwayne John Robinson. And the young man I hit is John Robinson."

Michael shrugged. "I'm trying to make this go away. But if they won't be reasonable, I may need you to step in."

She sat down in front of his desk. It was a big mahogany desk, the kind that spoke of wealth and importance. He knew how to make things go away. Just like how he put her mother in a nursing home so he wouldn't have to see or deal with her. And how he got Ethan's kindergarten teacher to promote Ethan to the first grade even though their son hadn't been ready. But Michael couldn't deal with Ella moving to the next grade without her brother, so presto, no more problem. But what did Alexis know about making things go away?

"I would contact them myself, but Peter thinks I should lay low. The last thing we need is to end up on the news with some nosy reporter connecting this accident with my company while we're in the middle of selling the business."

She put her hands in her lap. "John was hurt really bad in the accident. I don't know how to make that go away."

"Hon, I know you don't like dealing with these kind of things, but you talk people off ledges all the time. You're good at dealing with other people's drama. I just need you to convince those people to drop this court case and go to arbitration."

Alexis worked with mentally ill people who were transitioning from one difficult phase of life to another. She had never worked with a family whose child's life had been destroyed in an accident—and one she had caused, no less—but her husband didn't seem to recognize the difference. She got up and headed for the door.

Michael wasn't finished. "This needs to be handled quickly, Alexis. And if those people ask you to confirm that you were texting and driving, don't."

"The police already know what I was doing, Michael." She bit her lip again. "I don't know. You said you would handle this."

"What do you think our lawyer has been trying to do? Look, I tried to get it done quietly. But those people are being difficult, and I may need your help. That's all I'm saying, okay?"

She was about to say something else, but she could tell he was getting agitated with her. Yes, the accident had been her fault, but she needed Michael to take care of it and help that kid get better because she just couldn't deal with the fact that she had ruined someone else's life.

Leaving his office, she headed for the kitchen. Cut the cake. It was a half-white, half-chocolate cake, since Ella liked white and Ethan liked chocolate. Instead of taking it outside for the kids, she put about three pieces of the chocolate cake in a bowl, grabbed a spoon, and ate the cake so fast that her stomach protested.

Alexis scurried off to the bathroom, holding her mouth with one hand and her quivering stomach with the other. She made it to the bathroom, kicked the door closed with her foot as she lowered her head into the toilet, and threw up.

Her hat fell on the floor as she continued emptying the contents of her belly. When she finally stood, she took a moment to settle her breathing. She turned on the sink and splashed water in her mouth, straightened, then looked at herself in the mirror. She closed her eyes and breathed as if she were in a Lamaze class practicing breathing techniques. She then opened the bathroom door and headed back to the party.

In the kitchen again, guilt pricked her heart as one of the moms rushed over to her. "Someone ate some of the cake. I'm so sorry. I tried to watch the kids. But one or two of them must have slipped past me."

Alexis had destroyed the twins' beautiful cake. But she had also destroyed a young man's life. The sugar rush helped her to cope. She waved off the comment. "Ethan and Ella won't care." She picked up the cake plates and asked, "Can you help me get this delicious cake out there so the kids can enjoy it?"

CHAPTER 4

J ust another sad song. Marquita turned the radio off. She wasn't in the mood for some love-gone-wrong-cause-he-did-me-wrong song. Not when she and Moochie had just left the job center where she put together her first-ever résumé. The experience had not been pretty, especially when the social worker who helped her with the résumé had the audacity to ask, "Why have you had five jobs in one year?"

Really? The woman stared at her as if she demanded an answer. So Marquita asked her, "Why does the sun rise in the morning, and why does the moon come out at night?"

Ms. Fancy Pants social worker didn't have an answer for that. She just lifted the folder that held Marquita's résumés and said, "Working on your attitude might help you keep a job longer than two months at a time."

"Can y'all help me with day care? I'm still on the waiting list, and it will be at least two years before my number comes up with this dumb social service block grant in Charlotte." Marquita's head rocked from side to side, and she scowled at the woman as her voice elevated.

The social worker was still holding the folder with the résumés they had just created. She told Marquita, "I don't have any childcare vouchers. You'll have to check back with me. Or research to see if a church or day care has a subsidized program."

Rolling her eyes, Marquita took the résumés from the woman. She lifted Moochie's baby carrier and headed for her car. She didn't need a lecture from some woman who knew nothing about her. How was she to know why she couldn't keep a job? It wasn't like she didn't want to work. Things just happen. No rhyme. No rhythm. It just is what it is.

Arriving home, Marquita sighed deeply. She hated her apartment. Hated how winos were able to hang out in front of the building. She had complained to her slumlord, but he didn't care. All he wanted was the rent on the first of the month. "Come on, Moochie, let's get in the house before Larry asks for our spare change."

She passed the drunks on the porch and was about to put the key in the lock when she saw the eviction notice taped to her door.

"Looks like Ms. Thang has to find a new place to live," Larry said to his drunk buddy.

Marquita shot back at him. "Looks like Larry needs Alcoholics Anonymous and a quick lesson in 'mind your own business.'"

Snatching the ten-day notice off her door, she put the key in the lock and entered her apartment, slamming the door behind her. The building had four units. Larry the wino lived in the unit upstairs. Some guy who acted like he was hiding from the po-po lived in the unit across from Larry. She didn't know his name and didn't want to know it. The apartment on the first floor, across the hall from hers, was empty.

She threw the notice in the trash and then laid Moochie in the middle of her bed. No sense in thinking about something she couldn't do anything about. She didn't have the rent money and wouldn't have it until she got another job.

Marquita went into the kitchen to start cleaning and used her cell phone to turn on some music. Turning the volume up, she danced and sang as she washed the dishes and wiped down the kitchen counter. She then grabbed the broom and began sweeping. The fake pleather on the arms of the sofa and chair were constantly rubbing off. Each day, there were flakes of brown pleather on her floor. She'd bought the sofa and chair from a local Goodwill for fifty dollars. She wanted a refund.

Marquita didn't own a vacuum, so she swept the carpeted living room floor with her broom, then continued sweeping all the dirt and pleather into the kitchen until she had all the dirt in one pile. She was about to use her dustpan to pick the dirt up when her doorbell rang.

Marquita leaned the broom against the wall. She didn't know anybody in this neighborhood, so she had no idea why someone was ringing her doorbell. And if it was Larry, she was going to let him have it, just as she did the last time he had the nerve to knock on her door asking for money. "Who is it?"

"It's me, Rob. I'm here to collect the rent."

"What?" She put her hand to her ear.

"Turn down the music, and you'll be able to hear me!" he shouted.

Marquita slid her thumb upward on her cell phone and the music stopped. Walking to the door, she put her left eyeball against the peephole. It was her landlord. His dark-blue eyes stared back at her. He was balding at the front of his head, so he swooped the hair from the right side of his head to the left side.

Stepping away from the door, Marquita was clueless as to what to do next. She should have known he would come knocking. Her mother's landlords always banged on the door, demanding rent before they were thrown out.

"Did you hear me, Marquita? I need the rent money."

Leaning against the wall as if she expected the landlord to try to kick in her front door, she said, "I heard you, but I need more time."

"The law says I only have to give you ten days."

Adulting was harder than she thought, but being a kid had been no bed of roses either. Marquita never felt stable or like she could relax and call any place her mother moved into home. She didn't want that kind of life for her son. "I just got my résumés done today, so I should have another job in a couple of weeks."

"That's not going to cut it, Marquita. You're already two months behind. I've tried to be nice, but I can't let you stay here for free," Rob told her.

Marquita didn't like the way her slumlord demanded money like he was in the right and she was in the wrong. A boldness swept over her. She swung the door open. "What about the garbage disposal you never fixed?" She pointed toward Larry and his drunk friend. "And why you let these winos hang around the front porch like this?"

Larry slowly turned his head in her direction and stuck out his tongue at her. "I have a repairman scheduled to fix the garbage disposal, but that doesn't mean you can skip out on the rent."

Shaking a finger toward Larry again, she said, "And what about them? I have a kid in here. This don't even seem like a safe place to live."

Larry said, "You won't be living here much longer, so don't worry about us." He and his friend high-fived.

"Shut up, Larry, and get off my porch." Marquita slammed the door, not caring that the landlord was still standing there. In a huff, she sat down on her sofa.

Marquita's journal was on the coffee table next to her broken-down sofa. She picked up the journal, opened it to an empty page, grabbed her pencil, and started writing. When she was writing, nothing else mattered, even when she was writing about having a broken heart because the guy she'd had a baby by hadn't called, texted, or nothing since he made all those promises of love last summer.

She thought she had found someone to love her—someone who made her feel special. She thought they would build a life together. But like a dummy, she gave her heart to a guy who forgot all about her once he was back around all his college friends.

Moochie started crying, letting her know that he was either wet or hungry. She prayed he was just hungry, because the diapers were running low. Putting her journal down, she headed to the bedroom.

"Mommy's coming." She checked his diaper. It was wet and full of poo. Marquita rolled her eyes like they were trying to pop out of her head. She told Moochie, "I hope you got some diaper money, because you're using up these diapers too fast."

He cried louder.

"Okay, okay." She changed his diaper and then made his bottle. As she fed her son, she watched his lips tighten around the nipple of the bottle as those chunky cheeks of his compressed in and out, in and out. For a two-month-old, he sure did eat a lot. What was she going to do when he was two, or ten for that matter?

He downed the bottle. Marquita burped him and then laid him back down.

Moochie laid there and cooed while Marquita fretted and worried. "How on earth am I going to take care of you?"

CHAPTER 5

Help us understand what's going on, Dr. Phillips. Jon-Jon is strong. He's always been athletic. Why isn't he walking yet?" They were at the orthopedic office. Jon-Jon's doctor had a suite inside the same Novant hospital where Jon-Jon had his last two surgeries. Trish loved this place because it was fully equipped to handle Jon-Jon's needs—X-ray machines, nurses, and physical therapists on staff.

Dr. Phillips wrote something in Jon-Jon's file before putting down his pen and looking at Trish. "Jon-Jon gave me permission to speak with you and Mr. Robinson, so I was hoping we could discuss some observations that I think might be hindering his progress."

Jon-Jon had a physical therapy appointment today. Dr. Phillips had called yesterday and asked that they meet with him while Jon-Jon worked out with the physical therapist. Trish and Dwayne were now seated in front of Dr. Phillips's rich mahogany desk. "I don't like the sound of this," Trish said. "If he's not making progress, then . . ."

Dwayne interrupted Trish's conversation with the doctor. "He's saying that Jon-Jon done got lazy. And why wouldn't he? You do everything for him. You won't even let him lift himself up in that bed to get his own cup of water."

Like a mother giving her disabled son a glass of water was too much coddling for him. Trish shifted in her seat, trying to create a little more space between her and Dwayne.

"No, Mr. Robinson. That's not what I'm saying at all." Dr. Phillips spanned his gaze from Dwayne to Trish. "As I told you before, your

31

son's spine was severely damaged in the accident. His prognosis is an AIS grade B, where he has motor complete but sensory incomplete spinal cord damage."

"We know all that, Doc. You've told us several times that Jon-Jon might never walk again because of this"—Dwayne waved a dismissive hand—"motor complete thing you've mentioned over and over . . . which just simply means he ain't moving no muscles."

An inferno was building inside Trish. She put a hand to her temple and tried to massage away the ensuing headache. Dwayne was always shouting and interrupting and getting in the way of Jon-Jon's recovery. He couldn't just sit here and take in information, find out how he could help. Dwayne was just a pain "where the sun don't shine." She tuned him out and tried her best to listen to the doctor.

Dr. Phillips was saying, "I don't deny that his lack of motor functions means he may never walk again, but he hasn't lost all sensory functions, so there's a chance."

"Then why ain't he walking?" Dwayne demanded. "Why ain't he back on that football field? It's been six months."

Ain't . . . ain't . . . ain't. Did Dwayne have to mangle the English language like Ray Lewis coming in for a tackle that would leave his opponent twisted and shattered? Her eyes rolled to the back of her head.

And did everything on God's green earth have to center around that football field? You'd think Dwayne didn't want a son if he couldn't run up and down some field, getting tackled by guys twice his size, coming home bruised and bandaged. What was so great about football? She couldn't care less if he ever played again. She just wanted Jon-Jon to walk and have a normal life. But what was *normal* anymore?

"I don't know about football, Mr. Robinson. I don't even know if your son can ever walk again. But from what I know about this kind of injury, he's got a 33 percent chance of being ambulatory."

"Thirty-three percent is hardly any chance at all. And now you want more money for another surgery you can't even give us good odds on." Dwayne stuffed his hand in his pocket and came up with change. He counted out thirty-three cents and slammed it on Dr. Phillips's desk.

Trish jumped. Put her hand to her heart.

Dwayne ignored her and continued his assault on Dr. Phillips. "There, I just gave you thirty-three cents. Now, you tell me what you can do with that?"

Trish had just purchased a candle from Black Girl Candle Company called Headache Be Gone. She was going to light it as soon as she got back home. "Dwayne, will you please let the doctor speak."

Dwayne swung around, lashing out at her. "I am letting him speak. He ain't saying nothing we don't already know." He turned back to the doctor. "Am I right? Haven't we already been over this stuff? How many times you gotta bring us down here to tell us that my son might never walk again?"

Trish let out a long-suffering sigh, followed by eyes fluttering heavenward. "Do you have anything new to tell us, Dr. Phillips? Jon-Jon's been back in physical therapy for two months now. Is his physical therapist seeing any improvement?"

"That's actually what I wanted to discuss today. We really need to schedule that surgery as soon as possible to get the fluid off his spine, because 33 percent actually gives Jon-Jon a good chance at walking again. But his chance for recovery will seriously diminish if we can't get that surgery in motion. Another thing is—to be frank—your son has basically given up."

"Jon-Jon ain't no quitter." Dwayne shot out of his seat and paced around the room. "The boy's just gotten lazy." He pointed an accusatory finger at Trish. "If his mom would go back to work and stop treating him like a baby, maybe he'd do more."

"I don't treat him like a baby." Her son couldn't walk, and this man—the man she married—was giving her guff because she handed

Jon-Jon a glass of water rather than making him stretch his upper body to get it himself. "You like pointing that finger, but you need to ask yourself if you're helping enough."

"Helping enough!" Dwayne threw up his hands. "Who's putting food on the table, woman? Who's keeping that roof over your jobless head?"

Getting out of her seat, she huffed like a bull with a matador in sight. "If you say one more thing about my job, I swear for God, I'm going to—"

Dr. Phillips held up a hand. "I don't want to start an argument. I'm just wondering if either of you have noticed that Jon-Jon is depressed."

"Of course he's depressed. He can't walk," Dwayne barked.

"In my opinion, he's falling into a clinical depression. I don't think your son wants to live anymore, let alone walk."

"Wait . . . what?" Trish's hand went to her heart as she sat back down. They had lost so much since the accident. If they lost Jon-Jon after everything else, she honestly didn't know if her heart could take it.

"That's ridiculous." Dwayne put his hat back on his head and walked out of the office without another word to the doctor.

"I'm so sorry. I don't know why he acts like this. I'm so, so sorry." Trish was mortified, befuddled, and embarrassed by Dwayne's actions.

"Please don't apologize for him," Dr. Phillips said. "These are stressful times. I understand that."

Trish didn't have time to dwell on her foolish husband. Dr. Phillips had just told them that Jon-Jon didn't want to live anymore, and her husband was acting like a bona-fide fool. "Are you sure about this, Doctor? I mean, I know he's been depressed, but he's not thinking about suicide."

Dr. Phillips scribbled some information on a note pad, tore the page, and handed it to Trish. "He told me himself, but I'm not a psychologist. Dr. Vance works in this building. She knows her stuff. Why don't you make Jon-Jon an appointment?"

∽

The minute Trish, Jon-Jon, and Dwayne got in the car, Dwayne wagged his index finger close to Trish's face. "I guess you're happy about not contacting them blood-sucking attorneys to get the ball rolling on Jon-Jon's case, even though you know he needs his surgery."

Trish wanted to let Dwayne have it. How dare he put all of this on her? But she didn't want to upset Jon-Jon or make him any more depressed than he already was, especially after she saw how her son just sat in his wheelchair completely uninterested in the rehabilitation session. He'd looked like he just wanted it to be over—and not just the session but everything . . . his life.

A tear formed in Trish's eye as she watched the cars go by. Her eyes had cried a thousand tears over Jon-Jon's case, Dwayne's hardened heart toward her and her son, and everything in between. She sat in the back seat while Dwayne drove them home, and Jon-Jon sat on the passenger side. The way Trish saw it, the families who drove past them looked happy, like life was doing right by them. They'd found the right mate, gotten married, and had children whom God had blessed so they never had any spinal cord injuries. They'd probably never even heard the terms "motor sensory complete" or "motor sensory incomplete" or cared what they meant.

"I don't want you asking your mom to hand you stuff that's right next to your bed when you can just lean forward and grab it yourself." Dwayne's harsh voice shot through Trish's melancholy fantasies like a broken arrow. "You hear me? No son of mine is going to get soft."

"I'm not soft, Dad. Just tired of doing stuff that won't change nothing."

"Stop being lazy, boy. You lay in that bed all day, watching television and sulking. Ain't no son of mine just gon' lay around suck-ing up air while I go out and bust my hump on a job every day."

They were pulling into the driveway. Trish couldn't wait to escape the confinement of this car and get some space from Dwayne, but he just wouldn't stop. He wouldn't leave her son alone, and she couldn't take it anymore. "Will you shut up and leave him alone!"

Dwayne and Jon-Jon turned questioning eyes toward her. She gave them a yeah-I-said-it look. Dwayne didn't say anything else. For the love of God, he actually shut his blubbering mouth, turned off the car, and pulled Jon-Jon's wheelchair out of the trunk.

"You okay, Mama?"

She rarely spoke disrespectfully to Dwayne in front of Jon-Jon. And she'd tried her best not to do it in private either. Trish mostly just ignored him or gave him the silent treatment when he acted idiotic. But things were getting so bad between her and Dwayne that she couldn't hide it anymore—and didn't want to. "I just don't like him calling you lazy. You've always done more than was expected of you. Now that you can't do for yourself, it's our responsibility to help you, not call you names."

Dwayne opened Jon-Jon's door and helped him into his chair. Trish stayed in the back seat watching as Dwayne rolled the wheelchair up the ramp. *Breathe, breathe.* The thickness she felt in the air had suddenly cleared and she could breathe. She could think.

At that moment, Trish knew what she had to do. She got out of the car and walked into the house. Dwayne had put Jon-Jon back in his bed by the time she made it to her son's room. Seeing that she wasn't needed, Trish turned and walked toward their bedroom.

Dwayne stopped her. "I'm heading back to work, but when I get home, I think we should talk."

Trish didn't respond. He would figure out that she wasn't speak-ing to him when he got back home. In her bedroom, Trish waited until she heard Dwayne back out of the driveway, then she gathered up her toothbrush, soap, and nightgown and took them into the guest bedroom.

The guest bedroom was behind the kitchen where Jon-Jon's room was. A full bathroom separated Jon-Jon's room from the guest room.

"I will sing a fruitful song, in a barren land." She pulled most of her clothes out of her closet and took them to the guest bedroom. The closet in her new room wasn't as wide or long as her walk-in closet, but she stuffed as much in as possible. Then she piled her sweaters in the oversize chair she'd purchased from the Goodwill in Matthews township, where the rich white folks donated their old stuff. Like her mama always said, "One man's trash is another man's treasure."

The guest room didn't have a nightstand. Until now, Trish hadn't noticed the missing nightstand. They'd hosted at least twenty people in the ten years they'd owned this house. Why hadn't anyone complained about not having a nightstand? Trish kept her water or teacup on her nightstand along with all her vitamins and allergy pills. And in North Carolina, she couldn't go long without her allergy medicine before having a sneezing fit and puffy, watery eyes.

She went back into the master bedroom, took everything off the top of her nightstand, then jostled it as she relocated it to the guest room.

"Mama, what you doing over there?"

She hadn't realized how much noise she was making. "I'm just making some adjustments so I can be closer to you. Are you hungry?"

"No."

She wanted to go into his room to check on him, but didn't want him thinking she was treating him like a baby. The doctor told her it had been a miracle that she had been able to carry Jon-Jon to full-term. He wasn't just her baby; he was her miracle. All his life Jon-Jon displayed such promise, but this accident and Jon-Jon's "all but giving up" attitude just seemed like God was trying to take her miracle away.

As she lay down in a bedroom that essentially made her a guest in her own home, Trish wondered how God could have gotten this so wrong. How could He have let something like this slip? Could it be that her family just wasn't on God's top-ten list of things to do?

Trish really needed answers from God. Yes, she was grateful that Jon-Jon survived the accident. But after living for decades with the reality of not being able to have another child, was she really supposed to give up on all her hopes of having grandchildren to love and keep close to her heart? It just didn't seem right.

And it wasn't right or fair to Jon-Jon that she cried herself to sleep some nights, thinking about the shoulda beens that might never, ever be. Sighing deeply, she tried to shake it off. She couldn't blame Jon-Jon for not producing those three beautiful grandbabies that she would have taken to the movies, hung out with, and baked cookies for. Wiping a tear from her eye, she said, "It's not his fault."

She could forgive Jon-Jon for giving up, but that daddy of his was a whole other situation. She was tired of his you-need-to-go-back-to-work complaints, his attitude, and his comments about Jon-Jon just laying around all day. The boy couldn't walk, for goodness' sake. Everything about Dwayne irked her so bad that he ought to be glad she didn't have a job. Because if she did, she would be renting an apartment and filing for a separation.

❧

The next morning, Dwayne knocked on her bedroom door. She didn't say anything so he knocked again and again. "Your stuff is gone from our room."

She started not to respond. She had planned not to speak to Dwayne for a month of Sundays. She'd had enough of his toxic, woe-is-me filled words. But she heard the distinct sound of hurt in his voice. His voice had sounded like that when his daddy died, and Dwayne had tried so hard to be strong in front of everyone during the funeral. But later that night she'd heard him crying in the bathroom.

She'd walked out of their bedroom, sat on the back patio for a few minutes. If Dwayne hadn't wanted to cry in front of her, then she wanted to leave him with his dignity. So when she entered their master suite the next time, she made noise by knocking a few books off the TV stand and complained loudly as she picked them up. When he came out of the bathroom, his eyes were dry and he was hungry. Trish had made his favorite meal: penne noodles with chicken, shrimp, and alfredo sauce. She topped it off with his favorite dessert: a pineapple coconut cake.

She wasn't about to cook a single thing for Dwayne today, but she would leave him with his dignity. "I thought it would be better for Jon-Jon if I was next to him for a little while. That way I can hear him if he calls out to me in the middle of the night."

"Our room is just down the hall, Trish. You can hear Jon-Jon from our room and you know it."

"I think this is best for now."

"So this is how we gon' do things around here, huh?"

"I don't want to fight with you, Dwayne. I don't feel good. Can you just please get Jon-Jon up so he can use the bathroom and then fix him some breakfast?"

"But I thought you moved all your stuff so you could be on this side of the house for Jon-Jon? So shouldn't you be fixing him breakfast?"

"Will you just do it, please?" She was about to cry again. She'd cried all night long. Trish had turned up the TV and moaned into her pillow as the tears fell from her eyes. She tried her best not to let Jon-Jon hear her cry. She had to get a handle on herself. She couldn't let Jon-Jon see her like this. Her son was dealing with enough. She wanted to help, but she couldn't even go into his room right now. Not like this. She was just thankful Jon-Jon didn't have any sharp objects he could get his hand on in that room.

Trish figured that if she stayed in her room for the rest of the day, she might be able to get her emotions intact. Things had not been good around here for a while, but she hadn't expected Dr. Phillips to tell her that her son didn't want to live anymore. How could he be so ready to give up when the doctors all agreed that he might be able to walk again? But it was football—always football. Could football really be the end-all and be-all of life for Jon-Jon?

She had to find a way to make Jon-Jon see that life without football was better than no life at all. Yes, he had suffered a great loss, but couldn't Jon-Jon find a new dream?

Trish wished she could talk to Dwayne about this, but their conversations never ended well. She sighed deeply as her husband walked away from the door, because she was beginning to believe that life without Dwayne was better than life with him.

She went back to sleep. Sleep was her friend. Sleep didn't make her face the reality of life with a husband who was unbearable and a son who didn't want to live any longer. Trish wanted to lay in bed for as long as she could because she couldn't deal with the reality beyond this room.

Her eyelids were heavy as they closed and shut out the world around her. She didn't want to dream, didn't want to think. Jon-Jon needed her, but she couldn't make herself get out of bed.

Trish didn't know how long she had slept, but she heard someone messing with the bedroom door. The sound jolted her upright. Wiping the drool from around her mouth, she realized that Dwayne was fiddling with the interior door key that they used since Jon-Jon was in sixth grade whenever he locked himself out of his bedroom.

"What are you doing, Dwayne? I'm trying to get some sleep."

He finally got the door open. Trish was about to yell at him, but he entered the room with a tray of food. She looked down to see pancakes, scrambled eggs, sausage links, and grapefruit on her plate. There was also a cup of green tea with lemon in it. Her favorite breakfast, and Dwayne had fixed it for her.

"I already put Jon-Jon in the shower. He's eating his breakfast now, so you don't need to get up."

Trish didn't know what to say. She had been terrible to him, but he'd deserved it. *Shake off the bad thoughts,* she told herself, *just shake them off.* "Thank you," she finally said to Dwayne.

"It's the least I can do." Dwayne turned to walk out of the room. As he reached the door, he turned back. "I called out from work today. I'll take care of whatever Jon-Jon needs. Just get some rest."

He shut the door and left her to eat the breakfast he had cooked. But after only a few bites, Trish realized there was no cinnamon in the pancakes. "I should have known." For Trish, love was in the details, and Dwayne didn't get it. He didn't get her. As the tears started again, she wondered why she was wallowing in pity like this. Why couldn't she just get out of this bed and enjoy her day? Nothing was the same for them, that's why—and it never would be again.

Trish glanced over to her nightstand. The piece of paper with Dr. Vance's name and phone number lay next to her cell phone. She was going to call to make Jon-Jon an appointment for his depression. Trish found herself wondering if she needed to make herself an appointment too.

CHAPTER 6

Alexis squealed with delight as she gave Lillie Longmoor a big ole bear hug and then sat back down behind her small desk in the county building. "You did it, Lillie. I'm so proud to know you."

A puzzled look crossed Lillie's face. "How could you be proud to know someone like me? I'm nothing. Look at me, celebrating getting a job as a grocery store clerk, while my brother is an attorney and my younger sister is the vice president of marketing at a company she's worked at for ten years. I've never been able to keep a job longer than six months at a time."

Alexis put her hand on top of Lillie's shaky hand. "Your family loves you. Would your brother have allowed you to move in with his family if that wasn't so?"

"I'm in the cottage in the back of his house. And he's only doing that so I won't be on the street anymore. If our parents were still living, he wouldn't have anything to do with me. I've just been such an embarrassment to everyone."

Alexis had witnessed this self-sabotaging behavior with her bipolar clients more times than she wanted to think about. They knew their behavior could destroy relationships with family and friends, but they were powerless to stop it. "Things are going to be different, Lillie. Your doctor found the right medication for you, you have a job, and your brother wants you to stay with him as long as you need to."

"I know everything you're saying is true. I just don't want to mess up again."

Alexis put her elbow on the desk and her hand under her chin, then gave Lillie an easy smile. "What if you decide to take things day by day for a while? If you've had a good day, acknowledge that and give yourself some credit. Maybe one day you'll look back and discover that you've had three hundred sixty-five good days."

Tears welled in Lillie's eyes. She leaned over and gave Alexis another hug. "You are heaven-sent. Thank you for being so patient with me."

"Thank you for allowing me the privilege of being of service to you in your time of need."

Wiping the tears from her eyes, Lillie shook her head. "I just don't understand why a lady like you would come to this side of town to help out. I thought you rich people were too busy with PTA meetings, shopping, playing golf, and looking down on people like me."

Alexis had dreamed of going to college to either become a scientist who would discover the cure for mental illness or a psychiatrist who would help her patients reinvent themselves. But from the time she had turned sixteen, Alexis had started waitressing at night after school just so she and her mother could keep the roof of that double-wide over their heads. There had been no time or money for college.

That's why Alexis thought of Michael as her earth angel. Her American prince. He wasn't only a business wiz; he also had connections, and those connections allowed her to work in the mental health field. No, she wasn't a scientist or a psychiatrist, but she volunteered as a human services assistant. She helped clients recovering from substance abuse or who had mental health issues obtain benefits, repair relationships, sign up for job training programs, or obtain food or housing assistance vouchers.

People thought she was a saint because she spent one day a week working with people who were typically thought of as the dregs of society. They only thought this because they didn't know where she came from, and Michael would die of mortification if she told her story. He wished she would just work on the PTA at their kids' school, but she was passionate about the people she was able to help and wouldn't let him take that away.

"Lillie, now stop that. For all you know, I could live just two blocks away. Anyhow, wherever I live, it's no problem to drive into the city. I enjoy helping out. I just wish I could be here more often, but my kids wear me out." She glanced at the clock on the wall. Ethan and Ella would be out of school soon. She had to pack up her desk and head out.

Lillie gave her an oh-please look. "I might be on medication, but I'm no dummy. My parents had money. That's how my siblings received such distinguished college educations. I got kicked out at the age of seventeen for refusing to go to college. So, I know what people with money look like, and you've got it."

Putting a few files in her leather briefcase while reaching for her handbag, Alexis said, "But that doesn't make me any better than you or any of the other clients I see."

"Oh, honey, yes it does. But the thing I like about you is that you don't seem to know that. I just can't figure out why."

Standing, glancing at the clock again, Alexis said, "I am so sorry to cut this a bit short, but I have to pick my kids up from school." She handed Lillie an envelope. "Here is the furniture voucher I was finally able to get approved."

As Alexis left the social services building and hopped into her white Mercedes SUV, she prayed she hadn't made anyone feel uncomfortable around her. Alexis thought that putting on a pair of jeans and a sweater would help her blend in to some degree. She even wore her Target jeans, not the ones that were made in Italy. But who was she kidding? They all probably looked at her as some rich white lady doing charity work to ease her upper-crust guilt.

They would never know how much she understood them, how much she had been one of them, but she would hold her truth and just be thankful that she had the opportunity to help people like Lillie.

Each time she helped someone move forward into a better situation, she felt as if she was paying it forward.

Traffic was terrible, as it normally was in Charlotte. It hadn't always been this way. When she was growing up, this city had been like a forest with trees everywhere. She remembered playing hide-and-seek behind the trees in some of the many neighborhoods she and her mother lived in. When developers came to town, they knocked down most of the trees and turned Charlotte into the biggest city in North Carolina and the fifteenth-largest city in America. Alexis was now thirty-four and longed for that small-town feel again, especially while driving in traffic.

Her phone beeped, letting her know that she had just received a text. It was probably the kids, wondering what was taking her so long. Sad to say, but she was often late on Tuesdays when she helped out at the county office. Alexis got so involved in her clients or the assignment at hand that she often lost track of time. She had to ask Michael to pick the kids up twice. He hadn't been happy about it but had done it anyway.

Thankfully, she didn't need to call Michael today because she would only be about ten minutes late. The phone beeped again. She wouldn't dare reach for her purse to see the text. One thing was for sure; she would never check another text while driving for the rest of her life. The kids knew she wouldn't just leave them at school. They were far too impatient.

The phone rang. It was Michael. Alexis was okay with answering her phone while driving because she could keep her eyes on the road and just had to tap a button on the steering wheel. "Hey, hon, are you actually calling your wife before your workday ends?"

"Ella just called. She says you're not at the school yet."

"I'm turning the corner now and heading into the school parking lot. Your children are just as impatient as you, my love."

He laughed. "Well, at least they got their good looks from you."

"I'm here, so you can go back to inventing your next got-to-have tech project."

"We are trying to develop another program," he admitted.

"You are always developing a program. I am fully convinced that I married a genius."

"And I married the best wife and mother in this town."

"Oh, so I'm only the best in the city, not the whole world?"

"What was I thinking? I forgot that Ella gave you the Best Mother in the World award last year."

"Just don't forget it again," she joked. "Talk to you later. I'm pulling up to the school."

"Okay, and don't let me forget that I need to talk to you tonight."

They hung up as she pulled in front of the school. Long faces greeted her as Ethan and Ella hopped in the back seat. "You owe me another Marvel hero figure for this, Mom. This is the second time this month you've been late picking us up."

"I was three minutes late last time, Ethan." She glanced at the clock on her dashboard. "And seven minutes today. So in a whole month, I've only been ten minutes late picking up my two wonderful children. Do I get any credit for that?"

"Of course you do, Mom," Ella said. "I know you didn't mean to be late. You were helping people and time just got away from you."

Ella was her forgiving, understanding child. She'd told her how much it meant to be able to help people who couldn't help themselves and Ella had never forgotten that.

"I still want another one," said Ethan. "You can get me Thanos."

"I just bought you Thor. What did you do with that superhero?"

"I still have him, but I only have the good guys. My superheroes need somebody to battle with, like Thanos or Ultron. Oh, and don't forget that you already promised to get me Loki."

Alexis didn't understand this whole Marvel Universe thing. "But I thought you wanted Loki because he's Thor's brother?"

He gave her an oh-Mom-you're-so-old look. "Thor and Loki are always fighting. Loki's one of the bad guys."

Ella shook her head at her brother's antics. "All Ethan can think about is fighting. Just ignore him, but don't forget that I need a new dress for the father-daughter dance next week."

Her children were spoiled and loving life. Alexis enjoyed every moment she spent with them and would do anything for them, like buy tons of superheroes and hundreds of dresses.

In truth she would rather do anything than have this discussion with Michael tonight. She hadn't made contact with the Robinson family yet. How could she when her family's biggest issue was whether to get Thanos or Ultron for her son's superhero collection?

When they arrived home, Alexis took the leftover cheesy chicken casserole she'd made the night before out of the refrigerator. Her children loved this casserole and didn't realize how many veggies were mixed in with the pasta shells, chicken, and cheese.

She put the casserole in the oven along with garlic bread. She rarely made the kids wait until Michael came home from work to eat because her children were always so hungry after school. "Go wash your hands, change out of your school clothes, and then come right back to the kitchen."

"Can I bring my laptop to the table, Mom?" Ella asked.

"No, honey. You'll have plenty of time to do your homework. Just take a moment to eat your food first, okay?"

"Okay," Ella said as she and Ethan skipped out of the kitchen.

Alexis leaned against the counter holding a dry towel in her hand as she watched her children leave the room. It still amazed her how carefree they were. She wondered what made them feel so at ease all the time. Was it the house they lived in or was it that she and Michael had created a safe circle around them? Whatever it was, Alexis never wanted them to lose that skip in their steps.

After feeding the kids, Alexis sent them off to do homework while she took a hot bath. She then got comfortable on one of the lounge chairs in their massive master bedroom and picked up where she left off with the novel she had been reading. She usually was able to get about an hour of reading in a couple of days each week before someone had an emergency.

She had read five chapters of the suspense thriller when Michael came into their bedroom. He looked worn and weighed down. She put her book on the chair. "Hey."

"Hey yourself," he said while undoing his tie.

"You hungry?"

"Not right now. I just want to rest." Michael went into the bathroom, took a shower, and changed into a pair of pajamas. He then stretched out on the lounge chair next to Alexis.

She reached a hand over to him and rubbed his arm. "How was your day?"

"Exhausting."

"You did look like you wanted to just lay on the floor, like you couldn't go any further. I'm surprised you had the energy to take a shower."

"I almost fell in it." He laughed at himself. "But how was your day? Must have been something exciting going on down at social services for you to be late picking up the kids."

Alexis's eyes lit up. "As a matter of fact, there was. One of my clients got a job at the Publix in Steele Creek."

"A whole job? Well, oh my goodness, alert the media! Better yet, let's throw her a party."

"It's not funny, Michael. She hasn't had a job in over two years and had been living on the street. Things are going to be a lot better for her now that she's on the right medication."

"I shouldn't have made fun," he acknowledged. "It's just, you seem so excited about someone working at the grocery store. I guess I just don't understand people like that."

No, he didn't understand why Alexis's eyes lit up whenever she discussed the successes of the people she helped. Michael didn't see those accomplishments as successes. He thought those were just basic things people did in life. She was tired of trying to explain it to him and was just happy he didn't put up a fuss about the one day a week she did something that brought joy to her heart. "I guess you had to be there."

Snapping his finger, he said, "Before I forget. I need you to put together a dinner party on Thursday."

"How many people?"

"Two of the executives from Media Matters Inc. are coming to town on Thursday. Peter and I will be meeting with them and showing them around the office. Afterward, I want to treat them to dinner. Peter suggested that they might feel more comfortable here."

"That's fine with me. Whatever I can do to help."

Yawning and cracking his neck, he told her, "It would also help if you talked with those people before Thursday. Do I really have to keep asking you about this?"

"I have to be honest with you. I'm not comfortable with bothering the Robinson family. My recklessness has already cost them so much. I wouldn't know what to say to them."

"I told you what to say. We need to move this thing out of court and into arbitration. The last thing I need is for your accident to swing back and bite me."

Alexis felt awful on both ends. She had ruined a young man's life, and now she was hurting her husband's business deal. She felt powerless to do anything about either situation. Alexis couldn't deal with the knowledge that she had caused harm to someone else. She wanted to block the whole terrible nightmare from her mind.

"Put it this way, Lex. You like helping people, right?"

"Yes, of course I do."

"Well, the boy you hit needs another surgery."

"How do you know that?"

With a flick of the wrist, he waved off the importance of the information he was about to share. "The kid's attorney called the office claiming they didn't have the money for his next operation because the dad lost the job that paid for the previous operations."

"Is his dad working now? Will they be able to get the insurance?"

"If they drop this court business and go to arbitration, this whole thing would be solved."

"Why don't you stop postponing the case? Just let them have their day in court."

Michael shook his head. "They should have taken the insurance money. I'm not going to let them run over us and take what I've worked so hard for all of my life because you accidently hit that kid. That's what insurance is for."

"Stop being so stubborn, Michael. Why can't we just find out how much money they need and give it to them?"

"The kid's father is the one who's being stubborn. Our attorneys have made contact with their attorney, but the dad won't budge. He wants to go to court, but I'm not letting that happen. I will keep pushing the court date back so I can get through the sale of the company. So if that's the game the dad wants to play, then his son will not get that surgery."

"But you just told me that he needs that surgery."

Michael yawned, stretched, stood up. "I'm going to bed."

But Alexis couldn't sleep. She went into her walk-in closet, sat down on the floor, leaned her back against the wall, and stared at all the designer clothes and shoes in her oversize closet, wrapping her arms around her legs as she rocked back and forth. She cried and cried and cried. She cried so hard that snot ran down her nose and dripped onto her lap.

She felt like such an imposter. This wasn't the life she was supposed to have. Girls like her don't usually get fairytale endings. Girls like her who never go to college shouldn't still be able to buy anything they want. Her children were happy and healthy. They attended a good school and would be able to take care of themselves when they became adults. She owed it all to Michael.

She was terrified of what would happen if she ruined this deal for her husband. If he stopped loving her, what kind of life would she and her children have then? But the fear she had about ruining Michael's business deal paled in comparison to the terror she felt at facing the young man she had caused so much harm.

"What am I going to do?" She lifted her eyes heavenward. "I really need help. Can You please show me what to do?"

Alexis went into the bathroom, blew her nose, and washed her face. She prayed Michael hadn't heard her crying like a blubbering idiot. She didn't have the strength for that conversation. When she stepped back into the bedroom, Michael was asleep and snoring like a man who'd known peace and easy days all of his life.

If only, she thought as she sighed. *If only*. She climbed into bed and prepared herself for a sleepless night.

CHAPTER 7

Trish was on the back patio sipping iced tea with her mother. Her name was Lillian Thornton, but no one ever called her Lillian. All the family called her Sister because her baby sister couldn't pronounce Lillian, so she kept calling her Sister until that just became her name. Even Jon-Jon called her Grandma Sister. Not even the people at church called her by her given name. It was Sister Lil. For Trish, her mother was no sister. Lillian was too controlling and always in Trish's business, telling her what to do, to be a sister.

As the two women sat there taking in the moment of peace, Trish breathed in the fresh air.

"What's going on with you, girl?" Sister asked.

"Nothing's going on."

"Dwayne tells me you done moved out of y'alls bedroom and you're moping around this house as if you have no hope."

"Mama, can't we just sit out here and enjoy the fresh breeze and the warm sun?" One of the reasons Trish convinced Dwayne that they had to buy this house was because of the back patio. She used to sit out here, prop her feet up on the lawn furniture, take in the warm breeze, and look to heaven, praying about all the things that needed praying about that day. Since Jon-Jon's accident, there'd been no time to sit out on the patio and sip her tea, no time for happy-go-lucky moments.

"Now, I don't want to get into your business, Trish. I know you're a full-grown woman with a child of your own, but—"

"But you're going to get in my business anyway, right, Sister Lil?"

Trish loved her mother dearly, but their relationship was complicated. Sister Lil didn't think Christians should be sad or depressed because they had Jesus. But Jesus wasn't paying Trish's bills or healing her son or making Dwayne act like he had some sense.

Sister's lips tightened. "Don't hold that tone with me, Trish. I'm just here to tell you what's what."

This patio had been Trish's happy place, yet nothing seemed to make her happy these days—not the sun or the warm breeze, not the iced tea, and certainly not her mother with all her "what's what." Trish had had it with all the bad she'd been going through every single day. She didn't want to talk anymore.

"I'm going back inside."

"That's fine," Sister said, "but first tell me what's wrong?"

Trish leaned her head back and closed her eyes. She wanted to block out her reality and her son's. "How can you ask me what's wrong? Where have you been these last six months?"

"I know Jon-Jon got hurt, but that doesn't answer my question about what's wrong with you?"

Sighing deeply, Trish turned her head. She looked up at the sky like she was trying to find something she'd lost up there. "Jon-Jon doesn't want to live anymore, and I'm all out of answers."

"Sounds to me like you want to dig your own grave right next to his."

"Did you hear what I said, Mom? My son doesn't want to live."

Sister leaned forward so that she and Trish were eye to eye. "And I'm asking, what are you going to do about it? Are you going to fall apart or be the woman God created you to be?"

Here we go. She was about to get the "we don't act like this" speech. Couldn't her mother understand that life had done Trish and her family wrong? She and Dwayne used to laugh and joke together. They used to go to Jon-Jon's games. They used to go out to eat. They used to do a lot of things before everything changed with the blink of an eye. "Things have been so bad for so long that I guess I don't even know what to ask God for."

Sister nudged Trish. "You just said it, hon. If things are bad and you don't want them to be that way, why not ask God for something good and see if He don't come through for you?"

She heard her mother, but at that moment she was completely numb.

"When's the last time you took a hot bath?"

"It's been a while." One of Trish's favorite things to do was run super-hot water with lots of bubbles in the tub. She would then get in and soak until the water turned cool. Trish loved to listen to praise music or read a book during her private time in the tub.

"Why don't you let me hang out with Jon-Jon while you soak in the tub?"

She fixed her mouth to decline the offer, but the idea of a hot bath was too good to pass up.

While her mother went to Jon-Jon's room, Trish went to soak in the tub. She ran her water, put in her favorite bubble bath, turned her praise music on, got in, and managed to relax for forty minutes.

When she got out of the tub, Trish thanked her mother. "I needed that."

"I figured. It always helped when you were younger."

Grinning, Trish said, "You know me so well."

"I'm your mama. Don't forget that. And call me if you need help."

Trish agreed. "I will."

❧

When her mother left, Trish walked into the kitchen and opened the fridge to grab a snack. Dwayne was standing in front of the sink, washing the dishes.

"Are you ready to talk to me?" Dwayne asked.

She closed the door, swung around, and laid into him. "So you told my mother that I'm a basket case, huh?"

Dwayne took his hands out of the water and dried them off. "I didn't call you a basket case. I told your mother that you haven't been yourself lately. I'm sure I'm partly to blame for all of this, but we have to figure something out. If not for us, we've got to do something different around here for Jon-Jon."

"Why?" She put her hands on her hips. "So he can stop being so lazy and laying around while you go off to work?"

"Look, Trish, I don't want to argue. We've been arguing for months now and getting nowhere. Like I said, it's time for us to do something different."

He was sounding too reasonable for her. She couldn't argue with Dwayne while he was standing in front of the sink, washing dishes, and trying to talk calmly with her for a change. She didn't want to continue the conversation because things would soon go left if she talked to him for more than a minute.

Walking out of the kitchen and away from an issue she wasn't ready to deal with yet, she stepped into Jon-Jon's room for the first time since they arrived home from the doctor two days ago. It was time to deal with the giant that was trying to strangle the life out of her son. "How's my handsome son doing today?"

Jon-Jon had the remote control in his hand. He changed the channel to *Chopped* on the Food Network, then glanced in his mother's direction. "Grandma Sister said you weren't feeling well."

The bath had given her a moment's reprieve from all the ills of the world and allowed her to clear her head and think about what Jon-Jon needed from her, rather than her own selfish need to wallow in pity.

Leaning against the door jamb, Trish's lips twisted as guilt filled her heart. She'd been devoted to Jon-Jon from the day they brought him home from the hospital. His accident hadn't changed that. Jon-Jon made her smile just by being in his presence.

"I'm so sorry I bailed on you these last couple of days. When the doctor told us that you didn't want to live anymore, and I saw the way you just gave up during physical therapy, I don't know. I guess I just needed some time to regroup." He didn't respond to her telling him that she knew what he'd said to Dr. Phillips, so she went another route. "Has your dad been taking good care of you?"

"He's all right. Just wish I wasn't such a burden to you and dad. I wish I hadn't been on the road at the same time as that lady who hit me."

Trish wished he hadn't been on that road either. Wished that woman had some compassion and would let them have their day in court. She tried not to think about the woman who caused all these problems in their lives, because then she'd have to admit that she had another person on her list that she needed to forgive.

Stepping closer to his bed, Trish shook her head. "You got to stop feeling sorry for yourself, Jon-Jon." Her voice caught, and she got a lump in her throat. "And me and your daddy have got to stop feeling sorry for you and ourselves."

Jon-Jon slammed his fist against his mattress. "It's not fair, Mama! I'm supposed to be in my second year of college right now, getting ready to go pro."

"What happened to you isn't right nor is it fair, hon. Fact is, you need another surgery that we can't pay for right now. And if you don't get it soon . . ." She trailed off, not wanting to start crying again. "You looked so depressed during physical therapy, and it just about broke my heart."

"I was in pain. I'm in pain all the time, Mama." A tear rolled down his face. He swatted it away.

"That's because you need this final surgery and more therapy. Once you get that done, there's a chance that you'll be able to walk again."

"But not run . . . and I'll never be able to play football again. If I can't play football, then what good am I?"

Trish had thought she was all out of answers, but hearing her son say he was nothing without football caused anger to boil in her. "You are more than some football player. Think of it like this, Jon-Jon: the game runs out for most men around age thirty to thirty-five. The next half of their lives is spent without football being at the center of everything. Do you think they just call it a life, lay down, and do nothing else with their lives?"

With frustration written all over his face, he yelled, "What else am I supposed to do, Mama? I'm twenty years old and all I've ever been trained to do is catch a football!"

"Not true." Trish pointed at the television. *Chopped* was still on. You used to get in the kitchen with me or your Grandma Sister and bake like a pastry chef. I know you didn't want any of your friends to know you enjoyed baking so much, but maybe that's just another gift God gave you. And maybe you can make a career out of that."

He gave his mother an oh-really look. "I was trying to be the next Emmitt Smith, not the next Bobby Flay."

"Give it a chance, Jon-Jon. That's all I'm suggesting. Do you think Bobby Flay thought in his wildest imagination that he would become as well-known of a celebrity chef as he is today?"

"What am I supposed to do? Wheel myself around the kitchen, bumping into everything? Oh, yeah, that has celebrity chef written all over it."

"Boy, your mama is just trying to encourage you. Why you gotta be so flippant like that?"

Out the side of her eye, Trish watched Dwayne enter the room. She didn't know whether to thank him for setting Jon-Jon straight or to duck because the next verbal blow he'd throw would probably be aimed right at her. Her husband didn't know how to deal with conflict without yelling. Trish had put up with his behavior for so long that the yelling seemed normal at the Robinson household. But she was tired of it. No way would she live like this for a lifetime. So if he thought he was about to yell at her, she was going to let him have it. No more keeping quiet and letting things blow over. You come for me, I'm coming for you.

When he looked her way, she braced herself for a belittling comment about the way she was handling this situation. "I didn't mean to interrupt," he said, "but Jon-Jon was just being too flippant for me, when all you're trying to do is help him."

Trish's arms wrapped around her chest as if she were trying to protect her heart. Dwayne walked out of the room, leaving her confused and dazed as she stared at the backside of him that she had come to know so well. He turned his back on her every night when they went to sleep, before she moved into the guest room. He turned his back on her after Jon-Jon's accident, when he couldn't understand why she wasn't as angry as he was.

Somehow, as he walked away this time, it felt different, but she didn't know if this was the wind of change or a temporary sprinkle that would dry up and leave her feeling like the biggest fool God ever created for thinking Dwayne John Robinson could be anything but who he was. Even as she bet against her husband's ability to change, Trish began to wonder if there was hope for them after all.

Falling asleep was tough that night. She had a restless sleep and a crook in her neck when she woke the next morning. She pulled herself out of bed. "I will sing a fruitful song . . ." She helped Jon-Jon get to the bathroom so he could clean himself up in the walk-in shower that had a shower seat.

When Jon-Jon was done in the bathroom, she rolled his wheelchair as close to his bed as she could get it and then allowed Jon-Jon to lean on her shoulder as she lifted him onto the bed. It amazed her that she had enough strength to lift her son. She guessed it was like that woman who lifted a one-ton car to save a little boy. You never know how much strength you have until you're tested.

Dwayne came into the room, barking into the phone. "No! No!

That's not good enough. I'm starting to think you're getting a kickback from the other team."

Rolling her eyes, Trish turned back to Jon-Jon. "I'm going to finish your breakfast."

She went back to the kitchen, trying to get away from Dwayne and his irate phone conversation. She was sure he was talking to the attorney, and her head was beginning to hurt from lack of sleep, so the last thing she wanted to do was deal with any of what Dwayne had going on. She finished boiling the grits and frying the sausages and eggs. She was making Jon-Jon's plate when Dwayne came into the kitchen, yelling his head off. She knew that the real Dwayne would show up sooner rather than later. And here he was.

"I can't believe them. Those blood-sucking lawyers are in cahoots together, and you can't tell me no different."

"What happened now?" She didn't want to hear it, but she would be accused of giving him the silent treatment if she didn't respond.

"What's happening is that Jon-Jon's court case has been postponed again. How does she keep getting these postponements? You think a little bit of white privilege might be going on? Maybe she knows the judge . . . golfing buddies or something."

Taking the grits pot off the stove, Trish scooped a couple of spoonfuls on Jon-Jon's plate. "Why don't we just give up on the court stuff and take the insurance payment. We really need to get Jon-Jon's surgery scheduled."

Pointing an accusatory finger in her direction, he said, "You can quit talking to me about that insurance money. That policy is only worth a hundred thousand dollars, and Jon-Jon's injuries and lifetime earning potential is ten times more than that."

"I'm just saying . . ."

"You can stop 'just saying' and start doing. Like, go get a job so we can scrape up the money for that surgery ourselves."

Trish's nostrils flared. She had the hot grits pot in her hand

and was thinking about giving her husband the Al Green special. *Breathe . . . Breathe.* She hurriedly put the hot pot back on the stove and stepped away from it. She wasn't trying to catch a case by pouring hot grits on Dwayne and giving him third-degree burns. With a hiss, she replied, "Who is going to take care of my son if I go back to work? You don't do anything unless I ask you to."

He pointed toward the sink. "I just washed the dishes for you last night."

Her neck started rolling. "You didn't wash dishes for me. You washed dishes for the household. Everything is not on me, Dwayne John Robison. I'm not the maid around here." She practically spit out his name, she was so mad.

He stood there, staring at her, as if he was trying to come up with something to say. She didn't have time for this. She took the plate to Jon-Jon and lifted his bed so he could eat. As far as Trish was concerned, that conversation was over.

∽

When Dwayne came back in from work that evening, he walked right into Jon-Jon's room where she was sitting and watching *House Hunters* while Jon-Jon ate his dinner. Dwayne started in on her immediately as if he had something on his chest all day that he couldn't wait to unload. He didn't even speak to Jon-Jon.

"Before I left this morning, you informed me that you weren't the maid and everything wasn't on you. Well, everything shouldn't be on me either, Trish. I don't make enough money for all of our needs. You and I have always worked together on these bills."

"Things have changed, Dwayne." She glanced over at Jon-Jon, knowing that he couldn't feel good about what his daddy had just said. She wished he would just stop. She had always been the responsible one, making sure that their bills were paid on time and that they kept their credit score above seven hundred, but none of that mattered to her right now. If a few bills had to be paid late so she could take care of her son a few more months, then that's what it would be.

Dwayne wouldn't quit. "Maybe you can't work full-time right now, but you sure can work part-time, and you know it."

This man obviously didn't know how close he came to a hospital visit this morning or he would leave her alone. Getting out of her seat, she said, "You know what, Dwayne? You're right. I do need to get a job. And you need to get another place to stay."

"Mama!"

Jon-Jon sounded hurt by her words. But she didn't care anymore. "I mean it, Jon-Jon. He has got to go." She turned back to Dwayne. "I have had it up to here"—she lifted her hands above her head—"with your mess."

Twisting his lip, like he wasn't buying what she was selling, he told her, "You done fell and bumped your head on that one, because I'm not leaving my home."

"Argh!" Trish shook her hands in the air as if she was practicing having his neck in between her hands, strangling him. She then screamed, "Forget it! I'm done!" She stormed out of her son's room, went into her bedroom, and slammed the door. She paced back and forth, back and forth. She didn't know what to do. She was at her wit's end and ready to pack her own clothes and move in with her parents.

Thinking of her parents caused Trish to think back to something her mother said while they sat on the back patio. Sister had admonished her to pray, but how could she pray when she was mad at God? There, she admitted it. God was supposed to protect them from seen and unseen dangers, but He didn't protect Jon-Jon from that distracted driver. Trish was also mad at the lady who hit Jon-Jon. There, she admitted that too. She was supposed to be so forgiving, so full of God's love, but she was mad at everybody. "You weren't there, God!" she shouted as she looked heavenward. "Why weren't You there?"

She hadn't been able to get a grip on her day-to-day life, let alone her spiritual God-I-need-You life. Her mother had been right. If she truly thought things were so bad, then she needed to start praying for something good to happen for the Robinson family.

The radio had been softly playing in her room. She hadn't paid it much attention all day. But it was as if God was speaking to her through the radio. Kierra Sheard and Tasha Cobbs Leonard were singing "Something Has to Break." She had heard this song before, but as she listened this time, the words that must have come straight from the throne room of God were breathing new life into her. So much had gone wrong. So much had been weighing her down. So much had been against them, so as Kierra sang words inspired by Isaiah 53:4, "Surely he hath borne our griefs, and carried our sorrows," Trish stood up.

She had lost that anyhow-kind-of-praise after Jon-Jon's accident. But at this moment Trish wanted—no, needed—to get it back. With tears streaming down her face, she lifted her hands in praise to her God. "I'm here, Lord. Everything is falling apart, and I don't know what to do. But I'm standing right here because I know You care about what concerns me. You care about how things have been so bad that I can barely see my way through. I just need something good, Lord. Do You hear me?" She got down on her knees. "Something good. That's what we need." She lowered her head, and her body shook from the torrent of tears.

Here she was, feeling exhausted after having tried to take this battle on all by herself. Trish had been raised in church, she had been raised to believe that she and God were the majority. Trish saw God not just as her Jehovah-Raah—her Shepherd—but she also knew Him as Jehovah-Jireh—the Lord who provides. She truly needed God to be their provider. She needed Him to make a way out of no way.

Jon-Jon needed his final surgery. Trish was fighting hard to believe that her God, her Jehovah-Jireh, wasn't going to let these insurance companies and lawyers decide whether or not her son would walk again. She knew she needed joy back in her household, and she wasn't too picky about where the joy would come from. She just needed something good to overtake them and get her family back on track.

She had just told her husband to get out. In all the years they had been married and all the times he had gotten on her nerves, she had never told him to leave their home. What was wrong with her? Did she really want it to be over? Was she done loving Dwayne? Had Jon-Jon's accident been too much for them to handle together?

Lifting her eyes heavenward, she shouted, "I can't take any more, Lord! I need You now! Right now."

The waterfall kept cascading down her face. She would wipe tears away and before she knew it, her face was drenched again. She had never been in such a dark and unmoving place as this. She needed God to shine some light on her situation. She needed to feel joy again. "I trust You. I trust You with my whole life."

Even in the face of her crumbling marriage and all her other problems, she was beginning to believe again. She was beginning to believe that God could fix it.

It didn't matter that there was no more money in the bank, that the insurance company refused her son's surgery, or that Dwayne was still fighting and refusing to accept the car insurance payout for Jon-Jon's accident. It didn't matter that the guest room had now become her bedroom. It didn't even matter that she might never have those grandchildren that she so desperately wanted. It was just her and God, and she was going to praise Him until she got tired.

Turning up the radio, Trish started dancing around the room. Her God was an awesome God. Her God was mighty. Her God was powerful. He wouldn't let her down, He would come see about her.

"Turn it down!" Jon-Jon shouted.

She ignored him. Her son wasn't going to stop her praise, not tonight.

She heard Jon-Jon shouting over her music again. She didn't

want to be an inconsiderate neighbor, but she wasn't finished yet. "Hallelujah!" It was the highest praise. She kept saying "Hallelujah!" because she just felt like screaming it through a house that had lost the ability to praise, whether happy or sad, whether rich or poor. She swung open her bedroom door and shouted, "Let God be praised!"

Dwayne was standing at her door. He was about to knock and looked as if she had caught him off guard when she swung the door open. She started shaking her head. *Not now, devil, not now.* This man was not about to bring her down. "I'll be done in a few minutes, but I'm not letting you or Jon-Jon stop me from praising the Lord. This is personal."

"Didn't come over here to stop you." He walked past her as he stepped into the room.

Trish was about to object. This was her prayer and praise time. She hadn't asked for company, but how could she uninvite someone to prayer?

Dwayne opened the curtains wide and pointed toward the tree in their backyard. "Come see what has been perched on our tree since you shouted hallelujah."

Trish's eyebrows furrowed. Did he actually stop her prayer to have her look at their tree? She wished Dwayne would just get out of her room and let her get back to spending time with God. When he kept standing in front of the window with this look of awe on his face, curiosity got the best of her and she moved closer and closer to that window. The sooner she looked out the window, the sooner Dwayne would leave her alone. She knew she shouldn't feel this way, especially while in prayer, but things were complicated between her and Dwayne.

Her eyes traveled the distance, and then she saw it. Perched on one of the limbs was a North Carolina cardinal. The magnificent bird was a brilliant red all over, with a reddish bill and black face surrounding the bill. Trish's hand went to her face as she backed away from the window, furiously shaking her head in disbelief. "That can't be."

"I've never heard you pray like you did just now, Trish, and look what happened. Your prayers have called down heaven. God has sent a messenger to watch over us." He pointed toward the tree again. "Just look at him. I wonder how long he'll stay."

Her mother told her about cardinals when she was a child. This bird was symbolic of beauty in the midst of darkness, hope in the midst of sorrow—and her family had certainly seen a fair share of sorrow. Could this cardinal truly be bringing hope to them?

Still looking out the window in wonder, Dwayne asked, "Remember that old wives' tale you told me about when we saw a cardinal on our wedding day?"

She did indeed. Taking in a long, deep breath, like she was ready to exhale all the bad she allowed to dwell within, she exhaled as she said, "When a cardinal appears in your yard, it's a visitor from heaven."

Mystified, they stared out the window a little while longer, interested to see if the bird would fly away or do something. Trish really didn't know what she expected the bird to do. When it didn't move, she finally told Dwayne that she was tired and needed to lay down.

Dwayne left her room. Trish kept the curtains open and got in her bed. All the arguing and praying had worn her out. She'd had a rough night, barely sleeping at all as she kept waking from a nightmare.

The sun was going down and her heavenly visitor was still perched on the tree. She laid her head on the pillow and, for the first time in a long time, slept without falling into some kind of nightmarish dream that had her being chased or falling off of a building. Peace enveloped her, warmed her, and soothed her. How could she not be at peace? God had sent a heavenly visitor to watch over her.

Even if that old wives' tale wasn't true, for tonight, she chose to believe.

CHAPTER 8

"Mom, tell Dad to keep his promise."

Alexis was sitting at the kitchen table, filling out paperwork to get one of her clients approved for housing, so she was a bit distracted. "Promise about what, Ethan?"

Ethan shook her chair. "He promised he was going to race me today. Daddy's always bragging about being a better swimmer than I am, but I've been practicing and he still owes me a race."

Michael entered the kitchen, then did his best imitation of a Superman stance. Arms folded across his chest, legs spread apart, he said, "Ethan, my boy, you have no clue who you are challenging. Once we're in the water, there will be no turning back. No crying for your mommy."

Ethan came toward his father as if they were in the *Batman v Superman* movie. "I won't be crying to my mom, but let's just hope you don't run back in the house and call Granny to ask why they didn't get you a better swim coach when you were my age."

"Did you hear your son, Alexis? He really thinks he can beat me."

Alexis put down the forms she had been working on. She gave her husband a you-got-your-hands-full look. "I don't know. Ethan may have your number."

Michael backed away, hand to his heart. "You wound me, woman. How can you turn on your husband like this?"

"She's my mom. She's supposed to be on my side," Ethan told his father.

Standing up, Alexis shook her head. "I am not taking sides. I have a dinner party to get ready for, so I can't referee you boys right now."

"You take his side," Michael said, pointing at Ethan, "and accuse me of acting like a kid? Where is the love?"

"I have so much love for you, husband. I really, really do. I just don't have time for you two right now. I have to whip up a meal that will help you close the deal on this merger."

"Not exactly a merger," Michael corrected. "They just want the company, not the inventor."

"You'll invent something even better, Daddy." Forever Daddy's little girl, Ella had encouraging words for her father as she entered the room.

"Thank you, Ella. I knew someone in this house was on my side."

"She just wants to make sure you show up for her daddy-daughter dance and buy that awful dress she wants." Ethan stuck out his tongue at his sister.

Michael got back in his Superman stance as he turned to Ethan. "All right, kid, it's time for me to teach you a lesson for coming in here and stealing my wife's heart. You've got to pay for that."

"Daddy, Mommy is supposed to love us. We're her kids." Ella laughed at her father.

"Don't try to take up for him, Ella. He wants this fight, and I'm going to give it to him." Michael headed to the bedroom to put on his swim trunks.

Ella's eyes widened as she looked over at her brother. "Are you really going to race Daddy?"

Flexing his muscles, Ethan said, "I sure am. I beat you every time. I'll beat him too."

Looking doubtful, Ella asked, "You do know that Daddy has a bunch of trophies and almost went to the Olympics, right?"

"It's all in good fun, Ella. Just let your brother go swim with his father." Alexis put her paperwork up as the kids rushed to their rooms to put on their swimsuits.

Alexis loved the fact that Michael was in good spirits today and that he was taking a break from his work to spend some time with the kids. She didn't have time to splash around in the pool with them because they had a big night planned—an important night for Michael's business.

Media Matters Inc. was a global technology conglomerate. They didn't seem to come up with any new ideas of their own. They bought companies with proven success in the technology field. Michael and his business partner Peter's app came to their attention after Peter ran into an old college friend at a technology conference.

Nora Foster was vice president of new development at Media Matters Inc. She and one of the directors of the company, who was also a woman, would be coming to the house for dinner tonight. Alexis was a bit intimidated by the fact that these women were powerful enough to make buying decisions at their company. The biggest buying decisions she made each week was at the grocery store or online, ordering toys for Ethan and cute outfits for Ella.

Everything had to be perfect. If this dinner party was done right, it would go a long way to closing the deal. Lobster and steak were on the menu, along with asparagus and sweet potato puree with smoked paprika and brown sugar. She picked up a red velvet cake from her favorite bakery. After picking up the cake, Alexis started second-guessing herself.

She needed something much more than just slicing a piece of cake and putting it on a saucer. As she put the sweet potatoes on to boil, sprinkled her asparagus with minced garlic, Himalayan sea salt, and olive oil, her mind kept turning. *Dessert had to be special.*

Then it hit her. When she was a kid, some of her favorite moments occurred in the kitchen with her mother as they cooked a chocolate-cookie crunch trifle. It was chocolaty and rich from the pudding—a fluffy cookie delight with the added layers of whipped cream. The Oreo cookies her mother crunched up in the trifle only added to the yumminess of the dessert.

Rushing to the pantry to make sure the kids had not eaten all of the Oreos, Alexis glanced out of her big picture window. Ella was sitting on the edge of the swimming pool, yelling at Ethan as he splashed in the water. Michael was climbing the stones as he normally did just before diving into the water. She opened the patio door and yelled out, "Show off!"

Michael climbed past the waterfall that cascaded over the stones on the second level of the stone wall. He reached the top of the stones and then lifted his arms, ready to take flight.

Ella stood up. "One, two, three—go!"

Ethan took off as fast as his skinny legs and arms allowed him. After giving Ethan a head start, Michael dived into the water. Alexis smiled as she watched them. Her husband diving from on top of those stones was something spectacular to behold. He was her Superman.

She went back to work in the kitchen, not wanting to see the winner and be forced to take sides. Her boys were too competitive. If they were more like she and Ella, they wouldn't even be out there using unnecessary testosterone.

Alexis put the heavy cream, milk, and sugar in a saucepan, stirred it, and then let it cook on low heat. She grabbed a bowl, sifted some cornstarch and cocoa powder. Alexis whisked in the eggs and heavy cream to form a paste. She stirred the pot that was on the stove. Next, she put milk in the microwave to warm it. Once it was warm, she gradually poured it in her chocolate pudding mix.

She smiled as she put her pudding mix into a saucepan and began cooking it on low heat. Making this dessert felt like coming home. All of a sudden she was that nine-year-old girl, helping her mother in their small kitchen.

"Let me stir the chocolate, Mommy. I can do it."

"Okay, baby, you can stir the chocolate," Vivian told her.

Tears wet her mother's face as she stood at the stove, stirring the whipping cream. Her mother always cried when they made this dessert. All Alexis wanted to do was make her feel better. By the time Alexis finished stirring the chocolate, her mother had dried her eyes.

"You feel better now, Mommy?"

"Yeah, I'm just sorry you had to see me like that."

Alexis had seen her mother "like that" too many times to count. Her mother had been a whirlwind, a hurricane, and a tsunami all at the same time. She knocked things over and barreled over anybody who got in her way. But when they were in the kitchen making this chocolate-cookie crunch trifle, even if only for a moment, when her mom would wipe the tears from her eyes, things would become calm again. They would sit down and enjoy their special dessert and laugh at whatever they found to watch on their nineteen-inch television.

"Our guests will be here in two hours. Do you think you'll be ready?" Michael asked, bringing her back to the present. He had a towel wrapped around his waist as he dried his hair with the smaller towel that was in his hand.

"Have I ever let you down?"

"Of course not, but I still think you should have hired a caterer."

"I hired two servers. They will be here in an hour. I am more than capable of cooking an elegant meal that will impress these Media Matters people."

Ethan swung the back door open and would have slammed it if Ella hadn't been right behind him. She grabbed the door. "You almost hit me, jerk."

"I don't care." Ethan stomped out of the kitchen and kept on stomping up the stairs on the way to his room.

70

Glaring at her husband, she pointed the whisk she used for the chocolate pudding at him. Chocolate dripped on the floor. "What did you do?"

He shrugged and grinned. "I did what winners do. I won, baby."

Shaking her head at him, she said, "Michael Marshall, why can't you let your son win at something—at least once?"

Michael glanced in Ethan's direction. "He'll be all right, Alexis. My dad never let me win, and I turned out all right."

"We might need a second opinion on that," she joked.

"Funny, but your son still lost." He then warned, "And don't go upstairs babying him. He needs to learn how to win." Walking out of the kitchen, he added, "Nobody ever gave me anything. I earned every win."

Alexis wiped the chocolate off the floor. She wanted to be mad at Michael, but he was right about being a winner. Before she met him, her life had been a disaster, so she'd always taken his lead on what their children needed in order to be successful in life. Summer camps and extracurricular classes were all approved by Michael because he was the one who had the structure growing up.

Michael had given them a good life, so if he thought babying Ethan would stop him from becoming the winner he was meant to be, then she wouldn't rush up those stairs and wrap her son in her arms, even though she really, really wanted to. She wanted to give Ethan one of these chocolate cookie thingies and tell him how sorry she was for the way the race turned out.

She finished her meal, then made a pizza for the kids. When the servers arrived, she let them into the kitchen and provided instructions on how she wanted everything plated and brought out to the guests. Honestly, she would rather plate and serve the guests herself, but Michael wanted to project a certain image at this dinner party. His wife could not serve the food or it would appear as if they couldn't afford people to do that job for them.

The house was spotless because the maid service had spent six hours cleaning yesterday, giving the house its monthly deep clean. She always used A-1 Cleaning. Michael was impressed with how well they cleaned the house. If Alexis told him that she had helped the owner start her cleaning business after referring her to a psychiatrist who got her on the right medication for the illness that had stopped her from being able to keep a steady job, he would have gone through the roof.

In truth, Alexis would rather stay in the kitchen cooking and cleaning while Michael and Peter entertained. She just didn't have much in common with Nora Foster or Deidre Delaney. They were both high-powered businesswomen, climbing the ladder of success. She had been so nervous when Michael introduced her to them, though they had been nice to her.

"I hope you didn't go out of your way with dinner preparations. I would hate to interrupt your routine," Nora said while shaking Alexis's hand once she had arrived.

"No trouble at all. It's normally just me and the kids when Michael is working late, so it's nice having company."

They sat in the living room making small talk while the servers set the dining table. Alexis liked these businesswomen because they didn't go out of their way to make her feel less than because she was a housewife without a college degree. They made her feel at ease, and the conversation wasn't all business. Nora spent time catching up with Michael and Peter about their college days, while Deidre seemed genuinely interested in Alexis and the kids.

The ladies seemed to enjoy what she had to say. Deidre even told her, "The older I get, the more I appreciate that my mother was home to greet me when I arrived home from school."

"You don't have to say that." Alexis turned her head as her shoulders slumped and her eyes glanced toward the kitchen.

"I mean it," Deidre said. "My mom and I were really close when I was a child. Even today, there's nothing I wouldn't do for her."

Beaming with a bit of pride, Alexis said, "Thank you for saying that. It is important to me that I'm here for my kids while they're still young."

"It's commendable," Nora said, then turned back to Michael and Peter. "My mom sent me to college to find a husband. She never expected that I would choose corporate America instead."

Michael laughed. "Your mom got more than her money's worth, because you are kicking butt."

"That's funny. My mother never expected me to get married," Deidre added with a grin. "Never know, I just might surprise her with a grandchild one day."

The servers put their plates on the dining room table and the group sat down for dinner. "Oh, Alexis, you outdid yourself," Nora said while cutting into her steak.

"And lobster too?" Peter gave Alexis the thumbs up. "I may need to come over for dinner more often."

Silence fell over the room as the group dug into their meal. Then Nora snapped her fingers. "Whatever happened to . . . ?" Snapping her fingers again, she looked at Peter and then back at Michael. "You guys were always together. Always working on the next big thing. I thought he was your roommate."

Solemnly, Peter said, "Kevin. His name was Kevin Jones. He died in a car crash a couple of years after we graduated from college."

Putting her hand to her chest, Nora gasped. "Oh, how terrible. He was such a genius."

The servers came out of the kitchen with trays of the chocolate-cookie crunch trifle. Alexis started to second-guess herself. Or maybe she was third-guessing herself since she passed on the red velvet cake in favor of this chocolate treat. Now she was wondering if these high-powered women might think the crumbled Oreos was too juvenile to be elegant.

Michael was counting on her. She hoped that she hadn't let him down. The moment the dessert was placed in front of each dinner guest, they picked up their spoon and dug in.

Alexis held her breath until she heard the sounds of *mmm* and *yummy.*

Michael's eyes met hers. He was smiling. She smiled back.

"This is so good, Alexis. Where on earth did you order these from?" Nora asked.

"I ordered a red velvet cake from our local bakery, but I thought you ladies might enjoy something a bit more fun. So I made this dessert that my mom used to make for me when I was a kid."

"Wow, so your mom is perfect too." Deidre dug her spoon back into her pudding and put a heaping helping in her mouth.

She wished she could tell the truth—that Vivian hadn't been perfect, but she loved her anyway. The truth was that when they got married, Michael's one and only demand had been that she keep her past a secret. Her past had not been perfect, and Michael was uncomfortable with that. The night was going so well and Michael was smiling, so she didn't want to do anything to take away from the success her husband had earned.

She would smile at him and let everyone think that life was uncomplicated. Tomorrow, though, he would be picking the kids up from school because she was going to take her mother a chocolate-cookie crunch trifle and make another good memory with her.

CHAPTER 9

Trish woke refreshed, revived, and renewed with a mind to press on. She got out of bed, turned on her praise music, and started fiddling around the kitchen, turning on the coffee pot. She cut up some onions, celery, and carrots and put them in her crockpot with a pork tenderloin. She would later put on her pot of rice with some green beans and that would be dinner.

Since Jon-Jon's bedroom was so close, she could hear him snoring. No use fixing breakfast yet. It was 7:00 a.m., which was early for some, but not for Sister. Her mother was up by five in the morning, praying, and then watching the news or a preacher via cable television. Trish's cell phone was in her room, so she went and picked up her phone, and called her mother.

"Good morning, Mother! I wouldn't have called so early except I know you are an early bird."

"You got that right. I just finished my prayers, fixed your father's breakfast, and packed his lunch. Now I'm getting ready to watch the news and see what's going on in this big ole city."

Trish heard the television blasting in the background. "Give Daddy a kiss for me. Tell him I'll be over for a visit one day soon." Her father worked twelve-hour shifts four days a week, so when he wasn't at work, he lounged at home, refusing to lift a finger. Her mother put up with it because Daddy worked those twelve-hour shifts. Trish wished he'd come visit her and Jon-Jon more, but she understood. Maybe she'd see if Jon-Jon wanted to visit his grandfather.

75

"He's already out the door, but I'll tell him you asked about him. He'd love to hear from you more."

Trish had been Daddy's little girl when she was younger. When her father came home from work, he would go into his room where he hid his stash of Sour Patch Kids, which was absolutely Trish's favorite candy in the world. Her mother didn't like her eating the candy, so Daddy had to dole the treats in small servings or Sister would not be happy.

When he came out of his room, he'd say, "Where's my little sugar patch?" He wouldn't call her sour patch, like the name of the candy, because her daddy said she was too sweet to be sour.

Trish would come running to receive a few pieces of her beloved candy.

She missed those days because Albert Thornton seemed to get her like no other man on earth. However, as the years kept coming and she and Dwayne started their own family, her father seemed to distance himself. One day, Trish planned to ask her daddy about that.

"Mom, I called to thank you for your visit the other day. I know I wasn't all that pleasant to be around, but your words helped."

"Praise the Lord for that. I'm just glad I could be of service to you, daughter."

"Oh, you were. You allowing me the time to take a hot bath made all the difference. I felt like I could think clearer when I got out of the tub, but it took an extra day before I did what you told me."

"My word, what is becoming of these young people out in these streets. Help 'em, Jesus."

"Did you hear what I said, Mama?"

"I'm sorry, Trish. This news is just so disturbing. Young kids constantly killing each other. I just don't know what has become of this city. It used to be such a peaceful place."

"I'm just thankful that Jon-Jon didn't hang around kids who were always getting into trouble," Trish said.

"Jon-Jon is a good kid," Sister agreed. "You and Dwayne raised him right."

Crime had exploded in the lower income neighborhoods of Charlotte about fifteen or so years ago. Trish and Dwayne saved up enough to move to the southwest side of Charlotte ten years back, when several developers began building nice, affordable homes on that side of Charlotte. She had never imagined being able to get a $230,000 mortgage. However, with her salary as a teacher and Dwayne's salary at the factory, they were able to afford it.

Things were tight now, so Trish prayed they wouldn't have to move back into a watch-your-back kind of environment. But then she wondered who was watching the kids' backs who were living their day-to-day lives in crime-infested neighborhoods, and admonished herself to pray for those kids.

"I am thankful that Dwayne and I were able to provide a better way of life for Jon-Jon, although he ended up hurt anyway with that woman plowing into him the way she did."

"Didn't you tell me that the woman who hit Jon-Jon was distracted? Picking up her phone or something that fell?"

"It was her phone. At least that's what the police officer told us. I've never actually spoken to Ms. Marshall. I would really like to know why it was so important to reach for her phone when she should have been keeping her eyes on the road."

"Wait a minute." Sister redirected the conversation. "You asked if I heard what you said earlier. What did you call to tell me?"

"I just wanted to thank you. I know I've been giving you a hard time, but I prayed as you told me to do. I asked God to turn all this bad we've been experiencing into something good, and this morning I actually felt like getting out of bed. I'm getting ready to cook Jon-Jon some breakfast, and I truly feel good this morning."

"Don't forget Dwayne."

Trish's forehead crinkled. "What about Dwayne?"

"Breakfast—don't forget to fix your husband some breakfast."

She said she felt good, but that didn't mean she was rushing to do Dwayne any favors. That man was still on her list, and she wasn't going to let her mother make her feel guilty about that.

"Let me get going," Trish said. "I've got to get Jon-Jon cleaned up before I start breakfast."

She opened her bedroom door and headed next door to get Jon-Jon out of bed. She was surprised to find that her son's bedroom door was open and his bed was empty. She hadn't even heard any commotion in his room while she was on the phone with her mother.

Dwayne came out of the bathroom and was headed back to Jon-Jon's room with a towel slung over his shoulder. He must have noticed her questioning gaze because he said, "I smelled the crockpot. Figured since you were busy with the food, I'd help Jon-Jon with the shower." Pointing toward the bathroom, he said, "He's showering now. I forgot his pajamas."

"Oh, okay," was all she could say. Then, as Dwayne headed back to the bathroom, she called after him, "Would you like an egg and bacon sandwich for breakfast?"

"Perfect," he said over his shoulder as he went back into the bathroom with Jon-Jon.

What was going on here? Was she living in an alternate reality where her husband was suddenly the chief of doing stuff? She threw her hands up as she walked back into the kitchen. She had prayed for something good to happen to this family, and if Dwayne was being nice, she wasn't going to be petty. She would fix his breakfast just as she'd always done.

She cooked breakfast for her men, then cleaned Jon-Jon's room. Dwayne left for work.

After praying about it, she realized that Dwayne wasn't being all that unreasonable by wanting her to work part-time. She wished she could do substitute teaching or teach at a night school. Anything to bring in some extra money. But she didn't have anyone who could sit with Jon-Jon on a regular basis. If she was being honest with herself, taking care of her son all day, every day was wearing her down. She hadn't felt tired all the time when she was working full-time. Something had to give, but she didn't know how to let go. She would add that to her prayers.

"How's your morning going, son?" she asked while vacuuming his room.

"Not as good as yours."

She didn't like the way that sounded. Was Jon-Jon drifting further into depression? Had the argument she had with Dwayne the day before sent her son over the edge? Turning off the vacuum, she turned to face him. "What's wrong? Did you have a bad night? Is it something I did? Are you still in pain? I meant to give you another pain pill last night."

Lifting his hands, he said, "Calm down, Mom. I'm good. You just look like you had a good night's sleep or something."

Relax . . . relax. He's okay . . . Breathe. "I did sleep well. I'm trying to stress less. So do your mom a favor and smile for me every now and then."

He gave her an I'm-not-really-into-this smile. "Look, Mom, I know you're worried about me. And I'm really sorry that what I told Dr. Phillips hurt you, but I don't know what to do. I'm stuck in this bed. I can't even go to the bathroom unless you or Dad help me."

"You've got to have faith, Jon-Jon. I believe you'll walk again, but you have to believe it also. Can you do that for me, son? No. No, not for me. Can you do it for yourself?"

The phone rang. Trish held up a finger. "I'll be back so we can finish this conversation."

Rushing into the kitchen, Trish took the house phone off the charger base. "Hello?"

"Is this Mrs. Robinson?"

Dawg, why did she rush to this telephone? Most of her friends and family called on her cell phone. She should have known a bill collector would call this phone. Should have checked the caller ID. Now she was stuck. "Yes, it is. Can I help you?"

"This is Tiffany with Duke Energy. I'm calling about your utility bill."

"I know it's late. We will be paying it next week."

"I have to inform you that your electricity is scheduled to be cut off this week if we don't receive a two-hundred-dollar payment by tomorrow at five."

"Can you give me a little more time?" Trish did not want to ask her parents for any more money. This whole situation was embarrassing and degrading.

"We extended the time for you last month, and you did not complete the agreed-upon payment arrangement."

She felt like she was constantly begging for help. "I know we missed that payment arrangement, but we did pay as much as we could. I just need a little bit more grace here. We can pay the bill next Friday."

Tiffany was quiet for just a moment too long. Trish thought the girl was going to cut the electricity while they were on the phone. Then she said, "We can make the payment arrangement for next Friday, but it must be paid no later than 5:00 p.m."

"Thank you." Trish hung up the phone, went to her bedroom, and opened her computer. She googled "work from home jobs." She needed to bring some money into this house. Things were getting too drastic.

"Hey, Ma!" Jon-Jon called out from his room.

"Yeah?"

"Can I get a turkey sandwich?"

Trish closed her laptop and went into the kitchen to make Jon-Jon a sandwich. She stirred the crockpot meal, then headed back to her son's room. As she handed him the sandwich, she asked, "Have you done any of the stretching exercises your physical therapist showed you?"

Taking a bite of his sandwich, Jon-Jon shook his head. "What's the point?"

Trish wasn't into meditation, but she had to do something to stay sane around this I-just-wanna-give-up child. She wasn't used to this behavior from Jon-Jon. He had been an all As and Bs student who lettered in track, got a football scholarship to the college of his choice, and even played volleyball just for fun.

Breathe in, breathe out . . . Breathe in, breathe out. "You have a physical therapy appointment next week. You at least want to show him that you've been trying. All the man asked you to do was arm stretches."

"Nobody gave me the resistance bands. What am I supposed to do? Walk around this room and find them myself?"

Trish was taken aback when Jon-Jon acted like such a little snot because he had always been a respectful child. Even his teenage years hadn't brought much drama to the household. That had been a welcome surprise to Trish because she hadn't just given her parents headaches during her years of puberty; she'd caused so much tension that they kept telling her their dome was about to explode.

Jon-Jon didn't get in trouble much, so he wasn't acquainted with the types of whoopings her mother put on her. But, oh, how she wanted to knock him upside his head right now. She took another deep breath and pointed at the end table next to his bed. "Boy, those resistance bands are in that drawer. I told you I was putting them in there when he gave them to you three weeks ago."

"I must have forgotten," was all he said.

Trish folded her arms and stood there like a mannequin posing in the women's section of Macy's department store.

Giving in, Jon-Jon said, "All right, already. You don't have to stare me down like that."

"And you don't have to lay up in here acting all lazy, because I know you're not."

He pointed at her. "You got mad at Dad when he tried to call me lazy. How is it okay for you?"

"I said 'acting lazy.' I know that you are far from lazy." She opened the nightstand drawer and took out the bands. "You can do those resistance bands, Jon-Jon, so don't cheat yourself."

He finished his sandwich. Trish picked up the glass of ice water his father had placed on his nightstand earlier and handed it to him while still holding onto the resistance bands.

"Thanks, Mom." Jon-Jon drank from the glass and then handed it back to his mother rather than leaning over and placing it on the nightstand. He then took the bands out of her outstretched hand. "Okay, I'll tell you what. If you play a game of Scrabble with me, then I'll workout with the resistance bands."

"You know I hate Scrabble. I was a teacher, and I can never think of enough words to win. How bad is that?"

"Mom, you taught math. Nobody expects you to know as many words as an English teacher."

She shook her head. "Doesn't matter. You and your dad shouldn't be able to beat me so bad. Let's play Sequence. That's a game we're both good at."

He nodded. "Sequence it is."

Trish opened the hall closet to get the Sequence box. It had been a while since Jon-Jon had asked to play one of the board games. She was thrilled because she held out hope that this would put an end to his anti-social, just-leave-me-alone, hostile 'tude he'd had for a while now.

Before Dwayne lost the job he'd been on for fifteen years, his health insurance paid for two surgeries and Jon-Jon's electric hospital bed. She used the remote control to put him in a sitting position. Insurance had also paid for the kind of rollaway table hospitals use for their patients' mealtimes. Trish was grateful for these items because it made things a bit easier for Jon-Jon. She just wished Dwayne hadn't lost his job before Jon-Jon got the final surgery he needed, because the insurance provided through Dwayne's new job considered Jon-Jon's final surgery elective. How was removing spinal fluid a medical elective? She didn't get it but was going to keep praying. God would make a way.

Putting the Sequence game board on Jon-Jon's table, Trish then rolled it over to his bed and pulled up a chair. She counted out seven cards for Jon-Jon and seven for herself. Jon-Jon took the blue chips, and she took the green chips. Green had become her favorite color of late. Not money green, which might explain why they didn't have much of that. But sage green. The color felt calming, soothing to her. "Let's see what you got, young man."

"Oh, you know I'm gon' bring it. I just hope you can take losing in Sequence since you can't seem to take losing at Scrabble."

"You got all that mouth. Let's see if you can handle what I'm about to do." They loved teasing each other during game time. Trish and Jon-Jon were very competitive, but Dwayne was the worst. He once turned over a game board and let all the pieces fly after Trish beat him, like he stole something and the police were at the front door waiting to take him into custody.

He'd accused her of cheating, and she laughed her head off at how bad he was at losing. Later that night he admitted that she won fair, but then he asked for a rematch. Jon-Jon was just like his father. No sooner than she beat him in the first game of Sequence, he'd asked for a rematch.

Trish put her rice in the rice cooker and, as she came back to set the board back up for their next game, the doorbell rang. Shaking her head, she told Jon-Jon, "You got me all caught up in this game and you never practiced with those resistance bands."

"It's okay, Mom. I didn't want to do it anyway."

Scrunching her face, she pointed an angry finger at him. "I don't like that Jon-Jon." She took the bands off the table and handed them to him again. "You are a Robinson, boy. We don't give up, and we don't quit."

Jon-Jon mumbled something as she headed toward the front door, but Trish couldn't make out what he said and she chose not to concern herself with it. He was going to work with those resistance bands today and that was it. Period.

Trish looked through the peephole. A young woman with a milk-chocolate complexion, long lashes, purple lipstick, and sad eyes stood on her front porch with a baby on her hip. She opened the door. "Can I help you?"

"Hi, I'm Marquita." The young woman nervously cleared her throat and shifted the baby from one hip to the other. "I brought my baby to see his daddy."

CHAPTER 10

"Look what I brought you today." Alexis handed the jar containing the chocolate-cookie crunch trifle to her mother as she sat in the recliner in front of her television. Alexis then sat down in the other recliner. A round table was between them.

Vivian's eyes lit up. She took her spoon and dug in. "Mmmm. I haven't had one of these in such a long time." Then a strange look spread across Vivian's face. She sat the dessert down on the table. "I'm sorry. I don't know what I did, but I shouldn't have done it."

Vivian started tapping her scrawny hand on the table. Thick, green veins made pathways from her wrist to her fingers as if they were trying to find a way out of this place, just as her mother had tried to escape so many of the nursing homes she had been placed in.

Alexis took her mother's hand in hers. "You didn't do anything, Mom. I wanted to make dessert for Michael's business associates, and I remembered how you and I used to make this delicious dessert."

Vivian picked her dessert back up. "I bet they hated it. Our kind of desserts might be too cheap for Michael's fancy friends."

"Don't say that, Mom. The ladies were very nice. I told them I got this recipe from you after they told me how much they loved it."

"Well, isn't that just something." Vivian leaned back in her seat and dug back into the pudding, taking special delight as she crunched on the Oreos in the dessert.

Alexis turned the television on to a Western. Her mother loved old Westerns. She could sit and watch Marshal Matt Dillon and

85

Miss Kitty all day long. Vivian once told Alexis that Miss Kitty stole her job and was constantly stealing the scenes she had rehearsed.

Alexis was just a kid when her mother started telling her stuff like that. She and her mother would be sitting in their small living room watching *Gunsmoke*, and Miss Kitty would stroll into the salon, say one or two lines. Her mother's eyes would get big as a cartoon character's eyes when they popped out of their head. She would jab her finger at the television. "She's doing it again! She stole my lines again."

Back then, Alexis had no idea that her mother suffered from delusions of grandeur. Alexis remembered being so mad at Miss Kitty. If it wasn't for Miss Kitty stealing her mother's lines all the time, they wouldn't have had to move into so many trailer parks. They could be in a big, fancy house, like the one Alexis was sure Miss Kitty lived in.

But at last she grew up and realized that Miss Kitty had nothing to do with their lot in life. After that realization, she was able to enjoy watching these old Westerns with her mother, but only when her mother was on her meds. If she skipped taking her medication, then Alexis refused to watch television with her.

She and her mother had a really good day. Vivian was calm and wasn't plotting her escape from the holding cell the Russians held her in, waterboarding her until she revealed all of the military secrets she learned from her years of dating General Jim Mattis.

Of course, her mother had never even met the man, but ever since she heard about Mad Dog Mattis, Vivian told all her nurses that she was the reason the general never married.

Alexis had asked Michael to pick the kids up from school so she could spend the day with her mother. As she was driving home in good spirits, thankful for a peaceful day spent with her mother, she thought about ordering pizza. The kids would love it, but Michael was not a fan.

After the dinner party yesterday and then spending the day with her mother, Alexis was tired and didn't feel like cooking. There was an

Italian restaurant not far from the house. Michael loved their cheese tortellini, so she pulled into a parking lot, called the restaurant, and ordered salad, cheese tortellini, and a half-cheese, half-pepperoni pizza. Ella only ate cheese pizza and Ethan only ate pepperoni. They might be twins, but they were very different.

Ethan was shy, and it was hard for him to make friends. Once he made a friend, though, he stuck by them and championed them. Ella needed a social calendar to keep up with all her friends and their activities. However, Alexis noticed that as Ella added new friends, old friends seemed to fade away. She had planned to have a talk with her daughter about that, but she didn't want to be overly critical if there really wasn't a problem. Alexis could just be looking for problems where there were none.

Later, as she picked up the food order and loaded it into her car, her phone rang. It was Michael. She didn't answer because she was just two blocks away from home and didn't want to be driving and talking if it wasn't necessary. She'd be home in five minutes and could discuss whatever was on his mind then.

The phone rang again as she pulled onto her street. She hoped he wasn't trying to get her to pick up anything at the grocery store because that wasn't happening. Rounding the corner and about to hit the garage door button on the sun visor, Alexis saw an ambulance and fire truck in front of her house.

The. Ambulance. Was. In. Front. Of. Her. House. "Oh, my God!" Alexis tried to hit the garage door button, but her hand kept missing the button. She yelled at the uncooperative button as she banged her fist against the sun visor.

The phone rang again as she pulled into the driveway. She swiped right to answer the call. She was frantic. "Michael, what's going on? Why is an ambulance at our house?"

"Mommy, it's me. Please come home. Something terrible has happened."

It was Ella, she was crying. "I'm here, baby." Alexis tried to open the car door, but it was locked. Why was it locked? She snatched at the door handle several times before realizing that she hadn't put the car in Park, nor turned it off.

The walls in the car were closing in on her. *Inhale. Exhale.* She put the car in Park and turned it off. Getting out of the car, Alexis put her hand on her heart, taking deep breaths, trying to get control of her breathing. She then ran toward the house. The front door swung open, and Ella ran into her arms.

"Come on, Mommy." Ella grabbed her hand and pulled her toward the backyard.

Alexis didn't know what was going on. She didn't know if Michael or Ethan was hurt, but the feeling in the pit of her stomach told her it wasn't going to be good. "What happened, Ella?"

Ella was crying so hard and was so focused on getting to the backyard that she didn't answer. But the moment they entered the backyard, Alexis saw Michael standing next to the pool, wringing his hands like he didn't know what to do.

Firefighters were standing around while two paramedics were on the ground next to Ethan. *Oh, God. Ethan.* "Noooo!" Alexis yelled out.

This. Couldn't. Be. Happening. Alexis felt as if she was moving in slow motion as she ran over to them and tried to pull them off her son so she could get to him. Ethan needed her. She had to get to her son.

Michael grabbed her by the waist and pulled her away from the firefighters. "They're working on him, honey. I promise you. Ethan is going to be okay."

"Let me go, Michael!" She reached her hands out, trying to move closer to her son.

"Calm down, Alexis. We can't get in the way."

Ethan wasn't moving. Alexis watched in horror as one of the paramedics breathed into Ethan's mouth several times. Then the other paramedic with weight-lifting muscles pushed down on Ethan's chest. Alexis wondered if her son's pole thin body could handle the pressure from such strong arms. "Don't hurt him!" she cried out. "Please don't hurt him."

Ethan jerked and water spurted out of his mouth. The firefighters and paramedics seemed relieved as if something significant had occurred. Alexis didn't understand why they seemed pleased because Ethan still wasn't moving.

His eyes darted this way and that. "What happened to my baby, Michael?"

Sorrow etched across his face. "He tried to dive into the pool from the top of the stone structure."

"But he knows not to do that." Alexis couldn't think straight. She'd told Ethan on numerous occasions not to climb to the top of those stones. Michael was the only one who climbed to the top of that awful stone structure. Michael was the one who had it built onto the pool when she had warned against it.

The paramedics lifted Ethan onto the gurney. Buckled him in and rolled him toward the front.

"Where are they taking my baby?" She took off behind them.

"We've got to go to the hospital, Alexis." Michael grabbed her arm. "Come on. I'll drive."

"No, no! I'm going with Ethan." Rushing over to the ambulance with tears streaming down her face, Alexis called out to the paramedics, "I have to ride with him. You can't take him without me."

"It's okay, ma'am. Get in. You can ride with your son," the paramedic told her. Then he turned to his coworker. "Let's get a bandage for the back of his head. I see a gash there."

"He hit his head?" Alexis shut her eyes tight. Maybe, if she closed her eyes, she could block out all the wrong that was going on. Her son wouldn't be unconscious, he wouldn't have a gash on the back of his head, and he never would have dived in that pool.

The other paramedic said, "Got it."

As they cleaned Ethan's wound and bandaged the back of his head, Alexis opened her eyes.

Putting her hand on Ethan's arm, she leaned in close to her son. "I'm here, Ethan. Mommy is with you. I need you to open your eyes, son. Just open your eyes."

Sobbing uncontrollably, she put Ethan's smaller hand inside her hand. "M-Mommy's here, baby. Don't be afraid. There's nothing to be afraid of. You just had an accident. Y-you'll be just fine. Your father said you're going to be okay. He's on his way to the hospital. He'll meet us there." She kept talking, hoping that if Ethan heard her voice, it would help him open his eyes.

"He spit up a lot of water, ma'am. We just need to get him to the hospital so the doctor can take care of him."

Alexis looked over at the paramedic who had just spoken to her. He had red hair and the brightest blue eyes she'd ever seen. The name on his uniform was "Gerald." The muscular man's name tag read "Paul." She realized she hadn't thanked these men for what they did for her son. "Thank you. I'm so glad you were able to help Ethan, but why won't he wake up?"

"We don't know, ma'am. The doctor should be able to tell you. We're pulling up to the hospital right now. Since we've already called this in, someone will be waiting for him," Paul told her.

The ambulance drove over a bump as they reached the emergency entrance. Once the ambulance came to a stop, Paul opened the doors and then jumped out. Gerald unhooked the gurney and rolled it out of the ambulance. Paul pulled the legs from under the gurney and the two men rushed Ethan into the emergency room.

Alexis put her hand on the door hinge and stretched her leg to jump down as she had watched Paul do. But Michael grabbed hold of her and helped her out of the ambulance.

"I didn't think you were here yet."

"We followed behind the ambulance. I took every red light they took. Let's get in there." Michael tightened his grip on her hand.

"Yes, let's get in there." Alexis put an arm around Ella. She was still crying. "You okay, honey?"

"I'm just so scared for Ethan."

"I know you are. We all are. Let's just have faith and believe that he will be all right."

"Okay, Mommy." Ella tried to smile, but it fell short.

They entered the emergency room and went to the check-in desk. Michael told the woman sitting behind the desk, "We're here for my son, Ethan Marshall. He was just wheeled in."

"One moment." The woman left her desk, opened the emergency room door, and disappeared behind it.

"Where is she going? Why didn't she let us go in with her?" Alexis tried the emergency room door, but it was locked.

"Calm down, Alexis. Let's just see what she says when she comes back."

"No! You don't get to tell me what to do today." Wagging a finger in Michael's face, she said, "I warned you. Didn't I warn you about erecting that stone monstrosity around our pool? You wouldn't listen, so I'm not listening to you, Michael."

He tried to pull her into his arms. "I'm so sorry, babe. I never meant for this to happen."

Gulping back tears, she looked at her husband, the man she loved, and realized she didn't want to fight with him. She just wanted Ethan to live. "I-I know you didn't. It's not your fault that Ethan disobeyed us. I shouldn't have blamed you." She didn't want to blame her husband for this catastrophe, but if Ethan didn't pull through . . .

The front desk clerk returned and walked over to them. "The doctor is working on your son now. He will be out to talk to you as soon as he can."

"I want to go back there with him," Alexis demanded.

The woman shook her head. "I'm sorry. No one can be in the room right now. You will be able to see your son in a little while."

"What's going on, Daddy? Why won't they let us see Ethan?"

Michael put a hand on Ella's blonde head. "We will be in there with Ethan soon. We just have to trust that the doctors know what they are doing."

Alexis's heart felt like it might jump out of her skin, it was beating so hard. Pointing toward the emergency room doors, she declared, "That's our son back there. He might be scared or . . ." Gulping, her voice trailed off. ". . . Dying. We can't just sit here and trust people we know nothing about."

"Be reasonable, Alexis. Neither one of us knows how to help Ethan. Only the doctors know. So let's let them do their job. There are seats just right over there. Let's sit down."

Her head was pounding. She needed ibuprofen. Alexis tried to sit down, but then Ella started crying. "I didn't mean to leave him out there by himself. I know we're supposed to swim together, but I was thirsty."

"It's not your fault, Ella." Michael put an arm around Ella, comforting her.

Alexis fidgeted in her seat as if she was being attacked by killer ants. Popping out of the chair, she went back to the emergency room door. She wanted to yell at somebody. Tears fell from her eyes as she paced the floor. Her body ached from the pain she was feeling.

Then a nurse pushed a young man toward the emergency room doors to go outside. He was in a wheelchair. Immediately, she thought of the young man she hit with her car. He was now in a wheelchair. His parents must have spent countless hours at the hospital with him as he went through one surgery after another. Standing there, watching that young man being wheeled out of the hospital, Alexis could feel how much pain she had caused the Robinson family, and it overwhelmed her. She doubled over and sobbed out loud.

Ella and Michael ran over to her. They coaxed her back to her seat. Her chest heaved and constricted as she white-knuckled the chair. She closed her eyes, trying to blot out the pain of what had happened to her son and what she had done to another woman's son.

A woman in scrubs approached, and they stood up.

Alexis tried to read her expression as she asked, "Are you Ethan's parents?"

Michael, Alexis, and Ella got in her personal space to hear what she had to say. Even as they did, Alexis didn't know if her heart could take the words that were about to come out of the woman's mouth.

CHAPTER 11

E xcuse me? You say you're looking for *whom*?"

"My baby's daddy," the young girl with the sad eyes said.

When Trish first heard the girl say that she brought her baby to see his daddy, the church girl in her was ready to do the backstroke down this young girl's throat. She wished her first thought had been to pray, but Trish wasn't like her aunt Mabel when it came to stuff like this.

Her great-aunt Mabel once opened her front door to two little girls, each holding on to a suitcase. They had arrived in a yellow taxicab. The cab driver handed Aunt Mabel a note and the bill for the taxi ride. One of the women Uncle Stevie had been fooling around with was tired of taking care of her children, so she sent them to Aunt Mabel with a simple note that read, "These is Stevie's kids. Y'all can feed them better than I can."

Aunt Mabel raised those girls until they were full grown, then the trifflin' mama started making noise all over town about how Mabel and Stevie stole her kids. Come to find out, only one of those girls belonged to Uncle Stevie.

She'd always thought that her aunt was the most kind-hearted woman she'd ever known—raising her cheating husband's extracurricular kids like that. Trish's heart wasn't made like that. She would have packed Dwayne's clothes and changed the locks. Uh-uh, ain't nobody got time for that.

"Okay. And who is your baby's daddy? And why do you think he's

94

here? 'Cause you got some nerve if you're trying to claim your baby belongs to my husband."

"Huh?" Marquita shook her head. "I don't even know your husband. Jon-Jon is my baby's father."

Trish's eyes widened, and she took a step back. "Jon-Jon? But Jon-Jon hasn't left this house without me or his father in the last six months."

"We made this baby last summer, and *our* baby needs Pampers. He needs food, and I just lost my job, so it's time for Jon-Jon to step up."

"You sure are sassy coming over here talking about somebody needs to step up, when my son can't even walk right now." Trish couldn't help but glance over at the baby. He was a small little chocolate drop. He could barely hold his head up, and this girl had him casually resting on her hip.

Marquita's hoop earrings swished in the air as she crooked her neck. "I'm not trying to be rude because I really do feel sorry for what happened to Jon-Jon, but I didn't make this baby by myself."

Trish glanced around to see if any of the neighbors were outside. They were getting a bit loud, and she really didn't want anyone overhearing this conversation. She opened the door a bit wider. "Come in. Let's talk to Jon-Jon so we can get to the bottom of this."

Marquita stepped inside the house. Trish closed the door while staring at the baby.

"What's his name?"

"Marcus. I named him after my baby brother."

Trish took the young girl to the living room and asked her to have a seat. "And you might not want to hold him on your hip like that. He doesn't look old enough to hold his head in the correct position for long."

Marquita smacked her lips like she didn't like being told what to do.

Trish's hand flinched like she was gripping it around a belt. "Hey, you came knocking on my door, telling me I've got a grandson, so don't smack your lips at me."

Marquita had this "whatever" look on her face. Jerking her neck she said, "I wouldn't have come over here without calling first, but Jon-Jon changed his phone number like he hiding out or just don't want to be bothered. I'm not going for that no more. Jon-Jon needs to—"

"Look, Jon-Jon isn't hiding from you. His phone was turned off a few months ago."

"What's up with that?" Marquita's brow furrowed. "I mean, I know he was in an accident, but don't he want to talk to his friends?"

They didn't have the money. That's what was up with that, and Jon-Jon wasn't using his phone anymore anyway. "Let me get Jon-Jon so the three of us can have a discussion."

This young girl was working Trish's nerve. She'd just met her, and she already wanted to take a belt to her. Coming in here rolling her neck and accusing her son of running from his responsibilities.

"Who were you out there talking to?" Jon-Jon asked as she entered his room. "You wasting time, because I'm ready to play another game."

Trish closed the door as she stepped into the room. "Boy, hush up and listen to me." She got close enough to him so he could hear the low volume of her voice. "Do you know a girl named Marquita Lewis?"

A sinful grin eased across his face. He adjusted his position, tried to wipe the grin off his face. "Why you asking about Marquita?"

She kept a throw pillow at the bottom of the bed in between the mattress and the iron bars of his hospital bed. It was kept there so Jon-Jon didn't get his feet trapped. She pulled the pillow out and hit him with it. "That girl is sitting in my living room with a baby in her arms and you in here grinning like a cat with a rat tail hanging from your mouth."

"Marquita's here?" He sunk into his bed. Eyes darted this way and that. "Yo, tell her to go away. I don't want anybody seeing me like this."

"Did you not hear what I said? She has a baby with her." Those words didn't even sound right coming out of her mouth. How could her baby have a baby? Trish looked heavenward. "How can this be happening, Lord? Aren't we dealing with enough?"

"I don't want her to see me like this," he whined.

"You don't have a choice, Jon-Jon. And I'm texting your daddy."

"Wait, Mama. Don't tell Daddy."

"Just shaking my head. Just shaking my head." Giving him the talk-to-the-hand sign, Trish told him, "I can't with you right now." She stepped out of his room to grab her cell phone, mumbling, "Bringing some baby in here."

She grabbed her cell and then came back into the room with Jon-Jon. She texted his dad and then put the cell in her pocket. "Okay, let's go."

"But, Mama." He looked like he was about to cry.

"I don't like what's going on, either, but if this is your baby then you have to take responsibility." Trish pulled the cover off of him. She then placed the wheelchair next to his bed and swung his legs onto the right side of the bed.

"Mom, no, I don't want to go out there. You texted Dad. Why can't y'all handle this?"

This was a baby, and as much as she loved her son and felt badly about what he was dealing with, she was not going to let him be some deadbeat dad. That just was never going to happen. Not on her watch. "You didn't ask us to handle nothing when you was laying up with this girl." She popped him upside the head. "You know better than that."

He ducked his head and cast his eyes down. He looked repentant.

Sighing deeply, she helped Jon-Jon sit up and then sat down next to him on the bed. Taking his hand in hers. "I get it, Jon-Jon. I really do. You were *the man* in high school, and you were making your presence known in college. You have refused calls from high school friends and your college teammates, and all they want to do is wish you well."

"I don't need their pity, Mama."

"Maybe your father and I should have made you take a few of those calls. We thought we were protecting you." Letting his hand go, she then gently rubbed his stubbly chin as images of Jon-Jon from boyhood to this very moment played in her head like a this-is-your-life video. "We can't let you hide away and pretend this isn't happening. This is the day you become a man, son."

"But, Ma, what if the baby isn't mine and Marquita just wants to laugh at me and tell everyone that I'm in a wheelchair?"

"We warned you about dating fast-tail girls who didn't want nothing but the fame that was sure to come your way. Were you listening? Did you take in any of the things we said, Jon-Jon, because I don't talk just because I have a tongue."

He nodded. "Yeah, I listened. And I stayed away from a lot of girls who wanted to go out with me. I knew they weren't for the right thing."

Of course, a bunch of girls wanted to date her son, and not just because he was destined to be a football star. Jon-Jon was handsome. He had that coffee-with-a-hint-of-hazelnut-creamer skin tone and mesmerizing dark-brown eyes that were just like his daddy's. Jon-Jon was also kind and thoughtful. He would be a good catch for any woman. But this right here just didn't make sense. He wasn't raised like this, and even though she wanted grandchildren his behavior was unacceptable. She was so mad she could scream. They could hardly afford Jon-Jon's needs. If this boy had brought another mouth for them to feed . . .

"Do I really have to do this?"

"What would your daddy tell you to do in this moment?"

Jon-Jon sat up, cracked his neck, stretched his arms. "Help me into my chair so I can see this baby for myself."

Trish wasn't happy that Jon-Jon had been fooling around in a manner that could get him stuck with a baby, but it is what it is. She helped him into the wheelchair and opened his bedroom door.

"Wait." He held up a hand. "Can you put a blanket over my legs?"

She did as he requested, then started pushing him toward the door. Then he stopped her again.

"I can do it." Jon-Jon gripped the wheels of his chair and then thrust forward.

Trish wanted to clap and cheer for her son. The physical therapist had worked with him on wheelchair mobility, but Jon-Jon had refused to guide the wheelchair himself, preferring to be pushed.

Walking behind him, Trish's stomach did somersaults like Simone Biles was in there practicing for the Olympics. She wished Dwayne was here, but she couldn't have him leaving work, not when he had just missed two days to take care of her and Jon-Jon.

Jon-Jon wheeled himself into the living room. That grin appeared on his face the moment his eyes connected with Marquita's. Trish wanted to pop him in the back of his head. She bent next to his ear. "No more grinning like that until you're married and in your own place, you got me?"

His head swiveled as he looked back at her like she was a joy-killer. "Mom!"

"I said what I said."

Turning back to Marquita, Jon-Jon waited as Trish put the safety on the wheelchair. "Hey, Marquita."

"Hey."

"My mom just told me that you have a baby." His eyes drifted to the baby laying in her lap.

"We," she corrected. "*We* have a baby."

"But I don't understand."

Marquita's lips pursed, and her eyes crossed. "Don't blame me if your mama and daddy didn't tell you how babies are made."

This girl's stank attitude was a bit much for Trish. She was raised to be respectful, and she and Dwayne taught Jon-Jon to respect others as well. She would never enter anyone's home and talk out the side of her neck like this. "Girl, what is your problem?"

Marquita glanced over at Trish. "I'm not trying to disrespect you or nothing. I didn't want to bust in your house like this, because I know Jon-Jon's got problems too. But I'm out of work and Marcus still needs to eat, and I don't know what else to do."

"Now that sounds like an honest answer." Trish reached for the baby. Marcus's bubbly laughter filled the room as Trish lifted the baby out of Marquita's arms. He felt so warm and cuddly and smelled like the same kind of soap she used to bathe Jon-Jon with. "You use Aveeno?"

Marquita nodded. "He has dry skin."

"Jon-Jon had terrible dry skin when he was a baby, but it went away when he turned four."

"That's a lot of Aveeno until then, and that soap ain't cheap," Marquita said.

Trish sat down in the seat across from the girl. As she looked down at the baby, her heart filled with joy and fear at the same time. His eyes looked like Dwayne's. Could this really be Jon-Jon's baby or was she seeing things? "If we can speak to one another in a civilized manner, I think we can get to the bottom of this."

"I'm not trying to be rude. I guess I'm just too blunt for your taste."

Jon-Jon was staring at the baby as he cooed in Trish's arms. "If this is my baby, why didn't you tell me about him before now?"

"First of all, your phone is no longer working and that was the only number I had to reach you. Not that you used it to call me once you went back to school. You didn't care what happened to me." Her head bobbed. "So back up on that one."

"My phone has only been inactive for the past three or four months. You had plenty of time to tell me that you were pregnant. Now you want to come in here acting like I'm not holding up my end, when I didn't even know I had an end to hold up."

Marcus's lip quivered as if he was about to cry. "Lower your voice, Jon-Jon. You're scaring the baby," Trish told him.

Rolling her eyes at Jon-Jon, Marquita got out of her seat and took the baby out of Trish's arms. "Y'all living good in this nice neighborhood. Don't have to worry 'bout no drive-by shootings or winos stealing from you. I just want Marcus to have a life like that, but I should have known you weren't going to help me."

"I didn't say I wasn't going to help you!" Jon-Jon's voice rose again. "I just don't understand why you didn't tell me you were pregnant if the baby is mine."

"I didn't even know I was pregnant until I was five months along." Smiling at Marcus, she said, "I didn't have morning sickness, and my stomach didn't start growing until my fifth month."

Trish had to ask, "And you were still getting your menstrual cycle?"

Marquita shook her head. "I thought I wasn't getting it because of stress."

Trish's hand slashed through the air as she waved off that comment. "You are too young for stress."

"You don't know my life." Marquita put Marcus in Jon-Jon's lap. "You didn't ask to hold him, but I'm giving you a chance to hold your son before we walk out this door."

Trish took her cell phone out of her pocket. A text appeared from Dwayne with several exclamation points. She would get back with him. "Can I get your cell number, Marquita? I'd like to call you when my husband gets home."

"Am I going to be accused of lying again?"

"Nobody is accusing you of lying," Trish said, still holding her phone.

Jon-Jon bounced Marcus on his lap. Smiling as he looked at the little bundle of sweetness. "Asking why you didn't tell me you were pregnant is not calling you a liar, but I do think we need a DNA test. You should be able to understand that."

She snatched Marcus away from him. "I don't have anything to hide, Jon-Jon. Get your DNA test, and then I want my child support."

The girl looked hurt, like Jon-Jon needing a DNA test before believing her was the worst insult she'd ever received in life. As a woman, Trish could kind of understand, because if Dwayne had ever questioned Jon-Jon's paternity, she would have hit the roof. But this girl wasn't married to her son, so they were going to need that test.

Trish held out her phone and tried again. "Can I get your number, Marquita? If you want our help, you need to work with us on this."

Marquita snatched the diaper bag and threw it across her shoulder as she made her way to the front door.

Trish stopped her. "Marquita, please don't bite off your nose just to spite your face. You said you need help. Give me your number so we can reach out to you."

Through huffs and puffs of agitation, Marquita gave Trish her telephone number and then left the house like a bad wind swept her away as fast as it had blown her in.

CHAPTER 12

"Hey, bud. How are you doing?" Alexis was overjoyed as she stepped into the hospital room to see her son alert and watching her walk in the room.

He lifted his arm and waved at her, but his arm dropped as quickly as he'd lifted it.

Ethan had tubes and wires all over his body, and electrodes were spaced out on his chest. Alexis turned questioning eyes toward the man in the white coat, standing in the room holding some kind of chart.

He offered his hand to her. "I'm Dr. Thomas, and I will be caring for Ethan."

"He's going to be okay, isn't he, Doctor?"

"We still need to run a few tests. I've ordered an MRI. We need to make sure there's no swelling in the brain."

Her eyes widened. Michael put a hand on her back and rubbed it. It felt like he was holding her up as her legs wobbled. "Brain swelling?"

"He's all right, Alexis. Just look at him."

"Can I go home, Mom?" Ethan asked.

Alexis turned back to Dr. Thomas. He said, "That depends on what the tests say. We have him on oxygen right now to gently push air into his lungs. We won't be able to take him off the oxygen for at least twenty-four hours."

Michael asked, "Are you saying he can't breathe on his own?"

The doctor nodded. "He was struggling when he woke up."

"Okay, Dr. Thomas, do what you need to do. We just want him to get better," Michael said.

Alexis couldn't speak. It felt like something was attacking her throat. Closing it. She coughed. Her baby had been healthy all of his life. He'd run, jumped, swam, and played with his friends. She didn't want him to be limited from doing any of the things that helped him enjoy being a kid.

"Mommy, we prayed, remember? Ethan is going to be okay."

Alexis looked at Ella. The child had more faith than she ever did, but Ella hadn't known many bad days. She had never seen life switch up on her where one day things were going fine, then the next hour—the next minute—things became upside down again. "Thank you, Ella. Keep praying for your brother so that he can come home with us soon."

"He'll be in the ICU overnight, but if he remains stable, I'll have him moved to a regular room tomorrow."

"Can I get a rollaway bed? Because I'm not leaving my son." Alexis stared Dr. Thomas down, daring him to defy her wishes.

"That's fine. But we can only have one visitor in this room for a long period of time." Dr. Thomas left the room.

While looking at Alexis, Michael put an arm around Ella. "I'll go to the cafeteria and get you something to eat, and then I'll take Ella home."

"Thank you, Michael." She sat down next to Ethan's bed and held on to her son's hand. "Mommy's going to spend the night with you."

"Mommy?"

"Yes, baby?"

"I'm hungry."

Laughing, Alexis was reminded of the food she picked up earlier that evening. She'd ask Michael to put the food in the fridge when he got home. "Of course, you are. I'll ring the nurse to see if you can eat yet."

❧

It turned out that Ella was right. Within forty-eight hours Ethan had been taken off the oxygen and was breathing on his own. He was released from the hospital. When Ethan arrived home and went to his bedroom, he ran back out holding two new superheroes in his hands.

"Ethan, stop running. You just got home. Please take it easy." Worry etched on Alexis's face.

His run changed to a fast walk. "Mom, you got them!"

"Of course I got them. Did you think I was going to let you come home without Thanos, Ultron, and Loki?"

Ethan hugged his mom, but then a puzzled look crossed his face. "How did you get them? You were at the hospital with me the whole time."

"I ordered them on my phone and had them delivered."

"Wow, they're quick." Ethan turned and ran back to his bedroom, anxious to play with his new toys.

Michael pulled her into his arms, kissed her forehead. "Told you he was going to be all right."

"Yes, you did." She put her arms on his shoulders. "I'm glad he's running around, but I don't ever want him anywhere near that swimming pool again. I don't care if that means we have to move."

"We don't have to move, Alexis. I should have listened to you in the first place. I called the construction company who built the wall for me. They will be here tomorrow to tear it down."

His words were like a balm to her soul. Made her feel safe again. "Thank you, honey." She lifted on her toes and kissed him.

"Eww," Ella said as she walked out of the room away from her parents.

Alexis and Michael laughed. It felt good to hear laughter again.

Smiling, Alexis headed to the kitchen. "Let me get something on for dinner."

"Are you sure you're up to it? If you'd rather rest, I can order a pizza."

Michael's offer made her want to hug him again. "I know you don't like pizza. I'll just fix sandwiches for us and maybe a salad."

The salad was for Michael and Alexis. The kids had chips with their turkey sandwiches. No one even cared that she didn't cook a hot meal. The four of them were so glad to all be under one roof again that Michael even sat down and watched a whole movie with the family.

Later that night the kids brushed their teeth and got ready for bed. Alexis went to Ethan's room to check on him. She could hardly believe that he was already in bed and not crouched on the floor next to his superheroes doing battle with his newest additions. "Being in the hospital really tired you out, didn't it?" She pulled his Carolina Panthers blanket up to his chest.

"Mom, duck!" he yelled as he got from under the cover and tried to move her out of the way.

"Ethan, what are you doing?"

"I'm trying to watch the fight."

"Huh, what?"

"Boom!" Ethan clapped his hands together and then moved them apart like clanging cymbals in a symphony. "Thanos just hammered the Hulk. That was cool."

Ethan's superheroes were in the toy box he kept them in. Nothing was flying or fighting in his room. "Ethan, baby, calm down. You're just seeing things." She wrapped him in her arms and hugged him real tight. "What you're seeing isn't real, honey. Please lay down and go to sleep for Mommy, okay?"

She let him go. Ethan was calm as he stared at her. "You didn't see them?"

"No, baby, I didn't see anything." She helped him get back under the cover. Kissed him. "I want you to do something for me."

"Sure, Mom, what do you want?"

"When you wake up in the morning, if you see any more fights or flying superheroes in your room, would you please come and get me?"

"Do I have to do it right away?"

"Yes, I really need to know."

"But what if one of them gets blasted before I get back to my room?"

"You won't miss anything, Ethan. They won't disappear before you bring me back to the room with you." She touched his nose. "Because those superheroes of yours like an audience when they fight."

Ethan nodded. "Okay, I'll come and get you. I hope my Thanos decides to fight again tomorrow. He's big." He yawned and then curled up under the cover.

Alexis turned off the light but then stood at the door watching her son, making sure he wouldn't jump back up. He needed to rest.

Michael came up behind her, wrapped his arms around her, whispered in her ear. "You don't have to watch him sleep. Come to bed."

She loved when he pulled her close to him. She was his and he was hers. If fairy tales came true, they would be like this forever. "I'm on my way. Just give me a minute."

Michael left the room. She continued staring at her son, afraid to turn away from him. Afraid of what the morning might bring. A chill ran down her spine. She put her hand to her mouth and bit back her fears, sighed deeply, and walked away. She poked her head in Ella's room. She was already asleep, so Alexis eased the door closed.

Entering the master bathroom, she turned on the shower, let the water get hot and then got in. She let the hot, hot water assault her as heat filled the shower like a steam room.

Turning off the water, she toweled off and then put on her peach-colored nightgown. It had crisscross straps in the back and was about knee-length. Michael bought her this elegant silk gown a few years ago for Valentine's Day. She loved all of her gowns, but this one hung just right and Michael was extra frisky when she wore it. She needed his closeness tonight.

"Everything okay with Ethan?" he asked as she came out of the bathroom.

Michael was in the bed. He pulled the cover back so she could join him. "He seems to be doing okay."

"I heard him say something was flying when I passed his room to check on Ella. What was that about?"

A quick, nervous laugh escaped, but fell flat. "Fighting . . . He was talking about his superheroes. You know he loves to pretend the Iron Man and Captain America are flying off somewhere."

Michael's eyes traveled down the length of her. Their eyes connected. "Are you tired?"

"A little."

"It's nice to have you home, sleeping in our bed."

"I'm glad to be home. Those people at the hospital come into the rooms all night long. I don't know how the patients get any rest. They drew his blood, took his temperature, checked his blood pressure . . . It went on all night long, both nights."

Michael moved closer to her. His hands reached out and pulled her to him.

"Wait." She sat up. "I need to go check on Ethan."

Questions flashed in Michael's eyes. "You said he was okay. Did something happen while you were in the room with him?"

"No, no, I just want to check on him. I won't be long." She got out of bed and walked back to her son's room. She leaned her head against the door, taking a deep breath before opening the door.

If her son was in there playing with flying superheroes, Alexis would probably break down and cry. Not tonight. Please let him be asleep. She eased the door open. He was sound asleep. She wanted to go in, sit on his bed, and watch over him, but she was afraid to wake him.

Maybe a good night's sleep would clear Ethan's mind, but Alexis knew all too well that what was up could soon be down and things in her life could start spinning round and round.

Stop thinking. Just stop thinking, she told herself as she climbed back in bed with Michael.

Sounding groggy, Michael asked, "What's he doing?"

"Sleeping."

He pulled her back in his arms. The tension of these past few days began to fall away. She belonged in Michael's arms. All she wanted to think about for the rest of the night was the man she loved with every part of her being. In the morning she would discover if any more superheroes flew around Ethan's room, if he'd suddenly had tea with the queen of England or became a movie star.

She wouldn't be able to keep it from Michael for much longer. Not if Ethan was still seeing things in the morning. Michael would know something was off.

"Where'd you go?"

"Huh?"

Michael's hand was on the small of her back. "You looked like you were somewhere else?"

"I'm here with you, Michael. I don't want to be anywhere else. Don't want to think about anything else but us and how much I love you." All she wanted to do was love on her husband tonight because she didn't know what tomorrow would bring for Ethan. She didn't know if her perfectionist husband could handle something being wrong with Ethan. If Ethan's delusions continued, would Michael want to put him out of sight and out of mind?

Love—she just wanted to think about love tonight.

CHAPTER 13

W hy did you let that girl in this house?" Dwayne stalked around the house, throwing up his hands and blowing hot steam out of his nose. "She's just trying to cash in."

Trish didn't get that comment. They had lived comfortably when they were both working. Now every day seemed like a struggle so she didn't understand what Marquita would be cashing in on. "What kind of payday is diapers and formula for the baby? Because that's about all we can chip in at this point."

"You got to see the big picture, Trish. She probably thinks Jon-Jon already has the insurance money from his accident or maybe she thinks he's collecting disability." He tapped his head several times. "Think."

Trish's lip curled. She snarled at him. "Don't talk to me like that, Dwayne. I'm not an idiot."

"I'm not calling you an idiot, but we can't just accept what some young girl tells us as gospel." He pointed at the kitchen table. "And why you got all these old photos of Jon-Jon on the table?"

"I'm just looking at them." Her head cocked at him, like, mind yo business.

He stormed into Jon-Jon's room, nose still flaring with hot air. "Boy, what I tell you about getting involved with these girls?"

Jon-Jon hung his head, looking miserable, like he wanted to get out of that bed and flee his home.

"Child support!" Dwayne yelled the words. "I told you they

110

would be coming after you for child support, didn't I? And you gon' be attached to that mama for a lifetime if this baby is yours."

"I'm sorry, Dad. I messed up, but Marquita wasn't coming after me for some payday. It wasn't like that."

Dwayne stood over his son, hands on the sides of his slightly bulging stomach. "Oh, she's not like that, huh? Then what's she like? Because this is the first me and your mama are hearing of her. Got your mama out there taking a trip down memory lane."

From the kitchen Trish yelled into Jon-Jon's room. "The baby reminds me of Jon-Jon when he was a baby." Still searching through the pictures, she added, "What if this is your grandson, Dwayne? Do you really want Marquita poisoning Marcus against his father and his grandparents? Because if we don't help her, that's exactly what's going to happen."

Dwayne came back into the kitchen, giving her a don't-start-your-mess look. He lowered his voice as he stood next to the table. "We both know why you want this to be his baby, but that's not good enough for me."

She wanted to be angry at Dwayne's suggestion that she just wanted to put a baby on Jon-Jon, but in truth, she was becoming more agreeable to the idea of having a grandson. After Jon-Jon's accident, Trish had feared that he might never get out of that bed and might never get married and have kids. But now . . .

She turned her attention back to the photos. Laughing, she slapped her knee as she picked up a photo that had captured Jon-Jon blowing spit bubbles when he was about six months old. She headed into her son's room with it. "Jon-Jon, you have got to see this picture. Now, you tell me that you and Marcus aren't twins."

Jon-Jon took the photo from Trish's hands and inspected it as if he was looking for clues like LL Cool J on *NCIS: Los Angeles*.

Dwayne loomed large as he leaned against the doorjamb of Jon-Jon's room. "What you think, son? Could this baby be yours?"

Jon-Jon handed the photo back to his mom. "Look, Dad, I'm sorry if I disappointed you again. I don't know if Marcus is mine, but I was with Marquita."

Dwayne's eyebrows furrowed. "What's this 'disappointed me' stuff? I love you, son, and don't you ever forget it."

"I know you love me, Dad."

Stepping into the room, Dwayne sat on the edge of Jon-Jon's bed. "But you think I'm disappointed that you can't play football anymore."

Jon-Jon didn't respond, but his eyes were glued to his father's face.

"I'm not gon' lie. I've pushed you all these years because I planned for you to get drafted into the NFL, but not for my glory. I'd love you just the same if you were a dishwasher down at Red Lobster."

"I'm not busting no suds, Dad. That's out."

Trish laughed. "Oh, we know that's true. I couldn't even get you to wash dishes around here."

"What I'm saying is," Dwayne continued, "whatever you do is all right with me. Just do something." He squeezed Jon-Jon's right leg and then stood back up.

Trish followed Dwayne out of the room. "That was nice."

"I'm nice," he said, looking as if he didn't get why she didn't know that. "But that doesn't mean I'm going to let Jon-Jon be taken advantage of."

"Well, what do you want us to do, Dwayne? The girl showed up on our doorstep. It's not like we put an ad in the paper looking for babies."

"You and Jon-Jon can keep looking at baby pictures, but I'm going online to see if I can order a home paternity test." He started to walk away but then doubled back. "You can get mad about this if you want, Trish. But right is right and Jon-Jon ain't paying child support for a baby that ain't his."

"I'm not mad, Dwayne. That's why I texted you when the girl showed up. And Jon-Jon already told Marquita that we wanted a DNA test." They were talking civilly to one another so she confided in him. "I don't want to get attached to this baby and then find out he's not Jon-Jon's. That would probably break my heart more than anything."

"So we're agreed. If this girl don't agree to a DNA test," he waved his hands in the air, like wiping the slate clean, "then we don't get involved, right?"

She thought about the baby, saw those dark brown eyes looking up at her, looking like eyes she'd seen for twenty years.

∽

The DNA test arrived two days later. Dwayne and Trish sat in the room with Jon-Jon as he called Marquita. When she answered, Dwayne said, "Put it on speaker."

Jon-Jon turned away from his father as he said, "Hey, Marquita, how are you doing?"

Dwayne's voice boomed. "Don't play me, boy. I said put it on speaker."

Jon-Jon's eyes lifted until only the white showed, but he put the phone on speaker as requested.

"I'm looking for a job to feed our son, that's how I'm doing."

Dwayne's head swiveled in Trish's direction. In a low voice he said, "This one is mouthy, huh?"

"Real mouthy," Trish agreed.

Jon-Jon's lips tightened as he glared at his parents. "Look, Marquita, I'm calling because my dad ordered a DNA test and we wanted to know if you would bring the baby over so we can do the test?"

"I don't have to lie about who my baby's daddy is, Jon-Jon. I don't sleep around like that and you know it," she said, sounding more hurt than angry.

Trish reached her hand out. "Hand me that phone."

Dwayne pulled her arm back down. "Let him handle his business."

Gripping the phone, he said, "I'm not accusing you of sleeping around, Marquita, but you showed up at my house with a baby I knew nothing about. I'm not going to ask my parents to pitch in with a baby that I don't know for sure is mine."

Dwayne nodded, pumped his fist in the air, like "Yeah, that's my boy."

"Well, I need a babysitter," Marquita said.

Jon-Jon shifted in the bed. "What?"

"You heard me. I have an interview this afternoon, so if you want to do your little DNA test"—the lilt in her voice displayed contempt—"then Daddy needs to keep his kid for a few hours."

Jon-Jon looked at Trish. She looked at Dwayne. After Dwayne nodded, he told Marquita, "We'll keep him for you, but you better not be playing games. This better be my kid."

She hung up on him.

Dwayne's eyebrow lifted. "Boy, you got your hands full with that one. You better hope that baby ain't yours."

"Dwayne! Don't say stuff like that. If Marcus is Jon-Jon's son, then it's all good," Trish admonished.

Dwayne's head bobbed back. He pursed his lips as he harrumphed. "I'll believe it when I see it. Until then, Mama's baby, Daddy's maybe."

"Just shaking my head." Trish glared at Dwayne.

"You know I'm right."

Hands on hips, eyes narrowed, Trish said, "So I guess Jon-Jon is your maybe-baby. Is that how it works?"

Dwayne's eyes widened as he looked at Trish like she had lost her mind. "Now you're just trippin'. You and I are married, and Jon-Jon is mine. I know that like I know my middle name."

Jon-Jon laughed at that. "That's because my name is your middle name."

Dwayne gave Jon-Jon some dap. "You better know it, son."

A few hours later Marquita knocked on the door. When Trish

opened the door, her eyes darted downward to the faded and torn blue jeans and high heels Marquita wore. Was she dropping the baby off, then going back home to change? Or was she going to an interview like this?

As Marquita stepped into the house, she cradled the baby in her arms. She followed Trish toward the back of the house, her eyes got big as she looked this way and that. "Wow, this place is on point. I didn't look past your living room when I was here last. I love the color you painted the walls. These paintings are really nice too."

That made Trish smile. Years ago Trish had discovered African American artwork that displayed scenes of the ministry of Jesus. She purchased several pieces and hung them on the walls in her family room and hallway heading into the kitchen. "Thank you. I like warm colors."

Marquita put the baby bag down on the kitchen floor and handed Marcus to Trish. "I appreciate this. I didn't have anyone else to watch Marcus, and I really need a job, like yesterday."

The girl wasn't sounding as rude as she had on the phone with Jon-Jon, so Trish felt comfortable talking with her. "How long have you been out of work?"

"It's been almost two weeks."

"Oh, I didn't know." Then Trish popped her finger. "But now that I think of it, you did mention that you were out of work when you came to the house the other day."

Marquita's chest heaved, her eyes clouded over with sadness. "It's been harder to find a job this time."

Trish caught the "this time," and decided not to get in her business. They had bigger issues. "Jon-Jon's father is home. He'd like to speak to you for a minute if you don't mind."

Marquita glanced at the time on her cell phone, winced. "I'm running late."

Trish told her, "This won't take but a minute."

Dwayne came into the room. "Hi, Marquita. I'm Dwayne

Robinson, Jon-Jon's dad." He took the baby out of Trish's arms and looked at him. Marcus cooed. Dwayne grinned. Clearing his throat, he turned back to Marquita. "You go on to your interview. We just wanted to get your permission to swab this little guy."

Rolling her eyes, Marquita flicked her wrist. "Whatever. I don't even care. But while y'all swabbing my baby just make sure you also add some diapers to his baby bag because he's almost out." She turned her back on them and stormed out the door.

Dwayne looked at his wife, pointed toward the door that Marquita had strutted out of. "Did that just happen?"

Trish closed the front door. "I told you the girl don't have home training." Trish reached for Marcus and she took him back into her arms. "You done ticked her off, so we probably won't see Marcus after this visit."

Dwayne pulled out the cotton swabs. "If this baby is Jon-Jon's, home training or not, she won't be able to deny us visitation." Dwayne stared at the baby for a moment, watched him coo and make bubbles. Looking back at Trish, he said, "He is a cute little somethin' though."

CHAPTER 14

The nerve of Jon-Jon's daddy, coming at her like that. Marquita fumed. He barely even introduced himself before telling her about some paternity test. Like she needed to lie on their raggedy son. Jon-Jon was the one who chased after her last summer. She had been working as a convenience store clerk at the BP gas station on the south side of Charlotte. Jon-Jon came in to pay for his gas and asked for her phone number.

She wasn't mad though. Those cornrows and goatee Jon-Jon sported had been hot. He took her to the movies, out to dinner, and they walked around the mall together a few weekends in a row. At eighteen, Marquita had never dated a guy who spent real money and was happy to spend time with her . . . like she mattered.

He was home for the summer, and Marquita fell completely, totally, madly in love. When summer was coming to an end, and it was time for Jon-Jon to go back to school, she gave him what he wanted so he wouldn't forget her. But he went back to college and forgot all about her anyway. That hurt like a kick in the head. Or better yet, a kick in the heart.

She didn't mean to be rude to the Robinsons either. But it bothered her that Jon-Jon didn't believe her about the baby. Like, maybe he didn't think their summer together was as special as she thought it was. Maybe he had been running around with other girls, so he assumed she'd done the same. Marquita used the back of her hand to dot her eyes. She wasn't going to let Jon-Jon get to her and she wasn't going to give them the satisfaction of seeing her crying about the situation.

She didn't tell him about being pregnant because she felt some kind of way about how he forgot all about her when he went back to school. She didn't need him pretending that he wanted to be with her just because she had his kid. But when she was eight months pregnant, she did try to call Jon-Jon. That's when she discovered his phone was turned off.

She pulled up to Chipotle for her first interview of the day. She then had another interview across town at a Publix grocery store. Marquita opened her purse and pulled out her MAC Love Me Lipstick and smeared the La Femme purple color on her lips.

She entered the restaurant and asked for Joey. She wanted to get in line and order a chicken burrito with brown rice, spicy salsa, and extra cheese. But no job—no money. She sat down at the table and waited on Joey. Mexican food was her favorite. She would probably gain ten pounds if she got this job. But that didn't bother Marquita since she was only a hundred and fifteen pounds. She just hoped the customers weren't rude, demanding, or bougie. That got her in trouble every time.

"Sorry to keep you waiting." Joey sat down. "Can I have a copy of your résumé? Then we can get started."

Ah man, she'd spent all that time at the job center getting her résumé together and left it at her apartment. She snapped her fingers like she had just thought of something she shoulda-woulda-coulda done. "I got one. Can I bring it back to you?"

He hesitated, perfected his interviewer smile. "Okay, just bring it back to me when you get a chance."

Marquita could tell that Joey didn't appreciate her not bringing that résumé. He was smiling at her, but he rushed the interview and didn't even show her around the kitchen area. When she left, instead of driving straight to her next interview she drove back home to get those résumés. Wouldn't do to show up empty handed again.

But when she pulled up to the apartment and saw a police car and her apartment door wide open, she started hyperventilating. "No . . . no! This can't be happening." She banged her fist against the steering wheel and jumped out of her car.

Her mother would scream, fight, and curse the people out as they dragged her belongings to the curbside. Marquita didn't have the energy for all that right now. She was just so distressed, because all she ever really wanted was to not be like her mother. And here she was getting evicted.

Her landlord had a big black garden trash bag in his hands. "What are you doing?" Marquita stepped into the room.

"You haven't paid your rent in three months. I had the eviction notice taped to your door, but you tore it off."

That's what her mother always did. But Marquita was learning that the method of see-no-evil-speak-no-evil didn't work when the rent was late. "Give me another month. I'm interviewing for jobs now."

"Can't. I need to rent this place out."

"But where am I going to live?" Her mother, sister, and brother were currently living in a women's shelter as her mother waited for them to get her another place. Marquita didn't trust places like that. If she went there with her two-month-old son they'd probably turn her over to Child Protective Services. That was how she and her siblings found themselves being wards of the court for almost a year when she was younger.

Her landlord wasn't listening. He didn't care. Nobody did. She snatched the trash bag out of his hand and started throwing her clothes and Marcus's clothes in it. She threw the bag in her back seat. Her shoes went into the trunk of the car along with her important papers. Her résumés were included in the pile of paperwork thrown into her trunk.

She went back into the apartment as tears streamed down her face. Her heart ached as she filled a few more bags with her stuff and then pulled the bags out to the car. By the time she was finished, everything was covered in the car except Marcus's car seat.

"I'll be back for the rest of my stuff, so don't throw it away."

"I'll give you three days. If you don't have your bed and sofa out of the apartment, I'll put them on the sidewalk."

By the time she drove away from the apartment, Marquita had missed her job interview. Her hair was wild and all over the place. Eyeliner trekked down her face because she kept crying as she dragged each bag to her car. Life was just one big chunk of nothing as far as Marquita was concerned. Every time she tried to better herself, she was swatted back down.

All she wanted to do now was see her son. Marcus made life worth living. She didn't care what people thought about her being a single parent. She didn't even care what Jon-Jon or his parents thought about why she didn't call to tell him she was pregnant. They didn't know her and she wasn't about to let them judge her.

As Marquita pulled onto Jon-Jon's street, she burst into tears because she had no idea where she and her son were going to sleep tonight. "Why can't I do anything right? What is wrong with me?" As she pulled into the Robinsons' driveway, she stayed in her car because she wasn't emotionally ready to talk to people who thought she was a big fat liar.

Tears like a river streamed down Marquita's face. She couldn't get life right and didn't know why. She had friends who'd kept their jobs ever since they graduated from high school a year and a half ago. In the span of a year, Marquita had been fired from five jobs.

She tried to open her glove compartment to get some napkins to blow her nose, but her laundry basket with overflowing clothes and shoes blocked her. She took a shirt out of the basket, wiped her face, and then blew her nose.

Taking a deep breath to calm her nerves, she got out of the car and went inside. As she picked up Marcus, she held her baby close to her heart. Her eyes closed tight and a tear slid out.

"Are you okay? Did something happen at your interview?" Trish asked.

"I'm fine," Marquita said through gritted teeth. She didn't want to be in this beautiful home, looking at this family who had it all together when everything was falling apart for her. She picked up the diaper bag, noticed that it felt heavier.

She put Moochie down, opened the diaper bag and saw a new bag of diapers and a can of powdered formula. Shock crossed her face as she turned back to Trish. "You went to the store?"

Nodding, Trish told her, "You only had two diapers and your powdered formula was low so I sent Dwayne out to the store."

Her voice caught as she admitted, "I didn't have any more." Picking Moochie back up she rushed out the door. Marquita felt another rainstorm of tears coming on and didn't want to stand in front of Jon-Jon's family looking like a blubbering fool.

She put Moochie in his car seat, pushed some of the bags over so they wouldn't fall on him as she drove, then got in the car and drove off. The problem was, she had no idea where she was going.

Her mother had experience with these type of things, so she drove to the women's shelter to speak with Gloria. But as she parked her car at the facility, her hands shook from fear and she started hyperventilating again. "W-what am I going to do?"

Moochie was sucking on his fingers. She rubbed his belly. "I'm not going to let them take you away from me."

Marquita's mind traveled back to the first time she and her siblings went to a shelter with their mother. Gloria had gotten angry when the director of the women's shelter hadn't found them an apartment in the timeframe Gloria thought appropriate, so she busted out the windows on the director's car.

The police arrested Gloria, then they put her in rehab. Marquita was only twelve years old when the social worker showed up to take them to foster care.

"Put my sister down!" Marquita yelled at the woman as Marquita grabbed Mark and put him behind her to protect him from the mean lady who was trying to separate them.

"I'm sorry, Marquita, but your sister and brother are too young for the foster home we have for you. But we will take good care of them."

"No!" Marquita kicked the woman as she tried her best to pull Kee Kee out of the social worker's arms. "I can take care of them until our mom comes back."

The social worker turned to the security guard, who was standing in front of the door so they couldn't run out. "Can you help me?"

The guard stepped away from the door and Marquita used that opportunity to yell at Mark, "Run!"

But the guard grabbed her brother before he could obey her command. She started crying, her heart breaking as the social worker and security guard backed out of the room with Kee Kee and Mark. She reached out as they reached out for her. "Please . . . please, don't take them away from me. I'll take good care of them. I promise."

Her brother and sister had been placed in a home together while she had been taken to another home by herself, without anyone she knew or trusted. That was the most alone Marquita had ever felt in her life. She wouldn't let anyone take her son away, to cause him to feel alone and scared.

She backed out of the parking spot and drove away from the women's shelter, then headed back to her apartment and pulled into the driveway. She got out of the car to see if the door might have been left unlocked. But there was a padlock on the door now.

What was she going to do? It was getting dark, and although it was still hot outside, at least the sun had gone down. She got back in the car, rolled down the windows, leaned her seat back, and tried to get comfortable.

Her cell phone rang. It was Mark. Gathering herself, she took a deep breath, then answered the phone.

"Hey, sis, what time are you picking us up tomorrow?"

Running her fingers across her forehead, Marquita felt like crying as she remembered that she was supposed to pick Mark and Kee Kee up the next day. They were tired of being at the shelter with Gloria and wanted to stay with her for a while. "Umm, I forgot to call. I won't be able to pick you and Kee Kee up."

"But Marquita, you promised. This place is whack. Come get us."

Still rubbing her forehead, she lied, "That's just it, Mark. My car quit on me. So I can't come get you until I can get it fixed."

"Mama's car is down too." Mark sounded glum.

Marquita didn't like disappointing her siblings. She tried to be there for them. But life was falling apart for her, just as it was for them. The knowledge she couldn't help Mark and Kee Kee was like a gut punch. When he hung up, she burst out into tears. "I hate my life!" she screamed.

Later that night, she needed to pee. She got out of the car, opened the back door, and unstrapped Moochie. She then walked to the back-yard. Eyes darting this way and that, she held on to her baby with one hand in a manner she was sure Trish would object to. She then crouched down and used the bathroom in the backyard like an animal.

It was pitch-black when they got back in her car. Marquita feared putting Moochie in the back seat with the windows down, so she put him in the front seat on her right side. She tried to sleep, but it was hot and muggy out. She would close her eyes, then open them within the next few minutes and look around to see if anyone was sneaking up on them.

Moochie cried so much that night that she wondered if any of the nearby neighbors heard him. By morning she had her answer.

The landlord stood at her car door looking like he'd been chewing on rusty nails. "Did you sleep here all night?"

"I left some of my food, so I came back to get it but you padlocked the door."

His lips tightened as he gave her a disbelieving stare. "You didn't have any food in that refrigerator."

"I had some stuff in the cabinets. Just let me in so I can get it and I'll get out of here." She didn't know where she was going to go. But it was clear she wouldn't be able to stay there.

He let her in, and as she opened the cabinets, she glanced over her shoulder to see if he noticed that she only had a box of graham crackers and a moon pie in the cabinet. "Do you mind if I fix a bottle for my son before we leave?"

Shaking his head, the landlord told her, "Make it quick."

Marquita didn't like the way her ex-landlord stood over her as she took the three bottles Moochie had out of his diaper bag, washed them, and then poured in the powdered formula and water. She shook the bottles, wanting to use the microwave to warm them, but she shoved them back in the bag, picked her baby back up, and left the apartment.

"Call when you are ready to pick up your bed and the sofa. I don't want you loitering around my building." He padlocked the door again as they walked out.

She didn't respond. She simply put Moochie in his car seat, then got behind the wheel and drove off. There was no way she'd be able to get the rest of her belongings. So, just like her mother, all of her things would be thrown away and she'd have to start from scratch.

There was a rest area with a bathroom and picnic tables on the outskirts of town. She got on the highway and drove until she pulled into it. She parked the car, then put a few of the items in her passenger seat in the back of the car so she could bring Moochie's car seat up front with her.

Marquita took out one pack of graham crackers and ate a few of them. Moochie was ready to eat, so she pulled out one of his bottles and fed him. Looking down at her son, she said, "Well, Moochie, looks like it's just you and me."

Thank God Trish had purchased diapers and formula for Moochie because she wouldn't have been able to do it. She needed money, but she couldn't apply for benefits because she didn't have an address. She learned from her mother that the worst thing you can do is tell government authorities that you don't have an address, especially when you have a kid.

After feeding Moochie, she leaned her seat back, pulled out her phone, and scrolled through Facebook. So many of her old friends were enjoying life and doing big things. Her high school rival was in college and just pledged AKA. Life was an open door for that girl.

That girl had it made . . . guess they weren't rivals anymore. Her old frenemy probably didn't think about her anymore—too busy with college and joining sororities.

She put her phone down, chewed on another graham cracker. Her mouth got dry, so she got out of the car and sipped from the water fountain. She then rushed back to the car because Moochie had started crying. "I'm sorry. I didn't go far. But I won't leave you again."

But Moochie wouldn't stop crying so she started crying with him. People stared at them as they passed by. One lady asked if she was okay.

Wiping her face, Marquita said, "I'm okay, just a little frustrated."

Marquita took Moochie out of the car and went inside the rest stop to sit under the air-conditioning. He stopped crying then. "You were hot, weren't you?" she said as she stripped him down to his T-shirt. Then she wondered if Moochie could get heat stroke or something. It was really hot outside, especially now as the sun hung in the air and beat down on their car.

She decided to stay inside the building for a while. She wished she could use one of her wash rags to clean herself up, but she didn't want to risk someone coming in the bathroom while she washed. She was able to use Moochie's wet wipes to clean him up. Then she fed him again. After his second feeding, he threw up. His tummy wasn't used to taking in formula that wasn't warmed.

"Oh, Moochie, what am I doing to you?"

She called her mom and asked for advice. Gloria said, "Let me talk to the director at this women's shelter. They should be able to get you a bed."

She didn't want to do it. But it was too hot for Moochie to stay out in the sun like this. "Okay, call me back and let me know what she says."

The sun went down, and Gloria hadn't called back yet, so Marquita and Moochie went back to the car and stayed there all night long, watching the travelers drive in and drive out.

The next day she moved her car under a big tree with enough leaves to provide some shade. She only got out of her car during the hottest parts of the day and to use the bathroom or fix Moochie a bottle. At about six in the evening she was getting hungry. She reached for the graham cracker box but it was empty. That was when she started to cry.

Several cars pulled up. Marquita scrunched down in her seat and wiped her eyes. What was she going to do? How could she take care of her son if she couldn't take care of herself? "God help me!" she yelled up to the sky, even though she wasn't sure if anyone up there would care about her.

A man walked up to her car. Marquita had the windows down because of the heat, but she was about to roll them up when he lifted the bag in his hand. "I bought this a couple miles down the road, but I'm almost home so if you want it, you can have it."

"Just like that, huh? You'll give me your food—no strings attached?" He was young, probably in his midtwenties. Short afro with a dark-chocolate skin tone. But those eyes of his made her squirm in her seat. As he looked into her eyes, it seemed to Marquita that he was reading her life story.

"No, ma'am, I don't want anything from you. I just want to be of service." Shaking the bag, he said, "It's fried chicken with mash potatoes and green beans. I haven't even opened the box."

Marquita wanted to say no, but her stomach was aching from hunger. She took the bag. "Thank you."

He looked over at Moochie, reached into his pocket, and handed her a twenty. "I wish I had more on me, but it's all I've got."

His eyes were so full of compassion, so kind that Marquita started crying as she accepted the money. Then he asked, "Can I pray for you?"

She also accepted the prayer. After eating the food, she and the baby went to sleep. In the morning, her phone rang. It was Gloria. "Get over here fast. They need you to fill out some intake paperwork but they only have one spot available."

"I'm on my way." Her heart was heavy as she pulled out of the parking spot, heading to a place where she said she would never ever take her son. Halfway there her phone rang again. It was Trish.

"Hello," Marquita said as she answered the phone.

"Hi, Marquita. I'm not sure if you're busy today, but the DNA test came back, and we didn't want to open it without you."

"That was fast. It's only been three days."

"Dwayne paid for the expedited service," Trish told her.

Marquita suddenly had a thought. Maybe the Robinsons would keep Moochie for a few days while she looked for a job and a place to stay . . . That way, she wouldn't have to take her baby to the shelter with her. "I'll be right there."

CHAPTER 15

Dwayne and Jon-Jon were in the family room. Dwayne was seated on the love seat; Jon-Jon was in his wheelchair. The television wasn't on because the main event was laying in a manila envelope on the table with all eyes on it.

Trish was at the kitchen counter, the family room directly behind her. Their home's open floor plan made it seem as if they were all in the same room. While Jon-Jon and Dwayne only had eyes for that manila envelope, Trish was trying to balance a checkbook that just wouldn't do right. The gas bill had been paid as well as the electric bill and the mortgage. "Dwayne, did we pay the water bill?"

"Not yet," Dwayne answered.

Rubbing his hands together, Jon-Jon asked, "Did she say she was on her way?"

"For the third time, yes," Trish told him. "Let's give her a chance to get from her place to here."

Dwayne tapped his knee with his fingers. "You know, we could just peek inside and then close the envelope back up."

Trish shot that down. "If it was my baby, I'd want to be here when the DNA paperwork slid out of that envelope. Let's just wait."

Jon-Jon fidgeted in his chair. "I can't wait any longer. My back is bothering me."

Dwayne got up and started wheeling Jon-Jon back to his room.

"Will you be able to pay the water bill this week?" Trish asked Dwayne before he disappeared into Jon-Jon's room.

"I don't think so. Can you call and ask them for an extension?"

Trish hated how many times they had to get extensions on the bills. It was embarrassing letting bill collectors know that they didn't have enough money to cover all their bills. She couldn't deny that Dwayne was trying his best and working overtime to bring in money, but the ends just weren't meeting.

The doorbell rang. Trish put the checkbook down and went to the door. She looked through the peephole; her eyes did a double take. She swung the door open, and as Marquita stepped in, Trish's nose crinkled as it tried to fend off the stench of dirty clothes and an unwashed body. Was the girl on drugs? "What is going on with you, Marquita? Why are you coming to my house looking and smelling like this?"

Marquita couldn't look Trish in the eye. "Do you mind if I take a shower?"

"What's wrong with your shower? Do you not have running water at home?"

Tears rolled down Marquita's cheeks as she tried to cover her face.

Trish uncovered the girl's face. "This is not the time to be shy. Tell me what's going on with you."

"I got evicted. I've been sleeping outside since we left your house three days ago." The tears flowed freely now as her chest heaved up and down. "I don't have anywhere to bathe. I didn't know I smelled so bad." She lowered her head and looked away from Trish.

"Hand me that baby." Trish stretched out her arms.

Marquita held back. "No, no, don't take him from me. He's all I have."

Trish's heart nearly broke as this mouthy young woman, who thought she knew so much about life, crumbled in front of her. She leaned close and whispered, "Do you have any clean clothes in the car?"

Marquita nodded.

"I promise I won't take the baby away from you. I just want to hold him so you can clean up." Slowly, she stretched her arms out for the baby. "Is that okay?"

"Okay." Marquita handed Trish the baby and then opened the front door to go back to her car.

Trish sniffed around the baby's neck. "Bring in some clean clothes for the baby too."

While Marquita showered, Trish cleaned Marcus. He cooed, giggled, and wiggled until Trish dried him off. She was putting his clothes on when Dwayne knocked on the bathroom door.

"What are you doing in there?"

Trish had the baby in the bathroom next to Jon-Jon's room. She let Marquita use the shower that was in her and Dwayne's bathroom because she wanted the girl to have some semblance of dignity and privacy. She needed Marquita to rush though. She and Dwayne didn't like people in their space for too long. "A little patience, Dwayne. We will be right there."

She put clean clothes on the baby and then hurried into her bedroom to wait on Marquita to come out of the bathroom. When Marquita opened the bathroom door, Trish handed her a laundry bag for her dirty clothes. Then she asked the girl, "I don't mean to pry, but is there some reason you can't stay with your mother?"

"She's in a shelter right now. I was on my way there when you called, but I was thinking about asking you all to keep Marcus for a few days so I wouldn't have to take him there. I'm terrified that they might take my baby away from me."

Trish's eyebrow jutted up. "Why would they take the baby?"

"They took us from my mom when I was a kid. I just can't let that happen to my baby." Marquita started crying again. "I swore I wouldn't be like my mother, but here I am, headed to a shelter just like she does all the time."

Trish handed her some tissues. "Wipe your face and come with me." Still holding the baby, she led Marquita to Jon-Jon's room. "We're here."

Jon-Jon had the envelope in his hands. He waved it in the air as he looked at Marquita. "Last chance. You got anything to tell me before I open it?"

"Boy, please." Marquita put a hand on her hip. "I know who my baby's daddy is," was a phrase heard often on those paternity shows, only to discover that the woman did not know who her baby's daddy was.

"I'm nervous," Jon-Jon said as he slowly opened the envelope.

"No reason to be, unless you don't want to be Marcus's daddy." Marquita had this "you'll see" look on her face.

Trish walked over to the other side of her son's bed. He had changed these past few days. Knowing that he could be a father to a baby as wonderful as Marcus had done something to him. She prayed he wouldn't be disappointed and then wallow in depression again.

There was a lot riding on the contents of that envelope. Trish's stomach jumped like butterflies were dancing in there. "You don't have to open it, son. Marcus is yours. When I hold this baby, it feels just like how I felt holding you twenty years ago."

Jon-Jon smiled at his mother, took her hand, and squeezed it. "I feel the same way too. I think he looks like me, but I have to know for sure. Even if it means taking a grandson away from you, I still have to know. Is that okay with you?"

It was his decision. Trish relented. She would be devastated if Marcus wasn't his, especially since she didn't know if Jon-Jon would be able to have another child. "I understand."

Jon-Jon pulled the contents from the envelope. When he opened his mouth again, he said, "It says there's a 99.9 percent probability that I'm the father."

The room erupted with cheers.

"Oh, thank You, God! I have a grandbaby." Eyes wide and over-flowing with joy, Trish stepped out of the room while Jon-Jon and

Dwayne fussed over the baby. She went into her bedroom and looked out the window. The cardinal wasn't there, which surprised her because she felt like God had just visited their home, bringing them a sweet bundle of joy. A grandbaby. She had a grandbaby.

As those words danced around her head, she lifted her eyes to heaven and said, "Thank You." Then she rushed back into Jon-Jon's room and took the baby off Jon-Jon's lap. Trish bounced the baby in her arms. Excitement rang in her voice as she said, "Marcus, I'm your grandmother."

"My family calls him Moochie," Marquita told Trish. "Since you're family now, I guess it's all right for you to call him Moochie too."

Tears of joy danced in Trish's eyes as she continued bouncing the baby in her arms. "You look like a Moochie with them fat cheeks. Hey, you know who else looked like a Moochie when he was a baby?" Wiping the tears from her face, she said, "Your daddy."

Trish handed the baby to Marquita. "Don't leave. Sit in here with Jon-Jon and let him visit with the baby so I can talk to Dwayne." They now knew that the baby belonged to Jon-Jon, but Marquita was dealing with another issue that Trish couldn't ignore.

She grabbed Dwayne's arm. "I need to speak with you about something."

Leading him into their bedroom, she gave a rundown of Marquita's situation before voicing her idea.

"No! Uh-uh, no way." Dwayne waved his hands in the air as he shook his head so hard dandruff fell out.

"Dwayne, be reasonable. We have to let Marquita stay with us. She has nowhere else to go." They tried to talk as low as possible because sound traveled easily in their home, especially yelling.

"That's not our fault."

"It would be our fault if we let that girl walk out of our house and something happened to her and the baby."

"Didn't you hear how she talked to us when she dropped the

baby off a few days ago? You really want to deal with someone as dis-respectful as she is?"

Trish got it. She really did. But as a Christian, she couldn't see someone in need and not try to help. "The girl has no home train-ing. I told you that. But come on, Dwayne, you can't honestly be comfortable with Marcus sleeping in that car?"

He didn't respond. It looked like he was mulling it over.

Dwayne paced the floor in front of the bed, then rubbed his chin. "Tell me this, Trish. Where is this girl going to sleep? We only have three bedrooms. I'm in one, Jon-Jon is in another, and you have moved yourself into the third."

Trish grimaced as the corner of her mouth turned up. Dwayne had played her. He had her where he wanted her and they both knew it.

"How bad do you want to help this girl, Trish? Would your Christian duty allow you to move back into our bedroom so we can make that third room available to that mouthy girl?"

She turned her back to him and crossed her arms around her chest. Things had not been good with Dwayne for months. Trish didn't want to be married to a man who acted as if her thoughts and feelings didn't matter. But if she was honest with herself, Dwayne hadn't been so horrible these last few days. He'd been on her side on quite a few things rather than disparaging her at every turn.

Dropping her arms to her side, she waved the white flag. "You win, Dwayne. I will move back into our bedroom. Now can Marquita and Marcus stay with us?"

Dwayne clasped his hands together. "Yes, but she can't stay here indefinitely. We can give her a couple of months to find a job and get another apartment, but that's it."

Trish exhaled. She couldn't wait to talk to Marquita. The girl seemed like a handful, but having her here just might be helpful. She'd see where Marquita's head was, then she'd know if things might be changing for the better around here. "Let's go talk to her."

Dwayne shook his head. "You go talk to her. I'm going to move your stuff back to our room."

"Missed me that bad, huh?"

"You've laid next to me for almost twenty-five years, Trish. I still remember how we used to be, and I want it back." He walked out of their bedroom, heading straight for the guest room.

Trish didn't know for sure what was happening with her and Dwayne, but he was making her feel some kind of way. Good vibes . . . good vibes.

While Dwayne was moving her stuff from the guest bedroom back to the master suite, Trish went back to Jon-Jon's room and signaled for Marquita to follow her. She and Marquita went to the living room and sat down. "Let me ask you something, Marquita. Do you really want to go to that shelter?"

Marquita lifted her hands, then let them flop back in her lap. "I'm all out of choices. I was sitting in Jon-Jon's room thinking about my son and how I want so much more for him. But . . ."

The girl looked so dejected that Trish wanted to cry for her. "You know what, Marquita. I think you and I can help each other."

"How can I help you? I don't have anything."

"I don't want anything from you. Well, maybe just a bit of your time." Trish leaned forward in her seat as she explained. "Dwayne and I just talked. We want you to stay here with us while you find a job and save up enough money for another apartment."

Shock exploded in Marquita's eyes. "What?"

"You heard me. You and Marcus don't have to worry about where you're going to sleep tonight, because we want you to stay with us."

"I don't understand. I thought you might take Moochie for a few days. But . . . Why are you doing this?"

Those sad eyes of Marquita's seemed to question why anyone would help her, as if no one had ever extended her kindness. A tear escaped Trish's eyes. She closed them to stop the dam that threatened to break. "We want to help you and Marcus."

"And this is for real? You're going to let us stay here, in your nice home?"

"I don't know what I have to do to get you to believe me. Marcus is our grandson. You are the mother of our grandson, and we want what's best for the both of you."

"I don't have any money. I wouldn't be able to pay the rent."

Trish nodded. "Thank you for your honesty, Marquita. We know you won't be able to pay the rent. You have to find a job—and that brings me to how you and I can help each other."

Marquita was at the edge of her seat. "Tell me. Whatever you want. If I can help, then I want to do it."

"I quit my job so I could care for Jon-Jon. It has caused a huge financial strain, so it would help me to have someone at the house who could sit with Jon-Jon for about four hours a couple days a week. That way I could teach at a night school."

"Jon-Jon told me that you are a teacher. That's cool."

"So, what do you say, Marquita? Can we go to the car and bring your things to your new room?"

Hesitant, but only for a moment, Marquita asked, "How long can we stay?"

Trish stood. "I'm not going to lie to you. Dwayne doesn't want this to be permanent. He's okay with you staying a few months, long enough for you to find a job and save some money. Will that work?"

For the first time since she met Marquita, the girl smiled and her brown eyes brightened. She had a beautiful face. Trish could see why Jon-Jon had been attracted to her. "Dwayne and I will help you bring your things in. Then we'll go over the house rules."

CHAPTER 16

"Mom, Mom, guess what?" Ethan knocked on his parents' bedroom door.

Alexis's eyes were slow to open. Just as she recognized that Ethan was at the door, Michael sat up, put on his house shoes, and opened their bedroom door. "Are you okay, Ethan? Is anything wrong?"

Ethan ran past his father. "Everything is wonderful! Mom told me to come get her if my superheroes started fighting in the air again." He pulled on Alexis's arm.

No, no, no. Alexis's hand flopped across her eyes. Hopping out of bed, she put on her housecoat and ran out of the room with Ethan. She hoped that Michael was still sleepy and had laid back in bed.

"They were flying again, Mom. I swear they were. Come see."

"I'm right behind you, Ethan. Just calm down, okay?"

Michael followed them. "What is he talking about, Alexis?"

"Go back to bed, Michael." She kept following Ethan. When she stepped in the room, Alexis watched Ethan closely. Please don't let him see anything. "I don't see anything, honey. Do you still see them?"

The gleeful expression left Ethan's face as disappointment weighed down his shoulders. "What happened, Mom? I knew I shouldn't have left my room. They're gone again."

Michael brushed past Alexis, got on one knee in front of Ethan, and wrapped his hands around Ethan's arms. "Are you okay, son? What did you think was flying in here?"

"Captain America and Thor were fighting. Then Iron Man

136

jumped in, so the Hulk pounded on all of them. It was a really cool fight. Then I remembered that Mom told me if it happened again, she wanted to see it, too, but now they're gone."

Michael glanced up, looking at Alexis. Then he turned back to Ethan. "Again? When did you see them fighting before?"

"Last night when Mom came into my room, but she didn't see them then either." A puzzled looked crossed Ethan's face. He turned to Alexis. "Maybe they don't want to fight in front of girls, Mom. They might be hiding until you leave."

Putting a gentle hand on the back of her son's head, Alexis told him, "You bumped your head when you fell into the pool a few days ago. I'm thinking that you're seeing these things because of that, but Mommy needs you to get dressed so I can take you to the emergency room, okay?"

"Why do you look sad, Mom? I might have super-seeing powers now. That's nothing to be sad about."

Michael stood back up. With a stern expression on his face, he asked Alexis, "Can I speak with you in our bedroom?"

Sighing, Alexis patted Ethan on the head and then left her son to go deal with his father.

"I distinctly remember asking you if Ethan was okay last night," Michael said as he closed their bedroom door.

Alexis went into her closet to grab a jogging suit. "He is okay."

"He's hallucinating," Michael said, in a whisper, "like your mother."

Alexis's eyebrow lifted. She knew he would go there. "I act like my mother, Michael. She and I have similar hand gestures. I hear her when I laugh. And I see her when I glance at myself in the mirror."

"You know what I'm talking about." He put a finger to the side of his head and twirled it. "She sees things that aren't there. Now my son is doing the same thing, and you didn't tell me about this."

"I was going to talk to you about it today, but I wanted to see if he had the same issue this morning. I'm taking him back to the hospital to make sure he doesn't have a traumatic brain injury. I'm just as worried as you are." She took off her gown and threw on her jogging suit.

"Are you? Because it doesn't seem like you're worried. I know you grew up with crazy and you work with all those crazy people, but I don't want my son like that."

"Stop it. Just stop it. I'm not doing this with you." She brushed her teeth and then rushed Ethan to the car. She had no words for her husband at this moment. She had never wanted to do harm to her husband. He had always been her prince, but, so help her, she wanted to slap some sense of compassion in his head. He married her knowing that her mother dealt with mental illness. How dare he stand in her face and degrade her mother after all these years.

Michael didn't want anyone to know that mental illness was in their family, so he demanded that Vivian be put into a nursing home. She'd always assumed that Michael's strong feelings against mental illness were because he thought her mother's condition would hurt him professionally. Now she wasn't so sure.

For Michael, everything had to be right, look right, and appear right or Michael wasn't happy. She'd spent the last thirteen years ensuring that Michael's world was just the way he wanted it, but she wasn't concerned about her perfectionist husband right now. Alexis's concern was for Ethan.

The drive to the hospital wasn't as traumatic for her as the other day. Her son was alive. Now she just needed to make sure he didn't have a brain injury. She hadn't told Michael about it last night because she feared he would associate Ethan's hallucinations with her mother's. She just didn't know he would be so cruel about it.

They parked in the emergency room parking lot and walked into the hospital. She informed the intake nurse about her concerns. After a short wait, they were taken to a room and then Ethan was given a CT scan. The scan came back normal.

The ER doctor offered reassurance. "Mrs. Marshall, I don't think you have anything to worry about. Ethan hit his head when he fell in the pool. Sometimes patients deal with hallucinations after an event like that. He might have a concussion. But at any rate, this should go away, but if it keeps happening, bring him back in or take him to his family doctor for more tests."

Alexis took Ethan to get an ice cream cone, then they went home. Michael was in the kitchen waiting for her. When she told him the CT scan was normal, he said, "Oh, thank God."

She wasn't moved by his sudden show of relief. She tried to walk past Michael, but he took her hand and held onto it. She tried to pull away, but he stood in her way and moved closer.

"I'm sorry for what I said earlier. I was wrong. Your mother has nothing to do with this, and I shouldn't have brought it up."

"It would just kill you if Ethan turned out to be like my mother, wouldn't it?" She did manage to snatch her hand away now.

"He's not like your mother." Michael backed up a step, putting a hand in his pocket. "I shouldn't have expressed my thoughts the way I did. I know how sensitive you are about that subject."

"What subject, Michael?" He couldn't even say the words. "Are you talking about the fact that my mother suffers from mental illness or the fact that you don't want anyone to know that?"

"I'm only concerned for our family. I don't want anyone looking at our kids and wondering if mental illness will pass down to them."

"And what if it did? Would you love Ethan any less?"

"No, Alexis. I promise you. I wouldn't hold any mental issue against Ethan. He's my son, and I will always love him."

Alexis believed Michael when he said he wouldn't hold it against Ethan, but as she walked away from him, she wondered if he would hold it against *her*. Would he think it was her bad genes that had caused these problems and then wish he had never married her?

Before Alexis met Michael she didn't know how to dream of better days. She existed only to get up, go to her waitress job, help her mother pay the bills, and try to keep her mother out of trouble. Falling in love with Michael changed her whole world. She hated being mad at him and hated not being on his side, but she had to protect Ethan and get her son all the help he needed, whether his hallucinations were a result of his head injury or if it turned out he had developed a mental illness. She would not, could not, let Michael hide their son away like an embarrassment to Michael's perfect family fantasy. Alexis would never wish the way she grew up on anyone, but if Michael had experienced just a taste of what she grew up with, everything wouldn't have to be so perfect all the time.

∽

Two days later, Ethan ambled his way into the theater room, hands in his pockets and head hanging low. They were getting ready to watch a movie for their family night. Ethan normally loved family night, but he was acting as if someone stole his favorite toy.

"What's wrong, Ethan? Do you want to watch a movie tonight?" Alexis asked.

"I do. I'm just mad."

Michael was reclined in his theater seat, relaxing. "What are you mad about?"

Ella walked past her brother and took her seat. "Just ignore Ethan. He's been complaining all day about his superhero figures."

Alexis's eyes closed tight, and she wished they could skip this moment and just watch the movie already. She didn't want to see Michael's disapproving glare or hear what Michael might say if Ethan had indeed seen another vision of superhero figures fighting in his head. Alexis reached for the M&M's bag, took two handfuls of the chocolaty candy, and dumped them in her mouth.

Ethan continued. "It's not funny, Ella. Those superheroes were

140

fighting, but now they won't do anything unless I bang them together myself."

Michael shot up in his seat. "Your toys aren't fighting anymore?"

"No! Not even when I try to use my super-seeing powers." Ethan plopped down in his theater seat. He waved a hand toward the big screen. "Well, let's get this movie going so I can go to bed already."

"Wow, I hope those sour grapes won't last through the entire movie." Alexis was kidding with Ethan, but in truth, she was overjoyed because his words brought her peace. The ER doctor thought the hallucinations wouldn't last, so she prayed this was the end of it.

Michael took her hand and squeezed it. She looked over at him; he was smiling. Ethan would be all right. She believed it, and Michael's reaction showed her that he believed it too. She squeezed his hand and smiled back at him.

Michael turned on the movie. Tonight they were watching *A Question of Faith*. Alexis had grown up watching Kim Fields's reruns of *The Facts of Life*, so she was happy to see her now in this family movie. She leaned back in her seat, pulled her blanket over her legs, enjoying family night with the kids as they passed popcorn and nachos to each other.

Joy soon turned to heartache as she watched a young Black boy get hit by a car and saw how horridly the parents suffered as their son lay dying in a hospital bed. A feeling of unease pricked her. Ethan's accident had helped her to see just how quickly a family could deteriorate when dealing with the illness of a child. Now this movie was making her think about the Robinsons. She wondered how the family was dealing with their son's injuries.

She leaned over to Michael and whispered, "Did the attorney set the court date with the Robinsons yet?"

Michael kept looking at the movie screen. "It's been postponed."

"Again?"

"Yeah." He popped some popcorn in his mouth, eyes still focused on the big screen.

"What about the arbitration you mentioned?"

Fixing his eyes on Alexis, Michael said, "I told you the dad is being difficult."

"Mom, Dad, you're making too much noise. I can't hear the movie," Ella complained.

Alexis quieted, but not because Ella shushed her. As she watched the boy in the movie die, Alexis thought about John Robinson. Then she wondered how his mom was doing.

Alexis hadn't taken Ethan's accident well. The mom on the screen was devastated by her son's death. John Robinson didn't die from the accident, but he was paralyzed. How could Alexis ever make amends for what she had done to that family? She desperately wanted to visit the young man to check on him, but she wondered if the family hated her.

Alexis questioned everything she'd done in the last six months. Michael was nervous that her accident would hurt the sale of the company, so she didn't contact the Robinson family, even though she had wanted to do just that right after the accident.

How could she have gone on with her life without making sure John Robinson was all right? Why weren't the Robinsons agreeing to arbitration? They'd already said no to the insurance settlement. Michael was going to postpone their court case for as long as he could. She needed to figure out a way to help this family. No more ignoring the people whose lives she had changed in an instant.

CHAPTER 17

W hat in the world?" Dwayne sat up in bed and shook Trish.
"Huh? What's going on?" Trish yawned and rubbed her eyes.
"Did you talk to that girl about the house rules?"

Music was playing so loud that the walls were thumping. Trish
sat up in bed. "This can't be happening." Tossing the covers off, she
got out of bed, put her house shoes on, and headed toward Jon-Jon's
and Marquita's rooms.

Marquita's door was open, and the baby was stretched out, asleep
in the middle of the bed. How he could sleep with all the noise coming
from Jon-Jon's room, Trish didn't know. Jon-Jon's door was closed,
but the music was causing his door to bounce. Trish swung the door
wide open.

Jon-Jon was in his bed, popping his fingers and bobbing his head.
Marquita was dancing—it wasn't the holy dance of praise. She was
twerking and gyrating in a way that Trish's older bones couldn't think
about doing without a heating pad, massage, and some pain pills.
"Marquita! Jon-Jon!"

Jon-Jon stopped popping his fingers. Marquita jumped, stood
straight up, and put her hands behind her back. "Hey, Trish."

Trish pointed to her cell phone. "Turn it off. We don't play that
kind of music in this house." She then addressed Jon-Jon. "You know
better than this. Your daddy works hard for this family. Y'all not gon'
interrupt his sleep with this foolishness."

Marquita picked up her phone and slid her finger across the device to stop the music. "My bad. I was just trying to cheer Jon-Jon up. He's in a lot of pain this morning and was being all gloomy about it."

Trish turned concerned eyes in Jon-Jon's direction. "You need your pain pills?"

Blowing threw his nostrils, he said, "They don't work."

"You should still take them. Let me fix you something to eat, and I'll bring your pain pills." She was about to leave the room, but then she said, "This door stays open when you have someone inside with you."

Looking annoyed, Jon-Jon said, "That's fine, Mama. She only closed it so we wouldn't wake Moochie up while listening to music."

Hands on hips, Trish said, "Well, y'all woke me and your daddy. Moochie probably needs his ears checked because he's still sleeping." She didn't know how she was going to handle having two grown folks under her roof, trying to follow their own rules.

Trish pulled some pots and pans out and started cooking breakfast. Marquita inched her way into the kitchen, like she wasn't sure if she'd be welcomed. "Get on in here," Trish told her. "Do you like cheese in your eggs?"

An eyebrow lifted as her eyes sparkled. "Yes, I like cheese." Then she said, "I'm not trying to cause problems for you. I didn't know you'd get mad about the music, especially since I was just trying to cheer Jon-Jon up."

"I appreciate what you did for Jon-Jon, but we live a quiet kind of life here. The only loud music that gets played in here is gospel music, but I've never played it *that* loud."

Trish had forgotten to provide Marquita with the house rules because the girl had been beaten up enough the day she moved in. After breakfast she sat her down and gave her the rules: no swearing, no music with swearing, and no late nights on the town and then coming home knocking on the door, waking everybody up. Marquita just nodded her head. Trish hoped she was listening but only time would tell.

Trish went back to her bedroom. Dwayne was sitting up with his back leaning against the headboard. They had been cordial since she moved back in their bedroom, but that was about it. Nothing else had been resolved.

"I owe you an apology, Trish."

Trish's head bobbed backward, her hands propped on her hips. Did she just hear what she heard? She was going to stand right here and wait. Dwayne said he owed her an apology. Knowing him, this apology might not be all it's cracked up to be. "What are you apologizing for?"

"You know, for everything."

She shook her head. That wasn't going to cut it. "No, I don't know."

Sweat beads formed on Dwayne's forehead. He wiped them away. "This thing with Jon-Jon threw me for a loop. I'm supposed to be a man and provide for my family. How do you think I felt when I lost my job?"

"It couldn't have been easy," she acknowledged.

Flinging the covers off, he paced the floor. "Fifteen years I gave that job. Never used my sick days. I only took the vacation time they gave me. But the minute we have a serious family emergency and I have to miss work or I'm late a few times, they let me go."

Trish didn't say anything. She just kept listening, praying that he would finally say something that she could latch onto, giving her some glimmer of hope that things might be good with them again.

He sat down in the oversize chair that had been placed on the right side of their bed. "I had to take a job making much less, so now I'm working all this overtime just to keep up. And I'm still not keeping up. I don't know from one minute to the next if the lights or the water are going to get cut off because of all the late payments."

"Yes, it has been tough financially, but we're partners in this." Trish added, "And with Marquita here, I'm going to be able to at least take on some part-time assignments."

145

"Are we still partners, Trish?"

"I haven't thought about divorcing you this week, if that makes you feel better." She was trying to lighten up the moment, but the look on Dwayne's face told her she had done the opposite. "I didn't mean to hurt you, Dwayne. I was just joking."

"But you weren't joking. I've seen it in your eyes, Trish. You don't feel the same way about us. You're not happy, and I don't know what to do."

Sighing, Trish decided to show her hand and see if it would make a difference. "I want someone who sees me, Dwayne. I have needs, and I need them to be important to you."

Dwayne pulled her close. "Give me a list of some of the needs that I'm not meeting."

"I can't explain it, Dwayne, but it feels like you don't get me. After all the years we've been married, you should know what I like, right?" She couldn't even get him to get her sandwich order right. And to this day, Dwayne would order a sausage pizza when he knew she preferred pepperoni.

"I can try to do better, but you have to try more as well, Trish. I can't be in this alone." His eyes were sad as they pleaded with her.

Sighing, Trish told him. "I'm sorry for the way I've been acting lately. Things haven't been good between us."

He sat down next to her on the bed. "But isn't that what our vows meant by 'for better or worse'? We had a lot of good years, Trish. That ought to count for something."

"It does." She looked down at her feet, then over at her nightstand, any and everywhere except looking directly at Dwayne. She couldn't look into those deep brown eyes—those eyes that drew her in and made her want to be close to him.

He put a finger below her chin and lifted her face. "Don't you give up on me, Trish. I would never give up on you."

"You came out the bag on me so many times since Jon-Jon's

accident. I just need to know that I can trust you won't act like that if we go through hard times again."

"Babe, like you said, what we just went through was the hardest thing we've ever dealt with." He stood, pacing the floor, listing off all the issues they dealt with. "Losing that job and then not having health insurance to cover the surgery that Jon-Jon needed made me feel less than a man, like I wasn't pulling my weight."

"That doesn't make sense, Dwayne, because I know you were doing the best you could with the hand we were dealt."

"I get that, Trish. I'm just telling you how I felt. When you quit your job and I was having trouble making the mortgage payment, I was in a bad place. I know I took it out on you, but I've done a lot of praying. And I need you to forgive me and let us move on. I thought when you moved back into our room, things would be better, but you're still holding back."

"Give me some time, Dwayne. That's all I'm asking. I see you. I promise I do, but you broke my heart. I'm trying to find my way back. I'm just not all the way there yet."

He looked defeated. Trish wanted to reach out to him because it hurt her to see him like that, but she couldn't get her hand to move in his direction. It used to be so easy with them. Now everything was hard.

He turned so that his back was to her as he spoke. "When I met you, I thought twice about approaching you because you were this college girl and way out of my league."

"I was never out of your league, Dwayne. You've always been a wonderful provider for our family. Neither of us ever expected what happened to Jon-Jon."

"I know babe, but . . ." He wiped his eyes. "Remember when we got married and you were only working part-time?"

"Because I was still in school working on my master's degree."

He nodded. "I felt proud because my wife didn't have to work a full-time job. I made enough to pay for our apartment and the expenses so you didn't have to stop dreaming your big dreams."

She laughed. "I'd hardly call being a teacher a big dream. I certainly will never get rich with the career I chose."

"Trish, you were so good with your students. You care, and that's the most important part. Those kids will go on in life to be something, and it is because of what you and so many other educators do, day in and day out. I've always been proud of your decision to become a teacher."

The air was on in the house. The hot, humid days of summer were upon them, so the air conditioner was running nonstop. But to Trish it suddenly felt warm and cozy in the room. It felt like sitting in front of a fireplace, wrapped in the afghan her grandmother knitted for her while watching Christmas movies. "Thanks for saying that."

"But it's still not enough, is it? You still won't forgive me."

When she didn't respond, he continued pleading his case. "All right, okay, you say I broke your heart. But not being able to put things back to right around here broke me down. Yes, I took it out on you in ways I am ashamed of. I didn't realize how much I was tearing you down until you moved out of our bedroom, and that broke me down even more." His eyes implored her to understand where he was coming from. "I love you, bae, and I'm sorry for not being everything you needed me to be."

Stop it! Stop it! Stop it! was the internal voice bouncing around Trish's head. This man had bent over backward trying to make amends for his bad behavior. Why was he still asking for forgiveness? She put a hand over his. "Dwayne, you don't have to apologize anymore or ask for forgiveness. You and I are good. And anyway, I am the one who needs to ask you for forgiveness."

"You do?" His eyebrow lifted. He gave her a did-you-really-say-what-you-just-said look.

"I do, Dwayne. I never should have quit my job without talking it over with you first. I guess I thought you would handle things like you did when I was finishing college. Things are different now. We have more responsibilities."

A light appeared in Dwayne's eyes that she hadn't seen in a long time. "I can forgive you for that. Still, I wish I had handled it better, because I could see how much these last few months had taken out of you. I should have been a shoulder to lean on."

"Tell you what, Dwayne. Why don't we both try our best to wipe the slate clean and start from here?"

With a hopeful lilt to his voice, he rose from the chair. "Do you think you can do that?"

"I think I can try. I want to try. We have to work together, and maybe even pray together. I can't be the only one trusting and believing that God can bring about a change around here."

"You're right, Trish. I've been slacking, and I'm not going to do that anymore." He reached out for her hands. "Let's pray now."

Joy, that's what she was feeling right now. She'd thought joy was forever gone from her home, but Dwayne was standing in front of her asking for forgiveness and reaching out his hands to pray. She bowed her head as she took his hands.

Dwayne prayed for their marriage. He prayed for God to look down on Jon-Jon and take care of his needs. He prayed for Marquita and for baby Marcus. When he finished, all that was left was for Trish to say amen.

"Whew! That felt good," Dwayne said.

"It did. I have always loved the way you pray." She grinned at her husband, nudging him playfully as a truce was called.

"Believe it or not, I've been doing a lot more praying since we saw that cardinal in the yard."

She smiled. "Me too."

Dwayne leaned forward, about to kiss Trish, when the doorbell rang. "You expecting someone?"

Trish shook her head.

The only person who visited their home these days had been Jon-Jon's physical therapist. They had cancelled his sessions because Jon-Jon refused to cooperate. Trish headed to the door with Dwayne following behind.

"I hope it's not the water company. I haven't got around to that bill yet."

"Now listen, I can do without electricity, but if you don't get that water bill paid, I want to see how you feel when I walk around this house like the great unwashed for a few days," she joked with him. And that, too, felt good. There hadn't been much laughter in their home. Maybe Marquita and Marcus coming to them when they did had been a true godsend.

Trish looked out the peephole. Confusion danced across her face.

"Who is it?" Dwayne whispered, as if the person on the other side of the door hadn't already heard their footsteps as they made their way to the door.

"I don't know. Some white lady."

"What does she want?"

Trish laughed for the third time that day. "I don't know, Dwayne. She's still on the other side of the door."

With Dwayne standing behind her, Trish inched the door open. "Hello. Can we help you?"

The woman was biting her lip and looking nervous, as if she wanted to turn around but was trying to make her body line up and stay put.

"Are you okay?" Trish asked.

"Y-yes, I'm sorry. I'm a bit nervous. My name is Alexis Marshall. I came to see John Robinson."

"Alexis Marshall!" Dwayne's hand gripped the door and flung it wide open. "How dare you come to our house after what you did to our son."

150

Alexis took a deep breath and stepped forward. "I'm sorry that it has taken me so long to do this, but I'm here to help."

Anger flashed in Dwayne's eyes. "Then why do you keep getting the judge to postpone Jon-Jon's court case?"

Trish had a feeling about this. God was up to something, and she was not about to get in the Almighty's way. She wasn't a big fan of this woman either. Dwayne thought Trish was so forgiving, but in truth, she struggled to forgive Alexis Marshall. She put a hand on Dwayne's shoulder. "Maybe we should let her in so we can figure out why she decided to come here after all this time."

Dwayne looked like he was about to object, but then he stepped out of the way and allowed the woman to enter the house. Trish pointed Alexis toward the living room. "Let's sit down and talk a minute before we bring Jon-Jon in here." Alexis sat down in the large floral chair. Trish and Dwayne sat in the love seat next to her.

Trish thought back to the day she had felt as if she was at her lowest point. She prayed and asked God to do something good in her life. Then Marquita showed up and now Alexis Marshall herself. At this point, Trish wouldn't be surprised if those sweepstakes people came knocking with an oversize check in their hands.

CHAPTER 18

Alexis had been terrified about meeting the Robinsons. She half expected them to slam the door in her face. Although Dwayne Robinson was hostile toward her, his wife seemed a bit more gracious. She sat on the edge of her seat, looking at Alexis as if she was interested in what she had to say.

"Our attorney informed my husband that John is in need of another surgery. She opened her purse, took out a cashier's check, and handed it to Trish. "I want to pay for his surgery."

Dwayne's eyes bucked like they were going to fall out of his head. He snatched the check from Trish's hand. "This is twenty thousand dollars."

Alexis and Michael had a joint bank account, but she had kept the individual bank account she had before marrying Michael. Her husband gave her fun money from time to time. There had been occasional splurges, but Alexis managed to save most of the money. She had planned to do something special for Ethan and Ella when they graduated from high school. But she couldn't hold onto this money, knowing that John needed it.

"Thank you so much. It has been a real struggle trying to figure out how Jon-Jon would get this next surgery." Trish's voice caught. She wiped her eyes as she stood. "Let me go get Jon-Jon."

Dwayne stopped her. "Hold on a minute, Trish. No sense getting Jon-Jon out of bed if this check is some kind of bribery attempt."

Alexis's eyebrow furrowed. She never imagined they would think she was trying to bribe them. "No, Mr. Robinson, that's not my intent at all. You told our attorney that this surgery would relieve some of John's pain. I feel awful that he is still in so much pain."

Dwayne's lips pressed firmly together while she spoke, then he said, "So where's the document you want us to sign? We need to read the fine print."

"I don't have a document. You provided our attorney with the hospital information, so the cashier's check is written out to the hospital."

Trish narrowed her eyes on Dwayne and sat back down. "Stop grilling this woman and go get Jon-Jon."

"I thought you were going to get him?"

"I think you should." Trish turned to Alexis, gave her a quick, tight smile, then nudged Dwayne with her elbow.

Dwayne got up. "I'll go, but I just don't understand why they keep pushing our court date back if they are so concerned about Jon-Jon." He headed down the hall, mumbling all the way.

Trish gave Alexis another tight smile.

Alexis glanced above her head. "I love your coffered ceiling."

"Thank you, the ceiling is the reason I love this room so much."

Alexis was so nervous she couldn't think of any more small talk, so she sat there, staring at her hands. Her ears became attuned to the grind of wheels as Dwayne pushed the wheelchair from the back of the house to the living room at the front of the house.

Trish spoke up. "My husband may seem a bit angry, but it's been tough dealing with Jon-Jon's injuries. We've had to sit here, watching him be in pain, unable to do anything about it."

"I'm sorry I didn't come sooner," Alexis told her, and she meant it.

Trish looked as though she was about to say something else, but Dwayne entered the living room with the young man. Alexis's stomach clenched. Guilt pricked her conscience. As Dwayne locked John's chair in place, the only thing that kept Alexis from making some excuse, running out the door, and pushing this whole incident to the back of her mind was the knowledge that she could do some good for this family.

Her mother had taught her that trick. Don't think about it, and it doesn't exist. But John Robinson did exist, and she had done harm to him and his family.

"I wish I had come to see you sooner, John. I've wanted to tell you how sorry I was about the accident." *Don't cry. Don't cry.* But a few tears broke through anyway. Alexis wiped them away. "I wish this had never happened to you."

Jon-Jon nodded in agreement. "Wish I had taken another route that day."

She wished that for him as well. Regret hung on her heavy, like a soggy mink coat. "Our attorney told us that you were a college student with a football scholarship."

"Yeah, I was."

"Were you any good?" the minute she asked, she regretted the question. Small talk obviously was not her thing. It was wrong of her to make him think of things he would never be able to do again.

Rather than a look of loss and sadness, a gleam shone in Jon-Jon's eyes as he said, "Sure was. I was on my way to the NFL. Was gonna be the next Emmitt Smith." The smile dropped. Jon-Jon turned his head toward the wall.

"I'm sorry. I didn't mean to upset you." Alexis looked around the room, hoping that she hadn't offended John's parents.

Dwayne asked her, "Did your attorney tell you how the accident stole my son's life and left us without the means to get him the help he needs?"

"Dwayne!" Trish hushed him. "Mrs. Marshall is a guest in our home."

Shaking his head, Dwayne said, "Naw, Trish, she needs to know why it's important to get this court case going. Maybe they'll stop postponing if they know how much they took from Jon-Jon."

"Mr. Robinson, please believe me when I say that I do understand what I have cost your son. That's why I'm here."

"I'm not doubting your sincerity," Trish said. "But Dwayne has a point. Why do you keep getting the court date pushed back if you really want to help?"

It was reasonable for them to assume that she was trying to deny them their day in court, but seeing Jon-Jon changed everything. "My husband thinks we should go to arbitration rather than court."

Dwayne turned back to face Alexis. "Your husband doesn't want it getting out about how reckless you are, huh? Might hurt that tech company he owns, right?"

Maybe it was a mistake to come. Maybe she had waited too long. Alexis recognized she was not a welcomed face in their home. She needed to cut this short and get going. She opened her purse, took out a piece of paper, and handed it to Trish. "This is the information I have about arbitration. You can do your own research. It is binding." She turned to John. "And you'll get the money from arbitration a lot faster than waiting on the next date for court."

Dwayne crossed his arms. "It wouldn't be if your husband wasn't tying our hands."

She stood. "I probably shouldn't have come. I just thought I could help with John's surgery. I'm sorry that my husband feels the need to push the court date back, but you won't have to worry about any of that if you go to arbitration. I will not be contesting that the accident was my fault, so you are guaranteed a win."

"My dad told me that you brought a check for my surgery," Jon-Jon said.

"Yes, John." Her eyes softened as she looked at him. "I was informed that you are still in pain, so I don't want you to wait for court or arbitration to get this surgery."

Dwayne scoffed at that.

Jon-Jon asked, "What if I decline arbitration? My father wants our day in court."

"The money for surgery is yours. I wish I could do more, but I've given you everything I had in my personal account. I don't want it back. I want you out of pain." Her voice caught, but she held back the tears this time.

Alexis heard a door open, a baby crying, and then she heard someone say, "Ugh, I just fed you. Can't believe you're hungry again."

"Hey, pipe down back there!" Dwayne yelled at the girl.

"Sorry!" someone yelled back.

Trish said, "We will have to discuss this with Jon-Jon before we can agree to arbitration."

The baby was still crying. Alexis said, "I completely understand. I just wanted to come and express my concern for John and bring this information. The document I handed you has the telephone number you'll need to call if you decide to do it."

Trish handed the paperwork to John. "Thank you," she said.

"I won't take up any more of your time." Alexis put her purse strap on her shoulder and was about to walk out of the room when a young woman entered with the crying baby on her hip.

The young lady looked at John. "I don't have any more money for formula. Can you spare a few dollars so I can run to the store?"

Dwayne went in his pocket and pulled out a twenty. "Get him some diapers if you need those too."

She put the baby in John's lap. "You want to hold your hollering son while I run to the store?"

Alexis tried to remove the shock from her face, but her eyes were wide as she asked, "You have a baby?"

John grinned a grin that lit up his whole face. "Yes, ma'am. This is my baby." He then turned to the woman who handed him the baby. "This is Alexis Marshall, the lady who hit me."

"What?" Hand on hip, head bobbing, Marquita said, "Lady, you owe me some diapers."

Trish shook her head. "Marquita, the baby is hungry."

"Yeah, he is. And guess what? Formula is expensive too." Marquita eyed Alexis. "You owe me some formula too."

"Marquita, if you do go on about your business," Trish threatened.

"Okay, okay. But we all know that Jon-Jon can't pay for nothing Marcus needs right now and it's"—she pointed again—"this lady's fault." Marquita grabbed her keys and left the house.

"I'm sorry about that," Trish told Alexis. "The girl gets out of control sometimes. I want to work with her, but she does try my patience."

A tear drifted down Alexis's cheek as she looked at John holding his baby. "I am so sorry I did this to you. I shouldn't be here." She rushed out of the room and quickly walked to the front door. She couldn't take any more. Yes, she wanted to help, but this was too much. Knowing that she had destroyed John's life was hard enough, but now there was a child involved. A child that would never know the man his father could have been all because she tried to pick up a phone that she dropped. All because her mother had another episode.

She made it to her car, got in, and sat there for a moment. As a child, Alexis watched her mother destroy herself and the lives of the people around her. Alexis swore that when she grew up she would build others up and never tear anyone down. She'd seen enough of that for a lifetime. Seeing what she'd done to John Robinson and his family was something that would take Alexis a long time to get over, if she ever could.

As she prepared to pull off, her cell phone rang. A quick peek told her that her mother's nursing home was calling. She was not in the mood for whatever Vivian had gotten herself into today. Alexis didn't want to know about it, didn't care about it, so she let the call go to voice mail.

She drove off and focused on the road. On the highway Alexis was tempted to pull off at one of the exits that had a McDonald's. That Oreo McFlurry was calling her name. Talking herself out of the McFlurry, she kept driving.

Halfway home, Alexis received a call from Michael. She didn't feel like talking to him, either, since it was his fault that she had to go to the Robinsons house. Why did he have to postpone that court case over and over again, even though he knew the Robinsons needed the money?

Michael hung up but then called her right back. She had ignored his call when Ethan had his swimming accident, so no matter how upset she was with him right now, she knew she needed to answer the phone this time. "Yeah, what's going on?"

"Alexis, are you okay? Why haven't you been answering the phone?"

"You only called one other time, Michael. I'm fine."

"You didn't answer the phone for the nursing home either."

"They called you?" They never called Michael. She had told them not to bother her husband unless they couldn't reach her for an emergency situation. "Oh! Don't tell me she ran away again?"

"I need you to be calm right now, okay? Are you calm?"

"Michael, just tell me what happened. Are they threatening to move her again?"

"Not this time, baby. Your mom had a seizure."

Red light. Alexis pushed down hard on the brakes, not realizing how fast she had been going. "She what?"

"She had a seizure. They took her to the hospital. So, you need to get over there."

❧

When Marquita arrived back from the store, she handed Dwayne seven dollars. "Here's your change."

He handed it back to her. "Keep it. Moochie will need formula again soon."

"Right." Marquita took the money and shoved it in her pocket. She was about to walk away when Dwayne stopped her.

"The words you're looking for are *thank you*."

"Huh?" Her forehead crinkled.

With the flick of the wrist, Dwayne said, "Nothing. Go on and feed my grandson."

"Well, thanks for the money," she said. But as she turned away from Dwayne, she rolled her eyes. She went into the kitchen, fixed Moochie's bottle, then joined Moochie and Jon-Jon in his room. Marquita lifted the baby off the bed, sat down in the chair next to Jon-Jon, and started feeding her son. "I guess I'm supposed to say thank you around here, so thanks for watching your son while I ran to the store."

Sitting up in his bed, then wincing from the pain, Jon-Jon asked, "What's your attitude about?"

Lowering her voice, she told Jon-Jon, "I don't want to get thrown out of here or nothing, but your daddy just told me to say thank you for the money he gave me for Moochie."

"And?"

Moochie was sucking the nipple on the bottle so fast that Marquita pulled it out of his mouth for a moment to give him a chance to swallow. "And I don't think it's necessary. He is Moochie's grandfather. He should want to do things for his grandson."

"He does, but my parents think people should be polite."

Marquita shrugged. Moochie finished his bottle. As she burped Moochie, Jon-Jon told her about the arbitration Mrs. Marshall had asked him to consider. Then Marquita said, "Let me ask you something, Jon-Jon."

Jon-Jon's eyes were trained on her.

"Are you planning to go to arbitration or wait to go to court?"

Jon-Jon's lip twisted as he pondered the question. "I don't know. My dad is set on going to court. He had me turn down the insurance payout because he thinks we'll get more for my injuries in court."

"And you don't think you'll get as much in arbitration? Is that why you're hesitant?"

"Not saying I'm hesitant. I just want to research it."

Moochie fell asleep in her arms, she smiled down at her son. "I know what I think doesn't matter, but Moochie needs things. Your parents have already given us a place to stay, so I don't want to keep asking them for money."

Jon-Jon laughed at her. "You just want to get the money from me so you don't have to say thank you."

"They do have a lot of rules." She scrunched her nose at him. "You know I'm right. We shouldn't have to ask your parents for money like that. And since your mom is looking for a job, I don't think they have much money to spare."

"True that," Jon-Jon agreed. "It does make me feel some kind of way that my daddy has to give you money for our baby. I'll think about what you said, and when I make up my mind, I'll talk to you about it first."

It made Marquita feel good that Jon-Jon listened to her and was going to give her a heads up on his decision. He was acting like she and Moochie mattered. She then began to wonder if they mattered because he wanted to do right by his baby or if he wanted to do right by her too. Her heart couldn't take the rejection right now, so she wasn't about to ask him how he felt about her.

She got up and left his room before her moonie-swoonie eyes gave her away.

CHAPTER 19

What was she thinking, not answering a call from the nursing home? Alexis turned her car around and drove straight to the hospital. When they left the hospital two weeks ago with Ethan, Alexis never imagined that she would be right back in the same emergency room asking for her mother's room.

The doors opened and she was told Vivian Cooper was in bed twenty-three. When Alexis got there, the room was empty, not even the bed was there. Where was her mother? Vivian had had a seizure. Why wasn't she in her room? Her eyes darted from one side of the room to the next. Was she too late?

Frantically, she scurried to the nurse station just outside the room. "Excuse me. Excuse me. I'm confused." Scratching her head, she said, "I was told my mother was in room twenty-three."

"What's her name?" the nurse asked.

Alexis told her.

The nurse typed something into her computer, then looked back up, "Yes, Ms. Cooper is in that room. She's getting an MRI. She should be back in a few minutes."

Sighing with relief, Alexis ran her fingers through her hair as her stomach growled. She had forgotten to eat. "I need food."

She went to the cafeteria and purchased a sandwich, chips, and a bottle of water. She kept hearing Michael tell her that her mother had a seizure. What could have happened to cause a seizure? It wasn't as if Alexis thought her mother was in the best of health, but she never would have imagined something like this.

Back in the room, Alexis sat down in the reclining chair that was situated next to the wall. She took her phone out of her purse and scrolled Facebook to give her hands something to do while waiting on her mother. But Facebook proved to not be a welcome distraction as one of her Facebook friends posted a picture of her mother with the caption, "Rest in heaven."

She put her phone back in her purse and stared at all the gadgets on the wall. Her son had been hooked up to a bunch of tubes the last time she had been here. She wondered what her mother would look like when she came back to this room.

Within a minute the door opened, and her mother's bed was wheeled into the room. Alexis stood. She waited so they could re-position the bed and the monitoring equipment next to her bed.

"The doctor will be in shortly," the woman told her before leaving the room.

Her mother looked groggy, like they had pumped her full of drugs. Alexis wondered if they were aware of her mother's previous history with drug abuse. They had her hooked to an IV that led to two different bags of fluid. Hopefully, the workers at the nursing home informed them. She would have to speak with someone about that.

Alexis noticed those protruding veins again, but now she studied her mother's face and saw the wrinkles in her forehead, the crow's feet at the corner of her eyes, and the puffiness under her eyes. Vivian had lived her life like a roller coaster, with all the ups and downs—this way and that way, round and round, spinning and screaming. It was drama and trauma most days, and Alexis never thought it would end. Vivian was only sixty-eight, but she looked eighty. *When had she gotten so thin, so small?* Alexis wondered. Even Vivian's auburn hair, which matched Alexis's hair color, now had gray strands in it.

A knock at the door caused Alexis to turn away from the frailty of her mother that she was now forced to reckon with. A man with a white lab coat stood at the door. "Hi, are you my mom's doctor?"

"Yes." He stepped into the room. "Do you have power of attorney for your mother?"

Alexis nodded. "That information should be in the hospital records because she's been admitted here before." She then extended her hand. "I'm Alexis."

They shook hands. "I'm Dr. Gupta."

"Can you tell me what happened to my mother?"

He opened the chart he brought with him. "We've run several tests, and it appears she has suffered a brain aneurysm."

His words felt like a whooshing wind that knocked her off her feet. She glanced over at her mother as she sat back down in the recliner. She studied her, trying to see if she was breathing. "B-but I didn't think anyone could survive something like that."

"She's still with us. We gave her a sedative in her IV because she was worked up when she arrived."

"She was probably scared and confused."

He nodded. "We figured."

When he didn't say anything else, she asked, "What happens next?"

"I need to tell you the truth, so I hope you can bear with me."

"Go ahead, Doctor." This felt like déjà vu. Here she was again in a hospital room talking to a doctor while her loved one lay helplessly in the hospital bed.

"Your mother's vitals are not good. It's very touch-and-go at the moment."

"But she's only sixty-eight. There has to be something you can do. Some medicine she can be put on."

He looked over at Vivian as if disbelieving what Alexis just said.

"Sixty-eight!" Alexis shouted. Steadying her voice as she calmed down, she apologized. "I'm sorry. I didn't mean to yell. I know she looks older. My mom has had a hard life." Alexis had thought that one day things might turn around for her mother. Maybe a cure would be found, and they could all live a normal life. She just thought there would be more time.

"I understand," he told her. "Let's just get through the night, and then we can see what else we can do for her."

Get through the night? Alexis let those words roll through her mind as she leaned back in the recliner. Her mother had a seizure due to a brain aneurysm and now they had to hope that she would get through the night. She called Michael and informed him that she would be staying at the hospital with her mother. The nurse brought a blanket and pillow for her comfort.

"Well, this is life," she told herself as she pulled the wrapper off the sandwich and ate it. Wrapping the blanket around herself, she leaned back in the recliner, closed her eyes, and fell asleep. Not too much later, she was awakened by singing. It was her mother singing about flying away.

Taking her seat out of the reclining position, Alexis was horrified at the song her mother sang. "Mom, I've never heard you sing that. Where'd you hear a song like that?"

Vivian smiled at some distant memory. "My mama was a songbird. Did I ever tell you that?"

Alexis shook her head. "No, Mom, you never did."

"She used to sing in the choir. On Sunday mornings I would be so happy to sit in the front row on the church pew and hear her beautiful voice. 'I'll Fly Away' was one of her favorite songs."

"I've never heard that song before. I'd rather you sing something about staying right here."

Vivian glanced around the room. A look of sadness furrowed the lines in her forehead even more. "Where are my grandkids? Why do you keep them away from me?"

"I don't keep them away from you." That wasn't exactly true, but

Alexis felt the need to defend herself. "I just brought them to see you on your birthday. Remember?"

"Birthdays and Christmas," Vivian mumbled and turned to look out the window.

The sadness in her mother's voice broke her. Vivian had been so excited about being a grandmother. When Ethan and Ella were first born, she would have them around her mother all the time. Vivian gushed over her grandbabies, but as they got older, Alexis limited the visits to twice a year because she feared that her mother's erratic behavior would frighten the children. "You got me. I'm here. And I'm spending the night with you. Isn't that good enough?"

Still looking out the window, Vivian said, "I know you wanted a good life. I'm glad you found someone who makes you happy, but I've been on the outside looking in all these years. I just wish I could have been a part of your life too."

What had she done? Tears welled in her eyes. She put a hand on her mother's arm. "You have been with me every day of my life, Mom. I haven't forgotten you, nor will I ever. How could I forget how much fun we used to have?"

"Or how much pain I caused you. That's why you hid me away in all those awful places. You were tired of me."

Her mother was right. She had let her go for the promise of something better. Michael loved her, but he hated the thought of the world knowing he had a mother-in-law with mental issues. So she gave in and sent her mother away, effectively tearing her away from her grandchildren, just as Alexis had been taken away from the Coopers when she was five years old.

When she had asked her mom why they moved away from her grandmother and why she couldn't see Granny anymore, her mother had mumbled gobbly-goop, gibberish. Something like, "They want you to go to Hollywood, but you're not ready." Her mother could make believe that she was some fabulous actress, but when it came to

Alexis, she'd said, "Oh no, you're not ready to be an actress." It just didn't make sense.

It was hard to understand her mother and hard to love her mother at times, because she had to take the flaws and all. She had tried to do the right thing by putting her mother in only the best nursing homes. Vivian needed looking after, and those people could handle it better than Alexis could. This is what she told herself, and until this very minute, she had believed it. Could it possibly be too late for her to make this right?

"I'll do better, Mom. I promise I won't let you down again."

CHAPTER 20

Y ou're looking good," Trish said to her son as she stepped out
onto the back patio. Jon-Jon was seated in his wheelchair while
Dwayne used the clippers to cut Jon-Jon's hair.

"I felt good enough to get out of bed today," he told her.

Two weeks had passed since Alexis Marshall came to their home.
Jon-Jon had the surgery eight days ago and was now wheeling himself
around the house like it was nothing. "You gettin' all them matted-up
knots cut out of your hair because Marquita's in the house?"

Jon-Jon hid his face in his hands. "Dad, get your wife."

Lining up the back of Jon-Jon's head, Dwayne said, "Come on,
Trish. Don't embarrass the boy."

Trish sat down on the lounge chair. "I didn't come out here to give
Jon-Jon a hard time. I wanted to talk to both of you."

Dwayne's eyebrow lifted in surprise. "Yeah, what you know good,
Trish the Dish?"

Smiling, Trish got that butterfly flutter in her belly. Dwayne used
to call her Trish the Dish when they first started dating. She hadn't
heard that phrase from him in years. "I wanted to know what the two
of you thought about me going back to work?"

Dwayne turned off the clippers and stared to her.

Trish held up a hand. "I know how you feel about it. So, I guess
I'm really trying to get Jon-Jon's thoughts on this."

Wiping hair from his shirt as he looked at Trish, Jon-Jon said, "I know I've been bratty about everything that has happened since my accident, but I wasn't lying about being in pain."

"How is your pain level now?" Trish asked, concern etched on her face.

"It's getting better, Mom, so I want you to go to work and not worry about me so much."

"You hear him, Dwayne? Sounds like he's trying to grow up on us."

"He better," Dwayne said. "Babies don't raise themselves, and no son of mine is going to shirk his duties as a father." Dwayne turned the clippers back on and started shaving more off the top.

"Speaking of that, Dad. I know you want us to have our day in court, but I don't think it's right that you and Mom have to buy the things my kid needs, so I called Mrs. Marshall's attorney and agreed to arbitration."

Trish didn't say anything. This was a moment between father and son. Jon-Jon was showing his independence by making this decision without talking to his father first. It was the right decision in her mind. Still, she held her breath, waiting to see if Dwayne was about to go off.

To her surprise, Dwayne calmly said, "You made a decision that was yours to make, and you made it for the right reason. I'm proud of you."

Trish went back in the house, sat down at the kitchen table with her laptop, and filled out an application for a teaching job at the local community college.

Marquita came out of her room, humming some song Trish didn't recognize. She was reading something on her cell phone as she took a bottle out of the fridge. She turned and saw Trish sitting at the table. "Oh, hey, I didn't see you over there."

"You got your head stuck in the phone. I'm just glad you didn't trip over one of the floor rugs."

Marquita glanced back at her phone. "I was looking at this customer service job I want to apply for, but I don't have experience."

Trish wagged a finger at her. "Don't get stuck on experience. Customer service jobs are usually entry level. I would apply if I were you. The worst they can say is no."

"Right." Marquita nodded in agreement. She put Moochie's bottle in the microwave, then sat down at the table with Trish and started filling out the application.

❧

Within a few weeks of applying for the position at the community college, Trish had been hired. She was now working in the evening, helping kids study for their GED. She taught a two-hour class three nights a week, and Marquita sat with Jon-Jon while she was out.

There were fifteen students in her class tonight. Trish stood and greeted each one as they entered her classroom. "Good evening, students. I hope you all had a good day and are energized, because we are about to dive into some world history that may cause your eyes to glaze over. This information will be on the GED test, so stay with me."

Trish was a math teacher. She had been assigned to this history class because the GED program already had a math teacher, and they desperately needed someone to teach history. She was just thankful they didn't need a science teacher because she wouldn't have been able to take the assignment. She had minored in history in college, so she could handle this.

Teaching young adults was different than teaching fourth graders. She didn't hear a whole lot of whining about doing the work. But she kept in mind that the people she now taught had previously given up on school. Each night as she planned her lesson, she did it with success in mind. She wanted each of the students who attended her class to see themselves succeeding, passing that GED test, and moving forward with life.

"Our first quiz will be next week." She passed out study sheets to each student. "If you review everything on these sheets and read the first two chapters in your American history book, you'll be able to pass the quiz."

"I can't remember none of this stuff no matter how hard I study," Jerome said while pushing the paper away.

Trish asked, "Have you ever tried index cards?"

He gave her a blank stare.

"What I'm suggesting is that you take notes on index cards and then study those cards over and over."

"That will take a lot of work. We do have jobs and family, you know," Maria, the eighteen-year-old with two babies said.

"I understand that." Trish scanned the room, making sure to look at each student. Most of them were not complainers, but she wasn't going to let two students discourage the rest of her class. "This GED process is about how bad do you want it. It won't be easy, but you will have to find a study method that works for you so you can pass that test."

As she left the school that night, Trish stopped herself from feeling discouraged. She reminded herself that her students most likely felt discouraged every day. They needed someone to champion them. She decided to add each of them to her prayer list while continuing to show them best practices for passing that GED test.

Her greatest joy from this assignment would be if one or two of her students reconnected with her in a few years to tell her that they went to college after getting their GED, and that they not only have a degree but also a good paying job.

On her way out of the building, she noticed the community college course catalog for next semester was now available. She grabbed a copy for Jon-Jon. She wanted him to go back to college, even if he had to attend online classes at a community college.

Right next to the course catalog was the college newspaper. On the front page of the newspaper was a story about how distracted driving had killed two of their students last week. Trish's mind flashed back to the day she received the call about Jon-Jon's accident. It was a gut-wrenching feeling that she didn't want any other parent to deal with. The parents of the two teens received an even worse call than she had. "Lord, please send Your angels to these families," she prayed. "Mend their hearts, for I know the parents' hearts are surely broken."

Two lives lost because someone decided to text rather than pay attention while driving. She took a copy of that newspaper with her as well.

Alexis Marshall seemed like a nice lady. Trish was thankful that she had given them the money for Jon-Jon's surgery. Piece by piece, she had been letting go of the anger she had felt about the situation. What Alexis did was wrong and people needed to understand how harmful distracted driving was. How many more people have to die or be injured before these drivers start understanding general responsibility?

When she arrived home and went into Jon-Jon's room, Trish was shocked to see Marquita holding Jon-Jon's resistance bands on one end, and Jon-Jon holding the other end of the bands as he pulled himself forward.

"Come on, boy. You can do it," Marquita encouraged.

"I ain't nobody's boy," Jon-Jon said as he pulled himself up again.

"You aren't *anyone's* boy," Trish corrected.

Jon-Jon fell back against his pillow. He was sweating, so he leaned over to his nightstand, grabbed a tissue, and wiped his forehead. "Mom, you're a math teacher, not an English teacher."

"According to my night school principal, I'm a history teacher, and history teachers correct grammar on papers all the time."

"Whatever." He smiled at his mother.

"How's your back feeling?"

"Still doing good," Jon-Jon said.

Marquita added, "He didn't even want his pain medicine. He said it made him too groggy."

"Well, well, now. Look who's using his resistance bands." Trish smiled at her son. "I don't even want to know how it happened. I'm just glad that it did. I'm going to get out of the way and let you two carry on."

"He's almost done," Marquita said.

Trish glanced around the room. "Where's Marcus?"

"Sleep, in Marquita's room," Jon-Jon told her.

Trish handed Jon-Jon the course catalog for the community college. "The catalog for next semester is out. Since classes don't start for two more months, I thought you might want to sign up. They even have online classes."

"Okay, Mama. I'll look into it." He then went back to stretching with his bands.

Trish left them to it, and she went to her bedroom. She still had the school newspaper in her hand. She showed it to Dwayne. "Look at this. How many more people have to die from distracted driving like this?"

Dwayne read the article. "Makes my stomach turn."

Trish clinched her fist and boxed the air. "I'm thankful for the surgery, but this makes me wish Jon-Jon hadn't agreed to arbitration. If we could have gone to court, maybe a light would have been shone on this whole business of using cell phones while driving. North Carolina has laws against texting and driving, but people are still doing it."

"I used to do it all the time," Dwayne admitted. "But when that officer told us that Alexis had dropped her phone and was reaching for it when the accident occurred . . . now I just can't."

"It's wrong, and it's selfish, but you hardly hear anything about it on the news. Even when they show car accidents, they never come right out and say what the driver was doing before the accident."

"I wonder why that is," Dwayne said.

"I don't know, but something has to be done to change it."

"Well, before you get on your soapbox about that—"

"My soapbox?" Trish interrupted. "I'm not on a soapbox, Dwayne. Our son's whole life has changed because Alexis had to pick up her cell phone while driving. Now you tell me that's right?"

"I'm not saying it's right, Trish, but we can't stop people from driving recklessly."

"See, you say we can't, but I say we can." Her eyes brightened with excitement. "I'm going to do something about this, Dwayne. Look at the Mothers Against Drunk Driving organization. It didn't just materialize from nothing. Some woman started it after some drunk driver hit her child.

"I get it, Trish, but right now, I just want you to relax." He opened the bathroom door and waved her forward.

Trish's hand went to her mouth. She swung around with furrowed eyebrows. "You did this . . . for me?"

"Who else?" Her bathtub was filled with bubbles and red rose petals. "I put some Epson salt in there for you too. Why don't you get in and soak your body for a little while?"

She hadn't soaked in the tub since her mom gave her a break and sat with Jon-Jon. Taking time out for herself hadn't been at the top of her list for so long, Trish almost felt like she was doing something wrong to even think about getting in that tub.

She shook that feeling off. Jon-Jon was fine. It was okay to take a little time for herself. She got in the tub, leaned her head back, and listened to the soft music playing in their bedroom. She stayed in the tub until she felt sleep trying to overtake her. As she got out, toweled off, and slid on a nightgown, the music changed.

As she entered the bedroom, "I Found Love," a love song by BeBe

Winans, was playing. Trish's hand went to her heart. She and Dwayne used to snuggle up together and listen to the song all the time. "You still remember *our* song?" Astonishment lingered in her voice.

He took her hand and pulled her into his arms. "I could never forget our song." His head lowered, and he kissed her.

Trish had forgiven Dwayne. She knew she had. Still, there were some mornings when she got out of bed that something gnawed at her, not letting her fully commit to the forgiveness she wanted to give. She didn't know what the issue was, but it was there. So each time that little nagging feeling reared its head, Trish took a moment to pray about it.

"You're a good man, Dwayne."

As BeBe sang, Dwayne swung Trish around and said, "I love you, bae."

Love wasn't in the details. It was right here as she felt Dwayne's arms around her and breathed in the scent of sandalwood and musk that was so him. Love was in the showing up every single day, even when it was hard. She had love with Dwayne, and she was going to hold on to it with every fiber of her being. "You know what, Dwayne John Robinson, I love you right back."

CHAPTER 21

Since Vivian made it through the night, Alexis thought the worst was behind them, just as it had been with Ethan's hospitalization. Her mother would recuperate and then go back to the nursing home with her friends. But it seemed the doctor's only purpose for coming into Vivian's hospital room today was to wreck her whole life.

That song her mother sang about flying away rang in Alexis's ear as the doctor said, "Some patients live a long time after an aneurysm, but your mother's health is failing so I must be honest with you. I don't think she will live past the next six months."

"She only has six months?"

He shook his head. "I can't guarantee another six months. She could leave us at any time. I'm sorry I don't have better news for you."

He was sorry, but he would not take any of it back. A person who had the power to predict a death should have the power to take those words back.

"So, this is it," Vivian said as if she accepted the doctor's words as gospel.

"No, Mom. You aren't going to lay down and die just because one doctor says so. I'm going to get you an appointment with another doctor."

Vivian didn't look hopeful. "Can you bring my grandchildren to see me, please?"

Alexis sat down next to her mom. They had a complicated relationship. Yes, there were times when Vivian was hard to love, but

175

Alexis loved her still. She declared within her heart that she was going to do right by the woman who gave her life. "Mom, when the doctor releases you from the hospital, I want you to come home with me."

"For a visit?"

Alexis's mind was made up. Her mother belonged with her and the kids. "No, Mom, I want you to stay with us."

Vivian's head swung around to look at her daughter. "You want me?"

Tears rolled down Alexis's face. She wiped them away. "Yes, Mom, I want you with me. The kids will be so happy."

Vivian's eyes clouded over. "What about Michael?"

"Michael will be fine with it. You need me now, Mom. I promise I won't desert you." She'd done things Michael's way ever since they met. He would now have to adjust his perfect life to accommodate her mother. Alexis hoped her husband wouldn't disappoint her, but she wasn't sending her mother back to that nursing home no matter what he said.

❧

Vivian moved in with them and Alexis took her to see another doctor, but even her second-opinion doctor could not guarantee that Vivian would fully recover from the aneurysm.

"Mommy, Granny wants a sandwich!" Ella yelled from the top of the stairs.

"Okay, tell her I'll be up with it in a minute." Alexis went into the kitchen, opened the refrigerator, and started taking out lunch meat, veggies, and mayo. She placed the items on the counter as Michael came up behind her. He put an arm around her and kissed the back of her neck.

"Can you fix me a sandwich also?" He sat down at the kitchen counter.

Things had been tense with her and Michael since she moved her mother into the guest room three weeks ago. Alexis had been trying to keep the peace, but Michael was making it harder with each passing day. She made his sandwich and slid it over to him.

"Okay, I get it. You're still mad about the comments I made about your mom when Ethan was seeing things, but don't you think that moving your mom into our house was a bit much for getting back at me?"

She was slicing tomatoes for her mother's sandwich. She let the knife drop on the cutting board as she turned to Michael. "I'm not trying to get back at you. My mother doesn't want to be at that nursing home anymore."

"We've always found her a new place whenever she wore out her welcome. Why didn't you just find a new place for her, Alexis? This is too much. I don't like some of the things she says around our children."

"I don't like some of the stuff she says either, Michael, but she's my mother. Our kids deserve to know the good and the bad about their grandmother."

Michael took his sandwich off the counter and stood up. "This can't go on much longer, Alexis. Find her another nursing home."

"No."

Michael's back was to her as he was making his way out of the kitchen. He swiveled back around. "What?"

"I said no, Michael. You don't get to run everything around here. Not anymore." She had tried so hard to be the wife Michael needed her to be. She had never thought of herself as a rebel. Vivian had been rebellious enough for the whole family. Alexis was more a go-along-to-get-along type of person. "She's dying, Michael."

"Says who? That doctor told you he couldn't guarantee six months, but who's to say she won't live at least two years or more."

"Would that really be so bad?" For Michael, she knew the answer was yes and that made her sad.

His hand flew in the air. He gave her a look that said she was being unreasonable. Then he stormed out of the room.

She took the sandwich and a glass of iced tea to her mother. Vivian was in the oversize chair with her feet propped on the ottoman. Alexis put the food tray table down in front of her mother.

"How are you feeling, Mom?"

"I'm feeling wonderful." She stretched and rolled her neck. "The kids have been helping me rehearse my lines."

"Your lines?"

"Yeah, Mom." Ethan entered the room with a notepad and ink pen. "Here, Granny."

Ella came into the room. Around her shoulders she had wrapped the feather boa Alexis wore to a 1920s party Michael took her to last year. "Granny is teaching us how to write our own lines, just like the grand old Hollywood actresses did."

Alexis almost laughed as Ella stepped on the scarf while trying to strut around the room as if she was attending a red carpet event. "Well, you all are obviously in your own little world, so I'll get out of the way."

"No, Mom, stay and have fun with us," Ethan pleaded.

After the fight she just had with Michael, Alexis did not know if she wanted to encourage all of this pretending and delusions of grandeur. Maybe she should shut the door so they could play without Michael overhearing them.

"Come on, Alexis. You used to practice lines with me. Get on over here so I can teach these grandkids of mine how to get noticed when they audition."

"I don't think Ella or Ethan have any delusions . . . I mean, ambitions toward being actors." She tried her best to ignore the feather boa wrapped around Ella. That didn't mean anything. Her kids were not interested in acting.

"Of course, they do," Vivian asserted. "They have my genes. They will be wonderful actors, and they'll make much more money than I ever did. I can guarantee you that."

"Do you really think we can be famous actors, Granny?" Ethan asked.

"You betcha." Vivian moved the tray to the table and tried to get out of the chair. She was a bit wobbly, so she grabbed her cane as she tried to stand straight and tall. "When I was a younger girl, I was the talk of the town. If anybody got in my way when I was auditioning for a part, I would pulverize them." Vivian balled her fist and made a punching motion.

Ella's face turned from playful to horrified. "Granny, why would you do something like that?"

"Yes, why indeed?" Alexis wondered if her mom's medication needed to be increased or maybe Vivian needed to get some rest. She didn't understand why none of her mom's therapists had ever been able to get this Hollywood delusion out of her head. "Mom, you've been up long enough today. Please get back in bed."

"I can't, the kids and I have some lines to rehearse."

Alexis ignored her mother and helped her back to bed. "Okay, kids, give Granny some time to rest and let her eat her sandwich."

"But she wants to play, Mom. She really does," Ethan said.

"I know she does, but I need her to get some rest." Alexis turned to Ella. "Put that scarf back in my closet. Then you and Ethan can go play in the backyard for a little while."

"You don't want them to play with me?" Vivian sounded hurt.

Alexis didn't like that Vivian told her kids about her so-called Hollywood days, but she wasn't about to chastise her mother about it. She didn't want to make too big a fuss, especially not after the doctors told her that Vivian could experience a re-bleeding in the head and then life would just be over.

"It's not that, Mom," Alexis finally said. "The kids love having you home with us, but I really do want you to rest. I could hear you all last night pacing the floor. These all-nighters aren't good for you."

"I'm fine, Alexis. You don't need to baby me."

"Can you promise to get some sleep? Please."

"I am getting tired. Maybe I will go to sleep now. Will that make you happy?"

Alexis pointed at the sandwich. "Eat first, then nap."

"Okay, okay. You're worse than the wardens at all those prisons you and Michael put me in."

Sitting down in the chair that was against the wall in her mother's room, Alexis said, "We didn't put you in a prison, Mom."

"Oh, yeah? Then why did I have to bust out?" Vivian asked as she began eating her sandwich.

"I've wondered that myself, Mom. The homes we put you in were all very nice places. You had friends and lots of activities."

"It was no home at all if I wasn't with you, Lexi. Remember, it was always you and me against the world."

Alexis remembered. She and Vivian battled bill collectors, grocery store workers, landlords, and anyone else who told Vivian she couldn't do something she had already set her mind to do. Alexis had grown tired of the struggle and the you-and-me-against-the-world—a world that her mother created in her own head, and all she had wanted to do was escape.

Now she would give anything to add more restless days and sleepless nights. "Keep living, Mom," Alexis whispered as Vivian fell asleep. "Just keep living."

❧

That night, while Vivian slept the night away, Alexis barely slept at all. Michael wasn't speaking to her, and she didn't know what to do about that. How could she get her husband to care about the things that concerned her? All through their marriage it had been her job to care about what concerned Michael. Now she needed them to switch roles, just for a little while. The world would again revolve around Michael, but not now—not when her mother needed her.

As she tossed and turned, Michael lay next to her sleeping as if all was right in his world—at least that's how it seemed to her. She needed Michael. Why couldn't he see how much distress she was feeling and put his arms around her? Why couldn't he be there to tell her that everything was going to be all right? But Michael was consumed with what mattered to him.

She glanced over at the time on the cable box. It was two in the morning. *Go to sleep already.* She pulled the cover over her head.

In the morning, Alexis reflected that while she might not be getting much sleep, she was thankful that her mother was finally sleeping. Alexis hoped that Vivian would be in her right mind today. But after cooking the oatmeal that her mother loved for breakfast and taking it to her, Alexis found her mother in tears.

She put the breakfast tray down and rushed to her mother's side. "What's wrong, Mom?" She looked toward the television to see if she was watching something sad, but the TV wasn't on.

"I miss my mom. I haven't seen her in so long." Vivian's hand touched her heart. "It hurts."

Alexis could only imagine how much a lifetime of regrets could hurt. She wrapped her arms around her mother. "I wish things had been different for you, Mom."

When Alexis was a kid, her mom had got into a big blow up with her family. She'd cursed them all, and she and Alexis moved to another town. A few years later, Alexis's grandmother had died. Alexis wasn't sure if her mom remembered that and didn't know if she should remind her. The aftermath of her grandmother's death had been bad.

Vivian had gone on a rampage, destroying everything in sight. The trailer they lived in was beyond repair by the time the landlord got wind of what she was doing. They were kicked out of that trailer park. Alexis was sure the neighbors were all happy to see them go.

Alexis understood a little bit of the regret her mother was feeling. Ever since that day she hit John, or Jon-Jon as his family called him, Alexis had been filled with regret. She wished there was some way she could make amends, but how do you make amends for paralyzing someone? She had paid for Jon-Jon's surgery. That had at least taken some of the guilt off her shoulders.

"After all these years, I don't know if they will want to see me. My mother was very angry when I left. She never wanted me to get into the acting business. She never believed I was Miss Kitty." A look of shame crossed her face. "I don't want them to know that I didn't make it. I don't want them to know they were right about me."

Her mother was actually admitting that she wasn't an actress? Alexis wished she could stay in this moment. Just sit here with a mother who was in her right mind and let the rest of the world do what they may, but that wasn't the way life worked.

"Hey, remember that purple van I used to have?" Vivian asked with glee in her eyes.

Alexis had no idea if Vivian would become manic if she reminded her that Grandma Joyce was dead, so she was thankful to move on to another subject. Even if it was about that awful purple van. "I remember you made me sing 'Purple Rain' every time we drove around in it."

Vivian giggled. "You hated that van. Just never understood the beauty of having a purple van while others drove around in boring old white and gray vans."

"That's why you liked the van so much, because it was different?"

Vivian adjusted herself in the bed. She turned toward her daughter. "Look at me, Alexis. Haven't I always been a different kind of girl?"

Her mother had definitely been different—so different that Alexis had been embarrassed, mortified, and stupefied all at the same time.

She spent so many years trying to figure out why her mother was different from other mothers, but she'd never discovered any reason for Vivian's condition.

After talking with her mother, Alexis went downstairs to vacuum the living room and fill the dishwasher. She was in the kitchen rinsing the dishes before putting them in the dishwasher when Michael called. She hit the speaker and then sat the phone on the counter.

"Are you busy?" he asked.

"Just doing a little cleaning. How is your day going?" She hoped he was in a better mood today.

"My parents called. They wanted to spend the weekend at the house with the kids, but with your mother at the house, I'm a little worried how that might look."

He just wouldn't stop. She turned off the water and sat the dish she had rinsed on the counter as she scratched her eyebrow. She wasn't going to play his game. "I don't see why your parents can't spend the weekend here. We always give them the bedroom in the basement so they can have their privacy anyway."

"And Peter was thinking that we should do more dinner parties. And if you think Vivian won't become a problem at a dinner party, then I've got news for you."

She was so aggravated with her husband she could scream. He would be happy if they hid her mother away again. So happy if everything went back to the way he wanted it to be. But she couldn't do that. She couldn't turn her back on her mother, not now and not ever again.

"I know she's your mother, Alexis, but we're so close to having everything we ever wanted. Our home is a showpiece. We bought the house so we could entertain clients, and I don't think—"

Interrupting him, she said, "I thought we bought this house for our family. I don't want to fight with you, Michael. I know how much you have done for us, but our family also includes my mother."

"You have responsibilities to me, Alexis. I'm your husband, and I'm not going to let you ignore that fact."

She took a deep breath to the point where it felt like she was about to start hyperventilating. This was too much for her. "I'll see you when you get home." Alexis hung up the phone. She put her elbows on the sink base as her shoulders slumped. Michael was trying to make her choose between him and her mother. It wasn't fair because she wanted them both, but Michael had the power. He had given her this wonderful life and made everything she'd ever wanted possible. The things she had wanted so badly when she first met Michael were all tied up in escaping the drama that surrounded her mother.

After volunteering with social services and helping people who were like her mother, Alexis no longer wanted to escape. She wanted to lean in. She wanted to hold on to her mother and give her the ability to reconnect with her family, just as she had helped so many others do. She couldn't let Michael win this time. She just couldn't.

"He doesn't want me here, does he?"

Alexis jumped. She turned to see her mother standing behind her. "How long have you been standing there?"

Vivian held up the glass. "I came down to get a drink of water. I can do things for myself, you know."

Alexis took the glass and pushed the button for the icemaker. After several cubes fell into her mother's glass, she dispensed water from the fridge and let it fill up halfway.

"I could have gotten it from the sink," Vivian told her.

"The water from the fridge is filtered. Now, will you please lay down and rest as the doctor told you?"

"Are you going to let him throw me out?"

"No one is throwing you out, Mom. You live here with us, and we are happy to have you."

Vivian harrumphed at that as she headed back upstairs.

As she watched her mom slowly walk back up the stairs, her heart sank at the thought that Vivian would spend the rest of her days in this house feeling unwanted. Michael would have to fix this. There was no way she was going to allow her mother to feel unwanted—not anymore.

CHAPTER 22

A re you ever going to look at that college catalog your mother gave you? Classes begin in six weeks." Marquita picked the catalog off his floor so she could vacuum.

Sitting in his wheelchair, Jon-Jon was holding Marcus. "College was a lot of fun. I was halfway through my second year before the accident."

"I've always wanted to go to college, but I wasn't focused my last two years of high school and just barely had a C average when I finished. So, it's not like I would get a scholarship to go anywhere."

He pointed toward the college catalog Marquita set on his end table. "Community colleges cost a lot less than universities. Maybe you should be looking through that catalog yourself."

"The difference between ten dollars and a dollar don't make much difference to me because I don't have either." Marquita turned on the vacuum and pushed it around Jon-Jon's room until the baby started crying.

"Hey, you're disturbing Moochie." Jon-Jon put his hands over the baby's ears.

Marquita stuck out her tongue at both of them and turned off the vacuum. "I don't know how Moochie thinks I'm going to take care of our board and keep if he wants to cry every time I'm doing housework."

"My baby boy don't cry all the time. You scared him with that vacuum."

Marquita gave Jon-Jon the evil eye. "We weren't even talking about your crybaby son. I want to know why you haven't filled out

186

that college entrance form yet. Kids aren't cheap, you know. We need to figure out how to make some real money."

"I hear you," Jon-Jon said, more serious now. "Believe me, I had a good example growing up. My dad was always there for me, so I'm going to take care of my son. I just think it's better if I concentrate on my physical therapy before I go back to school."

When Marquita was with Jon-Jon last summer, she truly thought they had this forever kind of connection. She couldn't believe that she had found somebody to love and that he loved her back. But when he went back to school and didn't call and didn't text, she realized that nothing in her life had changed.

Now he was talking about how he was going to take care of his son. She wished she didn't want him to include her in that scenario, but like a fool in love, she did. She wished she could stop feeling love for Jon-Jon, but every day she was around him, her feelings kept growing stronger. She'd never tell him how she felt, because she wasn't about to be rejected by the same man twice.

The garage door opened, and Trish entered the kitchen. Marquita peeked out of Jon-Jon's room. "How was service?"

"Oh, it was wonderful. I really needed that tonight. Thank you so much for hanging out with Jon-Jon so I could attend Bible study."

"I heard that," Jon-Jon called from inside his room. "I don't need a babysitter, Ma. I'm getting around in my wheelchair now. I even fixed my own sandwich."

Marquita smirked at Jon-Jon's words. "Since he's doing so good on his own, I'm sure Jon-Jon won't mind that I have a job interview later this week." She wrapped the cord around the vacuum and then took Marcus from Jon-Jon. "I need to change his diaper."

Trish joined them in Jon-Jon's room.

Jon-Jon said, "Mama, tell Marquita that she's wasting her time with these penny-ante jobs when she could sign up for classes at the community college."

"One of us has to buy diapers," Marquita shot back.

Trish asked Marquita, "Do you want to go to college?"

Hesitant to answer at first, she bounced Marcus on her hip, wishing she could think of a joke to take the pressure off. She didn't need anyone laughing behind her back, or worse yet, making her believe something that was never ever going to happen. "I do, but it's probably best for me to just find a job."

"Why? You haven't been fired from enough jobs yet?" Jon-Jon laughed as if he had said something cute.

Trish and Marquita said simultaneously. "Shut up, Jon-Jon."

"Oh, it's like that?" Jon-Jon wheeled his chair on the other side of his bed, picked up his ten-pound weights. "Since no one needs my helpful advice, I'll just work out and build my upper body strength so I can throw that football to my son when he's old enough."

Trish's eyes lit up, but she didn't say anything else to Jon-Jon. She backed out of the room while signaling Marquita to join her in the kitchen.

"Did I do something wrong?" Marquita asked when she joined Trish.

"Marquita, you have got to stop asking that. Trust and believe, I will let you know if you do something wrong." Trish opened the fridge and took out an apple. "I work with kids who don't see a future for themselves, so I just want you to know that being a single mother does not mean you have to stop dreaming, okay?"

Marquita didn't respond. What could she say to something like that? Growing up the way she did taught her not to dream. She went into her bedroom with Marcus, laid her baby on the bed, and picked up her journal.

She didn't dream much, but she did write about all the stuff she could never, would never, dream about, like becoming a writer. When she was a kid, she gave her mother a poem for her birthday. Her mother actually had the poem framed. It used to sit in their living room, but her mother lost the poem after refusing to move from a house she had been evicted from. The police came and put her stuff on the sidewalk. That was the last time Marquita saw that poem.

Maybe one day she could write a book of poems like some of the greats, or maybe she would write a novel. No, no, no. She was letting Trish get to her. Trish and Dwayne were able to move to the suburbs after working their way out of the low-income side of town, but that was the only side of life Marquita had ever known. She couldn't even manage to hold on to a low-income apartment. *Dreaming—got to stop dreaming.*

Her cell phone rang. It was her mother. "Hey, Ma, how are you doing?"

"Doing good. They just found a house that I can move into, so I'm excited about that."

"How's Mark and Kee Kee doing?"

Gloria sucked her teeth. "If you cared about your brother and sister, you would have come to see about them."

"That's not fair, Mama. I've had my own issues."

"Marquita, you act like you're the only one who's ever been evicted. Life goes on. And I don't know why you didn't come to this women's shelter, because these are some good people. They helped me find a place."

The last women's shelter her mother stayed at threw her out after she cursed them out for getting in her business. "The Robinsons said I can stay here for a little while."

"Whatever, girl. Just don't come running to me for a place to stay when they throw you out."

Why did her mother have to act like this? Why couldn't she understand that Marquita wanted something better for herself and for Moochie? She couldn't win with this woman. "What did you call for, Mama?"

"Oh, now I can't call my own daughter unless I need something.

189

Don't get cute with me just because you finally found your baby's daddy."

Marquita wanted to scream. Just open her mouth and let one scream after another fly. This is why she had not called her mother. There was no letting up with Gloria Lewis. She did feel bad about not reaching out to her siblings though. She knew firsthand what they were suffering through and wished she could help them.

Maybe she should try to find a way to go to college. If she could get a degree and a good paying job, she would then be able to help Mark and Kee Kee do the same. They deserved a better life. Kee Kee was so smart. That girl could teach classes right now and probably do a better job than some teachers.

"I need to go to the store and put some food in the house, but you know my car isn't working."

Her mother's car had been in the shop for two months. The mechanic fixed it, but she didn't want to pay so she and the mechanic were still fighting. "When do you want me to take you?"

"Tomorrow. Can you pull yourself away from Moochie's daddy long enough to help your family get some food?"

Why did everything have to be a battle with this woman? "Yes, I'll pick you up in the morning."

It was a terrible thing, but hanging up with her mother brought Marquita's anxiety level down. She hated that she felt that way about dealing with her own mother, but them were her feelings. Pushing that conversation from her mind, Marquita bathed Moochie and put his onesie on. The two of them then lay down and went to sleep.

⁓

The next morning as she was in the kitchen fixing bottles, Jon-Jon called her into his room. "What you want, man? I'm busy fixing these bottles for your greedy son."

"I want to go to my physical therapy session this morning, but I don't want to bother my mom." He looked at her with so much hope in his eyes. "Would you take me?"

Trish told her that Jon-Jon had declined physical therapy because he didn't think it was doing any good. If Jon-Jon was now asking to go, she was going to help him get there because Moochie needed his father to be in the game. "If you got the gas money, I've got the car."

"I got to put gas in your car for a ride to the hospital?"

"If I had a job, I wouldn't ask. But I don't have a job yet, and the gas I have now is enough to get me to my interview on Thursday."

"That's fine. I'll get twenty from my dad."

She felt bad for asking so she whispered to Jon-Jon, "Don't tell them that I asked. They just purchased diapers and formula for Moochie."

"Look, my parents aren't like that. They don't mind helping. And anyway, I go to arbitration next week. We won't have to ask them for money after that. I should have enough to take care of us."

"Us?" she questioned.

Grinning, Jon-Jon repeated, "Us."

Jon-Jon was going to help her and do right by Moochie. From the moment she met him, Marquita had thought Jon-Jon was a good guy. With every passing day, she was more and more thankful that Moochie was a Robinson. She might not have done much right in her young life, but she picked a good father for her baby.

After Dwayne helped Jon-Jon get ready for his appointment, she, Jon-Jon, and Moochie set off for the hospital. It wasn't until they reached the hospital that her cell phone rang. "Oh, I forgot my mother!"

"Is that her calling?"

"Yes."

"Answer it."

Marquita shook her head. "I can't just answer the phone if I'm not on my way to pick her up. She will go ballistic."

"It's not that deep, Marquita."

Marquita got out of the car, opened the trunk, and took out Jon-Jon's wheelchair. She opened his door as her phone rang again.

"Marquita, just answer the phone and tell her you are on your way."

"I can't just leave you here."

"Yes, you can. Go pick her up, and I'll call my mom."

Marquita wouldn't hear of it. "Your mom has been too good to me. She deserves some time to herself." The phone kept ringing, so she answered it. "Hey, Mom, I'm on my way, so just sit tight, okay?"

Marquita hung the phone up, then told Jon-Jon, "I'll go grab my mom and then come right back here to get you. I'll be back before your session ends, so you don't need to call Trish. Okay?"

"That works."

Marquita took Moochie out of his baby seat and walked into the hospital while Jon-Jon pushed his wheelchair. "I just want to see where you're going to be before I leave."

"Physical therapy is on the second floor. I'll show you."

Marquita went to the rehabilitation area with Jon-Jon. She helped him get settled, then left the hospital and drove to the other side of town, about thirty-five minutes away, to pick up her mother. When Gloria got in the car, Marquita said, "I'm so, so sorry that I'm late. I forgot that I was supposed to pick you up this morning."

"How'd you forget when I called and asked you about this last night?"

Her mother's lip poked out like a petulant child. Marquita didn't want to tick her off further because Gloria could go from one to fifty in a matter of seconds, but there was no way she was going to leave Jon-Jon at that hospital while she spent hours with her mother. "I dropped Jon-Jon off at the hospital. I need to pick him up to take him back home, and then you and I can spend as much time as you want at the store."

Gloria let out a long-suffering sigh. "So those people mean more to you than your family, huh?"

Rolling her eyes, Marquita said, "I never said that, Mama. I'm just trying to do what's right. Jon-Jon and his family have been good to me."

"They aren't your family!" Gloria yelled at Marquita. "And if you roll your eyes at me again, I'm going to pop you in the back of your neck."

Marquita sped down I-485, trying to get back to the hospital as fast as possible. "Mom, calm down. You don't have anything else to do today but go to the grocery store. I promise I will get you there."

Gloria folded her arms around her chest and turned her face to the window.

Marquita was rarely graced with peace and quiet when in her mother's company, but Gloria didn't say another word to her all the way to the hospital. She looked at the time on the dashboard as she pulled into the hospital parking lot. She had been gone for an hour and twenty minutes. So, as soon as she parked, Marquita jumped out of the car. She opened the back door and unlatched Moochie from his car seat. "I'll be right back, Mama."

Gloria didn't respond. She just kept looking out the window as if she spotted something she couldn't take her eyes off of.

Marquita hurried to the second floor. Jon-Jon was at the receptionist desk scheduling his next appointment.

"How did it go?" Marquita asked as she stood next to him.

Jon-Jon put hands on his legs and rubbed them. "I'm sore. This was some hard work."

"Maybe you should take a pain pill before your next appointment."

"I'm going to need something because this was a lot." Then

Jon-Jon looked at Marcus. "But if it means I'll be able to do the things I want to do with him, then it's worth it."

Putting a hand on his shoulder, Marquita's eyes brightened. "Moochie has a good dad." They held eye contact for a minute before they headed for the door.

"John, wait a minute." A man in a white lab coat approached them.

"Hey, Dr. Phillips. It's good to see you." Jon-Jon shook the doctor's hand.

"It's good to see you. Your therapist told me that you had a really good session today."

"I'm trying, Doc." Jon-Jon then turned to Marquita. "Let me introduce you to my girl, Marquita, and my baby, Marcus."

Dr. Phillips shook Marquita's hand and smiled at Marcus. "So, am I looking at the reason for your newfound inspiration?"

"You better believe it, Doc. I'm going to do everything I can to make my son proud. I'm not giving up on these legs just yet."

As they made their way to the elevator, Marquita said, "So I'm your girl, huh?"

Sheepishly ducking his head while rolling the wheelchair inside the elevator, he said, "I didn't want to call you my baby's mama. Sorry if I overstepped."

"Boy, bye. You can call me your girl anytime. And you're right, it does sound a lot better than just being your baby's mama." She just wished she was truly his girl.

As the hospital doors opened and they headed toward the car, Marquita heard her mom yelling out of the window. "Ain't nobody paying you to watch me, so stop staring over here before I come over there and poke your eyes out."

Her mom got out of the car and stalked over to a car that was a few feet away. The driver backed out of the parking spot and sped off. "I thought so," Gloria said, then turned around and started walking back to Marquita's car.

"Mama! What are you doing?" Marquita rushed to the car.

"You told me you would be right back. How long am I supposed to wait out here with people gawking at me?"

"Were you talking to yourself again?" Her mother did that when she got really angry.

"No, I wasn't talking to myself," Gloria mimicked her daughter, then kicked her car. "I was stuck in this pile of junk, waiting on you, and people were staring at me."

"Mom, don't kick my car. This is the only transportation I have."

Jon-Jon rolled up to the car. "Is this your mom, Marquita?"

Marquita wanted to be like the Incredible Shrinking Woman and become so small that no one saw her. She always wanted to disappear when Gloria had one of her fits.

"Yeah, I'm her mama and that should mean something. I shouldn't be treated like secondhand trash for the likes of you."

People in the parking lot were staring because Gloria was causing a scene. Marquita had been through this a thousand times, but she didn't want Jon-Jon seeing this, not when he had just called her his girl and not when she was just starting to feel like she and Moochie might have a chance at a normal life. "Let's just get in the car and go."

Marquita put the baby back in his car seat and strapped him in. She opened the front door for Jon-Jon, then wondered what she did that for.

"I'm your mama. If anything, I should be getting in the front." Gloria started railing against all the injustices of the world again.

"Just help me get in the back. I'll sit next to Moochie," Jon-Jon told Marquita.

"But your mom said that you need to be able to stretch your legs out."

"I'll just walk!" Gloria yelled.

"Mama, please stop."

"Hi, John, is everything okay? Do you need help getting in the car?"

Marquita heard a woman talking to Jon-Jon. She swung around to see who it was and was instantly mortified. The white lady who caused Jon-Jon's accident was standing next to him while holding onto the arm of some old lady. "What are you doing here?"

"My mother has an appointment with her doctor. Can I help you with anything?" Alexis asked.

Marquita shook her head. "We're good." Why she said that, she didn't know. Anyone watching could tell they definitely weren't good.

Jon-Jon said, "I'd appreciate it if you can help Marquita get me in the car. My dad helped her before we left home."

Marquita turned back to her mother. "Mama, if you can just please get in the backseat. As soon as I drop Jon-Jon off, you'll be able to get in the front."

Gloria pointed toward Jon-Jon. "Why do you even care about him stretching out his legs? He wasn't the one babysitting Moochie when you first had him. That was me."

Her mother was exhausting. Marquita was about to cry. Their arguments often ended in tears and screaming.

"What's your mom's name?" Alexis asked Marquita.

"Gloria."

Alexis walked around to the other side of the car and introduced herself to Gloria. She then said in a calm and soothing voice, "I understand how you feel about this situation, but your daughter is just trying to help John out in his time of need."

"She should be helping me," Gloria complained.

Alexis nodded. "It looks to me like you did a good job with your daughter because she really cares about helping others. She had to get that from you."

Gloria looked over at Marquita. Her lips tightened. "Whatever. Let's just get going." Gloria opened the back door, got into the car, and slammed the door.

Alexis came back around to the front of the car and helped Marquita get Jon-Jon seated.

Marquita had first been mortified to have Alexis run up on them while her mother was acting like she was fresh out of a straight jacket, but after witnessing how well the woman was able to get Gloria to calm down and get in the car, she was so thankful. "How did you do that?"

Alexis winked. "One day I'll tell you my secret."

As Alexis walked away with her mother, Marquita got in the car and then backed out of the parking spot. She drove Jon-Jon home as fast as she could, all the while praying that her mother would not show out when they arrived at Jon-Jon's house. *Please Lord, just let her stay calm.*

CHAPTER 23

Alexis felt bad for Marquita. When she first met the young lady at the Robinsons' house, she thought the girl had a smart mouth and was a bit rude. But after seeing Marquita's mother, Alexis understood exactly why Marquita responded to people in the manner she did. She wished there was some way she could help, but right now her focus was on her own mother.

Vivian's doctor's appointment hadn't yielded anything positive or negative. She was holding on, and that was good enough for now. Alexis wanted to do something nice for her mother, so she googled the phone number to Coopville Farm. Her uncle Douglas was a farmer, just as his daddy and granddaddy had been. Her mother had gotten into some big fight with her family and had vowed to never return to the farm. Alexis hadn't seen her uncle since she was twelve.

"Can I speak with Douglas Cooper, please."

"Speaking," he said.

Alexis got excited. "I'm so happy to be speaking to you. It's been a long time."

"If you're calling for peaches, you might not be so happy when I tell you that they were destroyed in the storm. We still have plenty of chickens though."

Whenever she called family members for any of her clients, she pretty much got right to the point. So that's what she did now. "My mother's name is Vivian Cooper. This is Alexis, Uncle Douglas. I haven't heard your voice in so long. I'm just happy to have you on the phone."

Complete silence.

"Hello? Uncle Douglas, are you there?"

"I'm here. You just took me by surprise. I haven't seen you or my sister in more than twenty years. To be honest, I didn't think she was alive."

"She is." Alexis didn't know how much longer, but for now, her mother was alive. "I think it would do her some good to see you. Do you think you can visit her sometime soon?"

There was a heavy pause, he cleared his throat. "No, not possible. It's not a good time."

"I wouldn't ask if it wasn't important." Maybe if she told Douglas why this was so important, he would change his mind. "My mother may not have much longer to live. It would bless her heart to see you again." She didn't tell him that her mother had been asking for Grandma Joyce. She didn't want to shine any further light on her mother's mental state, neither did she want to say or do anything that might make him back out.

"I-I don't know. Vivian and I are like oil and water."

"Oh, but she would love to see you." She gave him her telephone number and address. "Please think about it." He agreed to think about it and then hung up.

Alexis put the phone down on the kitchen table and filled a pot of water for the spaghetti noodles she planned to cook for dinner. She opened the refrigerator and took out the hamburger meat, put it in an iron skillet, and started browning it.

Michael blew into the kitchen with Ella on his heels. "What in the world are you letting your mother tell my children?"

"It's no big deal, Daddy," Ella said. "Granny was just kidding. I didn't know you'd get so mad, or I wouldn't have told you."

Alexis turned off the fire underneath her meat. "What are you so upset about, Michael?"

"Why would you let your mother tell my children that school isn't important because actors don't need a formal education?"

Alexis knew that comment out of her mother's mouth wasn't going to end well. She thought Ethan would be the snitch because he told everything he knew. But since Ella was the one who spilled the beans, Alexis knew why and she wasn't happy about it. "Have you been quizzing them about my mother?"

"You allow them to be in the room with Vivian unsupervised. I have a right to know what she's filling their heads with."

Alexis turned to her daughter. "Ella, do you enjoy spending time with your grandmother?"

Ella's head bobbed up and down. "I do, Mommy. Granny is lots of fun."

"Can you go sit with her right now so I can finish dinner?"

"Okay." Ella bounced her way out of the kitchen.

Taking several deep breaths, Alexis turned back to her husband. Her eyes shot daggers in his direction.

"You have no right being mad at me. Your mother is filling our children's heads with nonsense."

"Oh, so now they are *our* children again. A minute ago, I was only hearing about your children."

"Of course they're *our* children. But it was irresponsible of you to bring your mother into this house. Ethan and Ella have not been exposed to this kind of stuff, and I don't want them knowing that there is mental illness on your side of the family."

She and Michael rarely argued. She wanted to make sure he was happy because he had done so much for her. But things had changed, and Michael needed to understand that. "She's not well, Michael."

"Then she should be in a hospital."

"Michael, please listen to me. The doctors don't think my mother has much longer to live." She was practically begging him to understand. To have some compassion.

But Michael just repeated, "All the more reason for her to be in the hospital."

She was done. He would never see things her way. She turned back to the stove and finished her meal while pretending Michael was nowhere in sight. She had no more words for him. They would live together in silence until he apologized for being such a jerk.

The following morning, Alexis fixed a bowl of oatmeal and then went upstairs to her mother's room. Each morning, Alexis steeled herself as she opened the door, not knowing if her mother might have passed during the night. Then her heart filled with joy as she caught a glimpse of her mother lounging in bed, watching television or reading.

"Good morning! How are you feeling?" Alexis would always ask while watching her mother's reaction, as if she would be able to tell if bleeding inside the head was going on by the way her mother responded.

"I won't be running a marathon this morning, but I'm fair for a square."

"Mother, I think you missed your calling as a comedian." Alexis sat the breakfast meal in front of her.

Vivian laughed. "Maybe I should try some stand-up."

"Eat your oatmeal before you go running off to some comedy club."

Michael had dropped the kids off at summer camp, so Alexis had several hours free. She sat down in the chair as her mother ate her breakfast and asked, "What would you like to do today?"

Putting her spoon down, Vivian turned to her daughter. "I'd like to get out of this bed and go for a drive that doesn't involve a hospital visit."

Alexis was about to give her mother all the reasons why they couldn't leave the house today. Michael's parents, Susan and Dave Marshall, were arriving to spend the weekend with the kids. She needed to whip up a meal befitting the Marshalls. But they have never liked anything she cooked anyway, so she might as well do take out. "Get dressed, Mom. We're going for a ride."

Thelma and Louise were about to bust out of the house. She would take her mother on an adventure like the ones Vivian used to take her on when she was a kid.

They drove around Matthews Township with the AC on and the windows down so they could breathe in the air. She and her mother played the Would You Rather and I Spy games. Then they got on I-485 and switched to the license plate game where players have to find a license plate from each state. The player is given a point for each state found. By the time they were taking the exit to get off the highway, Vivian had twenty points to Alexis's seven. "I guess you won," Alexis told her mother.

"Of course, I won. You had to keep your eyes on the road in front of you, but I was able to look all around to find my license plates. It was still a good game."

Alexis had never imagined that a road trip with her mother could be as much fun as it was. She was truly enjoying herself with this woman whom she hadn't understood for most of her life. Alexis pulled off the highway and headed up Carowinds Boulevard.

Vivian started humming the words to "I'll Fly Away."

Alexis found herself wondering if her grandmother had ever sung a song about living and striving to get through day by day at that church of hers. Alexis would love to hear something different from her mother.

When Alexis turned onto the road that took them to Carowinds amusement park, Vivian got excited. Alexis smiled to herself as she parked the car and then turned to her mother. "Remember when you used to bring me here so we could watch the fireworks on the Fourth of July?"

"We would sit in the Purple Rain van and see the best fireworks in Charlotte." Vivian's eyes were wide as she glanced around. "Are they doing fireworks today?"

"No. That was last week."

The light in Vivian's eyes dimmed a bit. "Oh," was all she said.

Alexis was second-guessing herself. She thought her mother would like to see a place where they shared a happy memory. Maybe she should have brought her here on Fourth of July instead. So much had been going on that she hadn't thought to do it last week.

Alexis glanced at the clock on the car dashboard. She then put a hand on her mother's shoulder. "You know what, Mom? Let's go pick up the kids. I have an idea how I can make up for this."

Vivian patted her hand. "You don't owe me anything. It was nice seeing Carowinds again. I don't need the fireworks."

Alexis heard what her mother said, but she also knew this woman. She needed the fireworks. They picked up the kids and went home. Alexis told the kids to change into their swimsuits and meet her out back. She and her mom put on swimsuits as well. Alexis made sandwiches. Then she took out her blender and threw some strawberries, lemons, ice, and a bit of sugar in it and made slushies.

While the kids were lounging by the pool with their grandmother, Alexis went into the garage and pulled out the leftover fireworks the kids had from last year. It was still daylight, and Alexis wasn't sure if any of these fireworks would light up after sitting in the garage all year, but she was going to give it a try. She just hoped none of her neighbors felt like calling the police.

"What do we have here?" Vivian put her slushie down as she sat up, eyes lighting up again as she saw the fireworks box.

Ethan was downing a sandwich. His eyes got big. "I didn't know we had fireworks. Why didn't we light them last week?"

"Mommy, are you going to light them now or wait until it gets dark?" Ella asked.

Turning to her mother, Alexis said, "It's your call, Mom. Now or later?"

"I've waited my whole life for this or that. I don't care that it's not dark yet. Let's do some fireworks."

The kids shouted, "Yay!"

Alexis found three ground spinners, two rockets, and a Roman candle. She lit the ground spinners first. Her mother propped her feet on the lounge chairs and Ella and Ethan jumped back. They all looked in wonder as the spinners turned round and round, releasing sparks in all directions.

"That was cool!" Ella shouted.

"Do another one," Ethan said.

Alexis took a bottle and lit up the rockets one at a time. Into the sky they flew and then burst into the air, with thunderous noise along with dazzling sparkling effects. Next, Alexis took the Roman candle out of the box and held it in her hand.

It looked like a long tube with the colors of the red, white, and blue flag draped around it. She lit the string that hung from the bottom and then stretched out her arm toward the sky. And then *boom, boom, boom.* One by one, colorful balls of light exploded out of the candle and seemed to dance in the sky. The colorful balls of light flashed, exploded, and crackled before they fizzled out. It was a beautiful display.

Vivian slapped her thigh, then bobbed her head back and forth. With wild eyes she cackled and cackled and cackled. In another time and place, the outburst would have unnerved Alexis. She would have looked around to see who was watching and wondered at the expressions on the faces of onlookers. But not today, because today she recognized the expression on her mother's face as joy. Vivian was happy and being her authentic self.

The thought that her mother was able to experience this moment of joy with her brought tears to her eyes. She wiped them away and then bent down and dug into the firework box one more time and pulled out sparklers. "Look, Mom, I found something you can handle."

Alexis handed one each to the kids and to the biggest kid of them all, her mother. She lit them and the four of them twirled and twirled around the backyard as the sparklers let off dazzling light.

They were so happy and so full of light themselves that Alexis forgot all about the fact that Michael's parents were due to arrive. That is, until Michael opened the patio door and stared at them as if they had committed some cardinal sin. "What in the world is going on out here? Were you the one letting off those fireworks?"

She, the kids, and her mother had been laughing and smiling while they twirled with the sparklers. Alexis was still smiling as she told Michael. "We were just having fun. The kids missed out on the fireworks last week because it was the furthest thing from my mind. So, we decided to shoot off the few that we had in the garage."

With a face full of irritation, Michael said, "The fireworks you just shot off are illegal in North Carolina. That's why we drive over to South Carolina to do our fireworks every year."

How had she forgotten that? "Well, we're done, so hopefully no one has reported us."

Michael stepped out into the yard. He glanced over at Vivian, who was still twirling with the sparkler that had lost its light. That's when she noticed Susan and Dave Marshall standing in the doorway. Dave had this disapproving frown on his face as he looked at her.

Michael's father had this way about him that made her feel like an interloper in her own home. She always felt like she needed to apologize for not being the person they thought their son deserved. She seriously doubted if they ever questioned if Michael deserved her. But she was beginning to wonder if loving a man like Michael was truly worth all that she had given up.

CHAPTER 24

F eeling both nervous and excited for what the day would bring, Trish dressed in a gray pantsuit with a soft pink shirt. Her pumps were two shades darker than her pantsuit. She was looking good and ready to go to war with her son at the arbitrator's office.

Dwayne had to go to work, so he could not attend the meeting with them. This may have been for the best, because if that arbitrator even looked like he wasn't on their side, Dwayne would probably bust a gasket. Their attorney already told them that they needed to be calm, present the facts, and even schmooze a little bit.

Dwayne was not a schmoozer, but he had been a tremendous help to her as they got ready for the meeting. He had even helped Jon-Jon get dressed.

Trish thanked him when she entered the living room and saw that Jon-Jon was ready to go.

"I didn't do much," Dwayne confessed. "Jon-Jon is getting stronger. He situated his wheelchair and got himself out of bed this morning."

Trish's eyes lit up. "Jon-Jon, I'm so proud of you."

Her son grinned. His expression showed that he was proud of himself as well. "I'm sorry I gave you such a hard time about physical therapy. It has really done wonders. My trainer is teaching me how to be self-sufficient."

"Good for you, Jon-Jon." She didn't want to make a big deal of it, so she took her keys out of her purse while praying that her joy wouldn't express itself with tears. "Well, let's get going."

Dwayne walked out to the car with them in case Jon-Jon needed help, but all he had to do was put the wheelchair in the trunk after Jon-Jon lifted himself into the car.

"I just hope Alexis keeps her word and doesn't contest anything during arbitration."

"She's a nice lady, Mom," Jon-Jon said. "I saw her at the hospital last week; she and Marquita got me back in the car when Marquita's mom flipped out on us."

"Marquita told me about that. It's a sad situation. I understand why the girl can't keep a job. When I met her, I did not think she had much home training and now I know why." Playfully nudging Jon-Jon, she added, "You sure can pick 'em."

"Ma, it's not like that. Marquita is a real chill girl. She doesn't even seem to mind that I'm in a wheelchair. She's just cool people. I give her mad props for that."

Trish kept driving, but she was not going to let this moment slip before instilling some godly wisdom into her son. "I am so thankful for Moochie because he brought so much joy back into our home."

"Yeah, he did that," Jon-Jon agreed.

"I know your dad already talked to you about this, but I need to make sure that you understand you weren't raised to have babies here, there, and everywhere. I always imagined that you would get married and then bring a bunch of rock-head babies to the house so I could spoil them rotten."

Jon-Jon put a hand on his mother's arm. "Mom, I hear you. I don't want you thinking you did anything wrong. You raised me right. I messed up."

"I didn't even know that you were seeing anyone last summer. You never brought her to meet us, and we've always been introduced to the girls that you've dated."

"You want the real?"

That was Jon-Jon's way of asking if she wanted him to tell her things she really didn't want to hear. "Yes, please give me the real."

"I guess I just got big-headed when I left for college. I had all these scouts looking at me, telling me I was going pro. When I came home that summer, I stopped going to church and hanging with my friends from youth group. I thought I was the man and didn't need all of that."

"Then you met Marquita," Trish finished. "And since you weren't listening to those God whispers anymore, you did what you wanted to do."

"Exactly." Jon-Jon turned his head away from his mom and stared out the window for a second. Then he turned back to her. "Do you think my accident was like a punishment from God or something?"

"No, Jon-Jon, don't think like that. God loves you and wants the best for you. Remember, the Bible declares that all have sinned and come short of His glory."

"So you think God is cool with Moochie? I mean, 'cause my son is innocent in all of this."

"All life is precious to God, and don't you ever forget that." Trish had no idea her son was allowing the Enemy to invade his mind with thoughts of unworthiness. God was not mad at her son. His accident was not a consequence of his actions. "Jon-Jon, you know something that I had to learn?"

"What?"

"Sometimes bad things happen to God's people, but even in the bad, if we keep praying for God to turn it around in our favor, we will eventually see the good in it."

They pulled up to the arbitrator's office. Trish turned off the car and turned to Jon-Jon with hands extended. "Can we pray?"

"I'd like that, Mom."

Together, they went before the throne of grace, asking for forgiveness and mercy. They asked for right judgment and favor with the arbitrator today. Trish believed God heard every word of their prayer.

She would keep speaking words of faith and encouraging herself in what God had already done for her and Dwayne through the years. In truth, she would never forget that red cardinal showing up in their backyard. It was like a sign to her that God's got them.

When they entered the arbitrator's office, Trish was surprised to see a lawyer seated on the side where Alexis should be. She and Jon-Jon sat down as the attorney introduced himself. "Will Alexis be joining us?"

The attorney's name was Bill Stevens. He said, "Ah, no."

"Okay, because I didn't think we needed a lawyer for arbitration." At least that's what Trish's attorney had told them. Maybe rich folks used attorneys whether they needed them or not.

"Mrs. Marshall had a family emergency to deal with, but she sent me here with full instructions."

They had agreed on one arbitrator for the hearing because the case seemed simple enough. Alexis hit Jon-Jon, and now she needed to pay for the damage she caused.

A man so tall he had to bend his knees and lower his head to get below the entryway, came into the room.

The man glanced at his watch and then sat down at the head of the table. "I'm Joseph Ridgeway, the arbitrator for your case."

Trish turned to Jon-Jon. "You ready?"

He nodded.

Mr. Ridgeway looked from one side of the table to the other. "This is a straightforward process. If you have written submissions, I will take them now."

Trish's attorney had secured written statements with witness signatures for this meeting. Her written statements came from three different people who stopped to help after the accident. They also gave statements to the police as to what occurred. She also included statements from Jon-Jon's high school coach.

Alexis's attorney told the arbitrator, "We do not have witness statements. We have already read the statements the defendant's attorney gathered and have no objection to those."

An eyebrow lifted, Mr. Ridgeway said, "Are you sure you don't want to submit any written statements?"

"My client was specific about that. She is not disputing that she hit Mr. Robinson."

"Then why are we here?" Mr. Ridgeway asked.

Clearing his throat, the attorney said, "My client's husband wants to ensure that the settlement is fair for all concerned."

Trish's eyes narrowed. "What's that supposed to mean? Do you think it's fair that my son is in a wheelchair?"

"No, ma'am, neither I nor my clients are happy about the situation Mr. Robinson is in."

Mr. Ridgeway turned to Jon-Jon. "Would you like to provide any information other than the written statements?"

Jon-Jon glanced over at Trish. Her son was still young. Even though he wanted to be grown, he still did not know how to handle himself out in the real world, but Trish recognized that she had already been speaking too much. "Go on, Jon-Jon. It's time to speak up for yourself."

Trish sat back in her seat and clamped her lips while Jon-Jon provided information about the career he grew up believing he would have. He also told the arbitrator about his new son and how he hoped to be able to provide for his son but wasn't sure how he could do that since he had to figure out another career.

Trish was beaming as she silently prayed for her well-spoken son. He would be just fine, of that, Trish was becoming surer as each day went by. Jon-Jon had struggled with the new reality of his life, but the just-don't-quit son she and Dwayne raised was back, and he was fighting for what was left of his life. No, it wasn't perfect, but it could still be very sweet.

"I think I have enough. I will review all of the information and then get back with you all very shortly," Joseph Ridgeway told them.

When Trish and Jon-Jon arrived home, her phone rang. It was Alexis. Trish answered it as she entered her bedroom to change into something more comfortable. "Hello?"

"Hi. Is this Trish?"

"How are you doing?" Trish kicked her shoes off.

"I've had better days, but I don't want to talk about me. I was calling to see how things went during arbitration today."

"I'm not sure. We'll be on pins and needles until the decision comes back," Trish said.

"My attorney said that Jon-Jon looked good. Did his surgery go well?"

Trish didn't know how much information she should provide. She could hear Dwayne as if he was in her ear, saying, *Don't tell 'em nothing. They're just trying to cheat Jon-Jon out of his money.* "The surgery was needed, and Jon-Jon is recovering."

"I'm happy to hear that. Well, I don't want to hold you. Just wanted to check in on you."

"Your attorney said a family thing kept you from attending the arbitration. Is everything okay on your end?"

"Thanks for asking. My mom is not doing well. I'm trying to get her to rest, but I don't think she knows how to do that."

"I'll say some prayers for her." Then Trish had a thought and, before she could formulate it all the way in her mind, blurted out, "I'm starting this program against distracted driving. I've lined up a few places where I will be speaking. Jon-Jon will also speak on what happened to him. I was wondering if you would be willing to team up with us? You could tell your story so others might understand how much harm distracted driving can bring to families."

Alexis didn't say anything at first, but slowly, very slowly, she said, "I, um . . . I really wish I could help you, but I don't think I can get involved with something like that. I'm sorry."

"Oh." Trish let the shock ring in her tone. "I just thought you'd be willing to do something like this. It's just that you seemed truly sorry for what you did. Others could benefit from hearing from you."

"I don't think I can do this. I'm sorry, but I've got to go." Alexis hung up.

Trish's eyes almost bugged out of her head. She couldn't believe what had just happened. Alexis had seemed so nice, like she truly cared about what she had done to Jon-Jon. Why wouldn't she want to help them bring awareness to an issue like this?

So much anger was boiling inside Trish that she wanted to throw her cell phone across the room. But she had cancelled the insurance on their cell phone to save money, so if she broke her phone, she wouldn't be able to go out and get another one.

A knock on her door took her mind off of doing damage to things she couldn't replace. "Come in."

Marquita nudged the door open and peeked her head inside. "Are you busy?"

Trish didn't feel like talking, but she didn't want to push Marquita away just because Alexis Marshall had just blown her off. "What's going on?"

"I wanted to talk to you." Marquita stepped into Trish's room and leaned against the wall, hands behind her back, head hanging low. "I got the job."

"The telemarketing job you interviewed for last week?"

Marquita nodded. "It's part-time, so I'll still be able to help with Jon-Jon."

"This is good news, Marquita. Why don't you sound excited about it?"

"I don't know. I guess I'm scared that I'm going to fail again. Jon-Jon is already making jokes about me getting fired within two weeks."

Trish wanted to go to Jon-Jon's room and give that boy a good thump upside his head. "Don't listen to him, Marquita. You can keep a job if you get in there and do your best."

"That's just it. I don't know what my best is. My last boss told me that I wasn't raised right and that's why I couldn't keep a job. I was mad when he said it, but I think he might be right. I just don't know what to do about it."

Trish's heart went out to the girl. She saw potential in Marquita, but it was raw and needed to be refined before she would shine like the jewel she was meant to be. "Do you want help?"

Her eyes filled with tears. "I can't figure out why I can't keep a job. I have this beautiful baby who needs both his parents to work hard so we can give him a good life."

"So, I'm going to ask again. Do you want help?"

"Yes, more than anything."

Trish patted the mattress. "Come sit down next to me."

Marquita pulled away from the wall and sat down next to Trish. "I want to make my son proud of me, the way Jon-Jon is so proud of you and Dwayne. But . . ."

Trish's heart bled for Marquita. The girl should be rejoicing over the fact that she had found a job, but instead her head was hung low as if she'd just received a horrible diagnosis from her doctor. "Have you ever heard the phrase, 'If you know better, you do better'?"

Shrugging, she said, "I don't know."

"I'm going to be honest with you, Marquita. When I first met you, I thought the same thing your old boss thought. I remember shaking my head at the way you talked to us and thinking, *This girl does not have home training.*"

Marquita's hands lifted as she shook them in the air, then dropped them to her lap. "How do I even know if I have"—she did air quotes—"'home training,' if I don't know what it is?"

"Give me the top three reasons you've received for being fired. What exactly did the managers say?"

"Let's see." Marquita started ticking off reasons. "Not coming to work on time and disrespecting customers. I also got fired from a job for fighting one of my coworkers. But you would have fought that woman, too, Trish. She had too much mouth and couldn't back nothing up."

Trish laughed as she scooted back against her headboard. This girl had a lot to learn. Trish had instructed fourth graders on proper etiquette for years. Marquita was a nineteen-year-old with grown woman responsibilities, so she hoped she could get the message across. "I noticed you called me Trish and my husband, Dwayne. Can I tell you that when I was growing up, I was taught to add Mr. or Mrs. onto the front of an elder's name?"

Marquita's nose scrunched, eyes squinted with confusion. "But you and Dwayne . . . I mean, Mr. Dwayne don't look all old like that to me."

In a moment of vanity, loving the fact that she didn't look her age, Trish put her hands to her face and said, "My mama told me that black don't crack." She laughed at her own joke and then became serious again. "It's a sign of respect, Marquita. Adding a Mr. or Mrs. onto the name of someone who is at least twenty-five years older than you says you understand that they have seen more of life than you have. It says that you understand they may have some wisdom to impart to you."

"Okay, but I don't see how that helps me on a job."

Marquita was being honest with her, and Trish liked the way their discussion was going, so she continued. "If you had learned to respect others when you were younger, by the time you started a job, it would have been second nature to you. It would have also helped you understand that being repetitively late to your job is disrespectful because it shows that you don't value other people's time."

"Yeah, but you know how bad the traffic is in this town," Marquita tried to justify herself.

Trish was not letting her off the hook. "Since you know how bad the traffic is, you adjust your schedule to make sure you make it to work on time. If that means leaving your house thirty minutes earlier than you have been leaving, then that's what you do."

Marquita's lip twisted. "One of my bosses told me to do that, but I thought she was being unreasonable and that she should have understood being that she lives in this town just like I do."

"And how did that work out for you?"

"She fired me."

Trish stared at the girl, then asked, "Do you get it now?"

"Okay, I get it. I need to wake up earlier so I can get to work. I can sit in my car and watch TikTok or something if I'm a few minutes early."

Or, Trish thought, *she could go to her desk and start preparing for her day.* Trish wasn't going to push that. If Marquita was willing to adjust her schedule to get to work a little early that was good enough for her. "Now, about this fighting coworkers and disrespecting customers . . ."

Marquita laughed at herself. "I've got this eye-rolling thing that I can't seem to control whenever someone says something that I think is real stupid."

"Aha! Another sign of disrespect."

"I can't help it."

"I want you to pray about your level of respect for other people. It appears to me that you view some of God's people as small and unimportant in the grand scheme of life. So, while you're praying, ask God to show you how important each and every human being is to Him."

"That's deep, Ms. Trish." Marquita leaned forward and hugged her. "Thank you for talking to me today. I'm feeling better about this job now. I'm going to try my best to do what you suggested."

Trish smiled as Marquita left the room. In her darkest hour, that girl showed up on her doorstep. At first sight she had wanted to close the door on her and make it all go away, but she was so thankful that she hadn't done that. Marquita was also a soul that was precious to God. Trish just prayed that she would be able to help Marquita move a little closer to the glory God planned for her on this side of heaven.

CHAPTER 25

A week after the fireworks incident, Uncle Douglas came by to see Vivian. Alexis gave him an ice-cold glass of lemonade and had him take a seat in the family room while she went upstairs to get Vivian. Alexis was thankful that Douglas came to see her mother, but this would be a day of reckoning for her because she had yet to tell her mother the truth about Grandma Joyce.

Vivian had asked to see her mother a couple of times in the last few weeks. Alexis had chosen not to remind her mother that Grandma Joyce died a long time ago because she feared it might set her mother off. She also hadn't wanted Uncle Douglas to be the one to break the news.

Stepping into her mother's room, she took a deep breath. She knew this had to be done, but at the same time she hated that she had to bring her mother back to reality about something like this. "How are you feeling this afternoon?"

Vivian picked up the remote and turned the volume down on *The Price Is Right*. "I was just sitting here wishing I was on this show." She pointed at the television. "I could have won that car and then painted it purple so I could give it to you as a birthday present." Vivian started laughing.

Alexis doubled over in laughter. "Don't do me any favors, Mom. I'm okay with the car I have." Alexis sat down next to her mother. "I have to tell you something, Mom. I have some good news and bad news. Can you handle bad news right now?"

Vivian's eyes lifted toward the ceiling, as if she wanted to linger in her happy place a moment longer. "Give me the good news first."

"Uncle Douglas is downstairs. He came to see you today."

Vivian turned questioning eyes toward Alexis. "Douglas? He wants to see me?"

"Yes, he's waiting to talk to you."

Vivian's eyes got big. "Did Mama come with him?"

Alexis took her mother's hand in hers, patted it. "Remember the bad news I mentioned?"

Vivian nodded her head.

"Grandma passed away."

Vivian drew a sharp intake of breath, then let out a long sigh. "Mama flew away?"

Alexis wanted to cry. Her mom had obviously suppressed this memory because it hurt too much for her to remember. Now, here she was making her mother face reality. Sometimes, reality sucked.

"Come on, Mom. Let's go visit with Uncle Douglas. You haven't seen your brother in a long time."

 ∽

The visit with Uncle Douglas went well. Her mother sat and reminisced with her brother for hours. When he left, Vivian hugged him and cried on his shoulder. Even though she had to bring her mother back to reality on the matter of Grandma Joyce, Alexis felt that she had made the right decision in contacting her uncle.

Later that evening she went to the kitchen and fixed a cheese and cracker snack with sliced green apples for her mother. She was about to take it upstairs, but then it hit her. She and Michael hadn't said two words to each other all day. They couldn't continue on like this. If she had to be the one to humble herself so they could get back to a good space in their marriage, then so be it.

Alexis walked to the back of the house where his office was. She was about to knock on the door, but she heard voices. She had not heard the door chime, but she wasn't surprised. Her brain had been frazzled lately. The kids could be shouting and breaking things in the house, and she wouldn't have noticed.

She could hear Peter. He sounded angry. Alexis started to turn and head upstairs to her mother's room, but then she heard Peter say, "Face it, Michael. We've been caught. Nora knows that Kevin was the real creator of our app, and she's refusing to complete the sale unless we add his name to the design."

"How did she find out?"

That was Michael's voice, and Alexis was absolutely shocked. She had expected Michael to say something like, "You know I designed that app. Nora doesn't know what she's talking about." But instead, he wanted to know how the woman discovered this information.

"You probably don't remember this, because you were so busy with the swim team back then," Peter was saying. "But Kevin and Nora dated for a few weeks during our senior year."

"So why is she busting our chops about this now? She knows Kevin is dead." Michael sounded as if it didn't matter that he'd ripped off a friend. Kevin was dead, so all's well that ends well.

"Nora says that their firm will not take on this liability. I told her about Kevin's kid, and she wants this matter taken care of."

"You told her about the kid?" Michael exploded. "How dumb can you be?"

"Hey, you can lie all you want, but Media Matters Inc. is not going to drag me into court and strip me of what I've worked hard for because we didn't disclose everything upfront." Peter sounded as if he'd had enough of Michael.

"And how are we supposed to find this kid? It's not like either of us kept up with her," Michael said.

"We should have. This could blow up the whole deal."

"So what is Nora's final on this? Is she really prepared to pull out?"

"She's worried that Kevin's app might turn out to be a PR nightmare," Peter said.

"Stop calling it that," Michael said angrily.

Alexis had heard enough. She opened the door and glared at her husband. "Why should Peter stop calling it Kevin's app? Kevin created it, right?"

All the blood drained from Michael's face as he turned toward his wife. "Alexis, what are you doing in here?"

She sat her mother's snack on his desk. "More secrets, Michael. Secrets, secrets, secrets. Everything has to be hush-hush with you."

"What are you talking about, Alexis?" Michael looked tired.

She hoped he was tired of keeping secrets. Alexis turned to Peter. "Did you know that he won't let me tell anyone that my mother has a mental illness? He also wanted to cover up the fact that I caused a kid to be paralyzed because I was reaching for my phone while driving."

Frustration rang in Michael's voice. "Alexis, it's enough already."

But she wasn't finished. She swung back around to Michael. "And now we have another secret. So, my accident didn't hinder the sale of your company at all. It was your secret that did it."

Peter stood up. "I'll call you later so we can finish our discussion."

Michael barely acknowledged Peter's abrupt exit. He was focused on Alexis. "You don't know what you're talking about, so just stop."

"I know exactly what I'm talking about." Her arms flailed in the air. "You've had me so stressed out all these years that if someone discovered my mother's secret it would ruin this make-believe world you created for us. But it's not my secret that's going to do you in, is it?"

"No one needs to know about your mother's illness."

Her eyes narrowed on him. "Would it be so bad if we decided to tell the truth in this family, once and for all?"

"I am always truthful with you. You're my wife, Alexis."

Her hands flailed in the air. "You're not even truthful with yourself, Michael. How could you steal your college roommate's app and claim it for yourself all these years?"

"That's not what happened."

She gave Michael an I-don't-believe-a-word-you-say look as her lips pursed. "Oh, really, then how did it happen?"

Michael's shoulders slacked. He shook his head and turned away from her.

Slamming her palm against his desk, raising her voice. "Don't turn your back on me. Not this time!"

He turned around as she commanded. "Sit down, Alexis. I'll tell you the whole story if you want to hear it."

He almost looked defeated, except the Michael she knew had never let anything defeat him. "What's the deal here, Michael? You made me feel like if I stepped out of line, I would tear down everything you've built for our family. I've kept so many secrets, and now I find out there is yet another secret."

"I know. I know. I should have told you about this, but Kevin died a few months before I met you."

"Why didn't you tell me that the app had been created by your friend? All these years I thought you created that app. Both you and Peter led me to believe that."

Michael sat down next to Alexis. "You have to believe that I was devastated when Kevin died. We were young and so ready to take on life. I thought that he and I would build a business together. And to tell you the truth, our business would be much more successful if Kevin had survived that car crash."

"You have your faults just like the rest of us, but I don't believe you wanted Kevin to die."

"Thank you for that," Michael said, then continued. "After Kevin died, I brought Peter on to handle the financial side of the business while I went to market with our offerings." Michael looked pained as he added, "Kevin's app has been our most successful product."

She put a hand on his thigh. "Oh, Michael, I wish you didn't think you have to be so perfect all the time."

"But I'm not perfect." His jaw clenched as he admitted the truth. "Kevin's app was better than mine."

"So what? You're the one who took it to market. Who's to say that Kevin would have been able to handle that side of the business? You don't do Peter's job, do you?"

Looking as if it almost killed him to admit another weakness, Michael confessed, "I suck at math."

"Exactly, that's why your son is so bad at math."

"It's not funny, Alexis."

"No, Michael, it isn't funny. It's actually very sad that you can't see how wrong you've been all these years."

"Hold on a minute." Michael stood up, paced the floor. "I've done pretty good by this family."

"Yes, you have, but you failed Kevin's family."

The pacing stopped. Michael turned back to Alexis. His eyes begged her to see it his way. "I didn't know what to do, Lexi. All I had was a photo with the baby's name on the back. How was I supposed to find her?"

Now it all made sense to Alexis. "The photo in your desk . . . She's Kevin's child, isn't she?"

He nodded.

"Why did you keep her photo all these years?"

Ringing his hands together. "Just couldn't throw it away."

No longer caring about the secrets her husband wanted to keep, Alexis rushed over to his desk and opened the top drawer and began searching through it. "Didn't you say there was a name on the back of the photo?"

"You don't have to look for it. I remember her name."

Alexis glanced over her shoulder at her husband. "Do you have some other secret in this drawer that you don't want me to see?"

"No, I don't. You can search the drawer if you want, but her name is Kee Kee. Kevin told me about her when she was born, and the name is on the back of the photo. I could never forget a name like that."

Closing his desk drawer, Alexis practically snarled as she confronted him. "If the child's name is etched into your memory, then why haven't you tried to find her? You owe that girl money."

"It's complicated," was all Michael could say.

"Then uncomplicate it." Michael was a real piece of work. It's always about the money with him. "You had the audacity to stress me out about what my accident could do to your company. Think about the PR nightmare you would have if it got out that you cheated a black man who was supposed to be a friend."

Alexis picked up the snack she fixed for her mother and stormed out of his office. For the first time since she laid eyes on Michael Marshall, she felt shame in being associated with him. She felt like he didn't deserve her. How could he have pretended that he developed that app and never bothered to compensate his friend's family?

She needed distance from her husband. She knew he was a bit selfish when she married him, but she never imagined that he was also a liar and a thief. She still loved him. Alexis didn't think anything could change that, but she was not happy with who and what he turned out to be.

When she arrived at her mother's door, Alexis heard the kids. She cracked the door and saw Ethan and Ella on their knees on either side of her mother's bed. Their hands were steepled.

"Okay, now repeat after me," Vivian said. "Now I lay me down to sleep. I pray the Lord my soul to keep."

The kids repeated the words of the prayer.

"If I should die before I wake, I pray the Lord my soul to take."

The kids repeated again.

Then Vivian said, "Now you can ask God anything that you want Him to do for you."

Ethan looked at his grandmother. "Mom and Dad have been arguing a lot lately. Can I ask God to make them like each other again?"

"You sure can," Vivian said as she glanced over toward the door where Alexis stood.

"Thanks, Mom," Alexis mouthed. She waited outside the door to allow the kids to finish their prayers.

When Ethan said, "Is it okay if I ask God for another Nerf gun? My best friend has one with a rip chain and it holds twenty-five darts," she knew it was time to go in.

"I thought you might like a snack." She put the plate on her mother's night table.

"Thank you." Vivian smiled at Alexis. "I was just teaching my wonderful grandkids the prayer my mother taught me when I was a child."

"I appreciate that, Mom. But I don't remember you letting me add gifts for myself in those nighttime prayers." Alexis pointedly glanced at Ethan.

Holding her stomach and laughing as if she was enjoying life, Vivian said, "You can't blame me for having such cute grandkids."

"Well, it's time for these cute kids to go to bed." Alexis shooed them out.

"Ah, Mom, do we have to go?" Ella asked as she stood up.

"Yes, hon, you have day camp tomorrow, so please go straighten your room and then get some sleep."

Alexis sat down in the chair next to Vivian's bed. She marveled at how Ethan and Ella lingered, even as they took their time giving their grandmother a kiss before leaving the room. When she was their age, she dreamed of being away from all the drama. She would have given anything for someone to take her away.

Now, all she wanted to do was spend as much time with her mother as possible. Vivian had experienced so much pain in her life, all Alexis wanted to do was bring her mother joy for the rest of her days. "How are you feeling tonight, Mom?"

"My body feels drained, like I ran the Boston Marathon. I'm hoping that I'll feel better by tomorrow."

"Your visit with Uncle Douglas must have worn you out."

"It did, but I won't complain because I had so much fun talking to him." Smiling as her head rested against her pillow, Vivian then said, "Thank you for calling my brother."

"I was happy to do it." Alexis leaned back in her seat. Not sure what else to say, she just wasn't ready to leave her mother's room. She especially wasn't looking forward to going to her bedroom tonight.

"Sweetie." Vivian's voice was low, like she was falling asleep, but had something she wanted to say.

"Yes?"

"You're finding your voice with Michael, aren't you?"

CHAPTER 26

Trish sat at the kitchen table with Jon-Jon across from her. It amazed her that her son had wheeled himself out to the kitchen and right up to the table.

"Whatcha working on?"

Looking up from her computer, Trish told him, "The schedule for the distracted driving events I told you about."

"So you're really going through with this?"

"You want a sandwich?" Trish got up and went to the fridge.

"We got any of those salt-and-vinegar chips left?"

Trish checked the pantry and came back with a bag of chips. "Got them. You want a turkey sub or an Italian?"

"Italian. And thank you. One day I'm going to make you a sandwich and grab you some chips so you can get some rest."

Trish closed her eyes and slowly inhaled, as though she was breathing in good, clean air after months of taking in smog and smoke-filled clogs of polluted air. Her son's words danced around her ears like a shimmy-shimmy, drum-beating song. "Yeah, well, you just remember that I don't like mayo. Your father has been bringing me subs with mayo for twenty-five years. I just don't understand it."

Jon-Jon laughed. "But you know why he forgets, right?"

She handed him his plate and then sat back down. "Please enlighten me."

"He likes mayo and lots of it. Every time I've gone to the sub shop with him, he makes sure they slather that stuff on his sub."

Trish's eyes rolled heavenward. "I know. That's why I don't ask him to get me a sub."

"Yeah, but Mom, you have to give him some credit. He at least picks up a sub for you when he gets one for himself."

"Whatever." Trish went back to working on her computer while Jon-Jon ate his sandwich. So far she had only received two confirmations for speaking engagements. One would be at Southwest High School and the other would be at the community college she worked at.

It seemed to Trish that most people didn't think distracted driving was such a big thing, despite the fact that one out of every four accidents in the United States was caused by someone texting and driving. If it was the last thing she did, Trish was going to make sure that people understood just how wrong-headed it was to text and drive.

Jon-Jon finished his sandwich, then rolled his wheelchair to the other side of the table. "I thought you were just working on your schedule." His eyes widened with surprise. "Did you create a whole website about distracted driving?"

"I sure did. I even have some of your football photos on the site. I hope you don't mind. I'm trying to get reporters interested in these events. It's important to me to reach as many drivers as possible."

"No, Mom, I don't mind. You are really serious about this, huh?"

Trish turned to her son and put her hand on his chin, feeling the stubble beneath her fingers. He still had a long way to go in his recovery. He wasn't allowing her to go with him to his rehab appointments anymore. Marquita took him. Her son wanted more independence, and that was okay. "I'm very serious, son. You are finally finding your way, and I'm thrilled for you. Still, this was and is the hardest thing this family has ever gone through. If I can stop one family from experiencing tragedy because of some inconsiderate texter, then that's what I'm going to do."

"Tell you what, count me in, Mom. When you go to speak to

these kids, I want to be there to show them the dangers of texting while driving."

"That makes me happy, Jon-Jon. But if it's going to put you into another depression, then I'd rather you not attend." Jon-Jon had completed three video visits with Dr. Vance. Things were going well. Her son was no longer talking about not wanting to live, and she wanted to keep it that way.

"I'm good. I'm free any day except this coming Friday. I'm going out with Marquita to celebrate her two weeks on the job."

Grinning at Jon-Jon, Trish nudged him. "Boy, when that girl first came into this house, I wondered what in the world you had been thinking, but I like her."

"Marquita's not perfect, but she's good people. Oh, and we both wanted to thank you for helping me babysit Marcus while she's at work."

"Anything to help that girl get to work on time, and I love having my little Moochie here."

"Yeah, but you didn't have to do it. You didn't have to do everything you've done to help me. I just want you to know that I appreciate you, and I'm so thankful that you are my mother."

"Stop, Jon-Jon. You are going to make me cry. I need to get this website up and running and I really don't know what I'm doing."

Jon-Jon leaned forward, picked up his mother's laptop, and set it in front of him. "I took a web design class in college. I can help you with this."

"Now I'm really about to cry. I can't remember a time when you volunteered to help me with anything. Remember how you used to run out of the room if I asked you to get me a glass of water or take a plate back to the kitchen for me?"

"Mom, I was ten."

"And now you're twenty and growing all up on me."

The phone rang. Trish looked at the caller ID, but no name

registered on the display. Before Jon-Jon's accident, she would have let the call go to voice mail, but receiving that call from the hospital changed everything for her. You never know when someone might need help. If it was a scammer on the other end, she would just hang up. "Hello?"

"Hello, this is Joseph Ridgeway. Can I speak with John Robinson, please?"

She handed Jon-Jon the phone. "It's for you."

After saying, "This is John Robinson," Jon-Jon spent the next few minutes nodding and giving a couple of mmm-hmms and "Yes, that sounds great." Finally, he said, "I'll speak to my parents and get back to you."

Jon-Jon was big-cheesing as he hung up the phone. He turned to his mom. "He's entering a judgment in my favor."

Jumping out of her seat, Trish hugged her son. "That's wonderful, Jon-Jon." As she sat back down, she said, "Tell me the amount. But tell it to me slowly, because if it's less than the hundred thousand you would have received from the insurance company, I'll be fit to be tied and ready for a fight."

"But you do your fighting on your knees, remember?"

She had told her son praying about a situation was like taking the fight to God and letting Him go to battle for us so many times as he grew up, but she never knew if he listened or believed her. Trish popped her fingers. "You got that right."

Tears wet Jon-Jon's face as he said, "The awarded amount is seven hundred and fifty thousand dollars. I have to sign off on it, but I told him I would speak with you and Dad first."

"Woot! Woot!" Trish stood up and started dancing as if a sweet melody was playing in her head. "With that kind of money, you can go back to school, get your degree, and start a business. That way you'll have something of your own."

"Mom," his voice was full of emotion as he wiped the tears from his face. "I'll be able to take care of Marquita and Moochie like a man, Mama, like a man."

Crying with him, she leaned over and hugged him. "You are a man, Jon-Jon, and I'm so proud of you."

"I can't wait for Dad to get home so I can tell him about it. I just hope he's okay with it. I'm tired of watching y'all struggle while trying to take care of me and these hospital bills."

"Are they covering your hospital bills?"

Jon-Jon nodded. "They will cover the hospital bills for the next three years."

Later that night when Dwayne arrived home, he looked tired and worn out. He put a bag of Sour Patch Kids candy on the kitchen counter and said, "Where's my sour patch?"

"Just shaking my head. Just shaking my head." Trish scooped up the bag of candy. "It's sugar patch, Dwayne. I'm too sweet to be sour," she said with her lip poked out.

"Then why you look like you're sucking on sour lemons?" Frustration showed on his face as he said, "My bad. I got the phrase wrong, but I got the candy right. So, it's all good."

"Oh, it's better than good in this hood," Trish exploded with excitement. "Go check on Jon-Jon, he's got something to tell you."

Trish stayed in the kitchen to eat a few of her Sour Patch Kids candies. She heard Dwayne say, "Are you serious? Don't play with me. Tell me the truth."

"It's real, Dad. All I have to do is sign the papers."

Trish walked over to Jon-Jon's room and stood in the doorway as tears rolled down Dwayne's face. He hugged his son. "Now, I don't want you spending this money like you're some baller. If you make the right money moves, this could set you and Moochie up for a good future."

They talked a little while longer. Then Trish went to her room and got ready for bed. She was about to turn the light out and let her head hit the pillow when Dwayne said, "How was your day, Trish?"

She thought about that for a moment, then smiled. "I had a good day."

"Mine wasn't too bad either."

"I'm thankful, because there's a lot less stress around here, even with a fuller house." Trish positioned herself on her side.

Dwayne went into the closet, then came back carrying a gift bag. "I know your birthday isn't until next month, but I bought you something."

Sitting up, Trish took the bag from her husband. She could feel her eyes growing wide with wonder. It had been a while since they had extra money to purchase gifts for each other. "When did you buy this?"

"Stop with all the questions, woman." He pointed at the bag. "Open it."

The box had some weight to it, so she knew it wasn't lingerie, even though she would have enjoyed having another nightgown. Putting her hand in the bag, she pulled out a deep-tissue therapeutic hand-held massager. "Oh, Dwayne, how on earth did you know I needed something like this?"

"I've watched you crack that neck of yours so many times that I've been worried it was going to fall off," Dwayne joked.

Like a giddy kid at Christmas time, Trish jumped up and down. "Plug it up for me." She pointed at a spot on her neck. "I need that thing right now."

Dwayne opened the box, pulled out the hand-held device, and plugged it up. Turning it on, he ran it across Trish's neck and upper back.

"Aww, now that feels like heaven."

"I thought you'd like it."

She didn't just like it. This was better than a nightgown. It was giving her new life. Trish shimmied her shoulders when he finished. "Thank you, babe."

They climbed into bed. Dwayne moved close to his wife, then pulled her into his arms. "Anything for my baby."

As Trish's eyes closed, she snuggled up to her man, loving the warmth that he brought into her life. Silently, she prayed, *Thank You for my husband, Lord. Keep speaking to his heart so we can grow more in love each and every day.*

CHAPTER 27

Parking her car, Marquita was feeling good. She'd now been on her job for two weeks, and this was the tenth straight day that she had arrived to work on time. Jon-Jon was taking her out to celebrate after his physical therapy appointment.

Breathing a sigh of relief, she looked at the clock on her dashboard. She had made it to work with ten minutes to spare. She turned off her car and used her cell phone to pipe music through her car. A few of her brown-nosing coworkers walked past her car glancing over at her as if she was doing something wrong.

She wanted to roll down her window and tell them to run on into work and collect their brownie points for being ten minutes early. Marquita didn't care what they did, as long as they stopped staring at her while she danced to the music in her car. How was that their business?

Eve, the dark-haired, blue-eyed devil who sat in the cubicle across from hers, got out of her car. She stood in the parking lot for a moment, putting her hands on her hips as she stared into Marquita's car and shook her head.

"What?" Marquita shouted at her.

Eve turned away, strutting into the building like she was running things and was about to be late for a meeting.

These white girls on this job were a trip. They were working this low-skill job, just like she was, but they acted like they were so much better, like they had stock in the company and owned fabulous homes.

Maybe they did. People like that got a lot further in this country than she ever would. Truthfully, Marquita didn't care if they owned the whole wide world. She just wanted them to mind their own business. Whatever. She only had four hours to deal with these people and then she would be hanging out with Jon-Jon and Moochie.

After doing a sing-a-long for the third time, Marquita turned off her music, got out of her car, and rushed into the building. If she didn't get in there in the next minute, she would be late, and nobody was going to accuse her of being late. She practically had to shove one of her coworkers out of the way so she could get to her desk. "Dang girl, why you always standing around, getting in the way?"

The girl looked at her, but didn't respond and didn't get out of the way.

What is wrong with these people? Why do they congregate in the halls, holding onto their coffee mugs and yapping it up when they should be working? Marquita put her purse on her desk, sat down, and turned on the computer. "Bring on the customers." Putting her headset on, she was ready for the day to begin.

Before receiving her first call, her supervisor peeked her head into her cubicle. "Can I speak to you for a minute?"

Marquita glanced around to see if another coworker was in her direct vicinity, sticking their nose in her business, before taking her headset off. She didn't know why she was being called to the office. The way Marquita saw it, she had been coming to work on time. She was being nice and helpful to each customer as they called into the office. So what could be the problem?

Sitting down in her supervisor's office, which was more like two cubicles put together with high walls and a door, she wanted to say, "I didn't do it—and don't blame me for something I did not do." Instead, she sat down and waited to hear what her supervisor had to say.

The woman stared at Marquita for a long moment. There was a quizzical expression on her face. "I can't figure you out," she said. "You come to work on time, you're getting good ratings with the customers, but I've received so many complaints about you from your coworkers."

"Ah, they're just some haters." Marquita rolled her eyes as those words flew out of her mouth.

The supervisor shook her head. "During orientation, we tried to express how important being a team player is. Some of your coworkers don't feel comfortable approaching you."

Marquita thought back to orientation. It was her first day on the job, and she was excited to be in an office setting for the first time in her working life. The orientation was a little dry, so she missed some of the information they provided. Even so, she didn't understand this at all.

"Also, this noise you're making in the parking lot is causing a public nuisance."

"How can playing music inside my car be a nuisance?"

"It's loud, and I have reports that when some of our workers look at you, trying to signal that what you're doing is out of order, instead of turning it down, you sing even louder than your music was already playing."

"They were just being nosy, staring in my car, like I'm loitering on the property or something."

The supervisor put an elbow on the desk and leaned forward. "We like working with team players, so if you can't find a way to get along with your coworkers, I'll have to let you go."

"Because of my music?"

The supervisor shook her head. "No, because you are creating a hostile environment with the way you treat some of your coworkers."

Eyes wide, she straightened in her seat. "What! But I just started working here. Can't you give me a warning?" Marquita's eyes filled with tears. How could she lose this job when she did as Trish said? She'd come to work on time and she'd treated her customers right.

"This is your verbal warning, Marquita. The customers give you good ratings, but you're not even making an effort to connect with your coworkers."

Marquita felt awful as she drove home. Well, it was more like her temporary home. Mr. Dwayne expected her to become independent and get her own place soon. How could she do that if she only worked part-time and was about to get fired?

If it wasn't for Moochie, she would give up. But her son deserved the best, and she and Jon-Jon were going to give it to him. She just had to figure out a way to keep her job. Marquita wished she could talk to her mom about things like this, but her mother had never been able to keep a job either. She decided that she was going to tell Trish the truth and see if she could help her figure out how to keep her job.

She walked into the house, took Moochie out of Jon-Jon's arms, and got an instant attitude. "He's wet. I hope we're not going to be late for your appointment, because I've got to change Moochie and clean him up since he soaked through his clothes."

Jon-Jon pointed at the items on his bed. "I'm getting them together now. I've got all of his stuff on my bed, and I was getting ready to change him before you stormed in here acting like Super Nanny."

"Well, I don't like being late."

"Since when?"

Rolling her eyes, like he was irritating her, she said, "Since I started this job. Not that it matters to anyone."

"We have an hour before my appointment, so Moochie not being ready is not why you came in here with this stank attitude. Something else is up, so spill it."

She folded her arms across her chest. "I got a verbal warning today, okay? So let's just cancel the date, because I'm not in the mood to celebrate a job I might not have very much longer."

"What you get a warning for?"

Marquita felt a headache coming on. She had done her best, and her best wasn't good enough. She heard a noise outside Jon-Jon's room.

Trish was in the kitchen. "Let me talk to your mom for a minute." She handed Moochie back to him and then went into the kitchen with Trish.

Trish was warming a bottle at the stove.

Marquita walked up on her. "Why you always warming the bottles in a pot of hot water? I put that bottle in the microwave and get it over with."

Trish smiled at Marquita. "I know all about this microwave generation. Y'all want everything to happen in an instant, but like the good Lord says, 'Better is the end of a thing than the beginning . . . and the patient in spirit is better than the proud in spirit.'"

"Ms. Trish, do you really believe all that stuff? For me it just seems like the harder I try, the more I get knocked down." Marquita pulled out a stool and sat down at the kitchen counter. She put her elbow on the counter and her hand under her chin as she pouted.

Trish turned off the fire and removed the bottle from the water. "You had a bad day?"

Marquita's lip twisted. "I got a verbal warning. My supervisor says I'm getting good ratings from my customers, but my coworkers keep complaining about me."

"Give me your arm." Marquita stretched out her arm, and Trish sprinkled some of the baby's milk on her arm.

"Too hot."

Trish sat the bottle on the kitchen counter. "We'll let it rest a bit. Let's talk." Trish sat at the counter with Marquita. "Now, tell me why you think your coworkers are having problems with you."

"They say I play my music too loud, but I'm in my car, minding my own business. I'm just listening to a little music before I go into work."

"Is that the only complaint they have?"

Scrunching her nose like she smelled something foul, Marquita said, "They think I'm rude."

"I wonder why." Trish started laughing.

"This isn't funny, Ms. Trish. I've really been trying to be a good employee. I don't understand why I can't get it right."

"You're young, Marquita. You are going to make mistakes, but you have to learn how to take constructive criticism. As they say, Rome wasn't built in a day."

"Who says that? I've never heard that."

"Okay, keep on reminding me how young you and Jon-Jon are." Trish laughed again. Then she added, "One of my favorite scriptures in the Bible is out of Galatians. It says, 'And let us not be weary in well doing: for in due season we shall reap, if we faint not.'"

"But those people are getting in my business and going behind my back to the supervisor."

"Remember our talk about respecting others?"

Marquita was about to say something else about them nosy coworkers, but it wasn't going to be respectful at all. So she said, "I have been very respectful to the customers who call into the company. My boss even gave me props about that."

"So, you're making progress. Pat yourself on the back, pray about what else needs to change, and then work on that. But don't give up."

Marquita stood and grabbed the baby's bottle. "Got it. Rome wasn't built in a day."

∽

On Monday morning, Marquita arrived at work about nine minutes before she was scheduled to start. She got out of the car and headed into the building. One of her coworkers got out of her car and started walking beside her.

"No rap music this morning?" Eve asked.

Marquita's eyes narrowed as she looked at the don't-know-how-to-mind-her-own-business woman. She was getting ready to give Eve a piece of her mind, but she could hear Ms. Trish saying, "Be respectful." Did she really have to show respect to people who weren't showing her any?

"I realized that my music was bothering you all, so I have decided not to play it anymore."

"Are you serious?" The expression on her coworker's face was one of disbelief.

Marquita ignored the woman and made it to her desk. She put her purse down, turned on her computer, and pulled out her headset. She had about seven minutes before the phone bank would receive calls. What was she supposed to do, sit there and stare at the walls?

Eve came over to her desk. Marquita braced herself, because if this chick came at her again, it was on. "What can I do for you, Eve?"

Eve put a novel on her desk. "When I come in early, I usually read. I just finished this novel, so if you want to read it, you're more than welcome to it."

"Are you actually being nice to me?" Marquita couldn't believe this.

"I know you got in trouble last week, but I can tell that you're trying to do something different, and I wanted to help."

"And you're being for real? This isn't some scheme to get me in trouble for reading at my desk?" Marquita wasn't about to give Eve another chance to run to the supervisor's office and tell on her. She was almost positive that Eve was the one who told on her. She had to think about Moochie and building a future for the both of them.

"I wouldn't do that. I'm not as bad as you think," Eve told her.

Marquita gave Eve a fake smile. "Okay, well, thank you."

"Or why don't you get some headphones and attach them to your cell phone if you'd rather listen to music?"

Eve didn't sound like she was on a mission to sabotage a coworker. She didn't look like the type of person who got off on doing stuff like that. "So this is for real. You're just trying to help?"

"I really am. I'm also sorry about how I've been treating you. I wasn't raised to treat people like that."

That comment intrigued Marquita. "Did your mom quote Bible scriptures at you and tell you to treat others with respect while you were growing up?"

Eve smiled, looked as if she was remembering some sweet memory. "Your mom was like that too?"

"Girl, bye. My mom is a complete wreck. She don't respect nobody, and she certainly hasn't read the Bible. But my son's other grandmother has been talking to me about respect, and I'm trying to follow her lead."

Eve stuck her hand out to Marquita. "Can we start again?"

"I think I'd like that." Marquita shook her hand. The phones started ringing.

"I've got to get that," Eve said. "We can talk more on our break if you want."

"Works for me." Marquita put her headphones on and answered the call coming into her line.

After that, the rest of Marquita's day was like the start of something special. By the end of the week, her supervisor came to her desk and said, "Hey, I just wanted to thank you for taking heed to our conversation last week."

Marquita was grinning like the sun was shining down on her and Pharrell Williams was singing "Happy" as she walked to her car.

Once she got in the car and started to head home, her cell phone rang. It was her mother. Marquita instantly tensed, wondering what might have happened. Praying that Mark and Kee Kee were okay, she answered. "Hey, Mama, how are you doing?"

"Not too good," Gloria told her.

They just moved into their rental home. She couldn't be having problems already, Marquita thought. *Come on. Please say it's something else.* "What's wrong?"

"I haven't seen my grandson in a few weeks, and I'm trying to figure out why you're keeping him from me."

"What? I'm not keeping Moochie from you. There's just been a lot going on."

"I used to keep him for you while you were at work. Now, all of a sudden, you don't need me no more and I can't see my Moochie."

Marquita almost reminded her mother of the day she told her to go find her baby's daddy. Well, she found him, and he don't mind watching his kid. She took a deep breath. "I'll bring him to see you this weekend."

"I'm not going to be home this weekend."

"Then why are you getting on me about this, when you don't even have time to see him right now?"

Gloria started screaming through the phone: "Because you ain't right, and I called to tell you about yourself!"

Her week had been going so well. Honestly, she would rather have not heard from her mother at all today. She would have stayed happy and could have continued to think of herself as someone of worth, someone who could make a change. But could she really have changed if she was this angry over a conversation with her mother?

Her mother hung up on her and that feeling of wanting to scream until she could scream no more came over her again. It was too much, so she screamed and then screamed again.

CHAPTER 28

D rives seemed to calm her mother, so Vivian had become Alexis's ride-along as she picked up the kids each day. When the kids got in the car and saw their grandmother, their eyes would light up. The oddest part about it was that Alexis was also enjoying herself with Vivian.

They were out on another drive when Vivian put her hand over Alexis's and said, "Thank you."

Smiling at her mother, she asked, "What are you thanking me for?"

"I enjoy spending time with you and the kids. I just wanted to thank you for allowing me to hang around."

"Mom, we are happy to be around you. You don't have to thank me for that."

"You haven't always wanted to be around me and you know it. Even yesterday, I could tell you were upset with me." Somehow, thinking about yesterday tickled Vivian's funny bone, and she threw her head back and cackled like her mind was half there and half somewhere else.

Alexis didn't care about that anymore. Let people stare. They would never know the true essence of Vivian Cooper. They would never know what a wonderful woman she was despite the mental illness that captured her mind so long ago.

Alexis didn't even care about the fit her mother threw in the house last night when it was time to take her medicine and she didn't want to take it. "I'm sorry, Mom. I wish I could go back in time and redo some things. You are truly a wonderful woman, and I am blessed to know you."

"You're doing fine, daughter. No need to redo anything. No time for regrets either."

"I just wish . . ."

Vivian patted Alexis's hand. "You know what we should have done last night, right?"

Alexis couldn't think of anything else they could or should have done. She had tried to do as many things as she thought Vivian would enjoy. "What else would you like to do?"

"We should have made our chocolate-cookie trifle."

Alexis laughed out loud like she hadn't in a very long time. Her mother knew she had acted out last night, but she also remembered what she used to do for her daughter after one of her episodes. "I'll tell you what. Why don't we pick up the items we need while at the grocery and then go home and make the dessert for the whole family?"

"The kids will love it," Vivian said.

They picked up the items at the grocery and then went home and got busy in the kitchen. Ethan entered the kitchen as they filled the jars.

"Awesome!" he shouted. "You're making those chocolate things again."

Alexis turned to her mom. "Ethan's the reason I only had one trifle that day at the nursing home. He ate all but the last one."

Vivian pinched Ethan's cheek. "I'll make sure you get an extra trifle tonight too."

"Thanks, Granny." Ethan skipped out of the kitchen, excitement in his eyes because of the extra dessert.

"Mom, you're spoiling these kids even worse than Michael and I do. I don't know how I'm going to get them in line after—" Alexis had a sudden intake of breath. The last thing she wanted to think about was her mother's death. *Think happy thoughts. Think happy thoughts.*

"You don't have to be scared, Alexis. Death is a part of life. Some people do great things with the life they've been given. Up till now, I've just been existing." Vivian did a tap-tap on her forehead. "Can't get this thing to work right. But you and my grandchildren have a chance to do great things, and that makes me happy."

Alexis didn't know what to say to that. Her mother had been doing so much better with the new medication. Maybe Vivian was the one who would do great things. She just needed the time to do it.

When Michael arrived home, they ate dinner and then enjoyed their dessert. Vivian went to her room to lay down and the kids took off before they could be asked to help with cleaning up.

"Everything was delicious, hon." Michael wrapped his arms around her as she placed the dishes on the counter, getting ready to put them in the dishwasher.

Michael's hands around her used to make her feel so special, like the world couldn't spin on its axis without their love. But at this point in their marriage, she was questioning everything. "Did you have any luck finding Kee Kee?"

He released her and moved her away from the counter. "I'm not the bad guy here, Alexis. All I did was provide for our family."

"I'm just thinking about Kevin's family. Doesn't his daughter deserve to be provided for also? Could you have ever imagined that you would do something like this to a friend who basically gave you the key that jump-started this wonderful life we have?"

"Can we please stop arguing for one night? I'm really getting sick of it."

She wanted to tell him that he started it, no matter how childish she might sound. He had, in fact, started arguing with her from the moment she brought her mother home. "Forget it. If you don't care, then I don't care."

"I didn't say that I don't care. I'm not saying that you aren't right.

I have been trying to find Kevin's daughter, but I haven't had much luck so far. I even hired a private investigator."

Okay, at least he was trying. Alexis put the dishes in the dishwasher and then sat down in the family room with Michael to watch the evening news.

"How is your mother doing today?"

Alexis side-eyed him, wondering why he would even ask about her mother—as if he cared. Then she remembered the scene Vivian made, screaming and running away from her last night. "She's been calm today. She enjoyed our drive. We've been apart for so long. She just wants to spend time with us."

"That's how you feel now, isn't it? Like I've kept you from your mother for years?"

"I'm not upset with you for that, Michael, because I had a part to play in putting my mother in all those homes too. I could have said no. I could have walked away from you and kept living life as I knew it, but I wanted everything being with you offered. I can admit that. And now I have to live with the choice I made."

Michael turned to her. He lightly rubbed her arm. She used to get goose bumps when he did that . . . Nothing.

"We have a good life, Alexis, don't forget that. You were all I ever wanted and, even after thirteen years, that hasn't changed for me. Has it changed for you?"

She shook her head. "I still love you, Michael, but I'm not the same girl you married. I want different things, and if our marriage is going to survive, you have to accept that."

"I'm sorry for the way I've been treating you and your mother since she's been in the house. I have to admit that, except for a few off-color things she's said to the kids and all the screaming she did last night, she hasn't been much trouble at all."

Alexis heard every word Michael said, but something on the local news caught her attention, so she couldn't respond. A reporter was holding a microphone and standing inside of a school auditorium, but that wasn't what caught Alexis's attention.

Trish Robinson was standing next to the reporter, and John Robinson was seated in his wheelchair. The reporter said, "You gave a very impassioned speech about distracted driving. Can you tell us why this is so important to you?"

"Yes, of course," Trish said as the reporter put the microphone in her face. "Distracted driving matters to me because it almost destroyed my family."

Trish looked to John and continued, "My son was in college on a football scholarship when a car accident with someone who had been distracted by their cell phone took all of that away from him."

The reporter asked, "Are you bothered by the sparsely attended event?"

John took the microphone and said, "Not at all. My mom told me that if she could convince just one of these students not to use their cell phones while driving, then she might have helped to save a guy like me from a wrecked future."

"And what does the future look like for you, young man?"

With a huge smile on his face, John Robinson took the microphone again. "If you would have asked me that a few months ago, I wouldn't have had anything good to say. But the future is bright for me. I'm more convinced than ever that despite my circumstances, I'm going to survive. No, no, strike that. I'm going to thrive."

Trish bent down and hugged her son. "I'm so proud of you, Jon-Jon."

Michael turned the television off as he paced the room. "How dare they be out there shooting their mouths off about the accident. I just paid those people seven hundred and fifty thousand dollars, and they have the nerve . . . I'm calling my attorney."

"For what?"

"I'm taking them to court for breach of contract." Michael reached for his cell phone.

"They did not mention my name, and how can they be in breach of contract if I am in total agreement with what they are doing?"

"You can't be. They are going to ruin everything."

Alexis couldn't believe she was standing her ground about this, nor could she believe the next words that came out of her mouth. "Trish did not say my name during that interview. So they aren't in breach of any contract. But they won't have to say my name because I am joining her at the next event, and I will tell my story to the audience myself."

The way Michael looked at her made her feel like she was in a Martin Scorsese movie and Michael was about to ask if she was going against the family. But she had to stand her ground. She had to do what was right.

"You don't care what happens to me anymore? Is that it? You're so anxious to get back at me that you'd sabotage my company and your own children's future?"

"No, you're not going to lay that at my feet." Her pointer finger jutted in his direction. "You sabotaged the buyout of your company when you stole Kevin's idea and acted like it was yours."

"Really, Alexis? That's how you see me? I'm a thief in your eyes?"

Folding her arms around her chest and giving him an I-don't-know-who-you-are-anymore staredown. "Find that little girl, give her what you owe, and I'll never say anything like this again. But until then, I don't know what to think about you."

Michael threw up his hands and left the room.

Alexis sat exhausted from the fight with Michael. She exhaled as she watched him walk toward his office. She was making things worse for him. That wasn't what she wanted at all. She loved her husband, but she couldn't keep sweeping things under a rug and acting like everything was fine.

Things were not fine and probably would never be again—at least not in the delusional, "hiding secrets to make everything better" kind of way that they had been living. Michael strived for perfection, but they didn't have the perfect family. Life could still be good if they worked at it.

With this last stand, Alexis didn't know if Michael would be able to forgive her for what she needed to do. She needed to talk to someone before making the decision that could cost her the very thing she thirsted for when she said yes to putting her mother in a nursing home.

Alexis went upstairs to her mother's room. She opened the door. Her mother appeared to be asleep. She looked so peaceful that Alexis almost backed out of the room. Just as she was about to close the door, she noticed that her mother's chest didn't have that slight up and down movement of sleep.

Tiptoeing over to the bed, Alexis had this strange feeling that she shouldn't be tiptoeing, but rather stumping and shouting. Her. Mother. Wasn't. Breathing.

She touched Vivian's arm. It was warm. Alexis grinned. She was just being silly and imagining things. Her mother was fine. Alexis shook Vivian's shoulder, "Mom, are you okay?"

No response.

No! No! No! This wasn't happening. Tears sprang to Alexis eyes as she shook her mother again. "Wake up, Mom. Wake up! Wake up!"

They'd had such a wonderful day. Everything had been good. Vivian had been calm. They even made their favorite dessert. It wasn't over. It couldn't be over. "WAKE UP!" Alexis screamed as she shook her mother's shoulders once again.

Ella ran into the room. "What's wrong, Mom? Why are you screaming?"

Alexis swung around to see Ella's eyes wide with fear. "Call 911. She won't wake up."

Ella ran out of the room, yelling and screaming all the way down the stairs.

Alexis climbed on the bed next to her mother. She wrapped her arms around Vivian and held onto her, never wanting to let her go. "Mom, oh, Mom, don't do this. Don't go now. I was just getting to know you."

Tears streamed down Alexis's face and fell onto Vivian like a sudden rainstorm. "Please, Mom, please stay here with me. Wake up. I need you."

Ethan and Ella stood at the foot of the bed crying and begging their grandmother to wake up.

"Grandma Vivian, don't go," Ella said.

"We don't want you to die," Ethan said.

Michael came into the room. He put his arms around Alexis. "The ambulance is on the way, baby. I'll stay here with you. Get down from the bed and sit in the chair, okay?" He was talking slow like he thought she didn't understand normal speech.

"I don't want to leave her, Michael. I left her alone for so long. I can't leave her anymore." She turned to face him. Her face was wet from the storm. "Can you understand that? I can't leave her."

He nodded. "I understand, and I'm so sorry, Alexis. I'm so sorry for everything. I never meant to hurt you like this."

Michael was crying with her. He held her as she held onto her mother. "Mom, remember Purple Rain?" Alexis asked as if she would get an answer. "I was so ashamed to ride in that van that you loved so much, but I really did enjoy singing that song with you in your purple van."

Drizzle ran from her nose, mixing with the tears. "I didn't understand you back then, but I do now. That's why I want you to stay. We've had so much fun. Don't go, Mom. Don't go."

The paramedics entered the room. Michael had to pull Alexis away from her mother so the paramedics could tell them what she already knew. Her mother was gone.

Alexis fell to the floor. Then, as Michael picked her up, she yelled, "Noooo!" But all the nos in the world wouldn't change the facts.

She missed out on a normal life with Vivian, but she never missed out on love. Since she was a child, Alexis knew that her mother wasn't normal, but she also knew her mother loved her. It would have to be enough. It was enough.

Michael wiped the tears from her face and pulled her into his arms. She closed her eyes, shutting out the world and shutting out the sorrow.

The paramedics contacted the coroner. Michael tried to coax her out of the room, but Alexis sat down in her mom's chair and propped her feet on the ottoman she'd gotten used to seeing Vivian relax in. Alexis leaned her head against the chair and inhaled the scent of lavender and orange blossoms.

Those scents came from her mother's favorite perfume. Alexis purchased Libre for her mother each year on her birthday. She smiled now because the reason she thought the fragrance would be perfect for her mother was because the perfume's ad campaign said it was for those "who live by their own rules."

Alexis didn't know how long she had been resting in her mom's chair, but when she opened her eyes, a blanket had been draped over her body and someone from the coroner's office was putting her mother's body on the stretcher and rolling her out of the room.

Throwing the cover off, she jumped out of her seat. "Wait! Don't take her yet." Alexis put her hand on the stretcher, halting their motion as she looked down on the face that was an older version of her own. "I'll miss you forever, Mom." She bent down and kissed her mother's wrinkly forehead.

"I'll never forget you, Mom, and I won't forget what you taught me about what death means to you." Through tears, she gave her mother permission to leave her. "Go ahead, Mom, fly away. Grandma Joyce is waiting for you."

As her mother's body was taken out of the room, Alexis cried. Ethan cried and Ella cried. As Alexis watched the emotion displayed by her children, she realized how much of a gift she had given them by allowing them to get to know their grandmother for a few months before it was all over.

Alexis prayed that Ella and Ethan would always remember the afternoons they spent with their grandmother, playing make-believe and listening to all the wild stories that Vivian concocted.

It was strange, but the sight of her children crying over their grandmother helped Alexis to heal. The only thing that made her feel better about losing her mother was the thought that she had given her children their grandmother for a beautiful moment in time.

CHAPTER 29

"We got us a celebrity now," Sister said as she stepped inside the house.

Trish blushed at her mother's comment about her being on the news. She then hugged her father as he entered. "It's good to see you, Daddy."

"I had a day off, so I decided to visit with my new grandbaby."

Trish put hands on hips and tsk-tsked. "Now that we have this new baby in the house, y'all two aren't thinking about the rest of us, huh?"

"Well, as big a star as you are, we didn't come to see you today. We want to hang out with the new kid on the block for a while. We even bought him a present." Sister opened the bag she brought with her to reveal a light blue and brown baby blanket.

"Mama, Daddy . . . It's beautiful. Thank you." Trish gave them both a hug, then hollered down the hall. "Jon-Jon, your grandparents are here." They sat down in the family room.

Jon-Jon came into the family room. He parked his wheelchair next to the sofa. "Here's the other star of the family." Sister's eyes beamed as she looked at Jon-Jon. "I'm so proud of you."

Jon-Jon blushed. "Grandma Sister, it's no big deal. It was just the local news."

"You think everybody on the local news is doing good for others?" Sister wagged a finger at her grandson. "Don't despise small beginnings, young man. You were born for greatness, and I'm just going to sit back and watch the show from this point on."

"Let me go get Moochie." Trish headed toward the back of the house.

"Mom, he's still asleep," Jon-Jon cautioned.

"Your grandparents came to see him, so I'm going to wake him up." Trish went into Marquita's room and lifted Moochie from the middle of the bed. She hugged him to her chest and loved how cuddly he felt. If anyone had told her how much she would love having a grandchild, she wouldn't have believed it. She didn't even want to leave him to do her job at night school. Unfortunately, she would have to leave in about two hours because her students needed her and she needed to help with the bills. "Here he is, Daddy."

Trish put the baby in her father's arms and then sat back down.

"Well, now, this is something."

"He really is, Daddy. I think I fell in love with him the first time I held him."

Sister reached out. "Hand me that baby, Albert."

He gave her the baby. Sister looked at Moochie as if he had hung the moon, the stars, and the sun.

"Watch it, Granny. You're not allowed to get another favorite grandson. I still hold that spot, and I'm not giving it up."

Sister leaned forward and put a hand on Jon-Jon's cheeks and squeezed lovingly. "Of course you're still my favorite grandson. Moochie here is now my favorite great-grandson."

"Oh, it's like that, huh?" Jon-Jon playfully glared at his son. "See what you did, Moochie? You done came up in here and took my grandparents from me."

Albert laughed at that. "You had your chance. It's all about the baby now. No more Christmas socks for you."

"Mama, you hear this?" Jon-Jon turned to Trish for help.

"Don't pay them no mind, Jon-Jon. I'll get you some Christmas socks if Daddy won't," Trish told him.

Her daddy objected. "No. You got to let him be a man. He's got a child of his own now. It's time for you to back up and let him handle his business."

Trish stared at her father. Had he used the same philosophy with her after she married Dwayne? He sure seemed to back away from her. They had once been so close, but her daddy didn't have much time for her after she married Dwayne. She needed to know what happened to them and felt that now was as good a time as any to ask. "Is that how you felt about me when I married Dwayne, Daddy? Did you back away from me so I could handle my business?"

"No, precious," Albert said. "I backed away from you so I wouldn't get in Dwayne's way. Your grandfather"—he thumb-motioned in Sister's direction—"your mama's daddy, wouldn't let up on me. That man never thought I was good enough for his daughter."

Trish turned toward her mother. "You never told me that Pop-Pop didn't like Daddy."

"He did like him once he got used to him." Sister giggled.

Trish's parents had no idea how this conversation had given her a whole new perspective. For years she had wondered what happened to her relationship with her dad. Now, she knew that her dad wasn't trying to distance himself from her. He just didn't want to step on Dwayne's toes.

"I am so enjoying my time with both of you." Trish beamed at her parents. "But I have to get dressed for work."

"Chile, go on. We didn't come to see you no way," Sister said.

Trish wondered how old she had to be before her mom stopped calling her "Chile." In her mother's eyes, she was still a little girl to be bossed around. Her father, on the other hand, now saw a grown woman with a husband and son. Trish didn't know which she preferred at the moment.

She went to her bedroom, took out a knee length dress, and then jumped in the shower. As she was putting on her clothes, there was a knock on her bedroom door. Trish pulled her dress over her head. "Come in."

Sister walked in, a mischievous grin on her face. "It's good seeing you back in your bedroom. How are you and Dwayne doing?"

Trish's dad never would have come in here getting in her business, but Sister didn't care. She got in other people's business like she was Dear Abby or that TV gossip, Wendy Williams. Her mother was no gossip, so maybe she should stop thinking of her as a Wendy Williams type. "We're not yelling at each other anymore."

"That doesn't sound very encouraging. Should I call the divorce lawyer now, or should I get you two a marriage counseling appointment at the church?"

"Dwayne and I don't want a divorce. We're just trying to get back in sync. That is, if we ever were in sync. Look, Mama, I don't know. I just don't know. One moment we're good, and the next I'm mad about some silly thing. But we are doing so much better."

"Okay, well, I can tell by the look on your face that I'm getting on your nerves, but allow me to ask one more question."

Looking at her cell for the time, she said, "Make it quick, Mama. I have to get to work."

"All right. Are you and Dwayne out of sync or is it just you?"

"Mama, why do you assume it's me?"

Sister took her daughter's hand and sat down on the edge of the bed with her. "I know you, daughter. You have always been so quick to forgive and move on, but something has stolen that gift from you. Don't let the Enemy win. You have to fight to get everything back that the devil took from you."

Her mother was indeed a busybody, but she would always be the voice in Trish's head, reminding her where her help comes from. "I get it, Mama, and I'm going to keep fighting, I promise."

❧

At school, Trish tried to concentrate on her students, but it was so quiet in the room as they took their exam that her mind betrayed her. She kept hearing her mother talking about forgiveness. She couldn't for the life of her figure out why this was so hard when it came to the man she planned to spend the rest of her life with. Dwayne had made some mistakes, but so had she. He'd tried to make things right, and had been very attentive to her needs of late. So, maybe it was she who wasn't doing enough. They were in a good place, so why couldn't she just roll with it?

"Mrs. Robinson, do you have an extra pencil? I don't have an eraser."

Trish handed him a pencil. She checked the time. "You all have fifteen more minutes. Do your best and try to answer every question."

A couple of students grumbled about needing more time.

Everybody deserves a second chance. She really wanted her students to pass the class. This exam would give them an idea of what they would face while taking the GED test. "Tell you what. I'll remain after class an extra ten minutes. Just keep working and try to finish as close to the time as possible."

She received a text from Dwayne asking her to call him as soon as she could. "Keep working. I'll be right outside the door."

She stepped outside the classroom and called Dwayne. He normally didn't call her while she was in class, so she hoped there wasn't some problem at home. Fear clenched her heart when she saw the text, so there was no way she would be able to wait until class was over to call.

"Hey, is everything okay?" she asked when he answered.

"Everything is fine at the house. I was just looking at the obituaries."

"Why are you looking at the obits? We're not old enough to do that kind of stuff." Her grandparents were addicted to the obit pages in the newspaper. They scoured it to see if any of their friends had taken that long goodnight. If they had, then they made plans to attend the funeral with a peach cobbler or pound cake for the repast.

"I look at the obits every now and then."

"Since when?" But even as she asked, she realized that Dwayne must have started his obit watching after Jon-Jon's accident. The call they received about Jon-Jon had put fear in both their hearts. Neither of them escaped this experience unscathed. "Are you looking for friends like my grandparents used to do?"

"You never know. Anything could happen," he told her. Then he added, "Anyway, as I was looking through the obituary, I saw that Alexis Marshall's mother passed away."

Trish's hand went to her mouth. Intake of breath. "Are you sure?"

"If her mother's name is Vivian Cooper, then yes, I'm sure. It lists Alexis as her only child and Michael Marshall as her son-in-law."

"Thanks for telling me, Dwayne. I've got to get back in the class-room." She hung up. As she walked back into the classroom, she was thinking about the type of floral arrangement she would send to the funeral home. If she had thought she would be welcomed, Trish would have attended the repast with her grandmother's famous peach cob-bler. She and Alexis didn't have that kind of relationship, but she felt bad for the woman.

❧

"How is work going?" Jon-Jon asked Marquita as they sat on the love-seat in the family room watching a movie. Moochie was in her arms as she fed him.

"I made a friend. Her name is Eve. I didn't like her at first, but she turned out to be cool people."

"That's good, Marquita. I'm happy for you." Jon-Jon picked up the remote and turned down the volume a bit.

"Me too. I normally don't make friends too easily, but she's nice."

Marquita put the bottle down, put Moochie on her shoulder, and burped him. "How was your day?"

"I signed up for fall semester at the community college."

Marquita's eyes lit up. "But I thought you wanted to wait?"

"I was just being prideful, not wanting people in town to see me in a wheelchair. I have to think about Moochie and building a future for him, so I'm going back to school."

"I'm proud of you, and I'm sure Moochie will be, too, when he's old enough to know what his dad did for him."

"Yeah, I told my grandparents about it. They said they're proud of me too. I thought they would get on me about having Moochie so young, but they didn't. They came over today and hung out with Moochie."

"So your grandparents came to see Moochie today?" Marquita rocked the baby to sleep.

"Yeah, and my granddad thinks Moochie looks just like me when I was a baby."

"Maybe you should have showed him a picture of me, then he would have seen who Moochie really looks like. All he has of yours is those deep, dark eyes and those dimples that cause women to hover around you."

"I don't see any women hover around me now, do you?"

Stop smiling at me, Marquita wanted to scream at him. Instead, she laid Moochie on the sofa. "You know what I mean. When you were out there being 'the man' on the football field, you had plenty of women running after you. I guess that's why you forgot about me like I was nothing but a distant memory."

"I never forgot you, Marquita. Things were just more complicated back then."

"Don't lie, Jon-Jon. You don't have to do that. I know I'm not the kind of girl guys like you bring home to meet their mother."

"And yet, my mother gave you a bedroom in our house."

Marquita's eyes clouded; she was feeling some type of way and needed Jon-Jon to know about it. "I'm grateful for what your parents have done for me. I just wish our summer together had meant as much to you as it meant to me."

"It did, Marquita. I promise you it did."

She shook her head and lifted Moochie from the sofa. "You're just saying this because you're in a wheelchair and I'm the only woman that hangs around now. But that's not good enough for me."

Marquita went to her room and closed the door. She felt tears coming on and didn't want to cry like a love-sick puppy in front of Jon-Jon. If she was being for real and true with herself, she had fallen more in love with Jon-Jon since moving in with the Robinsons than she was when they dated last summer. She changed into her night clothes and then she and Moochie climbed in bed.

Being around him every day and seeing how much he loved and accepted Moochie had caused her to think that he had love for her, too, but that wasn't reality. Reality was that she was a single mom who needed to earn enough money to get her own place and stop dreaming impossible dreams.

Marquita grabbed her journal from the nightstand, opened it, and wrote furiously, trying to get this boy-meets-girl, boy-falls-in-love-with-girl-and-never-leaves-her story out of her head. She had no idea what she would do with it, but she had to get the words in her journal. Her arm got tired, so she put the journal back on the nightstand and laid her head on her pillow.

But Marquita couldn't get comfortable as she moved around on the bed. Her restlessness finally woke Moochie, but he didn't cry. He was just looking up at her with those deep, dark eyes. Then he smiled at her. It was as if she was the only thing that mattered to him in this whole big world. She ran a finger down his cheek as her heart expanded with all the love she wanted to shower on him.

"I'm worthy of your love, aren't I, Moochie? You won't regret loving your mama. I'm going to be good to you. I promise I'm not going to flake out on you like my mother did too many times for me to count. I'm going to figure things out so I can make you just as proud of me as I know you're going to be of your daddy."

Moochie cooed and kicked his feet.

"Even if no one else in this whole world wants me, I know you do. And that's good enough for me."

CHAPTER 30

V ivian hadn't had many friends. She hadn't allowed too many people to get close to her, so Alexis was pleasantly surprised to see how many of the people from her nursing home showed up for her mom's funeral. There were even a few people from the social services facility where Alexis volunteered.

Alexis wanted a celebration of the life Vivian Cooper had lived, as complicated as it had been. So no tears were allowed today, only joy and good vibes.

A woman sang "I'll Fly Away," and Alexis did everything in her power to smile. She prayed that her mother was now with her grandmother. They could be together in heaven forever. At least, Alexis hoped it worked that way.

To take her mind off the song that meant so much to her mother, she focused on the beautiful standing sprays on either side of the casket. Some had lilies. Others had white carnations and yellow roses. The fragrance from the flowers filled the small room, and Alexis breathed it in. She had no idea who ordered the sprays, but she was grateful.

The funeral repast was held at Alexis's home. Alexis sat on the sofa and watched the people mill around. Almost forty people had helped her celebrate her mom today. Food covered the kitchen island and the table. Michael made sure that her mother's favorites were a part of the spread: the chocolate-cookie crunch trifle, macaroni salad, club sandwiches, green bean casserole, and on and on. Everyone was smiling and enjoying themselves and the memories Vivian had left behind.

Uncle Douglas came over to Alexis with a slice of pie in his hand. "Mind if I sit with you for a little while?"

She patted the seat next to her. "I'd love some company."

He took a couple bites of his pie, then said, "Thank you for allowing me to visit with Vivian. I don't know how I would have felt about myself if I hadn't made the effort before she passed."

"She was so happy to see you, so I'm the one who owes you a debt of thanks for bringing a smile to her face during her last days with us." Alexis sighed as she watched the people milling around.

"I wish I had come sooner," he admitted. "Vivian and I didn't get along when we were younger. I just didn't understand her. The one thing I always admired, though, was how she watched over you. Vivian loved you more than anything and she fought like the dickens to keep you with her, which is why she moved away from our town."

"What?" It felt like Uncle Douglas was revealing some new information to her. She turned to him, wanting to understand what he was trying to tell her.

"You were young when it all went down. Vivian and my mom were very close. However, when Vivian gave birth to you, Mama didn't think she was responsible enough to raise you with the way she was living. Mama didn't want to do it, but she contacted Child Protective Services.

"When Vivian found out, she blew a gasket. She packed and left the farm, and we didn't see her again until Mama passed. I'd never seen Vivian so distraught as she was at Mama's funeral. I think she regretted leaving the way she did. But to keep you with her, I think she still would have made the same choice, even if someone would have told her that she would never see Mama alive again. She just loved you so much."

"Thank you for telling me that, Uncle Douglas. Now I understand the full reason Mom never took me back to visit when I practically begged her to when I was a kid."

Uncle Douglas nodded and squeezed Alexis's hand. Alexis excused herself and went to her bedroom for a moment of solitude.

Knowing the reason for Vivian's choices didn't rest easy in Alexis's soul. It made this whole thing so much worse for her. The repast was still going on, but Alexis retired to her bedroom and laid down with her sorrow. Her mother moved away from her whole family so she wouldn't lose Alexis.

Vivian's greatest fear had been that her mother would take Alexis away from her. Even when her mind was reeling and conjuring up all sorts of weird things, Vivian had not lost sight of her end goal, which was to keep Alexis with her. Her goal cost her the relationship she had with her mother.

Alexis knew that Grandma Joyce's absence in her mother's life had hurt. That was why her mother had conveniently forgot that Grandma Joyce had died years ago. But Alexis never knew that Vivian destroyed that relationship because of the love she had for her little girl.

"I'm so sorry, Mom. I spent years being embarrassed by you, while you gave up everything to be with me." Alexis sobbed. All the years she spent ashamed of her mother should have been spent celebrating and championing her hero. She'd told herself that she volunteered as a human services assistant to pay it forward for her mother, but that wasn't the whole truth.

Truth is sometimes a hard pill to swallow. It didn't always go down easy or come up smelling like freshly cut lilies and carnations. The truth was Alexis had turned her mother away—the same mother who walked away from the only family she knew in order to keep Alexis. The same mother who hugged her and made her dessert to help her feel better. She had turned that woman away because she wanted and needed the life Michael offered.

Through tears, Alexis vowed from that day on she would live her truth. She would no longer be ashamed of the flaws that defined her. She was Vivian Cooper's daughter, and she would live her truth even if it cost her everything.

The door opened, and Michael peeked his head in. "Do you need anything?"

The one thing she needed Michael couldn't give her. No one could. "No, I just want to be by myself for now."

"Okay, I'll give you some time. I'll come back to sit with you once the guests leave."

Alexis sniffed, grabbed some tissue from the nightstand, and blew her nose.

Michael closed the door, but just as he promised, within thirty minutes he was back in the room with her. He handed her a chocolaty treat. "The kids are cleaning up some of the mess. I'll finish whatever they leave behind."

"Thank you." She had the treat in her hands. It would be so easy to soothe her pain with sugar, but she put the dessert on the nightstand and turned away from it. Just didn't seem the same without her mother.

Michael climbed into the bed and pulled her into his arms. They lay that way for a long while, neither saying anything. They just rested in what they knew for sure: they loved each other. After a while Alexis sat up. Her back was to her husband when she said, "I don't understand you at all."

"I love you, Alexis. Isn't that enough?"

She shook her head. "Not anymore. I want the truth from you. I need to know why I could never have my mother around for holidays, birthdays, or any of the events we had in this house throughout the years."

Michael repositioned himself to sit next to his wife. He lowered his head, but Alexis lifted it with a finger.

"Talk to me," she said as her eyes bore into his, imploring him to give her everything she needed.

"I-I was uncomfortable around her."

"Why? She never did anything to you or against you."

"But she wasn't right."

"You mean, she wasn't perfect," Alexis challenged.

"If you want to say it that way. Vivian didn't portray the image I want for my family."

"I used to think I understood you, that I knew what made you tick. I tried my best to do the things that kept you in this happy place you constructed for us. Then I discovered that you stole from someone you called a friend and never even gave the man credit for his work." Her hands rubbed at her elbows as if she'd felt a cool breeze. "That doesn't square with the person I thought you were."

"I've questioned myself about that decision for years now. Why do you think I kept his daughter's photo for all these years?"

"I don't know, but I wish you would tell me."

He stood. Hands in pockets. "I tried so many times to come up with an app on my own that would sell in the marketplace, but nothing I came up with was worth much. I kept hearing my dad say, 'Son, you can do anything in this world, just don't fail at it.' Kevin was gone, but I had his app and it was better than mine."

Michael swung away from Alexis. "With my dad, it was all about winning. Earning a B on a test wasn't good enough because winners got As. My silver medal in swimming wasn't good enough because gold medalists went to the Olympics."

Alexis knew that Michael's father was a narcissist from the first day she met and held a conversation with the man. His father had a great deal of influence on him, but she didn't realize that influence had caused Michael to become someone unworthy of the place he had claimed for himself.

"How could I admit to my father, or myself even, that Kevin was better than me? I couldn't do it. I couldn't put Kevin's name on the app." His voice broke as his shoulders shook. He put his hands over his eyes, wiping away tears. "I just couldn't deal with being a failure."

"If you had it all to do over again, would you make the same decision today?"

Leaning against the wall, Michael looked at Alexis. His eyes were still full with sorrow. "I don't know if you will believe me about this or not, but being married to you has made me a better man. I still want to win, but not at all costs."

"Thank you for finally opening up to me, Michael." She laid back down and tried to put her mind on something else, but Michael wasn't done.

"I admire how you care about other people. To you, a person's life really matters. You'd do the right thing to help someone else, even if it means that you'd come out on the losing end."

She sat back up. "But that's just it, Michael. I don't believe that helping others means I come out on the losing end." She then told him about her mother's great sacrifice.

"Wow," Michael said. "Your mother really loved you. I wish I had given her more of a chance, but I'm glad she was able to spend time with the children."

"I was thinking about that when you came to see about me earlier. My mom kept me away from my grandmother so that I wouldn't be taken from her. In the end I think God gave her time with her grandchildren to heal her heart from all the lonely years she spent missing her mother—and the years she spent missing me and the kids."

"I would have never seen it that way. The kids were happy spending time with her. I'm glad you didn't listen to me and send her back to the nursing home."

Now she was ready to tease him. "Oh, so are you actually admitting that you were wrong about something?"

With the humbleness of a man who was beginning to see the light, Michael said, "I've been wrong about a lot of things. I don't even know how you've put up with me all these years."

"It hasn't always been easy, Michael Marshall. But I know you love us, so I keep reminding myself of that."

"I've disappointed you. I know that, Alexis, but I wanted to talk to you about something else."

"I'm listening."

"I didn't tell you this earlier, but the Robinsons sent a standing spray for the funeral."

"Which flower arrangement did the Robinsons send?"

"I think it was the one with carnations and roses."

Alexis liked Trish. Even after what Alexis had done to her son and how she blew her off about the distracted driving program, Trish still went out of her way to send flowers. "I'll call Trish tomorrow to thank them. I also need to speak with her about the distracted driving program she started. I think she needs my help, and, even though I don't want to argue with you about this, I am going to help her."

Michael lifted his hands in surrender. "I don't want to argue with you about this anymore either. As a matter of fact, I want to help also."

"Help?" Did somebody spike the punch at the repast? Did her husband actually say he wanted to do something to assist someone else?

"Yes." He moved away from the wall and sat back down next to Alexis on the bed. "Distracted driving is a very big problem, especially since the invention of cell phones. My company does have apps that are used on cell phones, so it might be good PR if I paid for an ad campaign against distracted driving."

Alexis's eyes lit up. "Are you joking? Is this for real?"

"You have gotten behind any and everything that was important to me. Now it's my turn to do the same for you. Talk to Trish and see if she's on board. I think an ad campaign would bring more awareness when they speak at schools."

Alexis teared up. "I kept waiting. Somehow I knew that you would do the right thing." She wrapped her arms around her husband and kissed him.

CHAPTER 31

It was Saturday, and Trish had a meeting scheduled with Alexis in about an hour. At the moment, she sat in the family room holding Moochie and talking with Jon-Jon and Marquita. "I'm so happy that you registered for the fall semester, Jon-Jon. I know it isn't the college of your choice, but you can always transfer after a year."

"I'm good, Mama. I need to be close by so I can help out with Moochie."

"If you want to run back to that old college of yours, don't let us keep you, but you know how you get amnesia when you're not around." Marquita rolled her eyes.

"Girl, your eyes are going to get stuck like that one day." Trish laughed at her.

"Well, I'm sorry, but Jon-Jon needs to stop playing." Marquita's arms wrapped around her chest like she was trying to protect her heart. "He knows he wants to leave us again, so just do it."

"I didn't say I wanted to leave y'all. And for the record, I have never left Moochie."

"I know," Marquita snapped back. "Just me. I'm the one that didn't mean anything to you."

Moochie had fallen asleep. Trish stood. "I think I stumbled into a private conversation, so I'm going to lay the baby down and then get things ready for our meeting with Alexis."

"It's cool, Mama. You can sit with us. Marquita is just tripping."

Trish shook her head. "No, son. A wise man taught me to get out of grown folks' business and let them handle things on their own. So I'm going to let the two of you talk."

Kissing Moochie on the forehead, she laid him down on the bed. She then whispered in Moochie's ear, "Your parents need to get their act together."

Trish didn't have time for Jon-Jon and Marquita's drama, so she went to her room and grabbed her laptop, a couple of notebooks, and some pens. Trish was so excited about her meeting with Alexis that she didn't know what to do with herself. She had only imagined speaking at a few high schools and colleges to bring awareness to how harmful distracted driving can be. Only five teenagers attended her first event. After the first event, Trish started praying for fifty attendees at her next speaking event.

When Alexis called to tell her that her husband wanted to sponsor an ad campaign against distracted driving, needless to say, Trish was dumbfounded. They were going to do a commercial, design postcards, post billboards, do interviews, and speak on campuses and in corporate America. Kids weren't the only ones texting and driving. These high-powered executives thought they couldn't wait until they turned off their car to read a text message either.

Trish's excitement had quickly turned to dread when Marquita's mother showed up at the house acting a country fool, screaming and hollering outside, disturbing the neighbors until Trish let her in the house. Even that didn't satisfy her. Once in the house Gloria started ranting and raving without so much as a "How you doing?" Her car was parked in front of the house, and Trish noticed two teens in the car. She wanted to invite them in, but with the way Marquita's mother was acting, Trish didn't want to do anything to prolong this visit.

"Look, Ms. Lewis, you can't come up in my house acting like this," Trish tried to tell the woman.

"You got my daughter in here, and y'all done kidnapped my grandson, so I can come in here acting any way I want," Gloria told her.

Marquita came running out of the family room. "Mama, please stop. The Robinsons have been good to me, and here you come trying to ruin everything. You can't stand for me to have anything good in my life."

The doorbell rang again. Trish wished that she could snap her fingers and make this whole ordeal stop, but this woman was not ready to give up yet. Trish couldn't leave Alexis on the porch, ringing the doorbell. She opened the door, getting ready to apologize for all the yelling, when she noticed a young man and teen girl get out of Gloria's car and come up the sidewalk, heading toward her house. "Alexis, I'm sorry for all the noise," Trish said. "If you can give me a minute, I'll take care of this and then we can get on with our meeting."

"It's no problem. I think I heard Marquita's mother as I pulled up. I met her a few months back. If you don't mind, I might be able to help you with this situation."

Shock appeared on Trish's face. Why on earth would this woman want to enter a home with this much commotion? "Be my guest. If you can get that woman to quiet down, I'd appreciate it."

Alexis walked into the kitchen where Gloria, Marquita, and Jon-Jon were going at it. Trish turned to the two young adults at her door. "Can I help you?"

"My mom is inside with my sister. Can we come in?"

"You're Marquita's brother and sister?" Trish extended a hand. "Hello, I'm Mrs. Robinson, or Mrs. Trish, whichever you prefer."

"I'm Mark, and this is my sister Kee Kee."

As they entered the house, Gloria was saying, "I kept that baby for you free of charge. Now you act like you can't bring him to see me even though I told you I wanted to see him. That ain't right, Marquita."

"Look how you act, Mama. I don't want all of this drama around my baby anymore. Can't you just leave me alone and let me have some peace in my life?"

"Don't say things like that, Marquita. Mama loves you. Mark and I love you too."

"I'm sorry, Kee Kee. I love you and Mark too," Marquita said.

"Oh, but you don't love me? You don't appreciate nothing I've done for you. Is that what you're saying?" Gloria stepped closer to Marquita.

"I just want peace, Mama. The way you act is too much for me." Eyes rolling and hands flailing in the air, she said, "I look at you, and I see everything I don't want to be. I don't want Moochie to be around you anymore because I don't want him witnessing all the drama that you've put me, Mark, and Kee Kee through all of our lives. Can you just leave me alone?"

Shocked, Trish's mouth hung open. She couldn't believe the way Marquita spoke to her mother. In all her days and as much as her mother got all up in her business, she never would have had the audacity to say something like this to Sister.

She looked over at Alexis. She claimed she could help cool this situation down when she came into the house, but Alexis was barely paying Gloria and Marquita any attention. She was staring at Kee Kee with her mouth hanging open, as if she was in a daze or something.

Trish yelled at Gloria and Marquita. "Y'all gon' have to stop all this. I need to have a meeting. Visit with your grandson or don't, but you can't come here with all this confusion."

"I'm not trying to bring confusion to your house, but what's right is right," Gloria was yelling so loud, the sounds were vibrating off the wall. She jabbed an angry finger in Trish's direction, "And you are not Moochie's only grandmother."

This woman needed the trinity—prayer, Jesus, and a good whooping. Trish should have known that this upper-crust white woman wasn't going to come in here and handle this out-of-control situation. Yet, Trish was surprised that Alexis also hadn't ran out of the house. She didn't look afraid at all. She seemed more . . . transfixed. Whatever the case was, she needed her to snap out of it. "Alexis, you met Gloria, right?"

Alexis took her eyes off of Kee Kee and turned to Gloria. "Um, yes. Um . . ."

Alexis was out of her league with this woman. Trish put a hand on her hip and was getting ready to let Gloria have it when the garage door opened. Dwayne came into the kitchen carrying subs and a grocery bag. He sat them on the counter. "What in the world is going on in my house? I could hear all the yelling from the driveway."

Marquita turned to Dwayne. "I'm so sorry about this, Mr. Dwayne. I don't know why she acts like this."

Dwayne's eyes scanned the room. He turned back to Marquita. "You brought all this noise and commotion to my house?"

Jon-Jon wheeled himself in front of Marquita as if protecting her. "Dad, it's not Marquita's fault. Her mom came in here, going off on Marquita and Mama like she's got some kind of problem or something."

Gloria told Jon-Jon, "I don't have a problem. Y'all the one got the problem, because I'm about to turn up in here."

Dwayne's face had this oh-no-she-didn't expression as he turned to Trish. "Who is this woman?"

"Her name's Gloria—"

Gloria's head bobbed. "I'm Moochie's grandma, and I have a right to see him. Y'all can't keep him from me."

"Let me put it to you this way," Dwayne said. "I don't care whose grandma you are. You don't come up in my house and disrespect my wife. So, if you can't tone it down, and I mean right now, you got to go."

Gloria opened her mouth to say something else.

Dwayne stopped her. "Choose your next words carefully, because they may be the last words you speak inside this house."

271

Huffing loudly, then rolling her eyes, Gloria managed to lower her voice, "Is it all right if I spend some time with my grandson, since my daughter don't want to bring him around me?"

Trish started to add her two cents. She did think the woman should be allowed to see her grandchild, but she knew better than to get in Dwayne's way when he was handling a situation. Instead, she tapped Alexis on the shoulder. "Let's go sit down at the table."

"Okay." Alexis followed her to the table.

Dwayne looked from Jon-Jon to Marquita. "Are y'all going to let this woman have some time with her grandson or what?"

"It's not my decision." Jon-Jon glanced over at Marquita. "She's your mother. You make the call."

Marquita looked frustrated. "Mama, I just don't like how you came in here causing all this confusion. You know I don't have anywhere else to go right now."

"I miss Moochie." Gloria started crying. Mark and Kee Kee stood next to their mother.

"Don't cry, Mama. Marquita's going to let you see Moochie. Won't you, Marquita?" Kee Kee asked.

Relenting, Marquita asked Dwayne, "Can they go in my room and visit with Moochie for a while?"

"That's fine," Dwayne said.

Trish said, "Jon-Jon, can you sit over here with me and Mrs. Alexis? We have a lot of work to do if we're going to build an ad campaign that will get some attention."

As Jon-Jon wheeled himself over to the table, Dwayne pulled a serving tray out of the cabinet. He put the subs on the tray and then pulled bags of chips out of his grocery bag. He brought the tray over to the table. "I figured you wouldn't have time to cook, so I picked up some subs and chips."

"Thank you," Trish said while wondering what else was in the fridge that she could eat.

"Here's the barbecue chips you like." Dwayne handed Trish the bag.

Trish's eyebrow raised. "You never buy barbecue. You only bring the salt and vinegar chips that you and Jon-Jon like."

Dwayne said, "You like barbecue, so I got those for you." He then turned to Alexis. "I wasn't sure what kind of chips you like so I also grabbed a plain and a cheddar."

"I'll take the cheddar chips. Thank you. What kind of subs did you get?" Alexis asked.

"We have turkey and ham, club, and Italian. My baby's favorite is Italian." Dwayne winked at Trish. "Isn't that right, baby?"

"Yes, but your baby does not like mayo on her sub, so I'll fix myself something later."

Alexis said, "I'll take the turkey and ham. This was so nice of you."

Jon-Jon took the club sub sandwich.

Dwayne handed the Italian to Trish. "There's no mayo on the sandwich. I had them make it for you just the way you like it."

"You don't know how I like my sandwich," Trish said as she took the sub from him, opened it, and searched the sandwich like she was looking for a hair in her food. She looked back at Dwayne, astonishment on her face. "My sandwich is the exact way I like it."

"That's a good thing, right?" Dwayne looked a little nervous.

"It's the best thing ever." Trish hopped out of her seat, wrapped her arms around her husband, and kissed him with all the love she was feeling. Trish had given him a hard time for several months now. After talking with her mom and dad the other day, Trish knew she was just being bratty.

Dwayne was sorry for the way he had treated her. The dishwashing, the extra help with Jon-Jon, and the kindness he'd shown Marquita all helped her see he was changing. She had already forgiven her husband, but this Italian sub with no mayo was like an extra gift at Christmas.

"I love you, Dwayne. I'm so thankful that you are my husband."

Dwayne tapped Trish on the shoulder. Her arms were still wrapped around his neck. "Babe, I'm loving this. I truly am, but we have company."

Laughing like a teen caught making out with her high school crush, Trish released him and turned back to Alexis. "You must think this is a crazy house or something."

"Not at all. It looks like you and your husband need a little time to talk." Alexis took her cell phone out of her purse. "I need to call my husband."

"Of course, you do what you need to. I'll eat my Italian sub without mayo and wait for you to get back."

When Alexis stepped outside, Jon-Jon told his mom, "That was kind of embarrassing. You mauled Daddy in front of company."

"Shut up, boy. You need to worry about why Marquita is so upset with you, and ask yourself if you care enough to do the right thing."

"I don't even know what the right thing is, Mama. I'm focused on my son and my rehab. I can't think past that right now."

Dwayne put a hand on his son's shoulder. "Just don't play with the girl's heart. When I got with your mama, I knew right away that there was no other woman for me. Unless you feel that way, don't settle."

"I'll keep that in mind, Dad."

Dwayne leaned closer to his son and added, "The girl's mama is off the wall, so don't rush to join that family."

"Dwayne," Trish objected. "Don't do that. Marquita is really trying to make changes in her life. I don't want her being judged by the way her mother acts."

"You're right, baby." Dwayne looked at Jon-Jon and said, "You also need to make sure she can cook. The last thing you want to do is be in a house with an angry woman and your hungry stomach."

"I heard that." Trish nudged Dwayne. "You just got out of the doghouse. Don't get pushed back in there."

"You thought I was talking about you?" Dwayne stepped toward his wife. "Baby, I love everything you cook. You're better than Chef Boyardee."

"That's canned food, Dwayne." Her husband was talking himself out of the forgiveness Trish wanted so desperately to give him.

Dwayne snapped his fingers, like he was trying to come up with something. "Ooh, ooh, remember that time we dined at Emeril's restaurant in New Orleans, and I ordered the shrimp and grits?"

"Yes."

"If you remember, I didn't finish my plate that night. That's because it wasn't as good as yours."

Trish grinned wide. "Really?"

"Yeah, baby, you're better than Emeril, Bobby Flay, and that They-Call-Me-Ms.-Brown lady on the Food Network channel you like so much. I'm telling you, I'd rather eat right here in this kitchen than any restaurant in this country. You put your heart into each meal you cook for us."

Jon-Jon put a fist to his mouth. "Dang, Daddy, you overdid it. Mama's not going to believe that."

But Trish didn't care how over the top Dwayne was being. She loved every word that dripped from his gorgeous lips. She felt like crying and was so thankful Alexis had stepped out. This was a moment meant for her and Dwayne. After all these years of thinking that her husband didn't get her and never would, she was now thinking, *He gets me.* "I do put my heart into the meals I make for y'all. Thank you for noticing."

Dwayne gave an aw-shucks nod of his head. "I'm getting better."

"You're not just getting better, baby." Trish pulled Dwayne close again. Her hands went back around his neck. "You're the best, and I'm so thankful I get to spend the rest of my life with you."

They kissed again. This kiss was filled with all the passion they had denied each other for months on end. They were right back where they belonged, and they were going to hold on with everything they had left.

"I think I need to go make a call or change my socks or something." Jon-Jon left the kitchen and went into his room.

Trish and Dwayne looked at each other and laughed—and that laughter was good medicine, healing all that ailed them.

CHAPTER 32

Alexis thought her heart would beat out of her chest as she stood just about ten feet away from a girl named Kee Kee. She was not sure of this girl's age, but she was a teenager, no doubt. She also had the small beauty mark next to her nose, just like the baby in the picture. If the Kee Kee who was inside Trish's house was thirteen, then Alexis was almost positive that she was the girl Michael was looking for.

She didn't want to say anything yet. This had to be Michael's decision. When Trish and Dwayne got all lovey-dovey, Alexis used that as her cue to step outside Trish's house and call her husband. She giggled a bit as the phone rang because she was certain that Trish was embarrassed, but she shouldn't be. Alexis knew all too well what it felt like to be in love with a man she respected and cared deeply for. She wanted that feeling back and was praying that Michael wouldn't disappoint her again.

"Hey, hon, how's the meeting going?" Michael asked when he answered the phone.

"We took a break, so I'm calling you about something altogether different."

"Okay, what's going on?"

"Did your private investigator find any leads on the girl you are looking for?"

He emitted a heavy sigh. "No, I think Peter and I will have to face the fact that this deal is not going to happen. I wish I had known more about the mother, but all I remember is that Kevin was having the time of his life with an older woman who was a bit wild. He was this studious, nerd type so he couldn't believe a woman like that wanted to be with him."

"Kevin told you she was wild?" Alexis asked.

"Yeah, if I remember correctly that was the word he used to describe her. Beautiful and wild. If Kevin's parents were still living, we might be able to get more information from them, but they passed a few years ago."

"I need you to sit down and listen to me for a minute. You won't believe this, but your generosity with the ad campaign has led me to the very thing you need to move forward with the sale of your company."

Michael's voice quivered a bit. "What's going on over there, Alexis? Please, no more suspense."

"A teenage girl is inside Trish's house right now. Her name is Kee Kee, and she has that beauty mark on her face."

"What? Don't kid with me like this, Alexis. Are you serious?"

"I am, Michael. How many Kee Kee's could there be in Charlotte?"

"None that I'm aware of so far—at least none with a driver's license or property in their name."

His comment warmed Alexis's heart. "You really have been looking for her, haven't you?"

"I have. I know I disappointed you in the past, but I really want to make this right. I heard everything you said, and I'm ready to dig up this secret and expose it to the world if that's what needs to be done. I'll do it for Kevin."

Alexis let out a squeal of joy. "You don't know how happy I am to hear you say this. Let me go back into the house and do a little more digging. Then I'll get back to you."

"What type of digging? I thought you said you found her?"

"I know her name is Kee Kee, but I didn't ask if her father's name is Kevin Jones. I didn't want to do anything like that without talking to you first."

His voice softened. "We're back to being a team, aren't we, Lexi?"

Ooh, she loved when this man called her Lexi. She only wished she was in the same room with him so she could show him how much she loved being his wife. "I'm so glad you are my husband, Michael. God blessed me with a good man."

"You can still say that even after all that's happened?"

"I believe we are all entitled to redemption. And you, dear husband, are seriously about to earn yours. I'm proud to be married to you."

They hung up, and she went back inside. Trish and Dwayne were at the kitchen table eating. Trish put down her sandwich as Alexis approached. "Don't let me interrupt. Please keep eating. I need to speak with Gloria anyway."

Trish swallowed her food as she pursed her lips. "That ship has sailed, hasn't it? You told me you could handle her. All you did was stand there looking shell-shocked, so you might want to leave Gloria alone while she is calm. That woman is a special case."

"Believe me, I wasn't shocked by Gloria's behavior. I have dealt with 'special cases' all of my life."

"Oh, yeah, like when? And the Robinson family doesn't count." Dwayne laughed at his own joke.

"I work as a human services assistant, helping mentally unstable people find their place in society. You wouldn't believe how many people can't keep a job or are estranged from their families and are homeless due to mental illness."

"I don't know what to say." Trish looked around the room as if she were gathering words. "I wouldn't have thought you would be comfortable doing that kind of work. I don't see many rich folk doing stuff like that. In my mind, I could see you donating money to the cause."

"My mother dealt with mental illness, so I saw firsthand the unexpected damage it can do to families. I just want to help in any way

I can." It felt good to be able to say those words out loud and not look over her shoulder, wondering if her husband would be aggrieved over this confession.

"I didn't know. I'm sorry to hear that, Alexis." Trish's eyes filled with sadness.

Smiling from way down deep, Alexis said, "I'm not as sorry as I used to be. It actually felt good to tell you about my mom. I've never admitted that to anyone before. But you know what, even though Vivian Cooper dealt with mental illness, she was still one awesome woman. I will honor her for the rest of my life."

Trish stood up and walked over to Alexis. She took the woman's hand and squeezed it. "I know how you feel. My mom doesn't have mental illness, unless there's one for butting in everybody's business. Nonetheless, she is my shero. Moms are special people."

Alexis glanced over her shoulder toward the room Marquita and her mother had gone into. "I get the feeling that Marquita doesn't feel the same as we do."

"Marquita is trying to make her own way in life, and I think she feels like her mother pulls her down. So, she's been trying to avoid the woman."

Alexis told her, "Marquita and I are a lot alike. I used to be so ashamed of my mother. I hope that she and her mother get to the place of forgiveness."

"Is that what you want to talk to them about? Because I don't think either of them will want to hear that today," Trish admonished.

"No, actually, it's about Gloria's youngest daughter. I may have some good news for this family." Alexis walked over to Marquita's closed door and knocked on it. She took a deep breath, not sure how all of this would play out. But she knew she had to do the right thing for all involved.

"Yeah—I mean, yes? Come in," Marquita said.

Alexis opened the door. Mother, grandmother, auntie, and uncle were on different sides of the bed, looking down at the baby and making baby sounds. "I hope I'm not interrupting, Marquita. I would like to speak with Gloria if that's okay."

Gloria's back was to Alexis. She gave Alexis the hand that said, "Stop, uh-uh, no, and go away." Gloria then confirmed her hand action and said, "I am sitting in here with my grandson. I am not causing a disturbance, so you don't need to say nothing to me."

"I'm not here about that. This is about your daughter, Kee Kee." Alexis glanced over at the girl who was seated on the opposite side of the bed, playing with the baby.

Kee Kee put the baby down. "That's me."

Gloria swung around and put a finger to her mouth, encouraging her daughter to be quiet. "What's Kee Kee got to do with anything? She hasn't done nothing, so you can keep her name out of your mouth."

"I think I might have good news for Kee Kee. I just need to know who her father is."

Gloria exploded. She stood up so fast that she fell back on the bed. "It's none of your business who her father is. Why would you even ask me something like that?"

Dwayne rushed over to the room. "Hold on, Gloria. Alexis is a guest in our home just as you are. Can you give her a minute to talk to you? You just might like what she has to say."

Gloria harrumphed but turned back to Alexis. "What you want with Kee Kee?"

"I believe Kee Kee's father created the app that my husband's company was built on. If so, she is in line to collect a lot of money."

"What?" Gloria's interest was piqued. "Who owes my baby some money?"

"First, can you tell me Kee Kee's father's name?"

"What if I say the wrong name?" Gloria asked defiantly. "I'm not going to tell you his name. Just give us the money that you said is owed to her."

"Well, I don't know it's owed to her unless I know who her father is." Alexis didn't want to offend Gloria. After all, if Kee Kee was Kevin's child, then her husband had ripped this family off for years. But she couldn't promise her something that she wasn't sure belonged to her.

Kee Kee got up from the bed and stood next to her mother, eyes wide with excitement. "Tell her, Mama."

Gloria turned on her daughter. "I'm not giving information to a stranger." She swung back around to Alexis. "You tell them to give us that money."

Marquita got on her knees in the bed and waved her hands. "His name was Kevin Jones. I remember him. He died right after Kee Kee was born."

Gloria turned, screaming at Marquita. "You little turncoat." She lifted her hand and smacked her older daughter.

Marquita put a hand to her face as she jumped off the bed. "This is why I don't want you around my son. Leave us alone. Do you hear me? Just stay away from us."

Trish ran into the room and held on to Marquita, trying to comfort her. "You don't mean that."

"Yes, I do. She is a hateful woman, and I don't want anything else to do with her."

"Don't come crawling back when we get this money," Gloria told her.

Marquita wasn't backing down. "Oh, you better believe that if Kee Kee has any money coming to her because of something her father did, I'm going to make sure you don't get your hands on it and ruin her life like you tried to ruin mine."

"We'll see about that." Gloria snapped her head back and picked up her purse. "Come on, Mark and Kee Kee. Let's get out of here."

"Wait!" Alexis followed Gloria. "Can I get your contact information so we can arrange a meeting with my husband?"

"Lady, are you for real about this?" Gloria asked with her hand on the doorknob.

"I am, but first I need to know if you have anything that can prove Kevin is Kee Kee's father?"

Gloria snapped her finger while rolling her neck. "Sure do. Kevin and I did a DNA test on Kee Kee. I've got the receipts, lady." She snapped her fingers. "So you won't be able to take what belongs to us. No, ma'am."

Alexis backed up and lifted her hands in front of her chest. "I'm sorry. I didn't mean to offend you."

Gloria's tone softened a bit. "I always told Kee Kee that she got her brains from her dad, and now you're telling me that he created something that's going to benefit this family?"

Alexis nodded. "Kevin was a genius. He died before he could receive any of the fruits of his labor, but my husband wants to make sure Kee Kee gets it."

Gloria provided Alexis with her contact information and then left the Robinson house, declaring that she would never return where she wasn't wanted.

After Gloria left, Alexis went back to Marquita's room. Trish was sitting on the edge of the bed, trying to console the young woman who had had her heart broken by her mom.

Trish rubbed the girl's back. "I understand what you're going through, but you can't talk to your mother like that."

Looking at Trish, Marquita said, "How can you understand? I don't see your mother tracking you down just to yell at you and smacking you in the face for no reason. Why? Because your mother is normal."

Sitting down on the opposite side of the bed, Alexis sighed. She didn't know if she would be able to mend this mother-daughter relationship, but she had to try. "My mother wasn't normal, Marquita."

Marquita turned to face Alexis. She didn't say anything, but she appeared ready to listen.

"I tried everything, but nothing was able to get her to that place we call normal, because she had been broken for so long."

Wiping tears from her face, Marquita asked, "Did she act like my mother?"

"At times she was worse than your mother, because my mom suffered from delusions." Alexis realized now that her mother's delusions of being a movie star probably helped her cope with the loss of her family. She would never truly know why or how her mother got stuck in such a state. Alexis was just thankful that she was there for the final act of the drama that constantly played in her mother's head. It helped her understand her mother and have compassion for her like never before.

"My mother is trying to ruin my life. Sometimes I worry that I'm just like her. Until recently, I couldn't keep a job, just like her."

"You're not like your mother. You may display some of her behaviors, but that's only because you've been around her illness for so long that it begins to seem normal—like this is how people act and react, but it's not."

Marquita looked confused. "My mother has never said that she has any kind of mental illness. Are you sure? Or is she just an evil and angry woman who wants to terrorize me for the rest of my life?"

Alexis shook her head and looked at Marquita with sadness. "I'm not a mental health professional, so I can't diagnosis your mother. What I can help with is getting her evaluated, if she ever decides to do that."

"Okay, let's say she does have some kind of mental illness. Can she be fixed, or will she be like this for the rest of her life?" Marquita looked from Trish to Alexis, seeking an answer.

Alexis put her hand out like a stop sign. "I'm not definitely saying that your mother is mentally ill. I don't know that for sure. But if she is, the right medication could help her live a much better life."

Trish's lip twisted as she added, "I say she needs Jesus and a good whooping."

Alexis couldn't help herself. She burst out laughing and then hugged Trish as if she was a long-lost friend. "I needed that. Thank you."

"You laughing, but I'm serious. Marquita's mom needs a serious dip in the water. And when they bring her up, they should have that belt waiting to squash all her foolishness."

"Mrs. Trish, you are funny though." Marquita laughed also.

Trish looked at Alexis as if she had lost her own mind. "You think the woman who was just in my house acting a fool is going to agree to be evaluated for mental illness? She wouldn't even give you Kee Kee's father's name because she thought you were plotting to take the money away from her."

"Mrs. Trish has a point. My mother thinks the whole world is plotting against her. I don't see her letting some doctor test her for mental illness."

Knowing all that Alexis knew about mental illness, and from the way Gloria responded to her today, she had to admit they were right. She took a moment to think about the situation. Her eyes brightened as she looked at Marquita. "I think I know what we can do, but I'm going to need you and your siblings to help."

CHAPTER 33

Wow, just wow! Marquita still couldn't believe that her little sister was about to get paid. She had always known Kee Kee was some kind of genius, and now she knew where her brains came from.

Marquita didn't want Kee Kee or Mark to get stuck though. She didn't want them to think that since they had money, they didn't have to do anything in life but spend, spend, spend. Money comes and goes, but no one can take your education.

Admittedly, Marquita had allowed fear to consume her thoughts when Jon-Jon registered for college, wondering if he would begin to look down on her like he was better because of his education. But Jon-Jon had the right idea. After talking with Alexis and realizing that she could motivate her siblings if she went to college, Marquita felt a fire had been sparked under her.

She went down to the community college and applied for financial aid. Then she registered for the fall semester. Kee Kee and Mark were still young, but if she was able to show them that she could get through college with a kid and a part-time job, then they wouldn't be able to give her any excuses when it was time for them to register for college.

Marquita rushed home to show Jon-Jon her registration paperwork. "I'm in—well, as long as my financial aid gets approved."

Jon-Jon had been rubbing his legs with ointment when she entered his room. He glanced up at the paper. "Oh, Marquita, this is great news! I'm so happy you decided to go."

"What you so happy about? 'Cause you are going to be watching Moochie while I'm in class."

"And you're going to be watching him while I'm in class," Jon-Jon told her. "But the end result is we will both be able to get good paying jobs or build a business from the ground up when we finish with school. That's going to make a big difference for Moochie."

Marquita agreed with him. "I registered so that I could encourage Kee Kee and Mark to go to college when it's time, but you are right. Moochie is the one who will benefit because we are handling our business while he is still young."

"Are you nervous about the meeting with the Marshalls tomorrow?"

Marquita thought about that for a minute. "I don't think I'm nervous, but then again, I'm terrified out of my mind that my mother is going to do something to mess this up for Kee Kee."

"Your mother wants that money, so she's not going to do anything off the wall before cashing that check. Believe that."

"Jon-Jon, you don't know my mother. And if I get my way, she won't be cashing any checks. My mother would relapse, and Mark and Kee Kee would be left with nothing."

"I'm glad you're looking out for them."

"I've looked out for them since they were born. No reason to stop now."

"What's your major?"

Her eyes lit up. She was beginning to dream. "I'm doing liberal arts at the community college, but after that I'm going to get a bachelor's degree in writing."

Moochie was laying on Jon-Jon's bed. He turned to him. "You hear that, son? Your mom is going to be an author, and I'm going to own a business some day."

They were talking about the future and dreaming of a day when life would be good for them, and Marquita was ready to lean in to all of it.

"With the money I just received, we should be able to pay for a babysitter so we can take some classes together."

Jon-Jon received his payout last week. They were scheduling an appointment with child support so he could begin making payments. The child support would make it possible for her to get an apartment, so she was thankful. Now he was talking about taking classes together.

Marquita liked that Jon-Jon wanted to take classes with her, but she wasn't reading anything into that. She lifted Moochie off of Jon-Jon's bed. Then she felt eyes on her and glanced over at Jon-Jon to see him looking. It wasn't a regular look-see either. He was staring at her the way he used to gawk at her last summer, like she meant something to him. But she'd thought that before, and then he went back to school and forgot all about her. She wasn't going to let him put her in another trick bag, leading her on to pine after somebody who only wanted her because she was available and in close vicinity. "I'll take Moochie to our room."

"Do you want to watch a movie after you lay him down?"

Don't look at him. Just keep walking. "Not tonight. I need to clear my head for this meeting with Mrs. Alexis's husband tomorrow."

She felt like locking her door as she leaned against it. She was not going to let Jon-Jon play with her emotions. Marquita walked over to the bed and laid Moochie down. She kissed his forehead and then laid down beside him and whispered, "I'm going to make you proud, Moochie. You just wait. Your mom is going to be something good in this world."

She went to sleep dreaming about being a college student and walking through the school halls, holding hands with Jon-Jon. When she woke the next morning, instead of admonishing herself for dreaming, she smiled because in the dream Jon-Jon was on his feet. He was actually walking next to her and holding her hand.

She got out of bed, got dressed, and left for work like it was a normal day and not the day that her baby sister would become a millionaire. Whether Kee Kee was about to be rich or not, Marquita wasn't, so she still needed to get to work on time.

Marquita could barely concentrate at work. She kept watching the clock. As soon as the clock struck 1:00 p.m., she was out of her seat, racing to her car like she was a member of a NASCAR pit crew and had a need for speed.

The meeting was scheduled for one-thirty, and the office they were meeting at was twenty minutes away in good traffic. Marquita got on the highway and made her way across town as if her life depended on it, but it was more like Kee Kee's life and her future depended on it. She couldn't let her mother get her hands on money that was meant for her sister.

It wasn't that Marquita thought Gloria didn't love her children, but she had done things that brought harm to them. Marquita was tired of watching Mark and Kee Kee suffer because of Gloria's un-diagnosed condition. All that would hopefully end today, thanks to the plan that she and Mrs. Alexis devised.

Marquita parked her car and hurried into the building. They were meeting in suite 201. Marquita didn't want to wait on the elevator, so she took the stairs two at a time and found the meeting room. As she opened the door, Marquita was stunned to see about six people seated around a conference table. Two of the men had on black suits. The third wore a gray suit. Even the women were prim and properly dressed—one in a pantsuit, the other in a suit jacket and skirt. They were all white.

Her mom hadn't arrived yet. Marquita stood by the door, not sure what to do. She was totally out of her element. What was she doing in a room with powerful people like this? She was only nineteen. Could she help her sister, or would she mess things up even worse than her mother?

She wanted to open the door and run. She couldn't help Kee Kee. She couldn't help anyone. One of the black suits stood and came over to her. He extended his hand. "Good afternoon. I'm assuming that you are Marquita. Alexis told me that you would be joining us today."

She shook his hand.

"I'm Michael Marshall, Alexis's husband. You're the first to arrive, but you can have a seat with us at the table."

Have a seat at the table? She'd heard people who looked like her saying things about Black Lives Matter and how they needed to have a seat at the table. None of it ever really sunk in because Marquita had been so busy trying to survive her everyday life that all the stuff going on in the world didn't matter to her.

As she looked at these high-powered men and women who already had a seat at the table, she realized something about them. They all looked like money. Once Kee Kee received the money that her father had earned, she would be able to create her own table. That knowledge gave Marquita all the strength she needed to stay in this room and do what needed to be done to ensure a bright future for Kee Kee and Mark.

"Yes, I would like to sit down."

Michael led the way. He pulled out a seat for her. No sooner than she sat down did the door open and her family walked in.

Gloria did a dead stop in the middle of the floor when she saw Marquita. "What's she doing here?"

"I'm here for Kee Kee, Mama. Please sit down so this meeting can begin." Marquita prayed that her mom would do the right thing for once and not cause a scene that would get all of them thrown out of there.

Thanks be to God, Gloria sat down at the head of the table as if she was the queen being seated on her throne. Kee Kee gave her a smile as she sat down across from Marquita. Mark took the seat next to Kee Kee, and he rubbed his hands together, anxious for what would come next.

Michael began the meeting by introducing the other people at the table. The other man in the black suit's name was Peter Davis. Their attorney was in the gray suit. His name was Timothy Willey.

Michael then turned to the women at the table. The woman who sat at the other head of the table was Nora Foster. Then they were introduced to Deidre Delaney and finally to the attorney for the company, Media Matters Inc., which the ladies represented.

After the introductions, Nora stood. "I am very happy to meet all of you." Her eyes turned toward Kee Kee. "I went to college with your father. He was a brilliant man, so I'm thrilled that we are able to do something for his child."

"Thank you," Kee Kee said.

As Nora sat back down, Michael said, "As you know, Kevin created an app that helped Peter and I build our company. We are selling the company to Media Matters Inc., and they are requiring us to disclose the amount of the sale."

Marquita's breathing intensified. She thought she was about to have a panic attack. She thought that Kee Kee would at least get a million from Michael's company, but as Michael continued, her wildest dreams couldn't have imagined what he was about to say.

Gloria leaned forward, her eyes wide with curiosity.

"We are selling to Media Matters Inc. for two hundred million dollars. We will also be listing Kevin Jones as the rightful designer of our Go-Bo app."

Gloria got impatient. "How much will you be paying us?"

The attorney took the contract out and sat it on the table. "We are prepared to offer Kee Kee twenty million dollars."

"Twenty million!" Gloria spat the words out like they offended her. "Sounds like we deserve that two hundred million Media Matters Inc. is offering you."

Peter chimed in. "Kevin's Go-Bo app is not the only offering. Media Matters Inc. is buying the company as a whole, and we feel that twenty million is a fair price for the development of an app."

Gloria's nose turned up like something was foul in this room. "Y'all think because you're white, you're right. And because we're broke, we don't know nothing. But if I get a lawyer, we might just be splitting this money three ways."

They went back and forth, and to Marquita's surprise, Gloria was able to talk them into an increase of ten million. She wanted to high-five her mother for that, but Marquita knew what was to come and didn't want to seem phony.

They started shaking hands, and the women from Media Matters Inc. left the conference room. Michael then said, "We will make the changes to the contract and have it available for you to sign by Monday."

Marquita opened her purse and took out a document. She told Michael, "I'm not sure if my mom will be signing that contract or if I will."

Gloria swung around to Marquita. "W-What are you talking about, Marquita? You shouldn't even be here and now you starting a mess."

"I'm here for Mark and Kee Kee. They signed this document requesting that I become their guardian."

"I'm their mother. They don't need a guardian." Gloria pierced Mark and Kee Kee with her eyes. "I ought to break your ungrateful necks."

Michael held out a hand. "Hold on, Ms. Lewis. I will have to call security if you make any more threats."

"You need to call security on her." Gloria jabbed a finger in Marquita's direction. "She's trying to steal my kids so she can get her hands on this money."

"I don't want Kee Kee's money, Mama, but I also don't want you to relapse or spend all of her money before she can grow up and spend it herself."

"That's not your business," Gloria told her.

"We'll see what the courts have to say about that." Marquita turned back to Michael. "I suggest you hold onto that contract until the courts determine which one of us will have custody of the kids."

"Why you little . . ."

The door opened and Trish and Alexis came into the room. Alexis sat down next to her husband. Trish sat down next to Marquita and squeezed her arm. Marquita felt the love in that gesture. She tried real hard not to wish that Trish was her mother. God allowed Gloria to give birth to her for a reason, even if she didn't know what in the world that reason could be.

"What y'all want? I don't have any more kids to steal, because Ms. Thang here is already trying to take my kids."

A tear rolled down Marquita's face. It wasn't easy doing this to her mother, but she had to find some way to help her whole family. "I just want you to get help, Mama."

"We do, too, Mama. Isn't that right, Kee Kee?" Mark said and then he nudged Kee Kee.

Kee Kee cleared her throat. "They're right, Mama. You need help. I don't know what makes you so angry all the time, but it scares me."

"Ah, baby girl, Mama's not trying to scare you. I just get upset sometimes."

"And you can't stop yourself once your blood starts boiling, right?" Alexis asked.

"Right," Gloria admitted. "But I'm not the only one who acts like that. Marquita's a hothead too. Look what she's doing to me right now."

This woman had taught her every bad habit she had and hardly ever tried to encourage her to do better, or gave her a kind word. Marquita wanted to love her mother, but those feelings were buried way down deep. She hadn't felt true, uncomplicated love for Gloria since she was a child. But she wanted to dig those feelings back up, dust them off, and shower her mother with all the love she had to give if she would let her. "Please, Mama, you're not right. Something is wrong with you, but Mrs. Alexis says you can get better."

"Mrs. Alexis says you can get better," Gloria mimicked. She then pointed from Alexis to Trish. "This is your new family, huh? What you tell this white lady about me?"

Gloria turned to Trish. "How you even know Moochie belong to y'all? How you know Marquita's telling the truth?"

"Just like you got a DNA test for Kee Kee, they know Moochie belongs to them because we did a DNA test." Marquita knew that her voice sounded scornful, but why should she keep trying to help a horrible woman like Gloria?

Trish leaned closer to her and whispered in her hear. "Forgive, Marquita. She doesn't mean to hurt you."

Tears rolled down Marquita's face because this was the one time that she didn't believe Trish. All her life Marquita felt like the things her mother did were designed to hurt her, but she wasn't going to let this woman hurt her siblings anymore.

Marquita's unforgiving eyes darted in her mother's direction. "Here's the deal. I'm going to file custody paperwork for Mark and Kee Kee at the courthouse tomorrow. I'm sure I can contact past landlords and ex-friends of yours to verify everything I'm going to tell the judge."

Mark chimed in. "But Marquita won't go to court if you do the right thing, Mama."

Gloria smacked her lips together and slunk back in her chair, staring at them. "What's this, some kind of bad-mama intervention?"

Trish spoke up, "You can think of it as an intervention, or you can take a moment to see how many people care about you and want you to live a good life."

Taking a deep breath, Marquita said, "It's up to you, Mama. All we want you to do is meet with a doctor who can do a thorough mental evaluation. We want you to listen to the doctor and take medicine if need be."

"Oh, is that all?" Gloria mocked.

"There's more." Kee Kee took the floor. "I want the money put into a trust for me to access once I'm grown."

"Kee Kee, you're only thirteen. If we put all of that money into a trust, how are you going to eat and how will I keep a roof over your head? That's not fair to me. You know how hard it's been." Gloria looked around the table, her eyes pleading with someone to help her.

Peter, the accountant, chimed in, "There is a way we could set up a trust fund for Kee Kee and also have a monthly or yearly allotment paid out for expenses."

"What about a house? If we have this much money, we shouldn't have to rent a house," Gloria said.

All eyes turned to Kee Kee.

"You're my mother, and I love you. I don't ever want to see you homeless again. I'm thankful that I will be able to buy you a home and no one will be able to throw you out on the street ever again."

Kee Kee then turned to her brother. "I want to make sure you have money to go to college too. Marquita always believed that if we applied ourselves, we could go to college. Now we have the money."

Marquita smiled at that. "God works in mysterious ways. Who would have ever known that you would have enough money for you and Mark to go to college when I was badgering y'all about not missing school?"

"You can go to college now, too, Marquita. We can all do this," Kee Kee said.

"I already registered for school and applied for financial aid, so you keep your money in your pocket."

Trish whispered in Marquita's ear. "Take the money, girl. It's hard out here."

Mark turned to Gloria. "See, Mama, we are going to have a home, and Kee Kee and I are going to college. Please don't let us down. Can't you go to the doctor and just see what they say?"

Gloria turned to her oldest. "Y'all really think that something is wrong with me?"

Marquita nodded. "We do, Mama."

"And if I let some doctor check me out, will you tear up that custody paperwork?" Gloria asked.

"I will. I just want you to get better so that Mark and Kee Kee can enjoy being around you, like I used to when I was a kid, before everything changed."

Gloria looked as if she wanted to give in, but in the next moment she looked ready to fight.

Alexis popped up and said, "I'll go with you."

CHAPTER 34

On Saturday afternoon, two weeks after the meeting at Michael's tech company, Trish and Marquita found themselves lounging around the swimming pool in the backyard of Alexis's beautiful house. How the three of them had become friends was beyond Trish's understanding. All she had done was pray and ask God to take away all the bad and do something good in her life.

Her grandson showed up and changed everything for her household. Marquita was a welcomed surprise as well. She thought Marquita was all wrong for her son when they first met—she was loud-mouthed and defensive about everything—but Marquita had changed and was growing into a woman of substance.

When Alexis showed up in their lives, everything changed. Now Trish's son had the money he needed, and Marquita's family wasn't struggling anymore. God was so good, and Trish knew one thing for sure—prayer worked.

Marquita jumped in the pool, swam a couple of laps, then toweled off and took her place next to Trish again. "That was refreshing."

Trish covered her eyes from the hot, beaming sun. "Soon you won't be able to lounge around like this. Are you ready to be a college freshman?"

"Are you kidding? I feel like my life is finally about to start. I'm more than ready for college."

"It looks like we're all going back to school," Alexis said as she came back outside carrying a tray of Arnold Palmers in one hand

and a charcuterie board in another. The board was filled with salami, cured ham, pepperoni, and three different kinds of cheeses—cheddar chunks, brie, and a soft, spreadable herb cheese. There were grapes, apple slices, and crackers accompanied by pecans and almonds.

Trish glanced over at Alexis and smiled. Nobody on God's green earth could have told her that she would be friends with the woman who caused her son to lose his football scholarship and put him in a wheelchair. Alexis had made amends ten times over for the heartache she'd caused their family, and Trish was thankful she now considered her a friend. "What's this about school?"

Alexis put the charcuterie board and Arnold Palmers on the table and then walked over to her lounger and sat down. "Well, you're going back to school to teach those fourth graders, Marquita is starting her first year in college, and I got to thinking that I have always wanted to be a psychologist to help people who struggle with mental illness."

"You already help people," Marquita said. "My mother would have never received her bipolar diagnosis if it weren't for you. She might not be speaking to me, but Mark told me that she is in a much better place."

"I still say she needs to try Jesus too," Trish said. "And Alexis? I think you would be a wonderful psychologist."

"You do?" Alexis looked a little unsure.

Trish wouldn't allow the doubt. "Sometimes our greatest tragedies become the greatest gifts we can give back to the world."

"That sounds so beautiful." Marquita took a sip of her drink, filled a plate with some of the items on the charcuterie board, then added. "I was mortified growing up in an unstable family. We never knew how long we would live in this house or that apartment. People were always telling us to 'pay up or get out.'"

Trish and Alexis both put a hand on Marquita's shoulders, trying to provide comfort.

"That's why I want to be a writer," Marquita continued. "I know

I'll never be rich like my little sister, but I have stories that I want to tell. Stories that will let others know that no matter what they are going through, life can get better." Marquita looked down at her plate. "I need some cookies. You over here being healthy with all these fruits and cheeses."

"Sorry. I've given up baking for a while, and I haven't bought sweets since my mom passed. I'm trying to find another way of coping with my problems. My mom's way was sugar, and I gained ten pounds following her way."

Trish adjusted herself in her seat so that she was facing Alexis. "I can tell you a way to deal with the stress life brings and it won't put one extra pound on you."

Alexis put her hands together in a praying motion. "Please tell me, and hurry up, before I take up smoking."

Marquita and Trish laughed at that. Then Trish said, "Look at your hands."

Alexis looked down and then glanced back up at Trish, eyes saying, huh?

"Prayer is your answer. When I feel like life has taken me on a journey that I can't handle on my own, which is most of the time, I go to a room by myself and give all my problems to my Lord and Savior. He has always come through for me. I suggest you give it a try."

"You sure won't gain any weight from that," Marquita joked. Then said more seriously, "I just might try it myself."

"You two were the answer to my prayers. Matter of fact, before y'all showed up, I am convinced that God sent a cardinal into my yard to let me know that something good was about to come into our lives. Because that bird symbolizes hope in the midst of my sorrows." Trish choked up as she added, "I'm so thankful y'all came into my life when y'all did."

"Aww." Marquita put her plate down. "I love you, Ms. Trish, and I'm so thankful you are in my life."

Alexis seconded that. "I'm thankful for you all too."

They continued lounging, snacking, and talking. After a while, Trish leaned her head back. "It's such a beautiful day. I can't believe it's not humid out here."

"The weatherman said the humidity will be back tomorrow, so you won't miss it for long." Alexis stretched her arms and relaxed.

Ethan and Ella came out back with their swimming suits on. They waved at everyone and then jumped in the pool.

Pointing toward the pool, Alexis said, "I wonder if they will feed themselves today so I can continue lounging out here?"

"Probably not," Marquita said.

"Wish I could hang out here all day, but I have to prepare for tomorrow," Trish told them.

"Trish, you need to stop being a worrier. The event will go over fine. Just relax," Alexis encouraged.

"I think I need to send out more emails, pass out more flyers, or something. We rented out this huge auditorium. What if only five people show up again?" No matter how she tried not to compare, Trish kept thinking back to the first event. When the reporter described it as "sparsely attended," she had wanted to disappear.

"That was then, and this is now," Marquita told her. "Those commercials Mr. Michael paid for were impactful, and we reached many people with our social media ads. People are going to show up. Just you wait and see."

"Okay, if y'all don't think I need to do anything else, I'll just lounge around here, sipping on my Arnold Palmer and taking in the amazing view." Then Trish turned to Marquita and said, "White people got it made, don't they?"

Marquita glanced around the expansiveness . . . the beauty. "I actually don't mind being up in all this white privilege. I need to take pictures because no one will believe I was ever at a house like this."

"Hey," Alexis tsk-tsked. "We'll just see the type of house Kee Kee buys for herself after she becomes CEO of the world, then I want you two to tell me about," she did air quotes, "'white privilege.'"

Trish lifted her glass. "To Kee Kee taking over the world." They each raised their glass and cheered.

"But white privilege is a thing." Marquita couldn't let it go. "Just look at the way Alexis's husband took Kevin's app and made all that money on it for years while my family struggled, being evicted and homeless more times than I can count."

Marquita turned to Alexis. "I'm not trying to offend you, because you're a really nice lady, but why didn't your husband think he owed Kee Kee anything for that app before now? Like my mama said at that meeting, just because he's white don't make it right."

Alexis averted her eyes. "I wish I had an answer for you, Marquita. And I shouldn't have been so flippant about your comment about white privilege. But I will tell you that my husband did hire a private investigator to find Kee Kee."

"He did?" Marquita looked impressed by that.

Alexis nodded, then added. "I know how unfair life can be. And I will not deny that my family lives a privileged life. My hope is that we all work to be better and treat each other better."

"I know that's right, because—"

Trish cut Marquita off. "Let it go, Marquita. I don't care what is or isn't a thing. Alexis is my friend, and that's all that matters to me," Trish told her.

"Thank you for calling me your friend, because that is how I feel about you."

Trish and Alexis hugged.

Marquita said, "See, if more people in this world were like you and Mrs. Trish, then maybe we could all get along."

Trish opened her arms. "You get yourself over here and get some of this hug too."

Marquita joined them.

"After you conquer this whole distracted driving thing, maybe I should work with the two of you to tackle the stigma on mental illness," Alexis suggested.

Marquita squeezed in and hugged them back. "That's right, because people with mental illness can still live productive lives if they get the help they need."

The three of them had weathered many storms. They had learned the hard way that life wasn't fair. While the fight wasn't over, they were in it to win it, and that's all that mattered.

∽

The auditorium seated two thousand people and as Trish gazed over the crowd, she couldn't find an empty seat. All of her worrying had been for nothing. She looked to heaven and gave thanks. "Lord, You did this. Thank You!"

Alexis, seated next to her, leaned closer to Trish and asked, "You ready?"

"I wish Dwayne and Jon-Jon would hurry up and get here. Jon-Jon is supposed to speak first. The audience will get restless if we don't get started."

Alexis patted Trish's hand. "They'll be here, but I can go first so we can begin. You just go up there and thank everyone for coming and then I'll give my speech."

Trish's eyes widened. "Sounds like a plan." She got out of her seat, stood behind the podium, and adjusted the microphone. "Good afternoon, everyone. Thank you so much for spending your Sunday afternoon learning about the dangers of distracted driving. I don't know if you have ever experienced something like this, but the results can be devastating, and that's what we want to talk about today. This will not be an easy conversation, but if you take it to heart, it just might save someone's life."

Trish glanced over her shoulder at Alexis, then turned back to the crowd. "Right now, I want to bring to the microphone a woman I call a friend. At first glance we are the most unlikely of friends as two people can be, but God saw fit to bring us together, and for that I am thankful."

Alexis walked over to Trish. They hugged. Then Alexis stood behind the podium. She addressed Trish first. "Thank you for those kind words, Trish. I am so grateful you found the strength in your heart to not only forgive me for the harm I caused to your family but to also become my friend.

Alexis then faced the crowd. "I'd like to tell you a little bit of my story. I used to think it was no big deal to read my text messages or even to respond to text messages while driving.

"You see, I thought the things that were going on in my life earned me the right to ignore the rules of the road. My mother had mental illness, and she was always doing outrageous things that I thought had to be resolved the moment it occurred.

"My kids were always texting me. They needed this or that, and I had to respond immediately, or I wasn't being a good mom." Alexis shrugged, her body language reaffirming that she used to think texting while driving was no big deal. "Then one day, I got a text while I was driving, and I did what I've always done. I checked it. But this time, I lost control of my car and almost killed a young man in the prime of his life." Her eyes pierced the crowd. "Can you imagine how you would live the rest of your life knowing that you had accidentally murdered someone?"

Gasps were heard from the crowd. Trish prayed that they were truly hearing Alexis's heart and that the guilt she felt would somehow penetrate their souls and cause them to do the right thing. They weren't going to convince everyone to put down the phone and keep their eyes on the road, but the road would become a much safer place for the few who got it.

"Now imagine how you would feel," Alexis continued, "to know that you had paralyzed a young man and took any hope he had of becoming a football hall of famer. He told me he wanted to be like Emmitt Smith, but now he won't have that chance because of what I did. I have to live with that, but you don't. Please don't text and drive."

As Alexis took her seat, Trish stood behind the podium again. She touched her stomach as she felt a flutter. *Calm down*, she silently told herself. She looked out at the front row and saw Moochie bouncing up and down on Marquita's lap. Who would have thought that a little fat-cheeked baby would have brought so much joy into their lives?

Her heart filled as she exhaled. She was on this mission not just for Jon-Jon but for Moochie as well. When he grew up, she wanted her grandson to be able to drive down the street without fear of someone crashing into him simply because they weren't paying attention.

She pointed to Moochie as she began. "Many of you in attendance today are young and aren't thinking about having children, but my grandson is here today. Stand up, Marquita, and let Moochie wave to everyone."

Marquita stood and waved to the crowd while Moochie made gurgling sounds and played with her necklace.

"He's my son's firstborn. Jon-Jon would love to run and play with his son, but right now, he can't do it." She turned to Alexis and put her hand on her heart. "And even though my dear friend, Alexis, is so very sorry for the one moment she took her eyes off the road and then ended my son's hopes of a football career, I'm sure if she had it to do over again, she would pull off the road before trying to pick up her cell phone."

Alexis vehemently nodded in agreement.

The double doors in the back of the auditorium opened. Dwayne came into view as he pushed Jon-Jon down the aisle in his wheelchair. Trish smiled at the sight of her men but pressed on. "Did you know that cell phone usage while driving leads to 1.6 million crashes each year? And that one in four car accidents in the United States are caused by texting while driving?

"We don't want you to have to live with the pain of knowing that you needlessly injured or killed someone." Trish lifted a stack of papers that were on the podium. "Join us today and make the pledge to never text and drive and to not take your eyes off the road for even one second. That one second may just be the last one you have on this earth."

The audience broke into thunderous applause as Trish stepped away from the podium and took the microphone to where Jon-Jon was now seated just below the stage. His eyes beamed as he looked at her.

"Mom, look at all these people."

Trish scanned the crowd once more. In the third row she saw Michael Marshall and Alexis's twins. She thought it was kind of him to support his wife at this event. "God is good, son."

Jon-Jon took the microphone as he pumped his fist in the air. "Y'all heard my mother. We will be sitting at tables directly outside of the auditorium. Please come to our tables and sign the pledge and help end distracted driving."

Trish leaned toward Dwayne, who was seated next to Jon-Jon. "What took y'all so long?"

"Jon-Jon and his trainer did an extra session. We have a surprise for you when we get home."

Trish didn't have time to wonder about the surprise because the moment they ended the session and took their place behind the tables outside of the auditorium, the attendees flooded the tables, signing the pledge. Marquita, Dwayne, and Trish sat at one table, handing out the pledge forms and pens, while Jon-Jon and Alexis sat at the other table fielding any questions that were asked about their experience. That is, when Alexis wasn't fielding questions from her husband and her children.

It was a truly wonderful event. Trish believed they were making a difference and maybe even saving lives.

Looking from her table to the next, Trish was once again amazed at the people who were now in her circle all because she called out to God in her darkest hour. Her eyes lifted heavenward. "God, You are a wonder worker."

Life had taken them down unexpected roads that made them want to pull their hair out and just give up, but prayer, faith, and patience had changed everything. Life was good.

CHAPTER 35

SIX WEEKS LATER

Waking up in her own apartment, in a decent neighborhood, felt as if Marquita finally had her own little slice of heaven. Marquita was only able to afford a one bedroom, but that didn't bother her. Moochie was only five months old, and the crib Jon-Jon bought him fit perfectly in her bedroom.

She promised Trish that she would attend church with her today. So Marquita pulled herself out of bed, cleaned Moochie up, and put on his onesie that had a bow-tie imprinted at the top. Her little man was looking good.

Marquita took a quick shower, then looked through her closet. She didn't have any of what she would call churchy clothes. The dresses she wore to work were too short, and she didn't think Trish would appreciate her showing up wearing any of her blue jeans. She did have a pair of white jeans and a black blouse she could wear.

She pulled those items out of her closet and dressed as quickly as she could. Even though she tried her best to hurry, she and Moochie were still fifteen minutes late to church. The choir was on the last song as they walked into the sanctuary.

Marquita took in her surroundings as she looked for a familiar face. The carpet was blue. There were three rows of pews, and each row had fifteen long pews that could seat nine to ten people. Marquita hadn't attended church much because her mother wasn't into that sort of thing. This was the biggest sanctuary she had ever seen. It was grand, with chandeliers hanging from the ceiling. The pew benches were wooden with blue cushions for the seat and the back. She spotted Jon-Jon waving to her and rushed to the middle aisle about halfway toward the front of the sanctuary. She scooted into the aisle where Dwayne, Trish, and Jon-Jon were already seated. She put Moochie's baby seat down next to Jon-Jon, then whispered, "Sorry I'm late."

Jon-Jon smiled at her like it meant something to him to have her at church with his family. "You made it. That's what counts."

She and Jon-Jon had been to the movies, out to dinner, and to Carowinds Amusement Park since she moved into her apartment. It felt like they were building on something and Marquita was here for whatever was to come.

Jon-Jon took Moochie out of his carrier and sat him on his lap. Trish and Dwayne leaned forward and waved at her. Marquita mouthed, "Good morning."

The preacher stood behind the pulpit. He had on this white robe with black velvet center pleats on both sides of the zipper. Marquita noticed the preacher's eyes. They seemed all-knowing but kind, like he was the kind of man who would give his dinner to a stranger and then pray for them.

Pastor said, "Turn with me to the book of Isaiah, chapter sixty-one, beginning with verse one."

Aw, man, she didn't bring a Bible. She should have known she would need a Bible. Jon-Jon nudged her. He had his Bible open to Isaiah and slid it over to share with her. "Thank you."

Jon-Jon smiled at her. When he looked at her like that, making her feel special, she wanted to share more than this Bible with him. She wanted to share her whole life with this man.

The pastor started reading.

"The Spirit of the Lord GOD is upon me; because the LORD hath anointed me to preach good tidings unto the meek; he hath sent me to bind up the brokenhearted, to proclaim liberty to the captives, and the opening of the prison to them that are bound . . . To appoint unto them that mourn in Zion, to give unto them beauty for ashes, the oil of joy for mourning, the garment of praise for the spirit of heaviness; that they might be called trees of righteousness, the planting of the LORD, that he might be glorified."

Something stirred in Marquita as the pastor ministered. Felt like God was speaking directly to her through this preacher. God wanted to give her beauty for the ashes that had been her life. He wanted to give her joy, but was she ready to receive all that God wanted to do for her? Could she tear down this wall that had been constructed to protect her heart?

Pastor said, "I don't know who this message is for, but you're in here today and God is saying to you, 'Stop trying to figure it out. Just give it all to Me.'"

Pastor stepped out of the pulpit. His hands were stretched out wide as he stood before the congregation. "Come, son. Come, daughter. Give your problems to Jesus and let Him fix it."

Marquita felt a pull so strong that it forced her to stand up. She didn't know what she was doing. She just knew she needed to walk down the aisle and meet the pastor where he stood holding out his hands waiting for her.

Her heart started to feel funny, like it was expanding or something. Tears like a river flowed down her face as she made her way to the altar. As the pastor put oil on her forehead and then prayed for her, Marquita felt as if scales had fallen from her eyes and somehow she was able to see so much clearer.

This feeling in her heart was like nothing she'd ever felt before. She wasn't waiting on a man to love her, nor was she waiting on her mother to treat her the way she thought a mother should. Right here and right now, she was completely wrapped in the arms of Jesus. She cried until her body shook from the torrent of tears because it felt as if everything was finally going to be all right.

As she turned to go back to the pew to sit down, she wiped her eyes, thinking her vision was being impaired by her tears, because she couldn't be seeing what she was seeing.

Jon-Jon was coming down the aisle. But he wasn't in his wheelchair. He was holding on to a walker. Slowly and with intent, he walked past her and made his way to the altar.

Marquita had been taking Jon-Jon to his rehab appointments, so she knew he was making progress but had no idea he was making the stand-up-and-walk kind of progress. She went back to the pew she had been sitting in. Trish was holding Moochie. Marquita pointed toward Jon-Jon. "When did that happen?"

Trish's eyes lit up. "He brought that walker home from rehab yesterday. This morning he told us he wasn't going to use his wheelchair." Trish handed Moochie to Dwayne, then lifted her hands in the air and started to shout, "Thank You! Thank You! Hallelujah! Thank You, Lord!"

Marquita turned back to the altar. Jon-Jon was bowed down on the floor with his hands lifted in the air. The pastor prayed over him, then helped him stand back up. Jon-Jon wiped the tears from his eyes and then made his way back to where Marquita was standing.

The pastor gave the benediction, and as everyone was leaving the church, Marquita turned to Jon-Jon. "So, I guess this is why you didn't want me to take you to your session yesterday?"

He bobbed his head. "I wanted to surprise you."

"Well, you did that," she told him.

Jon-Jon steadied himself as he stood in front of Marquita. "You thought I was only interested in you because I couldn't walk and girls weren't hanging around anymore. Now what do you have to say? I'm standing in front of you, and I'm ready to tell you that I love you and want to spend the rest of my life with you and Moochie."

Her knee-jerk reaction was to protect her heart, but she had just given it to Jesus. Now it was ready to make room for Jon-Jon and to trust that God had something good in store for them. She wrapped her arm around him and allowed herself to be loved. "And I love you right back, Jon-Jon."

∽

Sunday dinner was at Jon-Jon's house. Marquita loved being around the Robinson family. They sat at the dinner table eating baked chicken and rice and gravy with cheesy corn muffins and green beans. Marquita was enjoying herself. But looking around the table at this happy family made her realize that she needed to be somewhere else. God had touched her heart that day and now she knew exactly what she had to do.

She excused herself from the table and got Moochie ready for a quick trip to Ballantyne. It was a suburb of Charlotte where the homes ranged anywhere from half a million to one million dollars or more, depending on which street you were on. All the streets were nice in this area of town.

The house she drove up to was a two-story beige brick-front home with four bedrooms, three bathrooms, an office, a game room, a screened-in back patio, and an open floor plan with granite counter-tops in the kitchen and white cabinets just like her mother wanted. The house had cost $649,000, and it was completely paid off.

As Marquita pulled into the driveway and got out of the car, she smiled at the thought that Gloria would never be thrown out of a house again.

Kee Kee swung the front door open as Marquita was taking Moochie out of his car seat, and ran out of the house. "Marquita's here!" she yelled.

Marquita put a finger to her lips. "Girl, you know you can't be all loud like that in this good neighborhood."

Kee Kee took Moochie out of her arms and ran back in the house with him.

Marquita walked up the stairs, getting ready to enter her mother's new home. Gloria came to the door wearing an attitude all over her face and with a hand on her hip, she said, "I don't have time for your foolishness today, Marquita. My kids are fine. They're in school, and I'm taking my medication, so I don't want to hear nothing you got to say."

As Gloria was talking, a cardinal flew by and landed on the hood of Marquita's car. She remembered what Trish had said about the North Carolina cardinal symbolizing hope in the midst of sorrow and that was just what her family had been given.

"I didn't come over here to get on your case, Mama. I came to tell you that I'm so sorry for never recognizing how hard things were for you. And even though it was hard, you still tried your best to keep us all together."

Gloria's eyes widened in complete and utter shock.

Marquita thought she had cried an ocean of tears at church, but tears started streaming down her face before she could get out everything she wanted to say. "I never gave you credit for completing that program the state sent you through and remaining clean all these years just so no one would ever take your kids away again. I stayed angry and bitter for too long, but I don't want to be like that anymore, Mama. I love you."

Gloria's hand went to her heart, then she opened her arms to pull her oldest child into the house with the rest of the family.

ACKNOWLEDGMENTS

I give all honor and praise to God for the gift of writing that He bestowed on me. He has never let me forget where this precious gift came from and that I was born to give Him glory through the written word. I love writing in this beautiful, inspirational women's fiction genre, and I pray many, many, many readers continue reading the books that are written in this genre.

I have to give a special thank you to my husband, David Pierce, because while I was writing *Something Good*, he came running into our room one Saturday morning all excited because he had spotted a North Carolina red cardinal perched on our tree in the backyard. I did not grow up in North Carolina and have only lived here for about ten years. So I had no clue why this was such a special sighting. But Google is a friend of mine, so I looked it up. And that's when I knew that God was trying to take the story of *Something Good* to a deeper level.

You see, the red cardinal is a symbol of beauty in darkness, hope in the midst of sorrow. There's even an old wives' tale that says when a red cardinal is in your yard, it is a visit from heaven. I knew immediately that the red cardinal would have to make an appearance in this story. So, thanks babe, your excitement about that bird truly helped to make *Something Good* something special indeed.

And to Natasha Kern, the best agent in this whole wide world, I just want to say thank you from the bottom of my heart. I had been away from traditional publishing for years, but the moment I told you I had more stories to tell and I wanted to find a publisher, you didn't hesitate. I'm so thankful that you took me on as your client all those years ago and cared about me even when there was no client relationship. I love you to life, Natasha, and I thank God for you.

I also want to thank Jocelyn Bailey, Laura Wheeler, and everyone on the Thomas Nelson team who believes in *Something Good* as much as I do. I am so thankful to be working with wonderful people like you to help bring this book to life and on the shelves of bookstores.

All of my family and friends are so special to me; I love you all dearly even though you all are too numerous to name. So, I'll take a shot at a few: My sister, Debra; my love-you-like sisters, Lala, Batina, Kim, Seana, and Rhonda. To my daughter, Erin; niece, Diamond; Tajiah, Dericka, and Kevona . . . I have many more family members but will list some in other books. Just know that you are all close to my heart.

To my grandkids, who have absolutely stolen my heart: Amarrea, Jarod, and Brielle. The best is yet to come for you all. Keep dreaming and trust God with your dreams.

Writing is such a solitary lifestyle. I sit in my office and plug away at the book in my head each day. But I have some awesome friends who also happen to write. They inspire me, and I have to acknowledge them here for all the encouragement they have provided while working on this project. First, to my critique partner, Michelle Lindo Rice—girl, you rock. You helped make *Something Good* a project I can be proud of. I am so, so grateful that you are my critique partner, even though you make me add more scenery when I don't want to. LOL.

Vanessa R., Pat, Rhonda, Kenyatta, Angela, and Jacquelin, my CBLR sisterhood, you all are the best. I love hanging out with you and appreciate all the encouragement while I worked on this project.

And finally, I would like to thank the Me and My Sisters group for our monthly write-a-thons. I need those monthly meetings to encourage me to get back on track if I have allowed life to get in the way of my writing. So thank you all for being there.

Something Good is the book of my heart. I pray it uplifts you, puts a smile on your face, and even inspires you to believe that God has something good just for you.

If you or anyone you know is dealing with mental illness, please talk with your primary care doctor or go to MentalHealth.gov or call 1-877-726-4727.

Many Blessings,

Vanessa Miller

DISCUSSION QUESTIONS

1. Marquita had a hard time holding onto a job and understanding that she needed to treat people with respect. Do you know anyone like Marquita? Have you ever been like Marquita? What are three things you would tell your younger self that would have made life easier?

2. How did it make you feel to read that Marquita didn't want to dream because she didn't believe anything good could happen for her? How would you minister to someone like Marquita?

3. Do you remember young love? I do, and it is sometimes painful. *I love him, but does he love me?* For Marquita this was compounded by her own feelings of worthlessness. What did you think about Jon-Jon and Marquita? Did they grow enough within themselves to truly have a lasting relationship?

4. Trish's once stable life was turned upside down after her son was left paralyzed. She kept trying to sing a fruitful song, even though she was in a barren land, but nothing she did was working. Things got so bad that she was ready to leave her marriage. Have you ever been so low that you didn't know how to get back up? What did you do to turn things around?

5. At Trish's lowest point she heard the scripture Isaiah 53:4, "Surely He has borne our griefs and carried our sorrows." Reading something like that let's me know that I can breathe easy because God's got me. But does that scripture bring comfort to you or the opposite? Why?

6. Jehovah-Raah is mentioned during Trish's prayer for something good. Jehovah-Raah means God is our Shepherd—our guide through all of life. Have you allowed God to lead you or have you, like Trish, been trying to handle everything on your own?

7. What did you think of the interactions between Trish and Dwayne? Was Trish too hard on him, or did you understand where she was coming from?

8. When tragedy strikes it can either bring a family closer together or tear them apart. When Dwayne realized his family was being torn apart, he made steps to right some of the wrongs. What did you think of Dwayne John Robinson?

9. Alexis was a complicated character because at first glance she seemed to have it all. The rich husband, two wonderful children, a beautiful home. But she also had a secret. Did you realize that her mother dealt with mental illness before she visited her in the nursing home? How did it make you feel when you realized that Vivian was being hidden away to protect the vision of the perfect life Michael wanted for his family?

10. I fell in love with the Alexis Marshall character because she dealt with more internal battles than anyone else. Alexis was loving and compassionate, but secrets and guilt weighed her down. What did you think of Alexis? Was she too much, or did you understand her and relate to the things that pulled her this way or that way?

11. Michael Marshall was a narcissistic character at times. I hated writing about him because he was all about himself and what he needed. But he loved his family. So, what did you think of Michael? Did he redeem himself in the end?

12. The North Carolina cardinal is a symbol of hope in the midst of sorrow, beauty in the midst of darkness. An old wives' tale says that when a red cardinal is in your yard it is a visit from heaven. After learning of this tale, I now smile whenever I see a red cardinal in my yard (I'm not saying it's true, but the story does bring me joy). What's your take on this? Could God use a bird to bring hope to a hurting family?

ABOUT THE AUTHOR

Photo by David Pierce

Vanessa Miller is a bestselling author, with several books appearing on *Essence* Magazine's Bestseller List. She has also been a Black Expressions Book Club Alternate pick and #1 on BCNN/BCBC Bestseller List. Vanessa has worked with numerous publishers: Urban Christian (Kensington), Kimani (Harlequin), Abingdon Press, and Whitaker House. Most of Vanessa's published novels depict characters that are lost and in need of redemption. The books have received countless favorable reviews: "Heartwarming, drama-packed, and tender in just the right places" (*Romantic Times Book Review*) and "Recommended for readers of redemption stories" (*Library Journal*).

Visit her online at vanessamiller.com
Facebook: @AuthorVanessaMiller
Twitter: @Vanessamiller01
Instagram: @authorvanessamiller